I0762122

COURT'S FOOL

by

Frost Kay

Copyright

Court's Fool

First Edition

Cover by Amy Queau

Formatting by Jay Cox

Copy Editing by Madeline Dyer

DEDICATION

This book is for all the readers who have stuck with me from my very first book. Your experiences in life and your willingness to share them with me is what created characters that stick with you long after the book is finished. Love you guys!

THE Five Kingdoms

Rooi

NAGALI

the Mort Walls

Janem

CASPERNRE OCEAN

the Mort Walls

SCYTHIA

FERMIA

Salvren

the Dregs

Sanee

the Blessed Beach

THALASSIAN SEA

N
Devil's Cage
Skigara
Laos
METHI
Sirenidae
the Wyver

TABLE OF CONTENTS

Prologue 1
Chapter One 2
Chapter Two 8
Chapter Three 18
Chapter Four 23
Chapter Five 27
Chapter Six 30
Chapter Seven 39
Chapter Eight 47
Chapter Nine 50
Chapter Ten 58
Chapter Eleven 66
Chapter Twelve 73
Chapter Thirteen 81
Chapter Fourteen 87
Chapter Fifteen 91
Chapter Sixteen 100
Chapter Seventeen 106
Chapter Eighteen 113
Chapter Nineteen 117
Chapter Twenty 122
Chapter Twenty-One 128
Chapter Twenty-Two 137
Chapter Twenty-Three 145
Chapter Twenty-Four 151
Chapter Twenty-Five 160

Chapter Twenty-Six 165
Chapter Twenty-Seven 171
Chapter Twenty-Eight 176
Chapter Twenty-Nine 186
Chapter Thirty 190
Chapter Thirty-One 192
Chapter Thirty-Two 199
Chapter Thirty-Three 204
Chapter Thirty-Four 213
Chapter Thirty-Five 223
Chapter Thirty-Six 235
Chapter Thirty-Seven 238
Chapter Thirty-Eight 245
Chapter Thirty-Nine 253
Chapter Forty 255
Chapter Forty-One 266
Chapter Forty-Two 273
Chapter Forty-Three 278
Chapter Forty-Four 286
Chapter Forty-Five 294
Chapter Forty-Six 296
Chapter Forty-Seven 300
Chapter Forty-Eight 306
Chapter Forty-Nine 309
Chapter Fifty 312
Chapter Fifty-One 319
Chapter Fifty-Two 322
Chapter Fifty-Three 324
Chapter Fifty-Four 331
Chapter Fifty-Five 334

Chapter Fifty-Six 340
Chapter Fifty-Seven 344
Chapter Fifty-Eight 348
Chapter Fifty-Nine 355
Chapter Sixty 363
Chapter Sixty-One 369
Epilogue 373

PROLOGUE

Dark Princes and Demon Kings.
Lady Spies and Assassins.
Pirate Queens and Spymasters.
Beast Masters and Dragon Songs.
Freedom and Captivity.
Consorts and Warlords.
Pain and Pleasure.
Death and Life.
Fables and Myths.
Betrayal and Love.
Truths and Lies.
All belonged in fairytales.
All were Sage's reality.

CHAPTER ONE

Mer

Sirenidae weren't supposed to drown.

Mer clutched at her throat, desperately trying to seal the wound that slashed through her gills. Blood leaked between her fingertips, creating a grisly halo of swirling water, debris, and blood.

She choked as warm liquid dripped down the back of her throat. Her stomach cramped and lurched as another casualty from above crashed through the surface of the unruly sea and began to sink.

A chill swept her as the faint notes of a haunting melody reached her ears. Mer cocked her head, and listened intently as the cacophony of the cannon fire and explosions of war raged above.

The hunt song.

Ice filled her veins at the clear words. Her magenta gaze darted to the soldier, struggling as he made his way back to the surface, his movements wild and unchecked. He was beckoning his own death.

Guilt pricked Mer as she pressed harder against her injury and kicked with all her strength toward the surface. The predators of the deep had no interest in the Sirenidae, but with copious amounts of blood, flesh, and prey struggling in the sea, it would be so easy for one of them to mistake her for something tasty.

Her legs ached as she fought her way toward the rippling surface. A deep-seated panic wrapped around her heart and squeezed when the muted, dull tones of death drew closer, and her waterlogged clothing began to drag her down once again.

Mer tore at her clothing, shedding the linen shirt, exposing her bare breasts and scratching herself in the process. Her feet tangled in her pants, and she found herself sinking deeper while she wrestled with the infernal garments.

Relief was a short-lived victory as she kicked free from her pants and caught a glimpse of a huge black fin.

Wicked hell. The leviathan. Time to move.

Abandoning her attempt to seal her gills, Mer clawed at the water and pushedtoward the surface. She had to get out of the water. Now.

Her lungs burned and screamed for air. Motion flickered at the corner of her vision, and she locked gazes with the soldier just as a shape formed with oil-slicked skin from the inky darkness.

Don't show fear.

With the last of her strength, Mer smiled at the man and held her hand out, betraying none of the guilt she harbored for not warning him. Just as he reached a hand toward her, the leviathan struck. She pulled back her arm and slowly moved toward the surface as the predator tore apart his meal so not as to attract his attention. Her gaze never moved from the red haze.

Where there was one beastie, there were always others.

Mer gasped as her head broke through the barrier of one world and into another. Seawater spewed from her lungs as she coughed and hacked. Lightheaded, Mer tried to make sense of the anarchy lighting up the sky.

Cannons thundered, metal shrieked, and the cries of a thousand men pierced the air. Disoriented, she craned her neck, searching for her ship. Lightning cracked across the night sky, highlighting the skeletal forms of sinking ships, floating debris, and phantom-like fins slicing through the ocean. She sucked in a breath as she spotted her ship to the right.

The Dauntless.

She inhaled deeply and sank beneath the waves, fighting the urge to allow the change to overtake her body. With careful, steady strokes, she worked her way toward the Dauntless, very aware of the dangers lurking above and below.

Her strength lagged as the hull of the ship grew closer, and darkness hovered at the edge of her vision.

Only a few more paces.

Mer crashed through waves and into the open air, the frigid wind stabbing her skin like a thousand needles. It was on the tip of her tongue to call for help, but she caught herself. If by some miracle someone heard it, she would have put a target on them and herself.

The ladder is here somewhere. Don't be lazy.

She moved along the side of the shuddering ship and grinned when she spotted the ladder the pirates had left for her kind. With blood and saltwater slickening her hands, Mer attached herself to the ropes. Now for the hard part.

Between her silvery-white hair and unnaturally pale form, she'd become a target the moment she scaled the ship.

Be brave.

Mer inhaled deeply and sprang into action, pushing past the pain, nausea, and fear. Hand over hand, she hauled herself up the rope.

One, two, three, four—

Heat seared her bare back, and agony sliced through the back of her right thigh.

"Damn it," she yelled, clinging to the rope as cannons fired on the Dauntless. Her muscles trembled, and bile flooded her mouth. Mer panted and yanked herself a little higher. A high-pitched ringing filled her ears, then the world imploded.

Her body soared through the air, and she crashed into the midnight waves, knocking the breath from her lungs.

Like a falling leaf, her body began to sink. Mer blinked until her eyes adjusted to the sea. Stillness settled over her soul as she came face to face with a leviathan. This was how she'd die. A memory flashed through her mind.

"I will love you for as long as the tides rise and fall." Ream's magenta eyes filled with emotion.

Mer blinked tears back, feeling like she would burst with love. "I will love you and stand by your side as sure as the moon fills the night sky."

No one was present for their bonding ceremony. Her grandfather certainly wouldn't approve, but she didn't care. It was her life, and they'd waited long enough. War was on the horizon, and time was precious.

Seahorses and jellyfish danced around them in the current as Ream leaned close to place a sweet kiss on her lips.

"I love you."

Her fingers tangled in his loose, white hair. "As I love you." Would this be the last time they saw each other?

Ream cupped her cheeks and smiled at her. "This is our beginning, not our ending."

She nodded, fear flooding her for the first time. It was happening. The Scythians were really attacking, and she'd committed treason to give the people above support. There was no going back.

"You're everything to me." Mer leaned her forehead against his and stared into his eyes. "Once this is over..."

His soft smile grew. "We'll spend copious amounts of time lounging in bed and celebrating our marriage and victory."

Mer snapped out of the memory as the beast glided closer, rows of daggerlike teeth gleaming in the patches of moonlight that lit up what had become a watery grave. Mer gazed blankly at the monster and hummed a few notes of the kin song in a last-ditch attempt to dissuade him from eating her.

He paused and slowed his approach, circling to her left. Mer kicked her good arm and leg and kept him in her vision. If she was going to die, it wasn't going to be from a sneak attack.

Again, she hummed a few notes of the kin song, something she was taught as a child to help the beasts distinguish her as friend instead of food. Her heart galloped in her chest as he drifted closer.

I'm sorry, Ream. I love you.

The beast did not attack. He bumped her chest with his pointed snout. Mer blinked in shock. Her fear dissipated at the affectionate greeting.

With slow careful movements, she ran her hand along his snout and down his back to his dorsal fin. Mer slid her good leg over his spine and laid her cheek against his rubbery hide, her fingers curled around his fin. She clicked gently, using the last of her air to politely ask for a ride.

A smile touched her lips as the beast glided forward in response. Her eyes turned toward the writhing watercolor surface of the sea as dots crossed her vision and the world blurred around her.

Death wasn't beautiful, but at least she'd finally know peace from the weighty guilt she'd carried around for far too long.

***

"Breathe, damn it!"

Mer spewed seawater, her throat burning. She coughed, pain wracking her body as the change took over.

"That's it," Sam crooned. "You're alright."

It didn't feel like she was alright. It was as if someone ran a fire poker along her neck and then shoved it down her throat. "What?" she croaked, blurrily staring up at Sam's bruised face.

He held a finger to her lips and cradled her against his chest. "Don't speak. You have severe wounds to your gills and neck."

She swallowed, wincing at the pain, and the taste of metal coins in her mouth, even as her eyes drooped. Damnation, she was tired.

"Don't worry. Ream will be here soon. Just rest a little and you'll be able to fight another day."

Oblivion washed over her.

Chapter Two

Sage

Blood sprayed across her face. Sage jerked her blade back as the warm, Scythian lifeblood ran down her hand and forearm. The warrior gurgled something unflattering and bared his scarlet-stained teeth before his lifeforce fled his body. His last breath froze in the winter wind for a moment before being swept away.

She stared at his body strewn across the first skiff of snow winter had to offer—his body an ugly reminder of what the days ahead of her held. Sage crouched and wiped her slick fingers on the warrior's leather jerkin, her eyes surveying the chaos and violence that rolled like the raging sea around her. She scarcely registered anything but her own heart beating frantically in her ears. Her lip curled as she spotted an Aermian soldier pinned down but fighting wildly.

Damn, Hayjen.

The frigid wind whipped across her face as she stood, and she caught Rafe's eye signaling her next move, then sprinted toward her uncle, leaving Rafe behind. He'd catch up soon enough.

A warrior spotted her and lunged into her path from the right, swinging a massive battle ax. Sage dropped onto one knee and slid in the muddy snow. Time seemed to slow as the ax cut through the space above her head, the slick soft sound of metal slicing the empty air. It was a sound she'd become familiar with; she'd managed to escape with her life for over three months, incurring more scars than she could count.

She twisted in the snow, then swung her sword backward, catching her enemy above his ankle, severing his Achilles tendon. The man bellowed and crashed to his knees. Pain echoed in every line of his face as promises of revenge fell from his chapped lips.

Sage pushed herself back to her feet and continued to run, the mud beneath her boots threatening her balance. She wobbled for a moment, then steeled herself, before she crashed into the melee surrounding Hayjen. Breaching the madness her uncle had waded into upped her chances of death—or worse, capture—a hundredfold. Her fingers squeezed the hilt of her sword, and she shoved the small prickle of terror away. It had been her constant companion for so long, her sense of fear had dwindled to almost nothing.

Except fear of the warlord, her mind whispered insidiously.

Her jaw clenched, and she narrowed her eyes on the Scythian about to cut Hayjen down from behind. The rush of her footsteps must have given her away, but not soon enough to change the outcome she had in mind for him. The warrior spun toward her, his black dreads flaring around him, as she sprinted up the remains of an old war machine and launched through the air. By the time she hit the ground, the warrior fell beside her. It wasn't guilt, or shame, or rage that fueled her—just a blank numbness and an animalistic need to save her family.

Hayjen was a madman. Scythian warriors came at him from every angle, but he never slowed, never faltered, even as some of their blows struck true.

A pair of hands seized Sage from behind and pulled her against an armored chest. "My lord will be so happy with my catch."

Doubtful. The Scythian warrior wouldn't take her anywhere.

He grabbed a fistful of her braid and yanked her head back. She hissed and spun toward the bulky warrior. He smiled at her, pulled her hair to his nose, and inhaled, his whole body shuddering in delight.

His mistake.

Sage lashed out with her dagger, cutting off six inches of her braid as well as two of his fingers. The warrior stared blankly at his bloody hand, then began to tremble. Now came the worst part: the berserker rage. It was a blessing and a curse. The rage made the warriors stupider, but they also became virtually unstoppable.

She geared up to take on the swelling monster of a man when Rafe attacked him from behind, dispatching the warrior without more than a flick of his wrist. He eyed Sage, seemingly scanning her for wounds, before slanting his gaze toward her uncle.

In unison, they attacked. It felt like coming home.

Every movement she made was calculated, and, no matter where she turned, Rafe was always at her back. Her arms shuddered with fatigue by the time they reached the center of the mayhem and closed ranks with Hayjen, who was covered in scarlet. His blood or their enemies', she didn't know.

"It's time to come in," she said, her voice rusty from disuse.

Hayjen shook his head, his ice-blue eyes searching the battlefield.

No doubt for another hopeless fight. "I can fight."

"Just because you can, brother, doesn't mean you should. The next wave of soldiers are coming," Rafe rumbled softly.

Hayjen shook his head and took one step forward.

"You're done." Her whisper cut through the air like her blade, icy and hard as steel.

Hayjen froze and glanced over his shoulder, his face pinched in stubbornness. "No."

"No?" she repeated, some of her numbness burning away as her rage surfaced. "I will drag you back myself. Get your ass back to camp."

"Is that an order, my lady?" he sneered.

"It is."

Hayjen snarled but took no further steps to wage war.

Sage glanced at Rafe, palming her blades. "Are you ready?"

Rafe graced her with a chilling smile that set the hair at the nape of her neck on end. "Any time you are, little one."

***

White flurries dropped from the dark clouds above, swirling in a pagan dance as their trio finally set foot in their camp. Soldiers bustled from tent to tent or lounged in intimate groups. Pots and pans clanged together as the camp's cooks prepared dinner, while horses nickered in the background. It was almost cozy if one could blot out the sound of the Scythian war drums and stench of death that followed Sage wherever she went. Her right knee buckled, and she wobbled before regaining her balance. She'd pushed herself too hard during this last round, and that was dangerous.

"You need to rest," Rafe said softly. She lifted her eyes and followed his gaze to the fiilee mulling at the far edge of the camp.

Sage nodded and rolled her aching right shoulder. She wouldn't be surprised if her entire arm was one big, ugly bruise. The Scythians hit harder than anyone she'd ever sparred with before, with the exception of Rafe. But her friend never fought with the hatred and rage that the warlord's warriors were capable of. They were madmen on the battlefield.

Her mind flashed to the memory of Zachael cutting down a massive Scythian warrior. The weapons master kept on moving, so he didn't see the monster push his guts back into his belly and force himself to stand, his predatory gaze latching on to Zachael's back. Sage had, and she'd attacked. It took herself and three other men to bring him down.

A shiver worked through her, but she ignored it as Hayjen broke from their group. Her eyes narrowed on his back. *Oh no, he did not.*

"A word," she bit out.

Rafe's eyebrows rose, and he passed her a knowing look. "I'll meet with you and Tehl tonight."

Sage nodded curtly but never took her gaze from her uncle's stiff form. "Follow me if you'll please, Hayjen." The *or else* was implied.

She turned her back on him and stalked toward her tent. Soldiers scurried out of her way with polite nods or bows, and she swiped sweaty strands of hair from her face, not about to force a smile for the friendly faces she passed. Too much weighed on her shoulders. Too much anger teemed beneath the placid surface of her expression.

Her tent came into view, and she didn't slow as she pushed through the outer entrance flaps. It was blessedly empty for once. She stopped at the edge of the round table that dominated the space and studied the map and the small pieces representing their soldiers and the warlord's forces. Her chapped lips thinned at the sight.

Scythia was winning. Their own forces were like locusts. The enemy never faltered, but kept advancing.

Hayjen entered, his footsteps stopped behind her.

Sage closed her eyes and tried to grab the inner threads that barely leashed her temper. She faced Hayjen and leaned against the table, eyeing her uncle. He looked awful. His light blue eyes had sunken into his pale face that now had too many sharp angles. He'd lost weight. So much so, that, despite his burly build, he reminded her of a scarecrow. Ropy muscle wrapped around his bones in a grisly sight. For a moment, her anger dwindled, cooled by empathy.

"When was the last time you ate?" she asked.

Hayjen's brows wrinkled, confusion evident on his face. Clearly, he expected another line of conversation. She'd get to that.

He rubbed his bristly jaw, and her stomach lurched. He'd wiped his blood on the short strands in a macabre painting on his chin. It was enough to set her off. Bile flooded her mouth. She'd warred for hours today, and nothing made her want to heave other than seeing his blood smeared face.

"I can't remember."

His comment snapped her out of her thoughts, and she swallowed hard, her breathing shallow. "That's not good," she gasped.

Hayjen frowned. "Are you all right?"

Sage waved him away and shoved her nausea down. She wouldn't puke over something so stupid. "Funny, I was going to ask you that same question."

His lips firmed into a thin, white line. "Nothing to report."

She laughed, the sound sarcastic to her own ears. "Nothing to report. I find that interesting."

He shrugged. "It is what it is. Now, I'd like to take my leave."

Sage glared at him. "We haven't talked."

Another damn shrug from him. "Nothing to talk about."

Her eyes turned to slits, and she slapped a hand against the tabletop. The small figurines rattled. Then she stabbed a finger at her uncle. "This needs to stop," she growled. "You almost died today."

"Men are dying every day."

"But you're *trying* to die. That's different." Hayjen stiffened, and she took a closer step to him. "How do you think that would make Lilja feel?" Her aunt's name seemed heavy upon her tongue.

Her uncle jolted and glared at her. *"Don't."*

"Don't *what*? Say her name?"

"Just don't."

Sage forced herself to laugh. "You and I both know what she'd say if she saw the way you were fighting. You're being reckless. She'd hate that."

Hayjen trembled, and his fingers curled into fists. "Stop it."

"Stop telling the truth? Never, and neither would my aunt."

"Enough!" he bellowed.

Now they were getting somewhere. Anger, she could work with—numbness, not so much.

Sage circled closer to him. "What did you think you were doing out there? Other than courting a death wish? Did you think you could fight your way *through* the warriors?"

"No."

"Did you think you could reach the warlord on your own?"

His upper lip curled, and he bared his teeth. "You know nothing."

"You're wrong." Her throat tightened as the words tried to stick in her throat, but she forced them out anyway, despite how they tasted like ash. "I know pain. I know suffering. I know loss. And I miss her so damn much." Sage rubbed her chest, her gaze earnest. "I can't imagine what you are suffering—"

"No, you can't," he bit out.

"But I know she wouldn't want you to give up like this."

"How am I giving up?" Hayjen exploded, throwing his shaking

hands in the air. "I am giving Aermia everything!"

"No, you're not! Aermia doesn't need soldiers who wade into the fray, heedless of their orders or the lives of the men around them."

"I've only risked myself."

"Wrong," Sage shouted. "You've left your battalion short a man and without the direction of someone who's skilled in battle. They're *boys* without experience, Hayjen, practically children."

"They'll die with or without me."

Sage jerked at his callous words. "Do you even hear yourself? She'd be so disappointed."

Holy rage lit in Hayjen's eyes, and he approached her quickly, stabbing a finger into her leather chest piece. "You're a child! How would you know what she wanted? You knew her for a year. I spent twenty years of my life with that woman. I knew her backward and forward, just as she knew me."

Sage slowly lifted her hands and clasped his fist between her fingers as he towered over her. "I know." He tried to pull away, but she tightened her grip. "I know you miss her."

Hayjen choked, a sob gurgling in the back of his throat. "There's not a word to express what I feel," he said raggedly.

Squeezing his hand, she let go and hugged him, her cheek flush with his metal chest piece. "When I came back from Scythia, I contemplated dying."

There they were. The ugly words that shamed her so much.

Sage continued on, "The pain seemed like too much, the emotions too bright and sharp, the nightmares too terrifying. What scared me the most was the isolation. I could be in a room full of people, and, yet, I'd feel alone, empty." She licked her dry lips. "I haven't suffered your tragedy, but I can recognize pain and self-destruction. You wear it like warpaint."

"He needs to die."

She pulled back and craned her neck to look her uncle square in the eye. "You and Lilja helped save my life when I couldn't even see why it was worth saving." Emotion swelled in her chest, and tears flooded her eyes. "You both gave me a life and showed me love that I could have never imagined, and I'll be damned if I don't fight for you like you fought for me."

Her words lingered between them, and a tear slipped down his cheek.

"You are not alone. You are loved." Her bottom lip wobbled. "I refuse to let him destroy your life. Don't let him win. Fight!"

Hayjen's whole body began to shake, and he snatched her up into a rib-crushing hug. She hugged him back fiercely, wishing she could imprint how much she cared for him into his skin. Hayjen silently wept, and Sage let her tears loose.

They grieved together.

Slowly, some of the tension in his body released, and he pulled back, his pale eyes overly bright in his haggard, dirty face.

"I don't feel alive," he whispered. "I feel like I died with her."

More tears flooded Sage's eyes. "You're not gone yet."

"I see so much of my sister in you." Hayjen smiled weakly and swiped at her cheek, her salty tears lingering on his fingertips. "And *Lilja*." Her name was said with reverence.

"We may not have shared blood, but she was blood. She changed my life."

"She *was* my life." Her uncle scraped a hand through his hair until the ends stood up, making him look so boyish, it caused her heart to clench. "I'll do better tomorrow."

"Tomorrow and all the other tomorrows after that."

"I'll try."

Sage knew he would. She had let him rampage for long enough. Today wasn't the end of his pain, not by any means, but it was a step in a healthier direction.

"Get some sleep."

Something haunted flashed through his eyes. "It's not so simple. The horror doesn't go away when sleeping."

Nightmares were miserable. "I'll have Mira mix something for you."

He nodded and lifted the tent flap, then glanced over his shoulder as he left. "Love you, baby girl."

Sage pinched the bridge of her nose to keep from crying. That was the first time he'd used the endearment since Lilja's death.

"I miss you," she whispered to the empty war chamber.

Wiping her face, she inhaled deeply to get ahold of herself, then latched onto her cold determination to destroy the warlord.

Sage flicked a glance at the map. Scythia might be winning, but the tide would turn.

If she had to cut every single warrior down herself to get to the bastard on the Scythian throne, she would. The warlord had claimed that he'd made her what she was today.

In that moment, he was right.

He'd twisted her into a killer.

In response, she'd forged herself into a weapon.

Sage pulled the necklace from her shirt and stared at the dainty poison ring hanging from the dull, silver chain. Lilja had given it to her before they rode out months ago. Sage toyed with it until the poisonous needle lunged from its hidden position, a translucent poison seeping from the tip.

It was only a matter of time until she destroyed the warlord.

Chapter Three

Tehl

The Scythian army buzzed with activity in the distance as the evening light waned. The clank of metal gears told Tehl his enemies were cranking the catapults. The warlord shouted orders to his men, and smaller machines rocketed forward as foreboding warriors rechecked their levers.

The first massive stone launched into the air from the distant war machines. The rock disappeared into the dark, swirling clouds and reappeared just before impact.

"Get down!" Tehl screamed as the crack of stone on stone filled his ears.

Another boulder launched into the air and came crashing down to the earth, the vibration under his feet causing him to stumble. The soldiers around him dove and created one massive shield to protect their battalion from the volley of arrows that followed in the wake of the stone.

Tehl lifted his head, ears ringing, and scanned the area around him. Soon, it would be too dark to see anything. They had to take out the war machines. Now.

Raziel crawled to his side, dirt smeared across his cheek. The Methian prince's amber eyes found the closest catapult. "Their machines are too powerful." He glanced at Tehl. "We need to take them out."

"My thoughts exactly." He pushed to his feet and eyed what was left of his battalion. "We're pressing forward. The goal is to destroy the closest ballista. We'll have the cover of darkness."

Grave but determined expressions rippled through his battered battalion. His attention paused on a scrawny boy who didn't look to be over the age of fourteen. He was hardly a man. He shouldn't be on the battlefield. Damn Scythia. Damn the warlord. Aermian children were dying.

"What's your name?" he asked gruffly.

The boy's eyes widened, and he nervously shifted from foot to foot, his sword looking far too big in his small hands. "Benjamin, my lord."

"Benjamin, I need you to report to Lord Zachael and inform him of our movements. Can you do that?"

"Y-yes!"

"Get on with you and be aware of your surroundings."

The boy nodded and sprinted toward their camp in the distance, the bloody mayhem swallowing his small form. Tehl's heart squeezed. He prayed that the boy made it back safely.

"That was well done," Gav muttered from his right. "The boy wouldn't have survived. He would've only been another distraction for us."

"Heads up," Raziel bellowed.

They tightened their circle just as the machines flung burning, tar-coated stones into the teeming mass of soldiers. Several fell short, exploding into the ground in a spray of earth, carving craters into the wet dirt. The other stones bounced into the fray, the explosion sending men flying like sticks in a children's game.

Fire-covered stones arced through the air like shooting stars, then crashed back to the ground, flames licking over men before flickering out, leaving scorched earth and death in their path. The wind rose and cut across the chaos with a whistle in a swirl of dust, smoke, and debris.

"Let's move," Tehl commanded. "The smoke will give us cover." They only had a short window of time to reach the machine before the enemy saw them. "Pick up anything you think will make a good torch. We'll burn that monster to the ground."

He smiled darkly as he slipped his sword into his scabbard and plucked an abandoned Scythian spear from the ground. He ripped fabric from the nearby slain Scythian and wrapped it around the tip of the blade. The warlord had inadvertently given them the weapon they need to destroy his catapults.

Raziel growled and spat onto the dead warrior. "Unnatural trash."

Tehl ignored the prince's comment and cautiously made his way forward, his eyes watering from the grit. The sickly stench of smoke and death invaded his nostrils, and he tugged fabric up and over his nose and mouth. He never seemed to be able to wash the stench from his skin.

The rattle of chainmail caught his attention, and Gav lurched forward. Tehl clapped a hand on his cousin's shoulder and shook his head, even though his heart was heavy. They couldn't help the pinned down soldiers. "We cannot stop and fight every fight along the way," he told Gav softly, firmly keeping anger out of his voice and off his face. Not anger at his cousin, but at the fact they were leaving soldiers to their deaths as Scythian warriors cut a swathe through them like a plague of locusts.

Gav's jaw clenched, and he wrenched his shoulder out of Tehl's grip, but he kept silent.

"If you want to drop out and foolishly die, then do so without argument," Tehl said. "I will not stop you. The rest of us have a mission, a vital one. We cannot afford distractions, no matter how many dire circumstances we come across. The machines are the huge problem here. If we don't take them out, we can't win this war. Either leave or be silent."

No one moved. No one spoke. So be it.

Sweat dampened Tehl's palms as they crept closer to the huge catapult, fire raging across the dry meadow grasses. The beat of the Scythian war drums echoed in his ears, along with his racing pulse. With each step, they got closer to the ballista, and he expected a swarm of warriors to attack them. He searched the darkening night for any hint of threats. Tehl paused when a low shriek filled the air.

His eyes widened. "Arrows!"

The soldiers lifted their shields, once again creating a barrier from the threat in the sky. Tehl hefted his shield closer to his chest and clenched his right fingers tighter around his spear as they waited out the fall of armor piercing projectiles.

"Do you think they saw us?" a soldier grunted from behind as the barrage continued.

"No," Raziel muttered. "If they knew we were here, we'd be dead already."

Gav snickered, and Tehl shot an annoyed glance at him over his right shoulder.

His cousin sneered at him and held up his hands. "You know I can't help it."

Gav had always been prone to laughing when things got tense or awkward. It seemed, even in war, that hadn't changed.

The smoke cleared, just for a moment. Tehl turned back and strained to peer through the deepening evening light to get a clear look at their destination. All sound ceased, and his vision dipped. The warlord stood two hundred paces from the catapult, laughing like a madman as he slashed his way through Aermian soldiers.

Before he knew what he was doing, Tehl sprinted toward the devil.

Chapter Four

Jasmine

The bone-jarring screech was what pulled her from her sleep. Jasmine gingerly touched her throbbing temple. Stars, her head hurt. Flashes of her kidnapping ran through her mind. They had drugged her. What else had they done?

She slowly blinked her eyes open and gritted her teeth as another explosion went off, rattling the window to her right and lighting up the curtain and the man currently staring outside.

Orion.

Her stomach bottomed out, and she jerked upright. The room seemed to roll, and Jas placed her left hand down to steady herself. The soft quilt and mattress beneath her palm caused panic to wrap around her chest. They'd placed her on a bed. Her hands shakily ran over her body. Her dress wasn't disturbed, and her body felt normal, but…nausea slammed into her, and she leaned over the bed to vomit.

Her eyes watered. Feeling fine didn't mean she was okay.

"Are you all right?" Orion asked, stepping toward her.

Jasmine thrust her hand out to stop him and scrambled backward until her spine met the corner. The leather of her thigh holster rubbed against her inner left leg. Sucking in a deep breath, she tried to calm herself. If they'd touched her, they would have discovered the blades and taken them from her. They'd left her unmolested, and she wasn't powerless.

Pain rippled across his handsome face, and he held his hands out in a placating manner. "I won't hurt you."

Traitorous tears sprang to her eyes. They already had. "Stay away from me," she whispered harshly.

Thunder rumbled, and a crack of lightning lit up the room, giving her a better sense of where she was. It was a small home with only one door and window. Across the room from where she sat held two chairs, a short table, and a screen which she assumed hid a chamber pot from the rest of the room. Her gaze darted back to the door. Only one escape, and Orion was guarding it.

He stared at her with remorse. "Do you need anything?"

Jasmine fought not to throw up again. He had always been the most caring and sensitive of her warriors. She froze. Not *her* warriors. Her *enemies*. Orion didn't get to care for her. "Where are we?" she croaked.

"Somewhere safe."

Safe. What a joke. Her arms curled around her belly as Orion dropped the curtain once again. His gaze paused on her bump, and a small smile lit up his face.

"You're a miracle." He said it with so much awe and what she refused to acknowledge as love.

Jas swallowed thickly, her throat aching and the cloying scent of the drug still stuck in her nose. "I need to go home." She scanned the simple room again. The daggers strapped to her thighs practically burned with the need to be used on the Scythian warrior. "Why am I here?"

"You know why," he whispered, his dark eyes soft. "We came for our family, for you and the babe."

Rage unlike anything she'd experienced burned through any residual fear she was harboring. *Family?* "I am nothing to you," she said coldly. "This babe is *mine*." And Sam's.

Orion winced and rubbed at his brow. "These aren't the best circumstances, but let me explain to you how much we—"

"No!" Jasmines sliced a hand through the air. "You get to say nothing to me. Let me go. I need to return to my children."

"They will join us soon."

Ice ran down her spine. "Excuse me?"

"We would never take you from your children, Jasmine. Mekhl and Phoenix are retrieving them."

Crippling horror settled over her. *No*. "Leave them alone! Don't you dare touch them!"

"We would never hurt you and yours." He moved back to the window and lifted the curtain, scanning whatever lay outside. "They'll be well protected."

Her plan of escape dissipated. There was no way she could leave without knowing if the warriors had Ethan and Jade.

Please, Vienna. Please have escaped. The older woman would take care of her children.

A tear dripped down her cheek. "You can't keep us. Please let us go."

"Jasmine," Orion whispered. "I cannot. You're breaking my heart."

"I'm begging you. I'm happy in Aermia. You need to let us go and forget this plan." She hiccupped and prayed he would falter. "Are you under command?" She edged toward him. "There's protection for you in Aermia. We can live there." A lie. "Please, don't take me back."

"You don't know what you're saying," Orion hissed, his gaze searching the room like there was someone listening to the conversation. "Be silent before we all die."

Jasmine placed her feet on the floor and began to tremble. "If you won't let me go, I promise I'll hurt myself and the babe." The words were a bitter lie on her tongue. She'd never hurt the babe, but he didn't know that. Orion faced her, his expression blank. "I know what you did," she choked out. "You know it was wrong."

He took a hesitant step in her direction. "You don't know what you're saying. I read books on breeding women. Your moods get out of control."

A bitter laugh escaped her, and she pinned him with a hard glare. "Try me. Do you really think I could ever love a child from a monster? A child of rape?" she shouted, shaking. The hateful words weren't true. She loved her babe without limit already. There was nothing she wouldn't do. But her words struck the intended chord. Orion looked like he was about to break into a thousand pieces.

"I wish you hadn't said that," he murmured, sorrow creeping into his expression.

That was her only warning before he attacked, pinning her to the bed. Jasmine screamed once before he placed a piece of sweet-scented linen over her nose and mouth. She bit his hand. Her struggles slowed, and her eyelids grew heavy, even as she begged her body not to give up the fight.

"I'm sorry," Orion whispered, his soft brown eyes watching her. "We can't take a chance of you hurting yourself or the babe. You're too precious." He drew a calloused finger softly down her cheek. "Sleep well, love."

That was the last she heard before darkness washed over her.

Chapter Five

Sam

"I don't care how you do it, but get them out of the city with minimum losses," the king commanded.

Sam brushed his dirty hair from his face and added, "It's a ploy to draw our attention from the bay. We can't allow them to get any closer. Our port is everything."

The king nodded to the captains of his fleet. "Dismissed."

Their men filed out, and Sam ran a hand down his face.

"Son, you look tired. You should get some sleep."

Sam nodded, not really seeing anything. "It's just beginning, and I'm exhausted already." He cast a glance east. "And the sun will rise within the hour."

His father moved around the makeshift table in their training yard and slapped him on the back. "It will only get harder from here. Go and spend time with your family."

"My lord?"

Both royals turned to face the Elite striding their way. Xav sketched a short bow before stepping closer. "I have an old woman trying to enter the palace gate."

"The order has been given that no one but military personnel is to enter," Sam said slowly.

Xav nodded. "Yes. We've followed protocol, but she keeps insisting to see you."

"Me?" Sam asked, his mind whirling. Was it one of his spies? He'd sent Marilyn out this morning. Did she have news already? If so, why was she coming through the gate? "Take me to her."

Sam followed the Elite across the training yard and to the heavily-fortified stone wall surrounding the palace. Xav waved a hand at the guard stationed at the entrance. The portcullis rose, and they exited. Sam scanned the darkened streets, his attention landing on a stern-looking older woman speaking heatedly to two soldiers. Her curly gray hair was a fuzzy halo around her wrinkled face. He'd seen her before. A little face peeked around her dirt-streaked skirts, and the world disappeared from beneath him.

Ethan.

Terror rushed through his veins. He launched forward, startling Xav. The older woman met his gaze as he barreled down on the group. Ethan released the woman's skirts and launched into his arms. Sam clutched the little boy to his chest as Jade followed suit. He dropped to his knees, holding both children to his chest, his heart thundering.

"Mama's gone," Jade sobbed.

Sam held them close as the twins cried, their little faces pressed into his shirt. A stillness settled over him as Jade's words finally registered.

Mama's gone.

He pinned his icy gaze on the older woman. "Where is she?"

The older woman didn't flinch. "The apothecary was attacked. We almost made it, but Scythians broke in. Jasmine sent the children with me."

Their enemy took Jasmine. They took *his* wife and babe. For a moment, he thought he'd suffocate.

"Papa, you're crushing me," Ethan wheezed.

Sam forced himself to loosen his grip on the twins. Time was short. The longer they dallied, the less chance they had to find Jasmine. A hand settled on his shoulder, and he turned to meet his father's eyes.

The king held his arms out. "Let me take one of them."

Ethan went easily into his grandad's arms, and Sam stood, Jade clinging to him.

"You come with me," Sam barked at the old woman. "I need you to tell me everything you saw. Follow me."

For the first time in his life, he was on the edge of breaking apart. He wanted to destroy something and kill. Whoever had taken his wife would pay. A dark smile curled his lips.

Blood would spill.

CHAPTER SIX

Sage

Sage used to think that *bloodstained hands* was a metaphorical saying. War had taught her otherwise.

The water turned pink and cooled, but still she scrubbed on, determined to clean the blood from her hands. Her skin ached as she pressed the rough bristles of the crude brush deeper into the grooves of her fingers and palms. Sage hissed when the cuticle of her thumb ripped, and she slammed the brush down, panting heavily. Her chafed fingers flexed against the small table while her gaze locked on the soiled water.

If only it was that easy to wash away pain.

Her conversation with Hayjen had left her feeling dull and out of touch with the world. It was so tempting to sink into the little black box in the back of her mind that offered numbness and shelter from the pain and loss their camp suffered each day.

Soldiers were dragged into camp—some dead, some alive—and, statistically, it was only a matter of time before someone close to her died on the battlefield again. She hung her head as Garreth and Lilja flickered through her mind. Tehl could be dying among the fallen right now—

"Stop it," she whispered. "He's all right."

Sage squeezed her eyes shut and attempted to calm her racing pulse. There was no use borrowing trouble. If that scenario happened, she'd cross that bridge then.

Inhaling deeply, she opened her eyes and straightened, her blurry gaze resting on their unmade bed when she spun around. Crawling in the bed and passing out sounded wonderful, but Sage knew what would happen. Even if she got into bed, sleep wouldn't come until Tehl arrived. Staring at the ceiling, imagining every peril her husband could be going through, wouldn't help anyone.

Sage exited their quarters and passed through the war room area of the tent. She paused at the tent flap, and doubled back for her dark green cloak. The times for strolling outside without a fur or wool covering from head to toe were over.

Clasping the cloak around her throat, Sage lifted the hood and slipped through the tent flap. Stars above, it was bloody cold. Winters near the mountains and plains were harsher than she'd ever experienced. An Elite stood to her left, and a Methian warrior to her right—both silent, watchful.

A pang seized her chest. It was at times like this when she missed Garreth the most. He'd been with her since she'd entered the palace. Sage scarcely remembered a time when he wasn't quietly following her, his footsteps almost silent. Tehl didn't say much, but she knew he mourned his friend.

"A walk, my lady?" Domin, the Methian soldier, asked softly.

They'd learned her nocturnal habits pretty quickly, although her radius for travel now stayed firmly inside the camp due to a raid that had gotten too close for comfort one week prior.

"No, tonight I seek the infirmary."

Sage strode forward, this time more aware of her surroundings. Fires scattered throughout the camp, casting warm light against the canvas tents. She smiled and murmured words of encouragement as she weaved her way toward the sick tent. She paused just outside the infirmary, her nose wrinkling at the smell wafting from it.

The place reeked of despair and death.

Puffing out a breath, Sage forced a smile on her face and stepped inside. A wall of heat slammed into her, and sweat beaded on her forehead immediately. She pulled her hood from her head and moved to the first bed on her right. The soldier rolled his bandaged head to the side and smiled, revealing his missing teeth. Reslin.

"Back so soon, Princess?" Reslin asked and gestured with his burned stump of an arm.

"With company like yours, how could I keep away?" she joked, all the while feeling like she was going to throw up. It wasn't the injuries that bothered her non-existent sensibilities, but the fact that she couldn't fix them, she couldn't take away their pain, that they'd suffer for years after the war ended. Her smile waned, and she jerked her chin toward his arm. "How are you doing, really?"

Reslin teetered his head back and forth. "The pain is gruesome, but I'm one of the lucky ones." His expression cooled. "I couldn't keep count of how many they brought in today, but I know six were taken out."

Sage nodded, her heart turning to lead. Six more dead. Mira was probably destroyed. "How is Mira?"

Reslin shook his head. "She's pale, and I haven't seen her eat all day."

"Thank you."

Sage smiled at him one last time and scanned the gigantic tent for Mira. She caught a glimpse of the healer sponging the forehead of a Methian warrior. There wasn't any way Sage would be prying her away for a meal anytime soon.

"Will you have someone bring some bread, cheese, and wine in?" she whispered discreetly to the Elite on her left. He nodded and ducked out of the tent.

Sage continued down the line of beds, speaking with every soldier. She halted next to the last bed and scowled at its occupant.

Blaise.

The Scythian woman scowled back at her and leaned against the tent wall. "Don't give me that look."

"I'm allowed to glare at you if I want to. You should be resting." Sage waved a hand at the pile of weapons resting in the center of the cot.

"I *am* resting. You don't see me walking about." Blaise stabbed her blade at the cot. "Sit."

Sage rolled her eyes and sat, mindful of her friend's leg, and picked up a stone and blade. The Methian warrior took his place near her side. She flicked a glance in his direction and watched as he scanned the room for threats. Sage turned back to sharpening the blade and both women fell into a comfortable silence, the slick sound of metal being sharpened.

"You need to prepare yourself," Blaise said in a low voice.

Sage paused and glanced at her friend. "For what?"

The woman held her gaze. "For the next phase."

"We're prepared as much as we possibly can be."

"When's the last time you saw him?"

There wasn't any doubt who the *him* referred to. Sage wet the blade in the bucket near her feet and started working the blade over the stone once again. "It's been a while."

"He's planning something."

She scoffed. "He's always planning something. He's always three steps ahead of us."

"He's had centuries to plan this."

Sage shivered at the reminder of what kind of creature they were facing. "We'll handle whatever he throws at us." Little blue toes flashed through her mind, and her jaw set. "He's tried to break us before."

Blaise readjusted her leg and rubbed at her knee, her brow furrowed.

Sage watched her then asked, "How is it healing?"

Her friend shrugged. "It's almost there. I'll be able to go into battle on the morrow, I should think."

Sage jerked and narrowed her eyes at Blaise. "You're not going onto that battlefield tomorrow, even if you have the advantage of speedy healing."

"That's exactly *why* I should be out there. I can heal faster than everyone else."

Sage wiped the blade against the blanket and placed it next to the other finished blades. "Do you know how many times you've been hurt?"

"Only a handful of times."

She glared harder at Blaise and held up her right hand, fingers spread. "Five times. Five times you've almost died. As soon as you enter the battle, you become the target. I've seen the way the warriors go after you. They aren't just out for blood. They're out for your pain."

Blaise held her gaze. "I'm a traitor."

"So you deserve to be raped and killed?" she hissed. Her stomach turned as she remembered Blaise's torn clothing and the pattern that had been carved into her skin.

Her friend blinked and stared at her lap. "In our culture, betrayal is the ultimate sin." She lifted her dark brown eyes and squarely met Sage's gaze. "Betrayal is disgraceful and begets disgrace."

"What they've been attempting isn't disgrace, it's barbaric. Animals don't even treat each other in that way."

Blaise shrugged. "I knew what the consequences would be when I helped you escape. I don't regret my choices."

"I regret a lot of things," Sage admitted.

"Regret helps no one. Move forward."

"I'm trying." She sighed and stood, her body aching.

"You're pushing too hard," Blaise said, her gaze running over Sage's form. "You'll get yourself killed if you don't slow down."

A wry smile touched her mouth. "That's a little like the pot calling the kettle black, isn't it?"

Her friend arched a midnight brow. "I'm Scythian," she said haughtily, as if that explained everything.

Sage shook her head, muttering, "You can take the princess from the palace, but you can't take the—"

Blaise growled and stabbed a short sword toward Mira's bustling form. "Go check the healer. She's pushing herself as hard as you, I suspect. Every day, I'm amazed she's still standing."

Worry filled Sage as she approached Mira, who had moved to the center of the massive tent and washed her hands vigorously with a strong-smelling soap. Sage snatched the pitcher up before Mira could reach for it and poured the warm water over the healer's hands.

"Thank you," Mira mumbled.

"You're welcome." She eyed the tent, spotting only two other healers. "Where's Jacob?"

"He went home today. They need a healer of his talent in the capital."

The capital: Sanee. Stars above, she was so glad they hadn't pulled their soldiers from the fleet before war broke out. If they had left them... Sanee would have been captured.

"It's come to a standstill from what I've heard."

Mira wiped her wet hands on a clean towel, blew the loose blonde strands from her face, and then smiled weakly. "Father doesn't like to be far from the king."

"It's good that Sam and Marq have Jacob as a support." Sage gave her friend a concerned look. "You need a break."

Mira shook her head. "No time. Bandages need to be changed, wounds cleaned, poultices brewed, fevers managed, and then the surgeries..."

Sage shivered. She'd already assisted in two amputations, and the sounds the men made would forever haunt her.

One of the Elite entered the tent with a loaf of bread and a bottle of wine tucked under his arm and a hunk of cheese in his hand.

"At least eat," Sage implored.

"I'm not very hungry."

She wouldn't be either if she had been dealing with pus, blood, and bone all day. "If you don't care for yourself..." The Elite paused by their sides, and Sage took the cheese and wine from him. "You can't care for anyone else."

Mira eyed the cheese tiredly. Then, she plopped onto the dirt floor and held her hand out. "Hand it over."

Sage broke off a large hunk of cheese and passed the bottle down to Mira before gesturing for the bread. The healer took a bite of cheese and then drank straight from the bottle. After a few swallows, Sage tactfully stepped in and took the wine. She tore off a piece of the rough wheat bread and handed it to her friend. Mira ate mechanically, like she tasted nothing.

Handing the rest of the bread back to the Elite, Sage knelt and pulled Mira into a hug. Her friend pressed her forehead against Sage's shoulder and shuddered.

"Six today. Six."

"I know," she whispered.

"I thought I was prepared for this." Mira's voice hitched. "I wasn't, I'm not—*six!*"

"You did your best," Sage crooned softly.

The healer pulled back, her blue eyes sad. "But it wasn't enough."

"It's enough that you're here."

Mira pasted on a bright smile. "And I'm not going anywhere."

"I know." Sage squeezed her once more and then stood, taking the leftover food from the Elite. She placed it in a clean towel and set it on the counter near some lavender. "Eat this."

"I'll do my best." Mira stood and kissed her cheek. "Be safe."

Sage nodded, then continued her round along the next wall of soldiers. By the time she reached the exit to the camp infirmary, her eyes felt like they had sand in them, and her bones threatened to collapse.

Tehl had to be back by now.

Once again, she lifted her hood and strode out into the freezing night air, her cloak stirring a flurry of snowflakes around her boots. The walk back to their tent seemed to take no time at all. She stood outside the entrance and stared at the tent flap. Anxious voices murmured just inside.

Her heart clenched, and fear started to rise when she didn't hear her husband's voice among them.

Be brave.

Sage prepared herself for the worst and stepped inside.

Chapter Seven

Sage

All voices ceased as she stepped into the tent. Four pairs of weary, concerned eyes stared at her with too much sympathy. Tehl wasn't among them.

The air was sucked from her lungs, and Sage couldn't get a decent breath.

No.

She began to tremble but forced the words from between her numb lips. "Does the crown prince still live?" she rasped, her voice almost failing.

Queen Osir gasped and strode from the war table, her amber eyes wide. "He's fine, little one. A few small injuries but fine." Sage's whole body sagged, and the Methian queen pulled her into a hug. "You okay?"

Sage nodded and pulled back. She pushed the loose hair from her face with a shaky hand and smiled weakly. "How goes it?"

Zachael eyed her and then the war map. "We're just discussing the movements of the Scythian army."

She squeezed Queen Osir's arm and moved around her to get a better look at the map. The Aermian and Methian soldiers were slowly being pushed backward, and the Scythians were taking over the south and the north. They couldn't allow the warriors to gain any more ground. If they weren't careful, their enemies would have them back up against the mountains.

Her gaze was drawn to the river that cut across the plains to the south. "They won't cross the river," she mused out loud. "They'd be bottled up."

Raziel hummed in agreement, the Methian prince looking more like a ragged pirate than royalty. "It would be the more difficult path. Logically, they should attack from the north."

Gav snorted, his lavender eyes filled with humor. "We all know how *logical* Scythia is."

Sage shot him a confused look. Why was he so chipper?

Raziel rolled his eyes. "More like crazy."

Zachael crossed his arms over his chest. "Crazy as the warlord might be, he's a tactical genius."

Gav's humor cooled, and something dark slithered through his eyes. "Some of our men were able to destroy one of his war machines today." A pause. "It wasn't easy."

Raziel scoffed. "It was a nightmare."

Sage leaned a hip on the table, her eyes feeling like they were filled with sand. Zachael squeezed her shoulder and moved to collect his cloak.

"Well done. The sooner we destroy every machine, the sooner the queen can launch the aerial attack and we can pull the fiilee from the coast." He tossed his cloak over his shoulders. "Our soldiers have their commands." He pulled his hood over his dark silver-streaked hair and held out his arm for the queen. "Tomorrow, we shall reconvene. My lady."

Sage nodded tiredly and didn't comment on how easily the queen took the weapons master's arm and disappeared out of the tent. Interesting. Maybe love had wiggled itself in, despite all the death they were exposed to.

Exhausted, Sage dragged her attention from the tent flap as Gav wove around the table and hugged her. She sank into his warmth and leaned her cheek against her friend's shoulder.

"I'll see you both in the morning," Raziel whispered before he slipped from the room.

She shuddered and hugged Gav tighter. "I thought Tehl had—"

Gav placed a hand on the back of her head and stroked what was left of her braid. "I know, I know. When I saw the look on your face..." He sucked in a sharp breath. "The fact is that he's okay."

"You were gone too long. How bad is it?" she murmured.

"A wound to the arm but not with a poisoned blade, thank the stars. He needs to be stitched."

"Thank you." She stepped back and studied her friend. His black hair had grown longer, and he'd taken to braiding the sides back in the Methian style. He used to carry an air of approachability. He was harder now. They all were, she supposed.

Gav kissed her forehead. "Get some sleep. Morning will be here soon."

"You too." She rubbed her forehead as he collected his brown cloak from the chair in the corner of the tent. If she wasn't mistaken, he smelled suspiciously like whiskey. Today must have been a close call.

He rarely drank. Her mind wandered to the long list of things she needed to take care of tomorrow. "The messenger is leaving with info for Sam tomorrow. If you have a correspondence for Isa, leave it here. I'll make sure it gets to her."

He smiled and pulled a letter from the breast pocket of his cloak. "I'm one step ahead of you."

Sage padded over to him and took the letter from his calloused fingers. "I know you miss her."

Gav frowned. "It's bizarre not to have her underfoot." His expression cleared. "Thank you and goodnight."

She watched him exit and rubbed her thumb across the rough parchment of his letter, then turned for their chambers. Tehl would come back when he'd finished with the healers. Hopefully, she would be able to keep her eyes open until then.

She lifted the flap and jerked to a stop at the sight that greeted her. Tehl was sprawled across their bed in his armor, sound asleep. Nali had wedged herself against his side and draped over the foot of the bed and onto the roughly woven rug that protected them from some of the chill of the frozen ground. The feline cracked a golden eye and rumbled a lazy hello. The fist around Sage's lungs loosened at the cozy sight.

Tehl was okay. Not dead on the battlefield somewhere.

"I wondered where you got off to," she whispered to Nali as she stepped fully inside. The feline huffed a contented breath and nuzzled the side of Tehl's neck. The man didn't even stir. She probably didn't want to know what had put him in such a state.

Sage toed off her boots and skirted around the end of the bed. She eyed his filthy armor and the bedding. It would need to be shaken out before they actually went to bed for the night.

"Tehl," she murmured.

Nothing.

"Tehl." Still nothing.

Biting her lip, she stared at the pillow and then his face. All she wanted to do was lie by his side and wake him gently, but that wasn't in the cards for them. He'd almost strangled her three weeks prior when he came out of whatever horror had plagued him while he slept.

"You might want to move, Nali." The leren didn't budge. "Your mistake."

Sage plucked the pillow from the head of the bed and, before she could feel guilty about it, smacked Tehl in the face with the feather pillow and lunged backward. Tehl exploded from the bed, gasping, weapons in both hands. Nali growled at being disturbed and slinked off the bed and out of the room.

Tehl's sapphire gaze followed the feline and then scanned the tent, settling on her. Recognition dawned, and he lowered his blades.

"Sage," he said with a half-smile. "The pillow again, love?"

Her heart clenched at the devastating smile on his face, and she forced herself to shrug. "I couldn't wake you."

"You didn't take my weapons?"

"You always hide them. I never know what you have stashed away." Her voice cracked.

His smile melted, and he squinted. "What's wrong?"

She swallowed. "Nothing is wrong. I'm fine." She wasn't at all fine. He'd come close to death; she knew it in her heart.

Tehl scoffed and shook his head, his midnight hair whipping around his face. "Not that word. Tell me what has you so upset."

Her bottom lip trembled and betrayed her as heat filled her eyes. She launched herself across the bed and into his arms. He'd dropped his blades when he'd stood, and now his arms snaked around her as she trembled.

"I thought you died," she choked out.

Tehl leaned back and cupped her face between his palms. "Whatever gave you that idea?"

Tears blurred her eyes. "You were late in arriving and then, when I entered the war room, you weren't among the war council. They all looked at me with so much pity. I just assumed..." An embarrassing hiccup escaped her.

He yanked her back into his arms and squeezed her against his chest. The metal from his breastplate dug painfully into her ribs, but she didn't care. He was real, alive, and whole. Sage ran her hands down his biceps, and he inhaled sharply.

Sage jerked back and eyed him with irritation. "You haven't seen Mira?" she demanded.

"I intended to. But I sat down just for a moment to take off my armor. Nali was purring, and I guess I fell asleep." He smiled sheepishly.

Men.

Rolling her eyes, she lifted her arms to the latches of his chest piece and began to unbuckle the right side. "Blaming it on the cat?"

Tehl grinned in amusement. "The cat? If that man-eating nuisance was here, I'm sure she'd be highly offended."

"Hmmm."

She finished up with the right side and moved to the left, her adept fingers making quick work of it. Sage grunted as she pulled the heavy breastplate away and leaned it against the small stationary washtub to the left of the bed.

"I don't know how you lug that around all day." She thumped her molded leather chest piece. "This is so much lighter."

"True," he said, running a knuckle across her left cheek. "But you're also a much smaller target. Harder to hit. Chances of an arrow finding your chest are slim."

She scoffed, helping him out of his pauldrons and depositing them on the floor. "I could make one stronger that was half the weight. Weight makes you slower. Slower means death."

Blood soaked the sleeve of his left bicep, and she winced when she saw the angry cut peeking out. "Do you want to go to the infirmary?"

Tehl released her and reached for the small, wooden box they kept at the end of the bed for occasions such as this.

He lifted the lid and pulled whiskey, bandages, and a needle and thread from the box. "Too tired." He held out the needle and thread to her. "Will you do the honors, wife?"

Sage took the needle from his fingers and gestured to their bed. "You know my stitches aren't as straight as Mira's."

Tehl tossed the supplies onto the bed and sat so he faced her. "Don't I know it."

She hid her smile.

"Help me with my shirt?"

He bent forward so she could help him pull the soiled linen shirt over his head. Blood rushed to her cheeks as she got an eyeful of naked chest and the small trail of dark hair that disappeared beneath the edge of his leather trousers.

Dirty and bloody.

Still, he was one of the most attractive men she'd ever laid eyes upon.

A goofy grin lifted her husband's lips, and his hands crept to her hips as he scooted to the side of the bed and tugged her closer to the mattress.

Sage arched a brow at him, knowing exactly what his game was.

"Not the time. We need to clean and stitch your wound."

With gentle pressure, he guided her into the space between his parted legs and rested his cheek against her lower belly. "You never know when the last time could be."

True.

She ran her fingers through his inky hair, and he tipped his head back so he could meet her eyes. It was moments like these that affected her the most. Quiet, humble moments when they held each other with love and affection. No outside world to interrupt them. She bent and placed her lips against his in a sweet kiss. Tehl's eyes closed as she pulled away, and she sat next to him, eyeing his cut. It was around three inches long and not terribly deep. More of an irritation than anything.

"Pass me the whiskey," she said briskly. They might as well get the worst of it over.

Tehl uncorked the spirits and took a heavy swig before handing the bottle over to her.

"I love you."

Sage startled and looked at him with surprise. Tehl showed love, affection, and devotion in his everyday activities. Rarely did he utter them out loud. Bloody hell, it must have been a really close call. Her pulse sped up, and she forced herself to take a calming breath. It wouldn't help anyone to think about what might have been.

"As I love you," she murmured back. Her gaze dropped to the whiskey. "But you might not by the time I'm finished with you."

CHAPTER EIGHT

Tehl

Tehl shifted to his side so he could stare down at his wife's face, the lone flickering lantern highlighting the contours of her skin. Sage's eyes flickered behind her eyelids, but she didn't otherwise stir. Even with dirt smeared on her cheek and a bruise forming around her left eye from a fight two days prior, she was still the most beautiful thing he'd ever seen.

She whimpered softly, and he reached out his right hand, gently stroking the downy hair at her temple. The furrows between her brows softened and disappeared. She snuggled closer to him and sighed deeply, her breath heating the bare skin of his chest. It was moments like this that he cherished the most. The unguarded way she sought his comfort even in slumber gave him a deep sense of satisfaction.

He ran his hand down her arm and carefully slipped his arm around her waist, gently tugging her closer into the shelter of his body, his wound burning. It had taken a lot to get them to this point, but even love couldn't fix everything. There had been some nights her nightmares were so vivid she'd attacked him. Her eyes had been open, but her mind was lost to the horrors she'd suffered in Scythia. His jaw tightened. The warlord had damaged her in a way Tehl couldn't fix. An invisible wound buried so deep in her heart that he doubted it would ever fully heal.

Tehl had promised that he would never hurt Sage to the best of his ability.

Today, he broke that promise.

The look on her face when he'd woken had absolutely gutted him.

Being pinned down hadn't terrified him, nor had the close call with destroying the war machine. It wasn't until they'd escaped and made it back to camp when the terror had set in, almost knocking him to his knees.

If Gav and Raziel hadn't taken care of the situation, Aermia would be down a prince and his wife would be a widow.

Guilt churned in his gut. The thought of death didn't scare him as much as the idea of leaving his wife behind with no one to protect her.

His lips twitched into the ghost of a smile. She would probably stab him for even thinking she needed someone to protect her. He traced her left, arching eyebrow with his fingertip and then ran it down the smooth bridge of her nose. A small part of him missed the little bump she used to have—a training badge of honor—one that had been erased by the demon ruling Scythia.

His lip curled.

The rage he hid from Sage sparked, and he had to release a slow breath to contain the urge to scream. It was a difficult thing to control;

one's emotions. Over the years, he'd thought he'd mastered the art.

Sage taught him differently.

He thought he'd known anger when she disappeared, when the warlord sent his letter, or at the mockery of a peace treaty. But it all paled in comparison to the fury he experienced when he'd watched Mira pry the metal thorns from his wife's neck. The devil had collared her—*collared her*—like an animal.

His gaze dropped to the silvery scars that circled her neck. She'd left Aermia bearing all the scars of her youth—accidents, fights, victories—only to return home with her past erased from her skin, and the warlord's actions imprinted there forever.

Tehl glared at the scars. Stars, he hated them. He'd die before he'd ever see her chained like that again. And he'd be damned before he let the warlord win the war and enslave the people of Aermia.

Sage shivered, and he pulled their covers over her bare shoulder.

He lay his head down and stared at the wall of their tent, his gaze blanking.

Today, he'd almost died.

Nothing in life was guaranteed, but today, he'd been too reckless. That recklessness had almost cost him his life.

He glanced back at Sage's face.

He'd let his emotions get the best of him. It was time to get them under control.

Tehl eased himself forward and pressed a soft kiss to Sage's forehead, his eyes drooping.

It was too late for midnight musings.

Tomorrow was coming all too soon, and, on the heels of it, more death.

CHAPTER NINE

Sage

Sage pushed her legs harder, her eyes locked on Lilja. Her aunt smiled sadly.

"Finish this," she mouthed.

A horrified scream caught in Sage's throat as the warlord's blade plunged through the Sirenidae's chest. Lilja began to convulse, and all sadness was wiped from her expression, replaced with disgust and disappointment. Blood dropped down her pale chin as she glared at Sage.

"This is your fault," her aunt spat, spraying blood. "You failed."

"No!" Sage screamed.

"You're worthless."

"I'm sorry," she sobbed, stumbling closer. "I tried."

"Not good enough."

Lilja lunged forward with a snarl and stabbed Sage in the chest. She gasped and gaped at the Sirenidae in betrayal.

"Why?" she gurgled, pain cutting deeply until she couldn't breathe.

Her aunt's magenta eyes darkened until it was the warlord's eyes looking out at Sage from Lilja's face.

"Because you've been found unworthy." Lilja leaned closer, her black gaze holding glimmers of hate. "Because you're mine."

***

Her eyes flew open, and Sage gasped, clutching her chest, the phantom pain disappearing. Goosebumps ran along her arms and legs as she sat up and scanned their tent, the warlord's presence still lingering in her mind. Nali huffed and snuggled closer to her left side between the mattress and the canvas wall.

She placed a sweaty palm on the feline's head and stroked her soft ears with shaking fingers. That dream was a new one. In the weeks since her aunt's death, she'd relived Lilja's murder almost every night. But, tonight, it seemed, the warlord had deemed to visit her.

A shiver worked through her, and Sage clutched the blankets closer to her chest as she scanned their quarters once more for anything unusual. One chair in the left corner with their discarded armor. A small washtub to the right of the bed. Nothing else. No intruder.

Even though she could clearly see no one was there, it still felt as though she was being watched.

Tehl's rough hand moved beneath the covers and squeezed her thigh.

"Nightmare?" he mumbled, still half asleep.

She swallowed hard and forced the tremble out of her voice. "The usual. Go back to sleep, love."

He scooted closer and wrapped an arm behind her back, then one across her thighs, effectively hugging her. He pressed a kiss to the exposed skin at her hip.

"You first..." His words drifted off, and he released a snore.

A sleep-deprived giggle slipped from her, and Sage slapped a hand over her mouth. Tehl still never believed her when she told him that he snored. She pulled her hand from her mouth and gently combed the black hair from his handsome face. He looked tired. Dark smudges lingered beneath his eyes, and, even in sleep, his expression never slackened. It was as if he was still battling.

Her brow furrowed. She wasn't the only one who had nightmares. He didn't always thrash or call out like she did, but, in mornings, the haunted look in his face gave him away.

Nali plopped her head in Sage's lap and purred. She smiled at the leren. "Are you jealous?"

The feline butted her in the belly with her head, encouraging Sage to scratch her ears. Sage touched Tehl's whiskered cheek one last time before she wrapped both her hands around her companion's pointed ears and massaged them. Nali's purr rumbled louder in pleasure.

"Hush or you'll wake him up."

Nali and Tehl both had a way of calming her down and helping her fall back to sleep. In no time, Sage's eyelids were drooping, and she found herself snuggling back into the blankets and her husband's body, one hand idly running through her feline's coat.

She was almost asleep when Nali's purr cut off abruptly, and the fur beneath Sage's palm stood on end.

Sage stiffened and slowly sat up, her ears straining to hear what the leren's could. What was coming for them?

Her right hand squeezed Tehl's shoulder, and she shook him. He jackknifed upward and blinked at her, sleep fleeing his eyes when he got a look at her expression.

"Something's not right—" she began to say when the first explosion shattered the stillness of the night.

Tehl crashed into her as he threw his body over hers. Nali snarled and then whined.

Sage tampered down the scream caught in the back of her throat, her fingernails digging into his sides. She peeked around his shoulder as the second explosion went off. Immense light flared outside their tent, showing the shadows of soldiers running past.

"Get up!" Gav bellowed. "Fire!"

"Wicked hell," Tehl muttered.

He jumped up, pulled Sage with him, and tossed his shirt over his head, then threw Sage's leather chest piece at her. Hastily, she slipped her arms through the straps and scurried over the bed to haul Tehl's metal breastplate from the floor. He moved to her, and they made quick work of his armor.

She jammed her feet into her boots just as Tehl tossed her cloak over her head.

"Put it on," he said gruffly, already disappearing through the tent flap.

Sage hastily swung her cloak over her shoulders and bounded after him, her boots thumping against the hard ground. She burst from the tent and froze. The blaze raged in the not-so-far distance, flames dancing above the sea of tents in a pagan dance. The hair at the nape of her neck rose at the tormented screams that sliced through the air.

"Princess?" She slowly turned toward the speaker; Domin looked at her with concern. "What do you need?"

Her mouth bobbed and she scanned the pandemonium, her eyes snagging on Tehl's wide shoulders. She shook her head and sprinted after him. Two soldiers flanked her as she barreled toward the blaze, her eyes locked on the light.

What had the Scythians targeted?

Her brows furrowed. There wasn't anything on that side of the camp except… Her breath caught, and she stumbled a step before catching herself and speeding up, her heart in her throat.

The infirmary. Mira. Blaise. Her friends.

Her stomach twisted as the scent of charred flesh entered her nostrils. A flash of burned bodies and pale blue lips hovered in the forefront of her mind. Sage shoved the thoughts aside and pushed herself harder, thighs and calves burning. Sweat dampened her temples as the temperature increased. She swung around the last tent and skidded to a stop, a wall of heat and light slamming into her.

Sage raised her arm and squinted at the ball of fire, her clothes instantly sticking to her. Soldiers scrambled from the front part of the massive tent, carrying the wounded and sick. She frantically searched for a blonde braid or long, black hair. Her panic ratcheted up a notch when she didn't see either. She had to get to them. Had to help.

She took one step toward the infirmary when a hand wrapped around her bicep. She glared into Tehl's determined expression.

"You're not going in there."

Sage tugged her arm out of his grasp. "I won't stand on the sidelines. They need our help." They were wasting time. They didn't have time to argue.

His gaze darkened as he pulled a bandana over his mouth and nose. "I'm not asking you to stand aside. Help those who need it."

He swiftly kissed her on the forehead, tore his breastplate from his chest, and waded into the fray. The fire swallowed his form when he rushed into the blaze.

For one second, she pondered obeying him, but then the wooden support beams of the tent released a pained groan. The ground seemed to drop out from beneath her. It was only a matter of time before the whole thing collapsed.

Once again, she scanned the fallen. At least half the soldiers from the infirmary were still missing. Someone needed to start working from the rear before the entire thing burned. She ran around the side of the infirmary, and terror flooded her as she took in the mangled mess. The rear of the tent had been hit the hardest.

Oh god. Blaise.

Soldiers collected water from the nearby horse trough and stream and tossed bucketfuls on the inferno. Gav appeared at her side, sweaty and soot-smeared, his black hair singed at the front.

"It's going to go any second," he shouted over the cacophony.

Sage ignored him and climbed into the horse trough, cloak and all. Frigid water caused goosebumps to erupt over her skin as she leaned back to completely submerge herself. Her fingers curled around the trough's metal edges, and she hauled herself from the trough, water streaming from her clothes.

"Have you seen Mira or Blaise?" she demanded and blinked the water from her eyes. They had to be there somewhere. Time was being wasted. Every second her friends were in the tent, they were closer to death.

"No."

"They're in there. I know it. Mira would never leave her patients behind." She turned her eyes on her friend. "Help me."

Gav cursed. "I'll cut the canvas. You stand back." He wrapped a wet scarf around his head and over his nose, then pulled his sword from the scabbard at his hip and pushed past the soldiers fruitlessly tossing water onto the inferno.

Sage shivered and pulled her soaking cloak tighter around her. Domin wordlessly handed her a wet piece of fabric to tie over her nose and mouth before doing the same to himself. Not once had he questioned or slowed her down. Only offered his aid.

Her legs tensed as she switched her attention back to Gav. They had minutes, seconds to help those inside. He sliced at the canvas and lunged back as a burst of flames, heat, and smoke billowed from the tent.

"Quickly!" he screamed. "Follow me and don't touch anything."

A flicker of fear flashed through her as she dashed into the tent after Gav. Her eyes immediately watered and then dried. The skin on her face and hands felt like it was cooking. She scrambled to the left, toward where she'd left Blaise, her Methian protector hot on her heels.

"Blaise?" she screamed, eyes stinging.

Steam began to rise from her cloak. Bloody hell. It was way too hot.

Her heart bottomed out as she found a cot with a charred body lying upon it. As much as she wanted to look away, Sage forced herself to look closer. The physique was too masculine to be her friend.

She swung around and carefully maneuvered through the disaster zone as the flames hungrily licked at everything they could get to.

"Blaise!" Her eyes skipped over the still bodies that she couldn't help. *Please let Blaise or Mira not be among them.* "Mira!"

"Here," a strained voice called over the roar of the fire.

Sage spun, her damp cloak slapping her leather breeches. She squinted, desperately searching.

"Got 'em!" Gav bellowed.

She scrambled toward his voice and winced as she passed too many unfortunate souls.

Domin ghosted beside her, checking for pulses as they quickly moved deeper into the room. Sage skirted around a collapsed beam and coughed as the smoke thickened. Where in the hell were they?

"Don't step on me," a dark, rough voice rasped.

Sage dropped to her knees and reached through the swirling smoke toward the familiar voice. "Blaise?"

The Scythian woman lay across the floor, her leg pinned beneath the beam. The burning beam.

"Oh, god," Sage whispered as the Methian warrior knelt and began to pull fabric from his pockets and wrap them around his palms.

"When I lift, you pull her out," Domin commanded.

She crawled around him and grabbed Blaise beneath her armpits. "Gav?"

"Right here," Gav huffed from behind her. "Found Mira. She's not well."

"Get her out," she commanded, her attention focused on Domin.

"I can't leave you," Gav snarled.

"You can and you will. We'll be right behind you."

Gav rushed by their side, his clothes steaming. "I'll be back."

Domin braced his legs and cast a glance over his shoulder. "Ready?"

"Do it," she gritted out. She stared down at Blaise, determined to get them both out. "This is going to hurt."

"I can handle it," Blaise growled. "Get me out of here."

The warrior grasped the wood and heaved. Blaise screamed as Sage pulled as hard as she could, dragging her friend out from beneath the beam. The Scythian shuddered, and her eyes rolled into her head.

"Damn it."

Sage pulled Blaise a few more inches and lifted her head to check on the warrior. Domin set the beam back in place just as the room groaned and let out a horrific shudder.

Their eyes connected as the burning roof gave up the fight.

Chapter Ten

Dor

Her life seemed to change by the hour.

A week prior, she'd decided that there was no chance in ever catching her breath. Dor had to run with it. But the dark, creepy tunnel was sending chills down her spine. She eyed the soaring ceiling that hosted a number of ominous webs. Wicked hell, she hated spiders.

"Are you coming?" a smoky, feminine voice asked. She turned her attention to Maeve, who hovered a few paces away. The woman's eyes danced in amusement.

Dor shot an annoyed glare in the woman's direction. They'd only spenta few weeks in each other's presence, but it felt like she'd actually known Maeve her entire life. Even so, Dor was still wary of the warlord's handmaiden. It was uncanny how the Scythian princess could go from laughter to bloodshed in the blink of an eye.

With that in mind, she slowly trailed behind Maeve. The tunnel sloped downward, and she cast surreptitious glances at the silent warriors who formed a loose circle around both women. They'd been trailing her since the day she'd stumbled into the stone room with Ada. She should feel safe, but they put her on edge. They were too silent, too big, and they'd always been her enemy.

Dor quietly followed Maeve deeper into the earth, the air cooling as they descended. It didn't bother her skin. After spending her whole life in the Pit, the cool, humid air felt like coming home. Her heart squeezed. The Pit. She'd unintentionally helped start a rebellion. In her mind, it had seemed glorious—romantic, even. In actuality, it was bloody. Blood was spilled on both sides daily, and while the Scythian society as a whole was corrupt, what went down in the Pit wasn't innocent. Every death weighed heavily on her conscience. How much blood would need to be paid for equality and freedom?

She shook her head and pulled herself from her morose thoughts. The silence stretched on, only broken up by the occasional water droplets falling from the craggy ceiling. Unable to stand it a moment longer, she asked, "Where are we going?"

Maeve smiled a secret smile but didn't answer. Dor rolled her eyes. That was nothing new. The woman collected secrets like her father collected blades. She huffed and continued the silent trek. The tunnel curved to the left and then to the right, sloping steeply downward. Her legs began to ache, and she gritted her teeth. It had only been a few weeks since she'd traipsed about the Pit's staircases, but she'd lost the muscle strength she'd gained, regardless of the relentless training the Scythian princess had thrown her into.

They swung around a curve, and her eyes widened when they approached a huge opening with enormous metal bars that ran from ceiling to floor like great, steel teeth.

Maeve halted and turned to face her, the dark maw behind the woman looking like it was about to swallow her. She gave Dor a piercing look that flayed her to the bone. It was uncanny. Maeve didn't look much older than herself, yet knowing Scythia's bloody history, she'd lived a long time.

Dor's skin prickled with unease. She crossed her arms to hide the goosebumps that had erupted along her forearms. It wasn't easy to trust the warlord's handmaiden. Well, work with her. She didn't really trust anyone.

The warlord's handmaiden tipped her head, her gaze intensifying.

Once again, Dor's skin crawled, and she shifted uncomfortably on her feet. Maeve had a way about her, like she could look inside your soul and delve into your deepest thoughts and feelings.

"What?" Dor barked, breaking the silence. "What are we doing here?" Was it another training exercise?

Maeve smiled and gestured toward the lever on the right-hand side of the bars. "Gentlemen, if you'd be so kind."

Three warriors broke off from their group, and each of them grabbed hold of the lever. They put all their weight into pulling the metal lever down. The stone around the opening groaned, and the giant bars began drawing upward.

Dor took a step backward, her instincts screaming for her to run. She'd never been a coward. She forced herself to stand her ground and face whatever was lurking in the darkness.

"Don't be afraid, Dorcus," Maeve soothed. "Your future awaits you if you're brave enough to face it." She stepped aside and held a hand toward the darkness. "Enter."

Her stomach bottomed out. "Weapons?" she croaked.

"You will need only what is strapped to your person."

Lovely. Whatever test this was, it would end up bloody. Although, they knew she couldn't outright die, so that was something. Dor cursed herself for not wearing better armor, or even bringing a sword. That was her father's number one rule: never go anywhere without a weapon. And while she harbored a few daggers, they wouldn't be enough if she went by the size of the bars. Whatever was hiding in the darkness wasn't an easy foe.

Woodenly, she took one step after another until she was standing in the immense doorway. "Light?"

Maeve gave her an amused smile. "In good time."

What the hell did that mean? "Am I to go in alone?"

"It's not my place to enter at your side."

Dor scoffed. Not the handmaiden's place? What rubbish. Maeve did what she wanted.

"You're hesitating."

"Wouldn't you?" Dor retorted, sarcastically.

She flinched in surprise when Maeve stepped close and cupped her left cheek. "Today is not a day of death, but of rejoicing. Step into the darkness like the warrior your sire raised you to be. Claim your birth right." With those cryptic words, Maeve stepped away and faced the darkness.

Dor scowled. The woman knew how to play on her pride. But pride never kept one alive. With careful, gliding steps, she moved past the entrance. She pursed her lips and whistled softly, the sound echoing around her.

A large cavernous space.

While stealth was usually the best form of attack, the creaking of the bars had already warned whatever was lying in wait for her that she was coming. The echoes at least gave an idea of what kind of room she was in.

It wasn't easy to put one foot in front of the other and stride toward the darkness. She paused and glanced over her shoulder as she hovered at the edge of the pool of lantern light, her ears alert to any sound.

At the entrance of the room, Maeve smiled, satisfaction clear on her symmetrical face. Dor stiffened and caught the slightest sound of something slithering against stone from her right. A snake? She squinted and searched the area around her for the threat. Was this an initiation? Her pulse thundered in her ears and a *shhhhh* sound came from the left. A second creature?

Precious one.

Dor froze at the familiar nickname running through her mind over and over. There was only one who referred to her in that way. Well, at least in her mind. She inhaled deeply, noting the metallic and musky smell she missed before. There was only one creature who smelled like that.

She stood taller and searched the darkness. "Illya?" she whispered.

A familiar click greeted her. *I am here.*

Dor gasped and stumbled into the darkness, holding her arms out in front of her, heedless of anything but reaching her dragon. It had been weeks since she'd seen him, and while she'd longed to visit, she didn't know Maeve's view on the creatures.

Her fingertips grazed warm scales, and a smile burst across her face. Carefully, she traced a scale, discovering the pointed edge that was razor sharp and tapered to his tail. Dor stumbled forward, determined to reach his face so she could give him a proper hug.

"I've missed you so much!"

Another series of clicks and hums greeted her. Some of her joy waned, and she paused, her left hand still on the dragon's side. She frowned. That didn't sound familiar. The scales seemed to expand and contract with the beast's breaths.

"Illya?"

Silence.

Real fear slammed into her, and she yanked her hand back. She'd imagined Illya, but the dragon in the room was very real. Her heart flew to her throat, and she took measured steps backward, trying to make herself seem as harmless as a fly.

"I didn't mean to intrude in your home," she murmured. "I'll leave you alone." Dor stiffened when the light disappeared behind her, and warm air blew across the back of her neck, a dry tongue licking her from shoulder to the crown of her head. She knew that familiar hello.

Welcome, precious one.

Tears burned in her eyes, and she spun around, opening her arms wide. She didn't imagine him.

Welcome.

"I can't believe you're here," she choked out, voice thick with tears.

Illya hissed softly and blew another breath into her face. He lowered his face, which was barely visible in the low light, and pressed his muzzle into her chest. She wrapped her arms around his snout, her forearm brushing one of his long fangs that stuck out from his mouth. Dor squeezed him tightly and leaned her cheek against him, her eyes closing. The small scales that covered his nose scratched at her skin. It was the best feeling in the world. She was actually here with him, no stone wall to separate them.

"Dorcus," Maeve called.

She opened her eyes and squinted toward the entrance, where Maeve's body was haloed by the light.

"Please ask your dragon if we may enter. We bear no ill will, and no weapons shall enter this sanctuary."

Ask her dragon... That was a weird request. Dor rolled her eyes and hugged Illya again. "May they enter?"

The Dragon Song and her protectors may enter.

Dorcus stiffened and lifted her head. Lanterns along the walls began to light, one by one. She stared at Illya, her mouth hanging open. She had no clue what a Dragon Song was, but she hadn't made it up. It had come from him. The dragon.

She stumbled a step away. Animals couldn't speak.

As the cavern lightened, her breath caught. He was massive! His black scales caught the faint light and reflected it like slick oil. Illya arched his long, sinuous neck and blinked at her with a large feline silver eye, like liquid mercury.

"You're magnificent," she breathed. Awe settle over her as she noticed his leather-like wings tucked against his back.

Precious one. Her attention was pulled back to his face. His clicks, hisses, hums, and soft purrs seemed to form the words in her mind. *It's time to speak and to plan.*

Dor blinked slowly, pressed her palms to each side of her head, and dropped to her haunches. Her eyes squeezed shut. What was happening to her? Before, she'd chalked it up to her overactive imagination and the need for friendship. Was she going insane?

"Dor," Maeve cooed. "It's all right. Take a deep breath." She inhaled slowly. "Now open your eyes."

The Scythian princess knelt a few paces away, not even glancing in Illya's direction. "I know you're overwhelmed, but it's going to be okay."

"Am I crazy?" she rasped.

Maeve smiled, and, for the first time since Dor met the woman, it seemed genuine. "No, you are not. You're a Dragon Song."

"A Dragon Song?"

"Yes." Maeve's smile grew bigger. "It's so very rare now, but once upon a time, dragons and Dragon Songs were very common."

"What are you saying? That I can speak to animals?"

"No, but you do understand the dragon language."

"Dragon language," Dor repeated, casting a glance at Illya.

Her dragon lowered his head to the obsidian stone floor.

Listen to the Dragon Song. She is wise.

Dor blinked. He spoke, and she understood him. Her legs turned to jelly beneath her, and she plopped onto her arse. "He speaks." With wide eyes, she turned to Maeve. "I understand him."

Warmth filled the Scythian's woman's face. "You do. You are so very special, Dorcus. You will change the world."

"Me?"

"You." Maeve stared at Illya. "Your bond is strong. One of five Dragon Songs left."

There were four more dragons? "Why am I special?"

I am Alpha. Her dragon's rumble held satisfaction.

"Your dragon is the Alpha, and you are the heir."

"The heir to what?" Chills ran up and down her spine. Somehow, she knew what the warlord's handmaiden was going to say.

"You, dearest, are the last remaining descendent of the Nagali royal house."

The world tipped on its side. A million little things snapped into place. Why she'd always been treated differently. She'd always assumed it was the color of her skin.

"What do we do now?" she asked, overwhelmed and lost.

Maeve's smile turned dangerous. "We free the dragons and reclaim what was stolen."

Chapter Eleven

Tehl

Tehl's lungs screamed as he carried a hacking soldier from the burning infirmary. His legs almost buckled as he moved away from the blaze, fatigue riding him hard. Soldiers rushed toward him and relieved him of his moaning burden. He bent over and placed his hands on his knees as he gulped huge lungfuls of air.

He flicked his eyes up when Zachael placed a steadying hand on Tehl's shoulder, and he forced himself to straighten, his back complaining in the process. Today, he felt old.

He yanked down the wet linen covering his nose and mouth. "Is that everyone?" Tehl shouted over the noise.

The weapons master nodded, his expression grim. "We got out all who were breathing."

The infirmary groaned, pulling Tehl's attention to what was left of the heavy structure. It swayed and then crashed to the ground, belching flames and smoke.

Tehl held his arm up to protect his face and tried to take small inhalations as smoke and ash rushed back at him. His nose wrinkled at the bitter taste of ash on his tongue, and his gaze locked on the inferno. They'd managed to save a fair amount, but it still wasn't enough.

Clenching his jaw, he dropped his arm and raked his sweaty hair away from his face. He scanned the crying mass of the wounded. Guilt swam in his belly for all those who had died. How many women had lost their husbands, children their fathers, and mothers their sons? He scanned the chaos of soldiers and the wounded, his gaze snagging on a Methian woman with half her face burned. Tehl swallowed hard. How many had lost their wives or daughters or mothers?

Too many.

"What about the rear?" he asked woodenly.

Zachael's expression hardened. "The rear of the infirmary took the most damage. There wasn't much to salvage."

Tehl swallowed hard and forced his mind away from the gruesome deaths the men and women must have suffered. There wasn't anything he could do for them now. Their focus needed to be on those who lived. They needed immediate care. Burns were painful, but with burns came infection. That's where the true danger lurked.

"Our healers?"

"Queen Osir has opened her tent as the new infirmary. Everyone with herbal or healer training has been instructed to gather there and attend to the wounded. I've been told the queen is an excellent healer."

"Then we are fortunate to have her skills. Jacob departed for Sanee, leaving Mira with the bulk of the responsibilities. Another pair of skilled hands will lighten the load."

"She's a capable healer," Zachael commented, his eyes narrowing. "Speaking of which, have you seen her?"

Tehl frowned and groggily tried to remember if he saw her among the fray. He didn't recall seeing a blonde. He reached out to a young soldier. "Check the new infirmary for Healer Mira."

The boy scampered off into the sea of tents toward the new infirmary.

Once again, Tehl scoured the cluster of wounded. Mira wasn't someone to stand by. She never waited in the infirmary for the wounded to be brought to her. She waited on the edge of camp for them. Mira had to be somewhere close by.

Tehl's brows furrowed as he scanned the group again carefully, looking for a blonde head. Where was she?

The young soldier jogged up to them, an apologetic look on his face. "She's not with the healers." He wrung his hands. "I'm happy to keep looking, my lord."

"Search the wounded," Tehl commanded, his stomach twisting.

The boy burst into action.

"Where is the healer?" Tehl asked hoarsely, his gaze focusing back on the inferno. She couldn't be in there.

The weapons master studied the chaos around them. "I don't see her, but that doesn't mean anything."

A sick sense of foreboding settled on Tehl's shoulders as he realized his wife was nowhere in sight, either. Wicked hell. Where was Sage?

"Sage," he gasped. "Have you seen her?"

Zachael stiffened. "No."

Tehl's eyes darted back to the blaze. She wouldn't have gone in, would she? Surely, he would've seen her. He closed his stinging eyes and tried to remember anything from inside the infirmary. All he could remember was smoke, heat, and the scent of charred flesh. He opened his eyes, gazing blankly at the fire.

"Search for the princess," Zachael barked at the remaining Elite guarding them. The men immediately waded into the crowd.

Where the blazes was she? Sage was supposed to stay here. But if Mira was missing...

"She wouldn't have left her friends behind," he muttered to himself. His heart thundered in his chest. Stars, he was so stupid. He knew exactly where she went. "The rear side."

Zachael's lips thinned, and both men started running toward the rear of the enormous fire.

The flames seemed to rise up and touch the stars. Tehl's breath shortened as they rounded the back of the collapsed tent and spotted a group of soldiers yelling at each other.

Gav knelt in the middle of them, a lifeless female form lying on the ground.

Tehl stumbled a step.

No. Not Sage. Please God, no.

He barreled through the group and skidded to a stop. The men quieted as he inhaled sharply. Blonde hair, not brown. *Mira*.

Gavriel didn't take his eyes from Mira as he placed a wet rag over a nasty looking burn on the healer's right shoulder and she took a shallow breath.

She shivered and moaned, coughs rattling her abused body. Tehl knelt and stared at her dirty, bruised face, and then pinned his cousin with a fierce look.

"Where is Sage?"

Gav lifted his head, his eyes holding pity. "Tehl," he said softly.

There was too much emotion in his tone. Loss. Guilt. Sorrow.

No.

Tehl wouldn't believe it.

A tremor worked through him, and he glared at Gav. "Where is my wife? Where is she?"

Gav held his gaze, pain and guilt written all over his expression. "It happened so fast."

Zachael placed a hand on his shoulder, but Tehl shook it off.

"You left her inside?" he roared.

"She was right behind me," Gav whispered. "One moment there, the next gone."

Gone.

It echoed in his mind, a morbid chant that he couldn't quite comprehend.

It wasn't possible. Sage couldn't just be *gone*.

Tehl shook his head and stormed away from the group, his eyes pinned to the fire as he moved around the far side of the infirmary. Maybe Sage had escaped and was on the other side.

But there was nothing there. No one.

His heart began to crack. She couldn't be inside. Surely, if she'd died, he would have felt it, felt something?

"Tehl…"

He shot a black look at Zachael. "Don't."

The weapons master snapped his mouth shut.

If Sage was inside, there was still a chance she lived. Tehl needed to get inside. Now.

He rushed to the horse trough, one thought in his mind: find her.

"I know what you're thinking, and I won't allow it," the older man said with determination.

"I'm the bloody crown prince. No one gives me orders," Tehl growled and dunked himself in the lukewarm water. He jumped from the trough and slicked his wet hair from his face.

Zachael placed himself between Tehl and the remnants of the infirmary. "You *are* the bloody crown prince, and as much as it pains me to say this—you're more important. You can't risk your life this way."

Tehl wanted to point out all the ways he risked his life every day, fighting monsters, but he didn't have time for that.

"Don't make me cut you down," he warned the weapons master. "Get out of the way!"

"She'll be long gone by now," Zachael said softly, pulling his blade from the scabbard at his hip. "I'm so sorry, but I can't allow it."

"Who's long gone?" a raspy voice coughed.

Tehl jerked around at the sound of Blaise's voice and scanned the bushes behind them. Blaise lay on her side just behind the trough, her muted clothing blending in with the blackened brush along the ground.

"My wife." He couldn't say her name.

The Scythian's forehead wrinkled, confusion twisted her face. "No, she's—" Blaise wheezed, her dark eyes closing as she struggled for breath.

Zachael moved to her side and slapped her on the back.

She gasped, a cry bursting from her mouth. "*Burns.*"

"Bloody hell," the weapons master hissed. He jerked his hand away.

Tehl rushed to her and knelt, his hands clasping either side of Blaise's face. "Where is she?"

Blaise opened her eyes, tears streaming down her face, and Tehl's heart cracked further open.

"Her guard took her to the creek."

He stiffened and blinked slowly, not able to understand her words.

"She's alive?" he croaked, his hands trembling.

The Scythian studied him. "I can hear them coming."

Tehl's fingers tightened momentarily, and he forced himself to carefully release Blaise. It was too good to be true. Woodenly, he stood and took two halting steps toward the creek. Sage pushed through the brush, soot-streaked and soaking wet. Her gaze locked onto his, and she froze as if detecting a predator.

His mind screamed for him to rush to her side and scoop her into his arms. To reaffirm that she was whole and healthy. Yet, his body refused to obey him. All he could do was watch her as numbness crept through his limbs. She was alive, but from the state of her torched clothing, she had gone inside the infirmary.

She'd risked her life and his heart, and she'd ignored what he'd asked of her.

Reckless and selfish.

Sage pressed her lips together and opened her mouth to speak.

He held up his hand. If she spoke, he would lose it.

Tehl ran his eyes all over her body one last time to affirm that she was okay before turning his attention to the Methian warrior standing by her side, his expression serene.

"Make sure she gets back to our quarters safely."

He spared his wife one last accusatory look and turned his back on her. He didn't feel the heat from the fire, nor did he take in the scenery around him. He only welcomed the numbness as he moved toward the chaos that awaited him.

She hadn't listened.

She'd almost died.

It broke something inside him.

Chapter Twelve

Sage

She'd messed up.

The look on Tehl's face wasn't something Sage would soon forget. She glanced around the new, makeshift infirmary and took in a shallow breath through her mouth. Charred flesh and singed hair created a pungent odor that had her frequently retching.

A moan sounded from her left, but Sage forced herself to keep her eyes pinned to her mud- covered boots as she shuffled to sit on a stool placed between Mira's and Blaise's cots. It was cowardly of her, but the burned remains of the soldier two cots down were just too much. The pieces of flesh didn't even resemble a human being anymore, more like a melted candle.

Her stomach rolled, and saliva flooded her mouth a second before she heaved into the tin bucket firmly planted between her feet. Tears sprang to her eyes as the contents of her belly revolted against her.

"You should get some rest," Mira rasped. "Being here isn't good for you."

Sage wiped her mouth with her dirty, trembling hand. "The moment I leave, you'll get up." She lifted her head and glared at the cot to her left. Mira stared back placidly through bloodshot eyes. "That innocent gaze doesn't fool me."

Mira wasn't in good shape. She'd inhaled a lot of smoke. Her voice was so hoarse, she could have passed for a man. She had burns everywhere and, while it could have been worse, she still was a bloody mess. Sage's gaze wandered to Mira's bandaged palms. The worst was her right hand. Apparently, she'd tried to move a burning tent support that had fallen onto one of her patients. It had to hurt like hell, yet Mira hadn't uttered one complaint other than the fact that she hated being a patient.

"I'm no good to anyone, lying here," Mira had argued. "There aren't any other healers of my level of expertise here. I'm needed."

Blaise had released a smoky chuckle. "Don't let the Methi queen hear you say that."

Now, Sage craned her neck and peeked over her shoulder at Queen Osir. The woman was an army in her own right. In the hours that had passed since the Scythian attack, she'd not stopped moving. She'd marshaled a troop of healers to help those who'd suffered in the fire.

A sniff pulled Sage's attention back to Mira, and her heart clenched.

The healer released a hacking cough, and a tear dripped down her cheek and onto the cot as she stared at the ceiling.

"Is it the pain?" Sage asked in concern. "I can get something for you."

Mira shook her head and croaked, "I couldn't help them. I couldn't save them."

"Don't think like that," Sage crooned. She placed her hand gingerly on Mira's uninjured shoulder. "You did your best."

Mira twisted her neck and met Sage's gaze. "It wasn't good enough." More tears tracked down the healer's cheeks. "How could someone do such a thing?"

That was the very question Sage had been asking herself for hours. It was inhuman. Monstrous. Mira released a gurgling, hiccupping laugh. "I should have known when Tehl brought you to me. I'd never seen someone is such a state." Sage hid her flinch. Her friend wasn't trying to hurt her. "We're dealing with a demon and his monsters. No one with any shred of humanity would cause the suffering and torture he does."

Sage nodded. "You're right."

Her friend angrily wiped at her face and sat up, her face creased in a grimace.

"Whoa!" Sage said, holding her hands out. "Take it easy."

Mira gave her a withering glance. "Like you do?"

"She's got you there," Blaise piped in.

Sage rolled her eyes at the Scythian woman. "What would you know about it?"

Blaise snorted and then released a chest-rattling cough, her whole body convulsing with the movement. Once she'd gained control of herself, all humor fled from her expression.

"I've never seen you hold still for more than a few minutes of time. You've lost weight. When is the last time you had a full night of sleep?" the Scythian woman asked.

Sage pursed her lips.

Before the warlord.

Blaise nodded as if she could read her mind. "I lived with that monster my whole life. I know what effects he can have. You're working yourself to the bone and if you keep it up, you'll break before we've defeated him."

Sage's jaw clenched, and she had to look away. She knew Blaise was right, but it didn't mean it was easy to hear. The warlord was always one step ahead of them. No matter what it felt like, she was fighting against a raging storm.

"You need to set boundaries and keep them," Blaise suggested.

Sage bristled. "Aermia can't afford any." She didn't even want to think about what would happen if they failed. The world as they knew it would cease to be. The warlord's dark smile flashed through her mind, and she fought back a shiver. It would be a bleak world indeed.

"They can't afford a dead queen, either."

Her eyes widened. "I'm no queen."

Blaise gave her a bemused smile. "Crown or no crown, you are these men's queen. They look to you for guidance. You need to set the example. Even in war, there must be rest for healing of the mind and body."

"I will try harder," Sage gritted out. It seemed impossible, but she vowed she would *try*.

"Do so." Blaise's attention wandered to something over Sage's shoulder. "Your mate is waiting for you."

Now it was her turn to snort. "I doubt it. He hasn't looked at me all night." Ever since he'd walked away from her earlier, Tehl had completely ignored her. It was as if she had become a piece of furniture.

"Maybe not in the way you're accustomed to, but he's been tuned in to your every move," Blaise said.

"I don't know what to say to him." If Sage told him the truth, it would just upset him more. Her gaze moved between her two friends. Her risk was worth it because the three of them were whole and alive.

That's what mattered. Sage couldn't lose either of them.

"Tell him you're sorry for being stupid," Mira wheezed. "And lay it on thick if need be."

"If I hadn't acted rashly, both of you would be dead," Sage pointed out.

Blaise reached out and squeezed her wrist. "Boundaries. Trust that others will take the training you've given them and be successful. Be humble. You can't do everything. When you make a mistake, even if the outcome is a positive one, apologize to the ones you've hurt. Your man is hurting, whether he's showing it or not."

That was true enough. Sage knew Tehl was the quiet sort who didn't show his feelings to hardly anyone. She'd also known, the moment he locked eyes on her near the forest, she'd angered him.

"Thank you," she said softly. "I'm blessed with wise friends."

"That's not the only thing you're blessed with," Blaise retorted, eyeing Tehl. "Make use of my advice."

Sage smiled. "Do either of you need anything before I go?"

Blaise quirked a half smile. "No, the healers will care for my burnt arse."

Mira inhaled sharply as she swung her legs off the cot. She patted Sage's knee and then leaned back, bracing her left hand against the cot. "Leave. We're well looked after, and you've done all you can. Stop putting off the inevitable."

She stood and glanced at her two friends. "I'll see you both once I get some proper rest."

"We'll be here," Blaise retorted, lacing her fingers together and then placing her head on them, the picture of relaxation.

Sage marshaled her thoughts and pasted a smile on her face. Blaise was right. She couldn't let the men see her down and beaten. It was bad for morale.

She turned on her heel, and kept the horror off her face as she passed the other fire survivors. The walk to the entrance of the tent seemed to go on forever as she passed cot after cot.

Queen Osir caught her eye and jerked her head toward the tent exit. Sage dutifully followed the Methian queen. Her breath came easier as she stepped from the cloying tent and into the fresh, early morning air. Her eyes lifted to the still-dark sky and part of her wanted to cry out to the stars.

Why? Why this?

"You did well," the queen said.

"Did I?" Sage frowned. "I puked."

"Lesser men would have never even stepped inside that hellhole." The queen narrowed her amber eyes and laid a hand on Sage's chest. "How is your breathing?"

She shrugged. "Fine."

The older woman gave her a skeptical look. "You need to rest. You're no good to us worn down."

"So I've been told," she muttered. Was she doing such a bad job?

"You'll be short of breath for several days. With luck, you won't get sick. I want you to stay off the battlefield."

Sage glanced at her sharply. "I won't agree to that." The Scythians were pressing forward every day. The Aermian army needed all the help they could get.

The queen's expression hardened. "What do you think will happen when you go out onto the field and your lungs seize? Your enemy won't wait for you to recover. You will be a danger to everyone around you—a distraction. My son fights with you every day. He tells me of your strength, but of your weakness, too. If you falter, he will fight to protect you." She stepped into Sage's space. "Rafe loves you. He will die for you. Are you really willing to risk my son's life for the sake of your pride?"

"There's no guarantee that would happen," Sage argued. "What if I'm not there to protect Rafe's back?"

The queen snorted. "My son can protect himself."

"Now who's prideful?" she said softly.

"It's not easy, is it?"

Sage frowned. "What?"

"Being a woman in power who is surrounded by men," the queen said. "We always feel the need to prove ourselves. It's never easy for us. Men often seek to dominate us or look for every flaw and weakness. I've learned over the years that a wise ruler needs to step back and take a look at the bigger picture." She touched Sage's cheek. "You are a fine warrior and will make a wonderful ruler, but only if you let yourself heal. I can hear how you're trying to cover the wheeze in your chest. Lying to yourself and to those around you about your health will help no one. It's okay to let others take care of you."

"It's not so easy," Sage whispered.

"No, it is not." The queen removed her hand from Sage's face. "Think about what I have said and take care of yourself, dear." She turned on her heel, her silver-and-black braid swinging behind her. She paused by the tent flap and turned, shooting Sage a menacing look. "If you decide to be stupid and my son is hurt, I will hold you responsible."

Sage eyed the Methian queen as she disappeared into the tent. She wouldn't want that woman as her enemy. She cleared her throat as the tickle became almost unbearable. How had the damn queen heard the wheeze in her lungs? Her lips pursed. While the Methian soldiers hadn't said anything outright, she had the sneaking suspicion they possessed remarkable senses. Rafe certainly possessed gifts she'd never seen in anyone—but the warlord—before. She swallowed, and her gaze drifted past their tents and the battlefield to the dark tents of the Scythians. What sort of secrets did the warlord have?

"I wish you could feel the hate I have for you," she whispered into the early morning air.

She jumped when the flap to the infirmary snapped open and Tehl's scent invaded her senses as he brushed by her without a word. Sage stared guiltily at his back and fell into step behind him as the Elite materialized from the dark and formed a loose circle around them.

Her lip curled in distaste. How much had they heard of her conversation with the queen? Nothing was private or sacred anymore. Her mind flashed back to her kidnapping. Even with the inconvenience of never being alone or having a private conversation, the protection was worth it. Never again did she want to be taken against her will.

Sage counted each step through the camp toward their chambers, feeling a prickling of doom along the bare skin of her arms. She shivered, and her brows furrowed. Where did she leave her cloak? In fact, when had she lost it?

But there were more pressing matters than her damn cloak. Raised voices pierced through the twilight air as they drew closer. Hayjen's voice was louder than the rest. Leave it to him to be the one shouting.

Her eyes burned, and her throat ached. She really wanted to go to bed.

Her gaze wandered to Tehl's back as they neared their own tent. She needed to make amends but now wasn't the time.

Aermia came first.

Chapter Thirteen

Hayjen

"We need to strike now!" Why were they all dragging their feet? Hayjen glared at the men clustered around the circular table in the center of the room.

"They will expect us to retaliate," Zachael said calmly. "We need to proceed with caution."

Caution? Caution got them nowhere. Lilja's crumpled form was still seared into his mind. Caution led to more death. They had to fight. "If we do nothing, the warlord wins." Did no one understand that?

Hayjen's gaze snapped to the entrance of the tent as Tehl and Sage stepped inside. His attention homed in on the blank expression on the crown prince's face. War wasn't ever pretty, but the destruction tonight was something else entirely. It was enough to break a man. He studied Tehl and slid his gaze to his niece. Sage flicked questioning glances at her husband as they joined the small war council. She looked concerned but not terrified. The prince hadn't been broken; he was just processing.

"Tonight's attack is most troubling." William ran a hand along his white, pointed goatee, and his bushy brows furrowed. "The Scythians have disregarded all war etiquette. Things are about to get infinitely darker. We need to tread lightly, or we'll lose ourselves to this madness."

Rafe snorted, and his brother Raziel chuckled.

"We're dealing with animals. What makes you believe that they will act like civilized, human beings?" Raziel asked sarcastically. "Mark my words, it will only get bloodier from here. We will have to match their efforts if we want to win."

Bloodstained lips taunted Hayjen from a ghostly, pale face, Lilja's pained magenta eyes dulling. He pinched the bridge of his nose and tried to control his emotions. Over the last several weeks, he'd been either numb or burning with rage. There wasn't a middle ground. Even in sleep, he couldn't escape the horror of his soul-rendering loss.

"We must destroy the rest of his war machines," Tehl said, his tone flat. "Soon."

"At what cost?" Sage whispered. "You saw what he did in retaliation tonight. We've lost many in one fell swoop."

Hayjen lifted his head at her anguished tone and studied the young couple. The crown prince stood as stiff as a board. Shadows slithered through his eyes, but his expression never cracked.

"You believe I'm to blame for the attack?" Tehl asked, never taking his attention from the war map.

Sage's mouth opened and then snapped closed. The members of the council all found somewhere else to look, but Hayjen watched the drama, a pinprick of jealousy stabbing him. He missed arguing with his wife. Marriage to a Sirenidae wasn't easy—hell, no marriage was easy—but he'd kill to be able to fight with Lilja one last time.

"It's no one's fault but the warlord's," Sage said after a moment of uncomfortable silence.

She shifted from foot to foot, reaching a hand toward Tehl and then dropping it before she touched him. Definitely trouble in paradise.

"This is on him and no one else. We need to tread carefully," she reasoned. "He'll anticipate our moves. We need to act rationally and not in anger."

"That's my specialty," Tehl said woodenly. "Can you say the same?"

Heat rushed into Sage's cheeks, and she glanced at the group, clearly embarrassed. Raziel coughed into his fist and side-eyed the tent flap. Hayjen scowled at Tehl. There was no need to embarrass her in front of everyone, no matter how angry Tehl was. Hayjen almost stepped in, but then good old William broke up the tension.

"Dawn is approaching, and we haven't had a full night's sleep in weeks. This needn't be decided right now. We will reconvene in a few hours when all our heads are clearer."

Sage smiled gratefully at the grizzled general while the Methian princes quietly departed. Tehl didn't say anything as he disappeared into the rear section of the tent where his chambers were.

Hayjen stayed put as William clasped Sage's shoulder in support, and Zachael offered a quick hug before both men left. Sage leaned a hip against the table and rubbed at her forehead, further smearing the spot of soot already lodged there.

She sighed. "Whatever you have to say, out with it. I'm exhausted and need to go to bed."

"I doubt you'll be asleep anytime soon," Hayjen murmured. Whatever was between the two of them, they'd work it out, but it would take time.

"What makes you say that?" Sage fiddled with a chain at her neck, avoiding his gaze.

Hayjen focused on the giant map and the small wooden carvings on it that marked the armies' locations. "I was married for a long time." He swallowed hard and soldiered on, despite how the words stuck in the back of his throat. "I can sense when a storm is brewing." He peeked at his niece from beneath his lashes. "And by the look of guilt upon your face, I suspect you have some apologizing to do, baby girl."

Sage darted a glance toward her chambers and then shot him a dirty look. "It's just a misunderstanding." She ran her finger along the dangling charm and flicked her finger against the clasp.

"Then why do you feel so horrid?" He straightened and crossed his arms, for some reason transfixed by her nervous movements. Something seemed so familiar about the necklace.

"He's angry because I disobeyed him," Sage hissed. "I never signed up to be his subordinate."

Hayjen squinted harder at her fingers. It wasn't a charm… Was it a ring? Damn, he'd soon need some spectacles. "What did he tell you not to do?"

His niece held the ring up and flipped open the lid. Recognition slammed into him, followed by fear. Sage inspected the needle of the poisonous ring and pulled it closer to her face to get a closer look.

Good god.

"Close the damn ring!" he barked, his voice louder than he intended. Sage startled but snapped the ring closed.

"You didn't have to yell," she said crossly.

Hayjen rushed around the table and snatched the ring from her fingers, pulling her along with the chain. He leaned closer and held the ring up to the lantern light. Stars above, how long had Sage had this jewelry? How many times had she opened the poison ring? "Do you know what this is?"

"A gift."

"Death," he whispered. How could she not know? "A horrid death. I assume Lilja—" he swallowed at the use of her name "—gave this to you?"

"She said to use it if I was ever captured again." A look of uncertainty crossed Sage's face. "It's my escape."

He nodded, his heart aching. "While that is true, she didn't explain how it works. The poison in this ring comes from some of the deepest trenches in the sea. It has been brewed to kill Scythian warriors. If even the smallest drop were to touch your skin, you'd die—no prick or cut necessary." Sage's eyes widened. "That's right. You were just playing with death." He carefully lowered the necklace and cupped her shoulders. "Never, ever do that again."

A tremble worked through Sage. "That would have been nice to know earlier," she croaked. "I've always liked dangerous things, but that's a little extreme. Even for me."

Hayjen huffed out a laugh. "Your aunt had an interesting idea of what was an appropriate gift."

"After my experiences, I welcomed her sort of gifts. Even if she didn't warn me that I was literally playing with death."

"Sometimes she forgot others around her weren't from the sea." He crooked a smile. "She never saw a difference between peoples. Everyone was the same to her."

"She was one of a kind," Sage whispered.

A pang of loss shot through him. He needed a drink, and some damn sleep before he went back to the battlefield. He leaned down and kissed Sage on her forehead. "Don't let the sun set on your anger. Fix what you need to before you sleep."

Sage sighed. "Mum used to say that all the time."

Hayjen pulled back and smiled softly. "That's because I taught her. Goodnight." He wove around her and lifted the flap.

"Hayjen?"

He paused and glanced over his shoulder at his niece, her face looking far too weighed down for someone so young. "Yeah?"

Something dark lingered in her gaze, but she blinked it away, and a small smile touched her mouth. "I love you."

He stiffened, and liquid heat burned at the back of his eyes. Hayjen nodded and gruffly choked out, "You too, *ma fille*."

He ducked out of the tent before he could make an ass of himself. He needed some bloody sleep and a heavy dose of whiskey. The sun had already begun to lighten the sky to the east. Damn it. Sleep would be short. Maybe his wife wouldn't torment him while he snatched a few winks of sleep. A twisted smile lifted his lips. He'd rather have her haunt him than have her not grace his nightmares at all.

Or worse: forget her.

He made his way to his tent and plopped down on his bed roll. He glanced at his pillow in longing. Better not. He'd need to get to the battlefield within the hour.

Hayjen swiped the bottle of whiskey from the floor and uncorked the top. He took a heavy swig, barely tasting the bitter swill. A single tear rolled down his cheek. Most would scold him for drinking so early. Most wives would berate their husbands. But Lilja would have grabbed a glass and had a drink with him.

"I miss you," he said to the empty tent.

Chapter Fourteen

Sam

Sam placed his hands atop the huge vanity and eyed his pale complexion in the tall, gilded mirror. He looked like hell. He scoffed. He was pretty sure he'd been there and back in the weeks prior.

A soft knock at the door.

"Enter."

Marilyn, one of his oldest spies, entered his chamber. He lifted his head and smiled weakly at her. She didn't smile back, her frown causing the wrinkles around her mouth to deepen. His heart fell.

"Nothing?"

She shook her head. "We've searched high and low, my lord. There hasn't even been a whisper of a woman of her description anywhere. If she were in the city, we would have found her by now."

"A person can't just disappear. You're not looking hard enough."

An unfair assessment, but he was so damn worried.

Marilyn didn't respond to his sharp tone—if anything, her expression softened. "We're doing our best."

"It's not good enough," he snapped. Sam immediately regretted his tone and closed his eyes, pinching the bridge of his nose. "I should not have spoken to you that way. Please accept my apology."

"There's nothing to be sorry about. These are trying times. I'm not sure how you handle everything without losing your bloody mind." Her gaze moved over his shoulder, toward the twins' room. "If you need someone to look after the wee ones again, I am happy to." The gruff older woman smiled, revealing crooked teeth. "Gems they are."

Sam nodded. His spies had been helping with the children more often than not. "I'll let you know if I need you. Keep your eyes and ears open. I'll send your next assignment on the morrow."

Marilyn nodded and left the room, the door clicking shut quietly behind her.

Sam stared blankly at the vanity. They had Jasmine. His wife. What was she going through? Bottles crashed to the floor, and he blinked at his hand. He'd just reacted. In *rage*. That hadn't happened before.

He laced his hands behind his head and stared at the ceiling. Losing his temper wouldn't help Jasmine. He had to do better.

"Papa?" a little voice murmured.

It was like someone had punched him in the gut. Sam turned toward Ethan, who stood in the entryway to the twins' room, sleepily rubbing his eyes. The little boy had called him *Papa*. His chest swelled with emotion, his throat clogged and heat built up behind his eyes. It wasn't the first time the children had used the endearment, but it floored him every time.

"Yeah, little man?" he choked out.

Ethan yawned. "I heard a loud noise. It scared me."

Sam swallowed and dropped to his knees in front of Ethan. He pulled his son into his arms and hugged him close. "I'm sorry. I promise to be more careful next time."

"S'okay, papa," Ethan whispered, wrapping his arms around Sam's neck.

Papa. "How about we get back to bed, huh?"

Ethan didn't say anything when Sam scooped him up and moved through the doorway to the twins' room. Toys littered the chamber, along with books stacked haphazardly and drawings pinned to the walls. His gaze snagged on one of Jas. *Where are you?*

Leaning down, he placed Ethan in his bed. He didn't let go.

"Stay?" his son whispered.

Sam sniffled and smiled. "Of course." He tucked Ethan in and then squeezed into the narrow bed, his hair no doubt tickling Sam's nose, but the child didn't move. The only time Sam had had even a modicum of peace since Jasmine's disappearance was when he was with the twins.

He pressed a kiss to the top of Ethan's head. "I love you."

"Love you too, Papa." A beat of silence. "I miss Mama."

"I know, Ethan. So do I."

"When will she come home?" Jade's high-pitched voice asked. Her covers rustled, and then she was clambering over Sam's side and wiggling in beside him.

"Soon, loves. Now go back to sleep."

Jade grinned and peppered his cheek with kisses. "All right, Papa."

The twins snuggled into the covers and quickly fell back asleep. Sam stared at their tiny faces.

"I promise to bring her back," he whispered.

Ethan huffed and tossed his arm over Jade, his pointer finger poking her in the nose. Sam chuckled and moved his son's hand. How did he get so damn lucky?

His arm went numb first, and a stitch cramped his side, but there wasn't a torture in the world that would move him from his spot.

For now.

Tomorrow, he'd once again board a ship and wage war.

CHAPTER FIFTEEN

Sage

Sage stared at the exit to the tent long after Hayjen disappeared through the flap. It would be so easy to go back to the new infirmary. And do what? Stand around some more?

Stop being such a sissy, Sage.

She reluctantly turned toward her and Tehl's chambers and frowned. Maybe he would be asleep? Sage shook her head. Facing angry men had never scared her before; she wouldn't back down now.

With soft steps, she approached their section of the tent, her fingertips grazing the canvas flap. She hesitated. Sure, she and Tehl had disagreed many times before, but this time was different. The look of disappointment earlier that night had almost gutted her.

Get in there.

Squaring her shoulders, she pushed through the flap, her heart racing as she spotted Tehl across the room, washing his face. She paused but forced her legs to move to the right side of the bed. He didn't say anything or even acknowledge her presence as he used a rag to wash his bare chest and arms. It was like she was a doormat. Invisible and unimportant.

Slowly, Sage tugged off her boots and sodden wool socks. She wiggled her chilled toes and then tucked them under the edge of the bedcover to keep them warm. Her lips pursed as she stared at the rumpled bed. Under normal circumstances, she would have stripped and crawled right into bed, but that felt too much like giving in. The tension in the air was almost choking her. A fight was coming, and she needed to have the high ground, so to speak.

If Tehl would say anything.

She cleared her throat. He said nothing.

This was not the response she was expecting. Sage expected him to yell, curse, something. Maybe he hadn't been pushed to the brink yet? Perhaps he wasn't as angry as she suspected.

"Are you going to look at me?" she asked softly. There, that was nonconfrontational.

He ignored her and began cleaning the back of his neck.

Sage let him have his silence for a few moments and observed him struggling to clean his back. The stupid, stubborn man.

She rolled her eyes and crawled across the mattress. He said nothing as she took the lemon-and-pine smelling cloth from his hands and stood, then began to wash his back with tender strokes. His muscles twitched beneath her touch, but even as she kneaded his back, the tension never left his frame. He really wasn't happy with her.

Her gaze darted down to the bed. It would be so easy to just climb in, turn her back on him, and go to sleep. Maybe they would both be more reasonable after a few hours of rest. A little time to cool down never hurt anyone.

Don't let the sun set on your anger, her uncle had said.

Sage's lips thinned. As much as she wanted to avoid this conversation, it wasn't going away. It helped no one to go to bed angry. And it was a sure way to have a poor night of sleep and an even worse morning. If Tehl wouldn't speak, then she needed to say something for the both of them.

She let her fingers wander upward and combed his damp, black locks with care, mulling over what to say. Sorry should be in there somewhere... but the problem was, she wasn't very sorry. In fact, she felt irritated at his high-handedness. Tamping down her own feelings wasn't easy, but one of them needed to be rational.

"Do you want to talk about it?" she asked.

Again, he said nothing, but he didn't move away from her massaging hands. That was something, at least.

She pressed closer and leaned her chin on his shoulder. "I'm sorry for not obeying you."

Tehl stiffened and pulled away from her, his movements jerky. She wobbled as he slowly spun to face her, his expression like stone. "That's what you think this is about?"

His voice held the chill of a bitter, winter wind. Sage shifted uncomfortably and fiddled with the rag. She hadn't heard him use that tone since he'd threatened the rebels into giving her a choice in marrying him all those months ago. Unease skittered down her spine, not from fear, but because, for the first time, she couldn't get a read on him.

"You commanded me to stay put, and I disobeyed," she responded, hating that she felt like a child about to get reprimanded by a parent. "I'm sorry."

"Unreal," he breathed. His deep blue eyes narrowed as he studied her. "For someone so intelligent, you're acting pretty stupid, and your apology needs some work."

Sage bristled. If there was anything that could ignite her temper, it was the word *stupid*. Men liked to throw it around to make women feel inferior to them. The fact that he would use it now angered her to the point of wanting to slap him.

She forced herself to uncurl her fists, and exhaled slowly before answering him. She could do this. A little patience and understanding never hurt anyone. "I would appreciate it if you would refrain from using that derogatory word when speaking to me."

"And I would appreciate it if you listened for once." He said it without any inflection—like he wasn't spoiling for a fight.

Lies.

"I'm happy to listen," she gritted out, "if you actually deemed to speak to me. You've barely said a word." Sage eyed him. "Would you please accept my apology?"

He pinned his gaze over her shoulder and nodded once. "Fine." Dismissing her, he kicked off his boots and began to unlace his leather pants.

Sage peered at him in confusion. It couldn't have been that easy, *and* he'd used the F word. Every woman knew what the word *fine* meant in a fight. It meant everything was certainly *not* fine.

"You're lying to *me*," she accused.

Tehl stopped untying his pants and his gaze rose, meeting hers, a hint of blue fire heating his eyes. "You wish to speak to me about lying?"

She almost took a step back at the vehemence in his voice, but she stood her ground, despite the way her toes curled into the furs covering their bed. "I don't lie to you, Tehl." They'd promised to be honest to each other, and she kept her vow to the best of her ability.

His hands clenched into fists at his side, the first show of emotion. "You looked me in the face and smiled as if agreeing with me to help those who needed it and then, as soon as my back was turned, waded into the fray."

"I never said I wouldn't do that," she pointed out. He'd just assumed she would obey him.

"That's splitting hairs and you know it. You should have listened."

"I'm your wife and your partner. I'm not a subordinate to be ordered around."

"You are so blind!" he growled.

"Then tell me what I'm not seeing!" What was he getting at? She was trying to make things better.

"It's not about obedience," he said raggedly. "Do you know what I felt when I got out of the fire with the last living man? As I lay him on the ground, I was thankful none of my family had been in there. I felt guilty that I would get to sleep next to my wife while others would never know the love of their women again." His gaze darkened. "But then, I couldn't find you. No one knew where you were." He raked a hand through his hair and then stabbed an accusing finger at her. "When I rounded the burning infirmary and Gav told me you were still inside..." His voice broke. "I... I couldn't breathe, and I wanted to be inside the fire with you."

Sage's bottom lip trembled at the emotion pouring out of her husband.

She *was* stupid.

It wasn't about her disobeying. It was about the danger. "I'm so sorry you had to go through that..."

"When you were taken into Scythia, that wasn't your fault. I managed, because I knew who to punish for my pain and anguish. It wasn't *your* choice to leave. But this time, you *chose* to go into that fire without any regard for my feelings."

A tear dropped onto her cheek. Was it just yesterday that she thought Tehl had died in battle? How could she forget how that felt? Inadvertently, she'd caused this pain for him.

"How would you feel if I disregarded your feelings and got myself killed? Do you know why I didn't want you to go into the fire, other than the obvious?"

She shook her head. It was only fair to let him have his say. It was better for her to stay silent and let him get it all out.

"Most of the wounded were men." He paced at the foot of the bed and shot her a glare. "Not that you can't hold your own in a fight, but do you think you could have slung a grown man over your shoulder and hauled him out? No, Sage. You couldn't have, not without endangering him, yourself, and everyone else around you because of your petite frame."

That rankled her, but she let it slide when he fully faced her, destruction and sorrow clear on his face.

"I thought you'd died. For five minutes, I believed I would have to walk this road alone, and I imagined every horror you would've suffered."

"I'm okay," she whispered and took a small step toward him.

He held up his hand and then dropped to his haunches, both of his hands pulling at his midnight waves, his gaze distant. "I can't bear this." His haunted eyes rose to her face. "I can't deal with the emotions. It's too much. I can't live like this. How am I to survive it?"

Her stomach flipped, and she dropped the rag, took three careful steps to the end of the bed, and knelt. She'd done this. Tehl allowed her to wrap her arms around his neck and pull him into a hug.

"I'm so, *so* sorry," she said, guilt churning in her belly. Tonight had been a close call. Death had crept too close. "I should have listened." She should have. But, even in her heart, she knew she'd do it again if it meant saving her friends.

He tipped his head back and scanned her face. "I know you're sorry, but we're going to be in this position again."

She wanted to deny it, but she couldn't. "It's possible."

Tehl cocked his head and brushed his thumb across her cheek, catching one loose tear. "I hate emotions. How am I to bear all of this without turning into a madman?" he asked hoarsely. "I don't know if I can do this. I'll turn into my father."

Sage wanted to cry, but she held herself together. "I guess you have to ask yourself if the good outweighs the bad?"

He pushed to his feet, slipped his hand behind her neck, and tipped her head back. She stood, ashamed tears streaming down her face.

"Love isn't easy," he rumbled.

"No, it isn't."

"There's no going back."

"Not for me," Sage whispered. "There's no one else but you for me."

"Until death do us part."

It was a grave, dark statement that resonated in her soul.

She wasn't sure who moved first, but all she knew was that she needed to be in his arms. Tehl's lips crushed hers, fierce and demanding. He wasn't gentle or careful. He kissed her like it was his last chance to ever touch her. Sage threw her arms around his neck and kissed him back with the same urgency. Who knew what tomorrow held?

Her hands fisted in his hair, and she parted her lips, inviting him in. Warmth swept through her middle as he deepened the kiss. His fingers slid down the sensitive skin of her neck, catching on her soiled linen shirt. He snarled and released her for a moment, then tore the worn shirt straight down the center. Sage jerked back and stared at him wide-eyed. That was new.

Cool air teased her belly, and a shiver worked through her at how his gaze burned through her. It was like he was devouring her with his eyes. Observing him closely, she shrugged her shoulders, and the tattered linen fluttered to the mattress along with her modesty.

"I'm sorry," she said genuinely. Tonight, she'd deeply hurt him. Sage shakily drew in a breath. "I'm so sorry." More tears blurred her vision. "I didn't mean to. I would never hurt you on purpose."

"No, no tears," he whispered.

His hand curled around the back of her neck, and he pulled her mouth to his once again. His lips trailed lower, nipping at her chin, then her neck, his tongue tracing the salt of her tears.

His fingers slid down the sides of her neck and over her shoulders, his mouth never leaving hers. She gasped when he pulled her hard against him, his hands finding the soft skin behind her knees. Wrapping her legs around his waist, he pushed her onto the bed. She squeaked as he came down on top of her, his weight pressing her into the furs. The rasp of his stubble against her neck arched her off the bed, and she dug her nails into his shoulders.

"Don't ever do this to me again," he said gruffly. Teeth grazed the twisted scars around her throat, a teasing bite that threatened and tempted. "Spare my soul the anguish."

How she wished she could give such a promise. "I'll do my damnedest to never hurt you."

He growled. "I guess that will do." His hands slid down her sides in feverish need and paused on her hips, ever the gentleman.

Sage clasped the sides of his face and forced him to look her squarely in the eye. "I love you."

His eyes burned like a blacksmith's forge, the heat blistering her scarred soul. “As I you, even when you tear my heart from my chest.” He had the power to shatter her. “But it’s worth the pain,” he breathed. The power to make her whole once again, too.

Sage kissed him eagerly, her hands sliding up his chest where she could feel the frantic rhythm of his heart beneath her palms. Tehl shackled her wrists and pinned them above her head. A flicker of unease washed over her, but his hard lips were there, capturing hers, ravenous and brutal. He tasted divine—like sin and redemption rolled into one. His kiss didn’t just steal her breath, for he owned, possessed, and punished her.

For once, there was nothing but Tehl and herself. Two halves that created a whole. All thoughts disappeared when his hand slid between the furs and the naked small of her back, pressing her harder against him, like he could imprint himself on her skin, like he was trying to make sure she was still with him.

Sage bit his bottom lip and his lips parted, his gaze becoming distant.

“Devilish woman,” he hissed. “Don’t tempt me.”

“Beastly man,” she taunted. “Don’t think you can handle it?”

His lips curled away from his teeth in a dark smile, and something hard and predatory slid over his face. “Be careful what you ask for, love. The beast might eat you all up.”

Her smile was devious as she crooked a finger at him. “I’ll take that gamble.”

Chapter Sixteen

Mira

Mira tugged the blanket higher over the shivering soldier and forced herself to walk away. He was lost to pain and a high fever. There wasn't anything more she could do for him.

Her feet dragged as she moved down the center aisle, scanning her patients as she drifted toward her herb station where the queen sat idly, brewing willow bark to help with the fevers. The Methian royal had been a godsend. Without her help, Mira doubted most of the men would have made it through the night. She rubbed at her eyes with her good hand and stumbled a step, her right hand knocking against the nearest tent support. Gasping, she clutched her right hand to her chest as colored spots splashed across her vision. The ground seemed to roll, and she lurched sideways as pain pulsed up her arms in waves. Her left foot caught on a worn rug, and Mira braced herself for the horrible fall. Huge hands curled around her biceps and steadied her. Dazedly, she looked up, way up into the face of Raziel, the Methian crown prince.

She opened her mouth to say thank you, but all that came out was a hoarse groan.

"Are you okay?" he asked in a deep timbre.

Was she? Nausea slammed into her, and she tried to jerk away as bile flooded her mouth. "Gonna be sick," she wheezed before puking. With every heave, jerk, and twitch, more pain flooded her body. By the time she came out of it, Raziel had placed her on a cot and had a bucket on her lap.

Mira leaned her cheek against the wooden edge of the bucket and took shallow breaths, the warrior's scent curling around her comfortingly. A large hand stroked her braid and rubbed small circles on her upper back. How embarrassing. Not the vomiting, because in truth, sickness was a part of life, but the fact she wasn't trying to get rid of Raziel. It was so bloody nice to have someone care for her, even if it was for five minutes.

She cracked one eye and gave the prince a silly smile. "Haven't run away screaming yet?"

He returned hers with a devastatingly handsome grin. "And miss the chance to hold your golden hair from your beautiful face? Never."

"You, good sir, are a pretty liar."

"And you, lovely healer, are too sick to be out of bed, let alone working." His expression turned serious. "You're to the point of collapse. When was the last time you slept?"

Sucking on her bottom lip, she debated lying to him, but the Methians had an uncanny way of knowing when a person lied. It was better to be truthful. "Since before the fire."

Raziel's eyes narrowed into golden slits that reminded her of the way Nali stared at rodents before she pounced on them. Thank the stars for the blessed feline. Mira hadn't spotted any mice at all.

"You mean to tell me you haven't slept in almost two days?" Raziel demanded.

She closed her eyes in an attempt to ignore the censure on his face. "What am I supposed to do? They need me." A calloused finger touched the delicate skin beneath her right eye. She flinched and opened her eyes.

"You're a healer, are you not?" he cajoled.

"A tired one," she said, trying to make a joke. He didn't crack a smile.

"So, you know how the body needs sleep to heal. You're doing yourself and these men a disservice when you don't care for yourself."

"Let me ask you a question," she said roughly, her voice still rusty from the smoke inhalation. "If they were your men, would you rest when you knew they needed you? When they suffered and you could alleviate that pain?" His silence answered her question. "I swore an oath when I took up this profession. I will do everything in my power to help them."

Raziel surprised her and brushed a stray hair from her cheek. Her chest warmed at the sweet gesture, but she shoved it down deep. He was just being nice. She'd seen how he acted with women in general. Plus, he was a prince and she a commoner.

"Beauty as well as intelligence, compassion, and loyalty. The day you were born must have been something special."

Heat filled her cheeks. "Save your sweet words for someone who will believe them," she retorted.

It was in moments like this that she loved and hated the most. Since she'd come to the battlefront as a healer, Raziel had slowly inserted himself in her life. It started out as little things, but now she looked forward to his visits and conversations every day. It was stupid of her, really. He meant nothing by it, but it was the first time a man had looked at her without the stain of her past or judged her for entering a predominantly male profession.

"You don't believe I think you're one of a kind?" he asked, his voice deceptively soft.

"I think you love women. With your charm, I'm sure you make all of us feel like royalty," she murmured, her pain slowly fading to a dull throb.

"You know, in my culture, you don't have to be royalty to be considered *royal*. It all comes down to your actions. Believe me when I say that you could be anyone's queen."

Such pretty words said in earnest. "You flatter me," she huffed. Mira slowly sat up and glanced over her shoulder to break the tension that was building between them. If she wasn't careful, he'd steal her heart before she knew it. "Your mother looks like she's almost finished. I should help her."

Raziel pulled the bucket from her lap and placed it on the floor, never flinching at the sloshing contents within it. He straightened and shocked her by cupping her right cheek. "You can pretend all you want, Mira, but you and I both know there is something here."

Her eyes widened. "You've known me for a handful of weeks."

"We don't court like you Aermians do. We judge a mate by their fortitude, loyalty, and caring nature. Spending time in your presence has taught me that you're by far one of the best people I've ever had the privilege of spending time with. Normally, courting couples come to an understanding and then one kidnaps the other."

"Kidnapping is *not* okay." All she could see were Sage's haunted eyes and the thorn-adorned collar around her bloody throat. His thumb brushed her cheekbone, pulling Mira back to the present.

"I understand your reservations, which is why I have moved slowly."

"Slowly?" she whispered. "Slowly is a six year courtship."

Raziel's nose wrinkled. "Why would anyone agree to that? Our time on this earth isn't guaranteed. Why waste time living it without those you love?"

"That's the point of courtship—it's to make sure you really love them. Marriage is forever."

He dropped his hand. "What you speak of is attraction and infatuation. Love grows over years of time spent together, or child rearing. Why would anyone base their relationship off infatuation? That's the perfect way to ensure an unhappy union."

She must have been more exhausted than she thought, because the damn Methian was starting to make sense. Perhaps she would take a bloody nap. It wouldn't be long until her body gave up on her.

"So, what are you really getting at?"

Raziel brushed a wine-colored braid from his face and leveled a determined look at her, filled with promise. "I am going to pursue you, my golden one."

A startled laugh escaped her. "Excuse me?"

"Don't pretend like you didn't understand my words. You know exactly what I mean." He leaned closer, his golden eyes twinkling. "I intend to make you my mate, Mira. Even if that means courting you the Aermian way."

"You're joking," she muttered.

"I am not. I wouldn't joke about mates."

"I'm not going to marry you," Mira said bluntly, even as her traitorous heart skipped a blasted beat.

"I'm not asking." A devilish look. "Yet."

Mira rolled her eyes. She had to be hallucinating. Maybe she had passed out and her overactive imagination had spun out of control. Raziel touched her chin and leaned so close that she held her breath. Stars, he better not try to kiss her. She'd just puked. He brushed his nose along hers.

"Seek your bed soon, or I will have to take measures into my own hands." With that last comment, he stood and strode out of the infirmary.

Mira stared after him in shock and confusion. Did that really just happen? She stood on wobbly legs and turned toward the herb table. The queen had a hip leaned against the table and her very familiar golden eyes focused on Mira.

"Run while you can, my dear. It's only a matter of time."

"Until what?" she found the courage to ask.

"Until he captures you."

Chapter Seventeen

Sage

The blasted rain made everything harder.

Sage shivered as cold droplets slipped down her neck, to her already soaked shirt. The linen chafed against her skin. She swiped the rain from her brow and blinked, searching the battlefield for Zachael. Steam rose from the wet earth, and fog hovered in the distance. The fog was a blessing and a curse. It gave them more cover, but it also hid their enemies.

Her boots slurped as the mud tried desperately to hold her in place as she slogged forward. Rafe panted at her side, his amber eyes constantly scanning the area for an immediate attack. The wind whipped through the chilly air, and she shivered as it moved right through her. Stars above, she hated the bloody cold.

The former rebellion leader cast a quick glance in her direction.

"We need to turn back."

"No, we've gained ground."

"Only because the warlord is letting us." Rafe tensed. "Incoming."

Sage hefted her sword higher, her damp fingers slipping on the pommel for one second. That wasn't good. Her stomach bottomed out as *six* Scythian warriors materialized through the mist.

Swamp apples. "Retreat," she breathed.

Rafe sprang into action. "You in front of me."

She didn't second-guess him as they bolted back the way they came. Where had all their bloody soldiers gone? They couldn't have disappeared. The hair rose along her arms. This was all a trap. A damned trap.

She yelped as her boot sank deep into the mud. Sage slammed her hands to her knees, her extremities screaming in pain. Twisting to the side, she desperately yanked at her foot, but the suction from the mud made it almost impossible to move.

"Come on, damn you," she muttered as the Scythian warriors closed in.

Rafe stepped in front of her and drew a second sword from the sheath at his hip. "Work your toes back and forth. Once you break free, you run."

"I'm not leaving you behind." Her teeth chattered as the rain fell harder, obscuring her vision some.

"You can and you will, little one."

Sage clenched her teeth and jerked her foot as hard as she could. "I won't."

"You have no choice." He threw his shoulders back. "I'll draw them away."

Her left foot popped free followed by the right and she lunged forward, only missing his cloak by a hair as he sprinted toward the soldiers.

"No!" Sage scrambled to her feet, mud and muck smeared across her body. She took one step forward before the voice from her nightmares slithered over her spine.

"Hello, consort."

Every muscle in her body froze, and Sage stared helplessly as Rafe engaged the warlord's men, refusing to acknowledge the hulking nightmare nearing her.

"Will you not look at me?"

She closed her eyes and inhaled deeply before spinning around.

The warlord stood a measly fifteen paces from her. He smiled softly and cocked his head, his gaze perusing her form. "You've lost weight."

Spots dotted her vision, and the world dipped. Oh god, she was going to pass out. Sage dug her nails into her palms and bit the insides of her cheeks until she tasted blood, the pain keeping her from blacking out. Self-loathing and shame crashed into her as she continued to stare at the monster that haunted her dreams.

"Are you eating?" he asked, like it was a perfectly rational question while on the battlefield.

Part of her numbness melted away at his asinine question. It wasn't like they were friends catching up over bloody tea. Anger boiled in her veins. "War has hardened me."

His smile grew. "I can see that. Battle becomes you."

She tensed when he took two steps closer, his movements like a leren on the hunt. Sage lifted her blade and stared him down. "Come any closer and I'll kill you."

"So much fire," he crooned. "How I've missed it."

Her stomach rolled. Oh, wicked hell, she was going to be sick.

"Are you ready to come home yet?"

"Home? With you?" she murmured, dumbfounded. *Attack him, do something.*

He arched a onyx brow and shook his head, reminding her of something her father did when he was trying to reason with one of her unruly brothers. Her gaze darted over his shoulder and then back to him. Where was Rafe? Was he hurt?

"Yes, of course."

"I'm not going anywhere with you," she mumbled. Sage would turn her own sword on herself before she ended back in his clutches. The warlord tsked, moving closer. She countered his moves and circled, her sword held up defensively.

Sighing, he paused and pulled his sword free from his scabbard. "You'll only tire yourself out. As much as I love a good fight, you could just come willingly."

"Never," she hissed, her fingers tightening on the pommel of her muddy sword.

A smirk touched his lips. "So be it, fiery one."

Sage jerked at the pet name as a flood of memories assaulted her. The warlord feinted several times, but she could see he never intended to strike. Yet. The scar at her neck burned at the reminder of his cruelty. He was trying to draw Sage into an attack, but she wasn't that stupid. He was older and more experienced, but she could outwait him if she had to.

"Don't be shy," the warlord whispered. "It's been so long since we've been able to come together."

He attacked, and Sage blocked his swing and dodged to the side, wincing when the handle of her sword jerked against her sore hands. She needed to be careful—her stiffness, the cold, and the raw skin of her palms might get her captured or killed if she wasn't.

The warlord pursued the attack, trying to use up her energy. Sage attempted to dodge more and block less in order to spare herself, but he was just too damn quick. His sword slammed into hers, and it reverberated throughout her entire body, her teeth clacking together.

Damn it. She growled and bared her teeth at him.

He grinned. "I love this side of you. I can't tell you how much I've missed this."

Pain wormed its way up her right arm and into her shoulder as he disengaged. Her palms stung, and warm liquid heated the pommel of her sword. Without looking down, Sage knew she was bleeding.

She blinked, trying to get rid of the moisture in her eyes. Had the warlord switched his sword to his left hand, or was he carrying two swords? If she'd believed in magic, Sage would have sworn he was using some sort of illusion. Weariness must have been the culprit. She shook her head, trying to clear her vision.

Don't give up now. Think of the children. Think of Lilja.

Her lip curled, unbridled rage unfurling in her chest.

"That's it," he murmured. "Let me have all of that anger."

He lunged at her, and Sage blocked his sword and thrust back, coming body-to-body with the warlord. But that was a damn mistake. The huge monster used his strength to force her slowly to her knees.

Stupid. She knew better than to go toe to toe with someone so much bigger than herself. Sage wheezed and broke away from him, dropping to the mud and rolling away. The warlord struck, cutting her shoulder as Sage rose to her feet, dripping rain and mud. She dodged back, cursing angrily.

He paused and began circling once again. Sage spared a quick glance at her shoulder, noting how the blood and rainwater mixed together and dripped down her soaking linen sleeve. It wasn't that bad, but it still burned.

"You cut me."

"As did you when you left me." His expression darkened before it cleared, a manic look of glee replacing it. "It's not deep, but it'll make a nice scar of our first duel." He switched his sword to the other hand. "Prepare yourself, love. The times for games are over."

She met his attack, and was barely able to follow his movements as he changed his sword from one hand to the other. Irritatingly, she was forced to admire his perfect technique—one her father had tried to drill into her over the years. And while she was an excellent swordsman, the warlord was something else. It was too damn bad he was such a demon. A pity for such talent to be wasted.

Her steps faltered, and her arms began to tremble. They were swiftly coming to the time in a battle where the lesser swordsman began to gasp for air, tremble, and make horrible mistakes. She refused to be that person today.

Dig deep for the strength you know you have.

She snarled as he switched swords, and she seized the brief moment by lunging in. Sage slashed his left arm. The warlord grunted as she cut through muscle. He jerked back and examined his wound. His fingers touched the bloody gash. Slowly, the monster lifted his head and drew his fingers across each of his cheeks, scarlet cuts marring his perfect set of cheekbones.

"And that is why you are my consort," he said softly. "You're the only one I'll bleed for."

Horror churned in her belly as he darted forward. She got in two good slashes before he knocked her feet from beneath her. Sage gasped as she hit the ground. Screaming, she ripped the dagger from her hip and sank it into his thigh, just as he stepped onto her right hand, forcing her to release her sword.

He hissed but otherwise didn't say anything as he knelt, his boot grinding her wrist into the mud. She cried out and attempted to twist the blade deeper. The warlord tore her hand from the blade and grabbed her by her braid, pinning her in place. He yanked hard on her hair, forcing her head backward, the vulnerable arch of her neck on display.

The warlord leaned close, his weight pressing her farther into the mud. His black gaze ran over her face. He leaned closer, and she did the only thing she could think of. She spit on him. He froze, and something scary crossed his face that had her quaking in her boots, but she didn't cower. He'd never see her cower again.

"I hate you."

"You think you do, but hate is easily turned into other things."

"Death is preferable to you."

Instead of her words making him visibly angry, he smiled. He released a soft chuckle. "All this time I thought I needed to steal you back." His smile grew. "How I was wrong." He pressed closer, his nose running along her jawline, and his lips rested on the shell of her ear. "You've been brainwashed. I'll not let you play the martyr." He slowly pulled back and placed a tender kiss on her cheek. "You'll come to me in good time."

He stepped back, and Sage immediately hunted for her sword. Her fingers found the pommel, and she jerked forward on her knees, slicing toward his calf. The warlord jumped out of the way and carefully pulled her dagger from his thigh. He held it up and then clasped it to his chest like a treasured gift.

"I'll be seeing you soon, consort." He backed into the fog as she got to her feet. "Don't keep me waiting too long. Every death from now on will rest on your head."

Sage screamed and charged him, but he was swallowed up by the mist. Squinting, she spun in a circle as his sensual laughter echoed around her.

"I'll be waiting."

CHAPTER EIGHTEEN

The Warlord

His body was overheating.

He barely felt the winter elements as he marched into camp. Warriors parted for him as he emotionlessly passed them. Blood dripped from the wound on his leg, but he didn't feel it either. All he could see were her fiery, green eyes and sinful lips.

Blair approached from the left, a jagged cut across his left pectoral. Very close to the heart. Was his commander losing his touch?

"Come too close to an Aermian blade today?" he asked softly, striding toward his tent.

His commander, ever stoic, didn't even flinch at the question.

He's too bold, too well trained. He wants our throne. We must watch him, the voices whispered.

He couldn't agree more. That was the problem with giving men power. When they held a position for too long, they eventually turned their greedy gazes on the Scythian throne. Zane had seen it time after time, and Blair was no different. It was only a matter of time until the commander made a grab for power.

"Would you like me to send for a healer?" Blair asked.

And let their incompetent hands touch him? Zane thought not. He waved a hand as they arrived at his tent. "Make sure no one disturbs me."

With that, he entered the enormous tent. Inside, it was divided into three parts: a war room of sorts, the washing area, and his sleeping quarters. The braziers were well-stoked and heated the canvas rooms to an almost balmy heat. Sweat beaded on his brow as he pushed into his bedroom. It was simple. Warm furs created the flooring. A large bed rested near the brazier, and his desk sat to the right of the entrance.

Zane moved to his desk and sat slowly, his gaze trained on the stab wound on his thigh. He leaned down and pulled a hand-sized notebook from his boot. To anyone else, the book would look insignificant enough, but to him, it meant everything. He tugged the desk's top drawer open and fished out a quill and ink. With care, he opened the notebook to his last entry and scratched out the date on the next open page.

He focused on his wound and studied the way it bled sluggishly. It wasn't a cause for concern, but... His lips pressed together. It wasn't healing as well as it should. Perhaps he needed to change his dosage?

Maybe the fools at your lab have made a mistake, the voices hissed.

His lip curled. Fools indeed. No matter how well he trained the next alchemists, they continually made mistakes, or they were intentionally trying to kill him. A wicked smile touched his lips. The last alchemist to try that had drowned in his own poison. There was poetic justice in that. Dying by one's own creation.

He unlatched the key from the chain at his neck and opened the bottom left drawer, the sound of tinkling glass filling the air. Zane sighed. There was something about the bell-like chime of glass bottles knocking together that calmed him. He lifted a purple bottle and examined the marks on the side, the liquid matching its marker perfectly. He cast a glance at his door and listened. He heard no one but the two guards at the entrance of his tent. Although, he knew no one dared to enter without his permission, there were still those who would like to see him dead.

Carefully, he inventoried his draughts and measured out his correct dosages, noting he was low on two. He'd have to send a message to Maeve. She was the only one he trusted with his tinctures. With precise movements, he made notes in the notebook on his wound and the dosage for the day. He also scratched out a coded message for his sister.

A wave a nostalgia washed over him. It had been her idea as children to create a code for themselves. He'd only warmed to the idea as the years passed.

He flushed out his wound and didn't bother to stitch it. It would seal itself shut by the next evening.

Zane leaned back in the chair and laced his hands behind his head, his armpits sweating. He hated sweating. While he understood the necessity, the uncleanliness of it bothered him immensely. It got particularly worse when wounded. The body ran a high fever as it tried to repair itself. But there were worse lots in life.

His gaze wandered to his bed and the trunk that rested at the bottom. A silky feminine article of clothing peeked out from beneath his bow in the open chest, taunting him. In preparation of retrieving his consort, he'd taken the liberty of having a few things created for her.

So close. In our clutches. You let her go. Weak. Weak. Weak, the voices taunted.

Not weak—smart.

He smiled as he remembered the fight earlier tonight. She'd looked wild, unhinged, and absolutely stunning. War became her. When she'd stabbed him, he'd never wanted to kiss her more. In truth, the voices had been screaming for him to take her, right there in the mud amongst the blood and war. But he didn't. He'd fought through the battle-lust and really examined her. While she'd changed for the better, his consort hadn't been ready to submit to him. That's what he craved the most.

Her capitulation.

It would be all the sweeter when she broke and came to him.

And she *would*.

While he didn't *want* to hurt his consort, he knew some types of pain shaped a person into something better, something great.

Something extraordinary. Someone worth the Scythian throne.

Zane rolled his neck and stared off into space as he went over the next parts in his plan. It may have pained him to leave her there on the battlefield today, but it was worth it.

The clock was ticking.

The two of them coming together was inevitable. He calculated that she'd come running to him in less than a fortnight.

His gaze wandered back to the blue silk.

She'd be home.

Chapter Nineteen

Sage

Sage scowled at the abused leather pants covering her knees. The fingers of her right hand tightened against the bottle of whiskey she was nursing. The pinch and tug of the thread and needle usually made her want to puke, but not today. All she could think about was the warlord.

He'd let her go. He could have dragged her through the mud by her hair, and yet, he'd left her. Why?

Are you ready to come home?

Her heart accelerated, and she lifted the bottle of spirits to her lips, barely tasting the whiskey as she swallowed. She relished the burn of the alcohol and how it heated her belly. Since arriving back at camp, she couldn't get bloody warm. Whether it was from the rain or her chilling experience with the Scythian warrior, she didn't know.

"You'll have to tell him," Rafe said, making sure to stay out of the healer's way. "And the war council."

She lifted her eyes and hid her flinch at his appearance. The man was a bloody mess. Sage swallowed hard. His entire face was practically an enormous bruise, not to mention all the cuts, a stab wound, and his two broken ribs. The stars only knew what would have happened if she hadn't shown up. Rafe was a beast in his own right, but if the warlord hadn't retreated when he had, Rafe would have died. Because of her.

Guilt settled on her shoulders. She was so tired of feeling guilty, but what was one more thing settled onto the chip she already lugged around?

"I know," she muttered. The war council didn't frighten her in the least, but after the rocky few days she'd had with Tehl, this was something she didn't want to talk about. He'd lose his ever-logical mind. "This changes things."

"It changes nothing."

"How can you say that?" Sage grimaced as the healer pierced the needle through her skin once more. Stars, she hated that.

"Our goals stay the same. We continue as we have been."

"I disagree." Her stomach knotted. "I have a feeling that things are going to be worse. Scythia's motives have changed."

Rafe snorted and then clutched at his ribs. "He still wants world domination. That's nothing new."

She couldn't put her finger on it but... "Something wasn't right." It was the way he dealt with her. It felt off.

"How so?"

"I don't know," Sage admitted. "I stabbed him in the thigh, and he didn't even cry out. It was like he didn't feel the pain at all." The memory of him swiping blood across his cheeks caused her belly to cramp and bile to burn the back of her throat. "He's changing."

"Into what?" Rafe asked.

That was the question. Was the warlord riding a berserker so high that he didn't feel the pain? Or was he dosing himself with some sort of draught? Either way, it made her uneasy. She rubbed her thumb along the glass bottle. "I can't shake the feeling that he's backing us into a corner we can't get out of."

Sage startled when Rafe lay his hand over her own. He pulled her left hand away and laced their fingers together.

"I'm sorry for today."

Her brows furrowed in confusion as she looked up. "What do you mean?"

"I should have protected you." His gaze darted to her wounded shoulder. "He could have taken you."

"But he didn't." She squeezed his fingers. "You almost got yourself killed out there protecting me. You did your best."

Rafe glanced away, his jaw clenching. "Not good enough."

"It *was* good enough. We are both alive. That's a victory in and of itself."

They fell into silence as the healer finished caring for and dressing Sage's wound.

Sage's shoulders slumped as they were left alone. This was something she loved about Rafe. They could just be in each other's company. There was no need to make conversations. It was enough that they loved and supported each other. Love. It wasn't something she said very often, but she'd promised herself that she'd work on it.

"You know I love you, right?"

Rafe jerked and scrutinized her. "You're not going to do something stupid, are you?"

Sage puffed out a laugh. "No." She chuckled but sobered quickly as she studied her dear friend. "We've been through many hardships together in the last few years. Never doubt that I truly care for you."

He smiled softly and leaned forward to her cheek. "I consider you my flesh and blood." Rafe pulled back. "While things didn't go as I expected them to, I still count myself lucky to love and have the love of such a fierce female."

She smiled. "It's funny how life surprises us, isn't it?" Her gaze moved past him to Blaise, who was currently sleeping. "Do you believe there is only one destined mate for a person?"

"No."

"I agree." Her smile turned wistful. "We could have been happy together before the Crown captured me. And though we may have been blissfully happy, I now can't imagine my life without Tehl."

"He is a strong mate for you, better than I."

Her brows raised. "Such humble words."

"I believe there are many potential mates for every person, and while you could make each pairing work, some just suit better." Rafe shrugged. "We would have made a powerful coupling, but you and Tehl complement each other in a way we never did." He smiled. "You were always a queen."

Sage rolled her eyes. "Such pretty words." Her smile turned smug as she caught him glancing in Blaise's direction. He'd been sniffing in the Scythian woman's direction for some time. "Something tells me your married future isn't far off."

"What makes you so sure?" Rafe asked, never taking his eyes off Blaise.

"Maybe it's the way you stare," she said bluntly. It felt good to talk about something light.

"She hates me."

"I hated the crown prince. Look where we are now."

Rafe smirked. "Soon, I'll be welcoming your fat, green-eyed babes into the world." He chuckled. "You should see the look on your face."

"Not anytime soon, I hope."

"There's only one way to control that..."

Sage blushed. "Enough," she said gruffly. "Are you ready to go?"

He stood slowly. "I've been waiting on you."

She untangled the fingers of her left hand from his and shook her head. "You always want the last word."

"And I don't know anyone like that at all," he retorted.

Sage threw her head back and laughed. It felt damn good. For a few minutes, her spirit was lightened. Darkness may have surrounded her, but, when one looked closely enough, there were always glimmers of light.

Chapter Twenty

Tehl

"Fall back!" Tehl bellowed.

His battalion of men sprinted away from the burning war machine as Scythian warriors gave chase. Tehl's arms pumped by his sides, and he changed direction when he realized a flaming stone was incoming. It slammed to the earth a mere three paces ahead of him.

Veering right, the Aermian soldiers flanked him, keeping pace as they pushed back toward their line. His breaths seemed abnormally loud in his own ears as his heart raced. Not too far to go until they made it back to safety.

The soldier on his left crashed to the ground. A spear stuck out from his back. Tehl broke stride for one second before picking up his speed. As much as it galled him to leave the man behind, there wasn't any choice. It was war. He shut his feelings away and focused on the task. The gray clouds darkened. That wasn't good. Either rain or snow. Neither was ideal.

"They're gaining on us. Move!" Gav yelled, his command spurring the small group of soldiers to move faster.

No one wanted to be caught by the enemy. While they'd managed to figure out how to take down warriors without as many deaths, the Scythians had the unfair advantages of speed, strength, and heightened senses. Damn them.

The smoke wavered, and Tehl narrowed his eyes. Did he see movement ahead? He studied the terrain. Did the hill ahead conceal the enemy? No time to turn back now or even find cover.

"Arms up," he shouted. "Be prepared." No sooner had he given the command when enemy warriors sprung from their hiding places. Tehl raised his sword and charged forward. The wicked devils had hidden themselves in the mud. They looked like bloody swamp monsters.

Tehl's sword crashed against an enemy sword with a clang that made his teeth rattle. He tore his dagger from his chest sheath and slashed at the Scythian's chest. He knew there were only a few moments to get one of the monsters down before they killed him. His knife drew a bloody gash down the man's chest. But the Scythian didn't even blink.

Wicked hell. The warrior was already deep into the berserker rage. Tehl danced back, and the Scythian lunged, his sword high. The crown prince danced out of the way and cursed when burning pain sliced across his shoulder. He clenched his jaw and ignored the pain. The cut was minor. If it had been deep, the pain would have knocked him to his knees.

Raziel rushed in from behind and chopped at the Scythian's bare, mud-covered back. The warriors were an arrogant lot. It was stupid to show that much skin in a battle. They were proud and it would be the end of them, he vowed. The Methian prince darted under the enemy warrior's guard and cut him across the ribs. Tehl blinked and circled the warrior while his attention was on Raziel. So, he planned on riling the enemy.

The Methian took one step toward the Scythian when he turned to face Tehl, snarling. Tehl lunged back and then forward, his right foot connecting solidly with the warrior's chest. It was like kicking a stone wall.

The Scythian stumbled but didn't fall.

"Weakling," the warrior spat. "I'll enjoy your death."

Tehl kept his gaze fixed on the warrior. He hadn't kicked the enemy to knock him down. The purpose had been to rile his anger, so that he forgot that death was stalking him from behind. Raziel struck without a sound. The warrior stiffened and choked, blood dripping down his chin. Tehl nodded to the Methian prince and turned from the gruesome scene.

He knew it to be ghastly, and yet he felt nothing. No nausea, remorse, or shame. Slowly, he was becoming desensitized to it all.

Tehl waded into the fray, hardly hearing anything around him. The world surrounding the crown prince faded, and all he could focus on was the next opponent, the perfect strike point, and the safest route for escape.

His sword bit into the flesh of his newest foe and he watched, completely unfazed, as life drained from the man's gaze. He released the warrior and lifted his own head, once again scanning his battalion, searching for who needed help.

The hair at the nape of his neck rose as he caught sight of Gavriel battling a warrior who looked to be twice his size. For the first time all day, he felt something.

Terror.

His cousin was sweating and fighting with everything he had. Tehl dug his toes into the ground and pushed forward, racing toward the duel. Gav couldn't see it, but the Scythian was toying with him. Tehl cut through the swathe, his heart pounding. Only a little farther. If he could reach them, then it would be a fair fight.

Snow fell from the sky, big heavy flakes like someone had cut a feather pillow and dumped it from above. The Scythian swept Gav's feet out from under him, and a cry stuck in Tehl's throat. The enemy slammed his boot down on Gavriel's ankle and then stabbed his spear into his left thigh. His cousin screamed in pain but never dropped his sword. The Scythian pulled a short blade from his waist and leaned closer to finish the job.

Tehl's focus homed in on the enemy who'd wounded his cousin. Gav wildly slashed his sword at the enemy, managing to hit the warrior in the chest. The man bellowed and lifted his blade, his attention locked in on Gavriel.

The crown prince smiled darkly, sprinting the last few steps. The warrior spun in time to see his death coming. Tehl drove his sword into the Scythian's chest. The warrior teetered for a moment and then crashed backward, taking Tehl with him. The crown prince rolled away and held out his dagger in case the warrior wasn't truly gone. He'd seen some of the warriors stabbed over ten times and still they kept fighting until they died of blood loss. It was like something out of a horror story.

This time, the Scythian didn't rise.

Tehl retrieved his blade quickly and turned to his cousin, dropping to his knees. Gav panted, his face creased with pain.

"How bad is it?" Gavriel gasped.

Tehl knelt and eyed Gav's wound. He carefully slipped his left hand under his cousin's leg and gritted his teeth. The warrior had stabbed him clean through the leg, pinning him to the ground.

Bloody hell.

"That bad?" Gav wheezed, sweat dripping down his brow and cheek.

Tehl didn't want to tell him. He unbuckled his cousin's belt and yanked it out from beneath him, not daring to look Gav in the eye as he formed a tourniquet around the top part of his left thigh.

"Just tell me. I already know my ankle is broken."

Tehl cinched the belt to stop the blood flow and met Gavriel's purple gaze, his heart in his throat. "The spear went clear through and into the earth. He pinned you."

Emotions raced across Gav's face too fast for Tehl to read before his expression melted into determination. "You must leave me."

No.

Raziel appeared on his right side, and a loose ring of soldiers formed around Gavriel.

"How bad is it?" the Methian prince barked.

"He's stuck."

Raziel cursed and dropped to his knees. He inspected the damage and probed the wound from below. "I think we can get the spear out of the ground, but we can't remove it here." *Or he'll die*, was the implication.

Tehl eyed the six-foot-long spear. They'd need to cut the staff down to mobilize him. His gaze darted to Gav's pale face. "We'll need to cut the spear before we move you as well. Prepare yourself," he muttered grimly.

A soldier to the right stepped closer and held out part of his shirt that he'd ripped away. "Bandages for our commander."

Tehl nodded gratefully as another handed him his belt. Wordlessly, he placed the leather strip between Gav's teeth. He stared at his cousin and touched his forehead to Gavriel's.

"You have a little girl at home. Don't you die on her. Hold on to Isa."

Gav nodded, and Tehl forced himself to place both of his hands on the spear. Raziel pulled a serrated blade from the sheath at his thigh and solemnly asked, "Are you ready?"

Tehl nodded, holding the spear steady. When Gavriel's purple gaze focused on the Methian prince, Tehl pulled with all his might. Gav's body arched, and he screamed once, before passing out as he pulled the spear from the ground. The crown prince released the spear and pressed the linen against the bleeding wound. Raziel knelt and began sawing the shaft of the spear off.

"It's a blessing he's unconscious for this."

"Let's pray that it stays that way," Tehl murmured.

They had a long way to go to get back to camp. Anything could go wrong in that time.

CHAPTER TWENTY-ONE

Sage

Sage burst into the infirmary tent, startling two healers. "Where is Gavriel Ramses?"

"The rear room, my lady," the older healer rasped.

She brushed by them without thanks, her legs shaking with adrenaline. News had spread fast through camp when their commander had returned hurt. *How bad was it?*

"Hold him down!" Queen Osir commanded Rafe and Raziel.

Sage rushed through the tent flap and into the commotion. People scurried about the room everywhere, but she ignored all of them when she spotted Gavriel. He lay on his right side with a spear pierced through his thigh. Tehl stood at the foot of the bed, cutting Gav's leather boot from his now-very-swollen ankle.

Stars above. Queasiness rolled through her, and she pressed a clammy hand to her forehead. Blood had never bothered her in the past, but the longer she was exposed to grisly scenes, the worse it got.

Get yourself together. This is Gav.

Swallowing her saliva, she pressed forward. Gav's glassy, purple eyes wildly searched the room. She stepped into his line of sight and smiled warmly at him. He froze and held out a trembling hand.

"It's okay," Sage crooned and dropped to her knees, both hands wrapping around his remarkably cool one. "You'll be all right."

"Hurtzzzz," he slurred through cracked lips.

"I know." She brushed her fingers along his heated brow and drew patterns on his cheeks. Her gaze caught the flash of Mira pulling scalpels from boiling water, and her belly flipped. Gav tried to look over his shoulder, but she released his hand and cupped the back of his neck. Scooting a little closer, she leaned her cheek against the cot and stroked his damp, dirty black locks.

"I'm not going to make it," he croaked.

"Don't talk like that." She mustered up the most reassuring smile she could. Not many would survive a wound such as this, but if anyone could do it, it would be Gavriel. "Soon this will all be over."

"Isa..."

"Isa will be so happy to see you when you're recovered. Just think how impressed she will be with your scars. I bet she'll ask you to show it to all the ladies in court."

"How scandalized they'll be when I start to unbuckle my pants," he gasped.

Sage laughed at the little spark of deviousness she spotted in his eyes. "They've been pining after you for years. I bet they'll take it as an invitation."

He nodded, but his gaze dimmed.

No, no, no, no. That wasn't good.

"Don't let him fall asleep!" Mira barked.

Sage removed her hand from behind Gavriel's head and pressed her fingertips into the hollows of his cheeks and pulled back. She shook him roughly. "None of that, my friend."

His head lolled, but his attention was once more focused on her face. She tipped her head to the side and shrugged her shoulder so the linen shirt slipped away from her neck, revealing the ropy scar around her neck. "Do you remember when Isa saw this for the first time?"

"She asked if a leviathan hurt you," he whispered.

"She did. Thankfully, Lilja was in the room."

Gav wheezed out a short laugh. "She really got a close view of a leviathan bite."

"We're ready," Queen Osir announced. "Anyone who is not assisting, get out!"

Sage watched the soldiers file out, and then turned her attention back to Gav. A familiar hand settled on her shoulder. She glanced up at Tehl, and her heart ached for the fear and pain naked on his face. He was covered in blood and muck. It was like he'd bathed in it.

"Are you assisting?" she asked.

He nodded and squeezed her shoulder. "Thank you, wife, for sitting with him."

She smiled and turned back to Gavriel, who watched them.

"I miss that," Gav murmured.

What was left of her heart shattered into a million pieces at his confession. "We love you, Gav. You're not alone."

Sage brushed an inky strand from his cheek.

Raziel and Rafe moved to the bottom of the bed as Zachael and Tehl moved to the top. When had Zachael arrived?

"The pain will soon be over." She leaned closer and made sure her face was all he could see. "I know you miss your wife, but your death won't bring her back. You have a little girl waiting for you to come home. This will be your hardest fight yet. I need you to give it your all. Can you do that for Isa?"

Gav nodded.

She squeezed his right hand as Tehl wrapped his hands around Gav's bicep and placed a knee on the cot to hold his cousin in place. Zachael helped pin Gav to the cot from the other side. Mira stepped around Gavriel and placed a thick strip of leather against his lips. He let her work the leather between his top and bottom teeth.

Strong lye soap and heated metal teased Sage's nose. She swallowed thickly and prayed that she wouldn't puke or pass out.

"You can squeeze my hand as hard as you need to."

Gav nodded, his fingers tightening a fraction.

"On the count of three. One, two..."

They never made it to three, because Queen Osir grabbed the head of the spear and yanked.

***

Sage leaned her forehead against her knees and closed her eyes. It felt like weights had been attached to her lashes. Sweat collected uncomfortably beneath her half corset, and her hair stuck to her neck and face. She rolled her neck and rested her cheek on her kneecap, watching as Mira stoked the woodstove in the corner of the canvas tent. More bloody heat. While she understood Gav needed to stay warm, she desperately wanted to cut a hole in the tent and let in some of the cold night air.

"How is your hand?" Mira asked, adding another infernal log to the fire.

Sage held up her red hand and wiggled her fingers. They ached but it wasn't horrible. "They're fine." Her hand would be bruised by the next day. In his pain, Gavriel had almost broken her fingers. She shuddered and swore she could still hear his inhuman screams echoing in her ears.

And the blood…

She nearly gagged and inhaled deeply, trying to keep herself from puking. Removing the spear from Gav's leg was a disgusting and messy business. In the end, it had taken two more soldiers to hold him down.

"You don't have to be here," Mira said softly, brushing her left hand against her apron. "He won't wake up for some time."

"*If* he makes it through the night," Sage muttered dully. The hole in his leg was a brutal mess. It would take a bloody miracle for him not to die. Heat built behind her eyes, but she forced the tears not to fall. Gav wasn't dead yet. She refused to mourn him now. He *would* get better. He had to.

She jerked when Mira touched her forearm and knelt in front of her. When had the healer moved? Sage hadn't even heard her. So much for being a paragon of observation.

"He won't even know you've gone," the healer said gently. "I've dosed him with enough herbs to keep him asleep for the night. Get your rest and then come back before he wakes."

It was a practical suggestion, but it didn't sit right with Sage. No one should recover by themselves. "I won't leave him."

She and Tehl were of the same mind. He would have stayed himself if he'd not been pulled into a war council meeting. He'd asked her to stay in his place.

Mira stood and held out her good hand. "Let's find you a better place to rest then, shall we?"

Sage stared apprehensively at her friend's hand. Stars, could she even lift her own arm? Everything hurt, and her ass had gone numb hours ago. She slapped her hand into Mira's and clambered to her feet, pins and needles running up and down her legs. Groaning, she rubbed her lower back and turned to stare at the cot Gav slept in. He looked so much like Tehl with his eyes closed. You'd have to be blind not to see the royalty in him.

"He'll be okay," Mira whispered.

"You have to say that," Sage said thickly. "It's your job as a healer."

The healer slipped her arm through Sage's and leaned her cheek against her shoulder. "No. It's my job to save lives. I promise you I will do everything in my power to help him."

"I know you will." Sage tipped her head against Mira's and soaked in the comfort of her friend. When was the last time she'd spent time with another female like this? A long time ago. She stifled a sarcastic laugh. It took Gav being stabbed.

"Come on," Mira said, pulling away.

She tugged on Sage's arm and led her to the cot at the far end of the room, nearest the exit. A cool breeze drifted through the crack of the flap, and she sighed. Sage slumped onto the cot and frowned when Mira placed the back of her hand against Sage's forehead.

"What are you doing?"

"You're flushed."

Sage arched a brow and gestured to the room. "The room is practically boiling." She squinted. "You're flushed, too."

Mira rolled her eyes and pulled her hand away. "Forgive me for worrying about your health." She sobered. "You look like a walking corpse."

Sage leaned against the outer tent post and tipped her head back, her eyes closing. "I forgot how flattering you are."

"I do my best, my lady."

Snorting, she shook her head. "Imp."

"Cretin."

"Since you're so fond of giving health advice, why don't you sit down for a little while?" Sage said, patting the cot she upon. "Gav isn't going anywhere." Hopefully.

The healer sat down and sighed. "My feet are killing me."

Sage leaned her head against Mira's slim shoulder and yawned. "Tell me something good. Something happy." After today, she needed to hear something light. Maybe it would keep the nightmares away. The least it would do was buoy her spirits before sleep claimed her.

"I'm… I'm being…"

Sage peeked up at her friend. Mira never hesitated. "What?"

The healer licked her lips. "I'm being courted." A pause. "I think."

What the devil? Sage kept her composure, even though she felt wide awake. "You think?"

"He spoke of his intentions a few days ago. Before that, I thought he was just a harmless flirt. Even now, I have a hard time believing that he's even interested in me."

That bothered Sage. "And why wouldn't he be?" she demanded. "You're a wonderful woman. Any man would be lucky to have you as a wife. Who is the man anyway?"

Mira's throat worked as she swallowed thickly. "Raziel."

Blinking slowly, Sage kept her mouth firmly shut, despite how she wanted to gape. It wasn't like Mira wasn't worthy of a royal husband… it was the fact that Sage hadn't the slightest clue he'd been interested in her friend. Her brows furrowed. Why hadn't Mira said anything before?

Probably because you've been too busy slaying the enemy.

Another stone to add to her mountain crafted from guilt.

"You don't sound excited," Sage said softly. "Does he make you happy?"

Mira shrugged her arm, her shoulder digging into Sage's cheek. "I don't know him very well. He's spent a lot of time in the infirmary, helping the wounded. He makes me laugh and is kind to those around him. I haven't heard him talk down to those who would be considered lesser. I find that appealing."

There was something in Mira's tone that bothered Sage. "But?"

The healer sighed. "But I've only just met him. It's been a month since we first met, and while we've spent hours in each other's company, I don't think that's enough time to decide one's future."

"Very wise."

"He said he wanted me for his mate."

Sage's eyes widened. "Bold."

"Everything about him is bold." Mira fiddled with the fabric of her apron. "I never thought I'd make a very good match with anyone."

"Why in the blazes would you ever think that?"

"I'm an orphan, Sage, and I work in a male profession. You know what has been said about me in the court. I'd planned on honing my skills and serving as a palace healer as an old maid. Raziel is… he is…"

"Scary," Sage supplied.

"Scary because he is the unknown. I've trained most of my life to become a healer, not a…" Mira huffed. "It feels ridiculous saying it out loud. I'm not a princess."

"Welcome to the club," Sage muttered wryly.

"I don't know what to do."

"That's the great thing about courtship. You have time to figure out what you want. Only time will tell if you are both suited for each other." Sage paused. "For what it's worth, Raziel is a good man. War can make beasts out of men. He's kept true to his honor." She reached out and held Mira's hand. "You're an excellent healer, but I think you'd make a marvelous princess, too." Sage chuckled. "I'm sure you'd do a better job of it than me."

"I don't know if I could do it."

"If you like him, court Raziel. Don't say no because you're afraid of change."

"Is that an order, my lady?" Mira said with a smile.

Another jaw-cracking yawn seized Sage. "Like you'd listen to me anyway."

Mira shook with suppressed laughter. "You know me all too well."

"Mmmhmmm." Sage's eyes closed, the siren song of sleep calling for her. She barely noticed when Mira helped her lay down on the cot and covered her with a light blanket. Slumber claimed her almost immediately.

Chapter Twenty-Two

Tehl

"More have arrived," Zachael said grimly.

Tehl hung his head. "Take me to them." His legs felt like lead as he followed the weapons master, accompanied by five Elite, Rafe, and Hayjen. He flicked a glance in Rafe's direction. The former rebellion leader looked like hell. They all did. There were some things that no person should ever see.

Their group reached the outskirts of the camp, snow still falling softly to the ground. Two men stood next to something covered with a horse blanket. It might have been cowardly, but Tehl wanted to turn around and never look under the blanket at the inevitable horrors awaiting him. He forced himself onward, their group silent except for the squelch of mud and snow beneath their boots as they reached the two men.

The taller man held the lantern higher, casting light over his sharp cheekbones and dark eyes. Blair. The Scythian commander. If he'd taken the risk to meet with them, circumstances must be dire.

Tehl halted when they reached Blair and William. William's face glowed a sickly pale yellow in the light. He looked the old man in the eyes, and his stomach dropped. William was holding back tears. Whatever the warlord had done, it had wrecked the older man. He'd never seen the general cry. Ever.

Hayjen stepped from the group and clasped forearms with Blair. "Well-met."

Blair nodded. "You might not say that when this is all through."

"What has happened?" Tehl asked, eyeing the pile, his stomach rolling.

"The warlord has prepared another gift," Zachael spat.

"Will you not say what he's done?" Tehl murmured.

The weapons master began to speak, but his voice cracked. He clamped his mouth shut and shook his head.

Tehl glanced around the silent group. No one could speak. He steeled himself and took the final step to whatever terror lay hidden. His fingers trembled when he dropped to his haunches and clasped the sodden edge of the blanket, pulling it back.

At first, nothing made sense. The shapes were wrong. They couldn't be bodies... Tehl froze when he spotted a familiar face. Bile burned the back of his throat, and he placed a hand over his nose and mouth. Benjamin's face stared up at him through sightless eyes. He was just a boy. A child. The sound of retching filled his ears, but he couldn't look away. He reached out and brushed a thumb along the dead boy's cheek. A lone tear dripped down his cheek, cooling in the winter wind. No one deserved a death like this.

Tehl forced himself to look at the others. The bodies were

unidentifiable, but from their statures, it was apparent they were all young ones. Chills rippled up and down his arms as he looked at each unmarked face. Trembling, he shot to his feet and stalked away, his chest heaving with labored breaths. How could someone do such a thing? Acute pain, so piercing, stabbed him in the heart. Tehl screamed as if it would somehow release the emotions that were trying to drown him. He placed his head in his hands and stared at the white, snow-covered ground, tears rushing down his cheeks.

A hand touched his shoulder, and he shrugged it off. He couldn't bear the comfort. It should have been him, not the boys. It was *wrong*, so wrong. Angrily, he scrubbed the tears from his cheeks and pressed his palms to his eyes as if it would stop him from seeing their little faces again. This couldn't go on. Every time he thought he understood the depravity of the warlord, the devil stooped to a new, disgusting low.

His stomach revolted, and he vomited.

Little ones.

His mind could not comprehend that sort of cruelty. Children were to be protected, not desecrated. He heaved again. Tears and snot mingled on his face. Only someone truly evil could commit such a crime. He straightened and wiped his forearm across his face, turning to his men. They all looked as haunted and destroyed as he was. Old William was openly crying, his big grey beard collecting tears.

"Was this…" Tehl cleared his throat. "Was this where they were found?"

Zachael shook his head. "No. They were found on our side."

Tehl swallowed as more bile pooled in his mouth. "Did you retrieve all of them?"

"What we could, there were parts…" William paused, swallowing hard. "We did the best we could."

Tehl's gaze turned to Blair, who looked as disturbed as the rest of them. "Why would he do this?"

Blair's mournful dark eyes met his. "These are the consequences for Sage's perceived disobedience."

Sage. Oh god. It would kill her when she heard of this. The prior killings this week had torn her apart. What would these killings drive her to do? For a moment, he considered swearing everyone to silence. But he knew that would never work. They couldn't cover up something this heinous, and the boys deserved to be honored and have a proper burial.

"I don't want to tell her," he said to no one in particular.

"We can't keep this from her," Hayjen said gruffly.

"I know," Tehl bit out. His wife wouldn't forgive him if he hid something like this from her. They didn't lie to each other. He needed to trust that she wouldn't do something stupid. Or at least, not without him being part of the plan. "We need to identify all the boys and then notify their families."

"I will take care of that," William said. The old man broke from the group, pulling an Elite with him.

Tehl turned his gaze on Rafe. "We need blankets for each of their bodies and more soldiers to carry them."

"Done," Rafe said, his tone brusque. He jogged after William.

Tehl turned his attention to Blair. "We need to prepare these little ones for burial, but I need to speak with you. Can you risk staying for a while?"

Blair nodded. "I will see this through."

Tehl nodded absently, his hands jittery at his sides. He felt like he needed to be doing something. Part of him wanted to cradle Benjamin to offer comfort to the youth. The other part of him felt like it would be disrespectful to disturb the body further.

On wooden legs, he approached the line of children and pulled the rug up and over their corpses, protecting them from the elements.

"I'm so sorry," he whispered.

He didn't know how long he stood there, staring at the blanket. The snow fell harder and slowly covered the material, camouflaging what was hidden beneath it. For some reason, it made him angry. A crime like this shouldn't be covered up or forgotten.

Flames of vengeance lit in his chest. Tehl lifted his head and stared across the whitewashed battlefield. He was tired of being one step behind. Right there, he made a vow: he would sacrifice whatever it took to avenge the boys.

His soul had already been damaged.

Tonight, what was left of it burned to ash.

***

"Can you tell us what his movements will be?" Raziel asked.

Blair frowned and pointed to the map on the center of the table. "I only have a piece of his plan. I've told you all I can."

William scoffed. "You're his commander. Surely, he shares with you more of his plans than what you've told us?"

Blair grimaced, his white teeth a stark contrast to his swarthy skin. "That madman trusts no one. Least of all, me."

"Why is that?" Rafe asked softly from his perch in the corner.

"He distrusts anyone who holds any sort of power in his court. He gives us each a piece of the puzzle and keeps us all suspicious of each other. That way, we'll be so divided, we'll never rise up against him."

"That's brilliant," Zachael muttered, and Hayjen shot him an irate look. "I didn't mean I condone it, but it's an intelligent move. Strategically, it makes sense. Crazy, he is. Stupid, he is not."

A heavy silence settled over the group. Blair's intel helped, but it wouldn't win them the war.

"We appreciate what you've given us," Tehl said. "But it's not enough." He stared the Scythian down. "We need more information. It's key to the warlord's downfall."

Blair gazed back evenly. "I can't risk exposure. Many people will die if he suspects me more than he already does."

"People are already dying. Children are dying," Tehl said softly.

Blair flinched, but his expression blanked almost immediately. Clearly, he wasn't as impervious to death as he pretended to be.

Tehl continued on, "Every day, he pushes us farther back. Soon, our troops will be trapped against the mountains. If that happens, we lose. He'll massacre us. We need to take a hard stand now."

"My people aren't ready," Blair responded. "Even if I could, by some miracle, gain more information, it would do you no good. You don't have the manpower to implement such a plan without my troops. There are too many working parts to rush in. We wait."

"How soon will your men be ready?" Zachael asked.

Blair's lips thinned. "One to two weeks, at least. Moving undetected through the forests of Scythia is no easy task."

"Who's leading your warriors?" Rafe probed.

Tehl nodded. He wanted to know as well.

Blair's expression became unreadable. "Someone I trust."

"You're sure they won't betray you?" Hayjen muttered. "Scythians aren't known for their trustworthiness."

"I've entrusted them with my wife and daughters."

Interesting. In Tehl's experience, a man didn't leave the protection of his family to someone who didn't deserve that trust. If Blair trusted this person, that was enough for Tehl. For now.

He turned his attention back to the map, scowling at how the Scythian markers on the map stood too close to the Aermian troop line. "So, our lots are cast." They had no choice but to hang on and wait. There would be consequences. The children were at the forefront of his mind. "What happened tonight will not happen again."

"What happened?" his wife asked, her voice sleepy.

Dread filled his gut as he turned to the entrance of the tent. Sage stepped fully inside, her clothing rumpled. She even had a blanket crease across her cheek. She looked wholly appealing in that moment. All he wanted to do was carry her off to bed and hold her tight. He swallowed hard, sickened at the news he had to give her.

"There was another attack."

Her sleepiness visibly sloughed off, and she joined the group, circling the war table. "How bad is it?"

"Bad," Zachael muttered.

Her emerald gaze studied the group before settling heavily on Tehl. "Don't sugarcoat it. Just tell me."

He nodded and forced the ugly truth from his mouth. "Bodies were found along the troop line." He swallowed hard but continued. "Little bodies."

Sage stiffened, her eyes darting to each of the grave expressions on the men's faces.

"Children?" she asked raggedly.

Tehl nodded curtly. "The warlord targeted the young boys helping around camp, and those flying our banners."

Sage staggered against the table and leaned on it for support. "How many?"

"More than ten is what we gather," William whispered hoarsely. "Their bodies… It was difficult to guess."

A tear dropped down his wife's cheek. "He said this would happen."

Chills ran down his spine. "The warlord?"

She nodded and dashed away a tear, just for another one to replace it. "He warned me."

Tehl held his breath as he watched Sage wrestle with her feelings. She bowed her head and sniffled loudly. Hayjen placed a hand on the back of her neck, and Tehl looked at him gratefully. A good friend was hard to come by. He was appreciative that they had such support.

Sage drew in a deep breath and lifted her head, her jewel-like gaze meeting his own. "Where do we go from here?"

"Our first priority is to hit another ballista and hold on until Blair's troops can arrive," Tehl replied. "We may have a hard time pressing forward, but we won't allow him any more ground."

"How long until your troops arrive, commander?" his wife asked.

Blair answered, "A minimum of one to two weeks."

"The warlord knew it would come to this." Sage placed her elbows on the table and held her head. "Why am I surprised? We only have one choice." She chuckled darkly and lifted her gaze.

Tehl narrowed his eyes. What was she going on about?

Sage smiled sharply. "It's time I handed myself over to the warlord."

Chapter Twenty-Three

Sage

Sage cradled her chin in her palms and watched emotionlessly as chaos and shouting erupted around her. All the while, she remained strangely calm. Once the words left her mouth, peace had settled over her. She wasn't afraid, only resigned. Deep down, she knew it would come to this.

Her attention narrowed to the only two people not arguing or shouting.

Tehl and Blair.

She stared down her husband as he glared daggers at her. He may not shout and scream, but his icy anger affected her all the same. Sage didn't dare look away. He'd fight her on this, it was clear.

Blair was a different story. He didn't react, but she could see the calculation gleaming in his eyes. He understood the warlord better than anyone in the room. If he deemed it a valid idea, things would go much smoother in convincing the others.

"You will not sacrifice yourself to that monster," snarled Rafe.

Sage arched a brow. He did not get a say in this. "Really? As much as I love you, don't you think that's a little like the pot calling the kettle black? How many times did *you* sacrifice *me* for the greater good?" She crossed her arms, and his mouth snapped shut. "I can see you plotting, commander."

Blair cocked his head, his dark braids falling into his face. "And what exactly do you see?"

"A way to defeat the warlord once and for all."

"And how do you suppose we do that? You're skilled, but have you forgotten about the last time you dueled? You lost. How do you expect to win?" Zachael asked frankly.

She pulled the long chain from her shirt and held up the poison ring. She grinned at an unsmiling Hayjen. "I have it on good authority that this can take down a Scythian warrior, even one in a berserker rage."

Her uncle's face turned purple. "That's for the average Scythian. That demon is not normal."

"True, but it would slow him down. Perhaps enough to dispatch him." Her gaze flickered to her silent husband doing his best imitation of stone. Tehl was *not* happy.

"You would risk your life for a maybe?" Rafe demanded.

"I would risk *everything* if it meant a real chance to rid our world of him." Her statement seemed to sober the group, dousing some of their fire. She once again focused on Blair. "I have a sneaking suspicion that even if this poison did not work, a concoction better suited to destroy the warlord would make itself available." Sage hadn't forgotten about the poison ring Maeve had gifted her when she escaped Scythia. She'd bet the warlord's sister had more things up her sleeve than anyone knew about.

Blair arched a brow in return. "I have no such skills, if that's what you're referring to."

"I'm sure. Your skills lie in combat. We both know a person with exceptional skills for deception, and a hatred that encompasses both our own."

"All of you, get out," Tehl said softly, his tone so wintery it brought goosebumps to her arms. "I need to speak with my wife privately."

She held his gaze evenly as the council glanced between them, before silently filing out. She waited thirty seconds before speaking. "My plan is valid."

He said nothing.

"I know you don't like this." She took a deep breath.

"You know nothing of how I feel," he said, his voice whisper-soft. "If you did, you'd never have suggested such an idiotic, haphazard plan."

"It hasn't been rounded out yet," she admitted. "But it's the only chance we have left."

"How can you say that?" He pointed toward the wall. "There's an army fighting for us, and they have reinforcements on the way. There are choices."

"And how long can they keep up?"

"We're doing our best!" He placed his palms on the table, his attention locked on the positions of the two armies.

"I know," she said calmly. "But it's not enough."

Tehl sucked in a sharp breath.

Sage edged around the table and laid her right hand on top of his. "I know you can see it. We've had our triumphs, but they are not enough. Soon, they'll pin us against the mountains if we don't do something."

"If only we could destroy the last three war machines," he growled.

"That would be a miracle." Sage reached out gently and touched his chin. He faced her, his expression grave. "Your men have succeeded at wrecking two ballistae, but at what cost? You never said how bad it was the first time, but I saw the haunted look on your face. You almost died out there." Tehl didn't deny it. "The second time, we almost lost Gav." They still could, but she couldn't think about that.

"Part of the Methian army is useless because of those war machines." He looked away from her, his jaw working. "We need to get them into the air."

"I can help."

Her husband shook his head. "By handing yourself over to the warlord?"

Her stomach flipped, but she tamped it down. "The only reason you're so angry is because you know I'm right." Tehl glanced at her sharply. Sage popped up onto her toes and cupped his cheeks. She smiled and ran her thumbs along his cheekbones. "Even if I can't kill him, my arrival would be enough of a distraction for your men to reach the other catapults."

He stared at her for a long time, his deep blue eyes serious. "I hate this."

"I know," she whispered, her smile trembling.

"How can I possibly allow you to go back?" he rasped. "It's not right. Everything inside me is screaming to snatch you up and run in the opposite direction. You're not safe there."

"True." She wouldn't lie to him. "But I'm not safe now. Every day that I march onto the battlefield could be my last. Life is not guaranteed."

"He's a different kind of danger."

That was an understatement. "I won't be alone. Blair will look out for me."

Tehl scoffed. "As much as he did in Scythia? You returned a mess."

Sage traced his cheekbone and ignored the need to be defensive. Her husband was worried for her. "I would have suffered at the hand of other monsters as well if he hadn't stepped in. I know where he stands. Things won't be easy, but he won't let me die."

He cocked his head and brushed a lock of hair from her face. Sage kissed his palm and gazed up at him, soaking in the love and anguish that was shining through the cracks in his mask.

"How are you so calm about this?" he asked quietly.

That was something she didn't even understand. "I don't know. When you told me what happened, it was as if everything quieted around me. It makes it easier to focus on what needs to be done." She pressed her lips together. "What happened tonight can't happen again."

Tehl nodded. "My chest hurts when I think of it."

"I know, love." Sage pulled him into a hug and wrapped her arms around his wide chest. Tehl squeezed her and rested his cheek on the top of her head. "That's why I need to go. I'm the only person who can give you a chance to destroy all three of the machines." She shrugged as her gaze went distant. "Maybe I'll be able to cut him down in one fell swoop."

His arms tightened. "Will you sneak away in the night if I forbid you from doing this?"

Sage mulled it over. "I wouldn't, but you and I both know you forbidding me from doing this would be the wrong choice. Look past your emotions. Strategically, you know this is right move." She pulled back and peered up into his face. "I want your support. I can't do this without you."

"Are you sure you can go back?"

No, but it was what needed to be done. "I imagine it will be the most difficult thing I have ever done." She paused. "But if it saves our people and others from a fate similar to mine, I'll pay whatever price. I can do it."

"You shouldn't have to."

"You know better than I, that with privilege comes responsibility. I chose to marry you. I meant my vows when I said I would fight for the good of Aermia and sacrifice whatever was needed. If you were in the same position, we both know the decision would already be made."

"I can't ask this of you."

"You're not asking me. I'm volunteering. I would feel better going into this if I knew I had you on my side."

Tehl leaned down and rested his forehead against hers. "I am *always* on your side."

Her bottom lip trembled at the passionate declaration. "I love you."

"As I love you."

She laced her right hand with his and pulled him toward their chambers. "All the details don't need to be set in stone tonight. Come to bed and hold me."

Sage squeaked when he lunged and swept her into his arms. Her eyes widened when he stooped low and kissed her heatedly. Her tongue tangled with his as he pushed through the tent flap.

"If you must go," he growled. "I want the taste of you on my lips."

Chapter Twenty-Four

Mer

Mer hurtled through the water toward the human body sliding through the current. She grabbed Sam beneath the arms and hauled him to the surface, gasping as the painful change overtook her. Her body expelled sea water, and her lungs inflated as a sharp spray of water hit her face, stinging her eyes and cheeks.

She kicked her legs to keep them both afloat, her eyes darting to Sam's pale face. How long had he been under? "Come on, Sam. Hold on!"

His ship released a heavy groan and creaked under the stress of the howling wind. Punishing waves tossed them about the sea, but she kept his face above the waves. Just barely. Fatigue threatened to overtake her, but Mer kept pushing on. He would not die.

The spymaster in her arms coughed and threw up the seawater

he'd swallowed as he tried to fill his lungs with air.

"That's it," she murmured. "Breathe. We're almost there."

Mer held his arm, keeping his head above the water as she shifted in front of him, his body pressed against her back. Another wave crashed over them, but she managed to swim back to the surface. She pulled his trembling arms around her neck.

"Don't let go," she shouted over the roar of the winds.

Sam mumbled something incoherent, but his grip tightened on her as another rolling wave tried to tear them apart. From the surface, the sea looked black; the only shocks of color were the foaming white tips of the dangerous waves trying to suck them down.

"Damn it," Sam bit out. His nails scratched her collarbone as he clutched her shoulders tighter.

Mer kicked her arms back and forth to keep the two of them afloat and scanned the turbulent ocean, spotting their ships. "We're close." She caught the sight of a few fiilee in the sky battling the winds. "Wicked hell." Mer said a quick little prayer for the survival of their riders

She made certain Sam's arms were secured around her before she swam toward the ship. It seemed to take ages. When her fingers curled around the ladder soaked with saltwater that hung from the side of the ship, she sighed. They'd made it.

Hand over hand, Mer hauled herself and Sam up the ladder, her muscles bunched and flexed, the burn heating her blood. Her foot slipped, but she gritted her teeth and found her balance, Sam's limbs wrapped around her. Finally, they reached the top of the ship. Mer sucked in lungfuls of air, and Sam rolled from her back, eyes glazed over.

The Lure.

"It's a good thing you're too weak to chase me," she wheezed.

Mer wiggled away from him and called out to the crew, who were shouting and rushing about on the deck. Her melodious voice cut through the wind and rain like a magic spell, just enough to be heard. A young sailor boy caught sight of her and rushed forward. She held her hands out to keep him away. If he caught a whiff of her Lure, he'd be no use to Sam.

An older man grabbed the boy by the back of the shirt and yanked him backward. "Don't be dumb, boy. Remember the Lure."

Mer inched farther away from Sam, so his men could pull him from the edge of the ship without having to worry about her scent snaring them. The ship groaned, and the waves slammed against the sides. She wrapped her arms and legs around the bars of the guardrail while she caught her breath. Her gut twisted as Sam's fellow sailors and Elite dragged their spymaster somewhere safe. Shouts of gratitude were lost in the winds, and she waved them away. Hopefully, he'd recover well. When he'd been pitched from the ship, she'd sworn her heart had stopped.

It was a lucky thing she'd found him when she had.

Her heart slowed, and her breathing evened out. She wanted to crawl into a hole and sleep to regain her strength, but every moment she dallied was another life lost. Mer was preparing to throw herself back into the water when a fiilee dove from the sky. The feline landed on the nearest Aermian ship, its rider sliding from its wet back in one smooth movement.

The Methian prince Raziel.

She'd know his wine-colored hair anywhere. Her lips parted. She'd heard of the handsome Methian prince, and had even caught glimpses of him in the last several weeks as he launched aerial attacks on the Scythian fleet, but she'd never been this close to him. Her gaze narrowed when the fiilee flared its wings and knocked two Scythian warriors from the ship. Raziel launched an attack, and she cursed, noting that the ship wasn't just fighting the storm, but Scythians. How had the bastards boarded it in this weather? She'd barely managed it.

Lightning lit up the night sky, as if the storm wanted Mer to have a better look at the hulking prince. Raziel. His clothing was soaking wet, clinging to his body, and the sharp lines of his face twisted with effort as he fought with a dark figure. They turned, and she got a good look at his adversary.

Ream.

The chill of the wind and the spray of icy water disappeared, and Mer forgot where she was and what was happening. All she could do was stare at the familiar shock of white, braided hair filled with pearls and shells she'd given him on their bonding day. Her brain couldn't make sense of what was happening. Why was Raziel attacking Ream? Ream was on their side!

The thunder rumbled, and lightning illuminated the sky above the maudlin scene. She blinked in confusion, and her breath caught as she realized the Methian prince carried a sword, the side broader than her arm and nearly as long as her legs. Mer lurched to her feet, her fingers digging into the wet handrail.

"Stop!" she yelled. What the bloody hell was happening?

Raziel hefted the sword and swung. Mer screamed, her sound of fear and anguish lost to the storm. Ream managed to roll out of the way and launched toward the Methian prince, sinking his blade into Raziel's back.

"No!" she whispered.

A heavy creak preceded a fresh burst of shouts as the mast on the other ship gave way. Raziel whipped his sword and jabbed backward, stumbling toward the ship's side. Ream's mouth opened in a silent shout before the two men pitched over the edge of the ship into the waiting arms of the sea.

Horror rose inside her. Not Ream!

Her mind screamed at her to move, to do something, but she couldn't. She was frozen. The air seemed to be cut off from her lungs. Shivers began to wrack her body.

Raziel had attacked her husband.

"Move!" Sam's familiar voice bellowed.

She glanced over her shoulder as the blond prince stormed toward her, his steps surprisingly even as the ship rolled on the waves.

"Mer!" he barked. "Bring him back."

Still, she didn't move. Ream had stabbed the Methian prince. It didn't make sense.

Sam seized her by both arms and shook her, his blue eyes dark. "I need you to bring him back."

"Ream?" she whispered.

"Raziel."

"Mer." Another shake. "You have to work through this. We can't lose him. He's too important."

She nodded, not really feeling anything. Sam always had a plan. Ream couldn't be gone. He was a Sirenidae. The water was his home.

Lurching toward the end of the ship, Mer jumped, twisting in the air to land in a perfect dive. She sliced through the water, her movements mechanical. Her lungs seized as she forced herself to inhale water, and her gills opened. She scanned the current for the men. Raziel floated with the water, his dark-red hair looking more like tendrils of black blood. Her heart pounded as the scent of blood hit her full-force. Water rushed past her ears, and panic sharpened her senses. Where was Ream?

He's a Sirenidae. He'll be okay. Focus on the Methian.

Mer fought the water and debris until she reached Raziel. She'd always known he was a large man, but it didn't prepare her for his actual size. She didn't even try to wrap her arms around his chest. Even if she could have gotten a grip around his broad shoulders and torso, his clothes and armor would have made it impossible. Quickly, she used the blade from her waist to cut off his chest plate and armor. Once that was done, she grabbed one of his wrists and hauled him toward the surface. As she fought for his life, Mer realized her eyes burned. Shock radiated through her system. She was crying. They weren't going to make it. It had been too long.

Don't give up.

Mer dug deep and swam with everything she had. Chunks of debris sliced at her skin, but she didn't stop until they reached the surface. She broke the waves with a jagged cry. Her body seized, and she spewed sea water from her lungs, her gills sealing. Mer thrashed around to get Raziel's head above water. She doggedly worked toward Sam's ship, the drag of Raziel's body slowing her. Mer grunted and fought against his weight.

Snakes of blood spread from the Methian's head. She clutched him closer in desperation. Leviathans were around. She needed to move fast. Adrenaline rushed through her veins, and Mer found the strength to reach the ship. She latched onto the ladder.

"Help!" she screamed. There was no way she could get his huge body up the side of the ship.

Sam popped his head over the side and tossed a rope down. "Cinch the loop beneath his armpits!"

She struggled to keep Raziel's face above the surface as she slid the rope under his arms and secured it. "Done!"

"Pull!" Sam shouted.

The line went taught, and Raziel's limp form began to lift from the sea. Mer tiredly clung to the ladder as the Methian prince disappeared over the edge. She'd done her job and saved his royal arse. Waves crashed over her from all sides as she released the rope, sinking into the inky water. The change painfully overtook her once more.

Mer stared up at the turbulent surface as she drifted deeper into the depths of the sea.

Move. Find Ream. Figure out what the hell happened.

With the last bit of strength she possessed, she glided through the salty water. The saltwater was tainted with blood—human, animal, and Sirenidae. Her stomach dropped as she followed the scent of Sirenidae blood. It grew stronger.

It can't be him. It just can't!

Her eyes scoured the darkness until she spotted him.

Ream lay on the sand, his hands on a massive gut wound, blood leaking through his fingers. Too much blood.

Mer burst into action. Her knees caught some coral, but she didn't pay it any attention as she met his shiny gaze. Her fingers fluttered over his.

"What do I do?" she croaked. She scanned the ocean floor. There weren't any sea herbs nearby.

Ream placed a hand on her own, pulling her attention back to him. "I'm sorry," he said, more blood leaking from his mouth.

Mer's bottom lip trembled. "It's not your fault."

"I didn't have a choice. They had my daughter."

She blinked slowly, her heart thundering in her ears. Ream's daughter had died years before. "It's okay," she crooned. "No one has your daughter, love. Just hold on."

He shook his head. "They have her. I had to do as he commanded to keep her safe." His eyes seemed to plead with her. "I didn't have a choice. I'm so sorry."

Mer stilled. "What have you done?"

"What was necessary to protect my only child." He winced. "They know Aermia's movements and there are other Sirenidae helping the Scythians. Beware who you trust."

No. "Tell me you're lying," she rasped.

"I'm so sorry." He seized her hand, blood clouding the water around them.

Her throat clogged. "We'll figure something out."

"There's nothing to be done."

"Shhhh," she whispered. "Everything will be okay." Nothing would be okay.

Ream squeezed her fingers. "Listen carefully to me. A woman is being held on one of the Scythia ships. She's pregnant."

Mer's head spun. *Jasmine.* "How long have you known where she's been?" They'd been looking for her for weeks.

"Long enough." His magenta eyes were full of pain. "Look for the ship with the black leren painted on the side. You'll find her there." He gave her a tender smile. "I've always loved you, Mer. I'm sorry for hurting you. Just know that."

His body seized, and the life from her husband's eyes faded.

"Ream? Ream!" Mer screamed, her hands shaking as she clasped each side of his face. "Please don't leave me."

He didn't answer.

"No, no, no! This isn't how it's supposed to go," she cried, lifting his torso onto her legs, and cradling his face to her chest. "Forever, remember?" Even knowing what he'd done, it didn't diminish her love for him.

Time ceased to exist as she rocked her dead husband. Sobs wracked her body as she mourned the boy who'd been her best friend her entire childhood. The boy who had grown into a man she loved with her whole heart. The man who married another, only to have his wife and child die in an accident after five years of marriage. The man she'd nursed back to life. The man who supported her rebellion against her grandfather in order to fight for what was right. The person she planned on having a family with.

The man who'd betrayed her.

Unbidden, a mourning song flowed out of her. Leviathans drew close, forming a circle, their haunting hums adding to her song. They mourned with her. When the last note passed her lips, the beasts receded into the deep, leaving Mer with the soul she'd loved her whole life.

"I will love you as long as the moon shines in the night sky," she whispered.

CHAPTER TWENTY-FIVE

Tehl

Morning arrived with a bitter chill.

He turned onto his side and watched his wife sleep. It was something that he knew was probably improper, if not a little eerie, but he couldn't stop. It was addictive to see her without her armor, so unjaded. Free.

Unable to help himself, he scooted closer and kissed her bare shoulder.

This might be the last time you kiss her.

He froze, his lips pressed to her olive skin. Slowly, he pulled back and tried to imprint her form into his mind. He was a wretch of a man to agree to such a plan. What sort of worthless rubbish would agree to send his wife back to her abuser? He hated the idea. What he hated more was that he could see the logic in it.

Damned logic.

When Sage succeeded, and she would, it would change the tide of the war.

But at what price?

Would Sage go back to being the ghost she was after escaping Scythia? His gaze focused on her once again. It would be so easy to knock her out and drag her away to some place safe, away from this mess. Away from the madness of this plan.

You promised a partnership.

Tehl squeezed his eyes shut and pinched the bridge of his nose. His wife was the fiercest person he knew. While he loathed every bit of the plan they'd formed last night, he knew he couldn't throw her in a tower somewhere. She was a warrior, through and through. They were equals, partners.

At least in this, they took the risk together. They'd be working as a team. He smiled darkly. The warlord wouldn't be prepared for that. He dropped another kiss to her skin and rolled out of bed. It was early, but he needed to check on Gav. Mira had said the first night would be the most dangerous. While Tehl would have loved to wake up his wife with his incessant need for her, she was right about one thing: with privilege came responsibility. Gavriel was more than a responsibility. He was family, and he deserved someone looking out for him.

He pulled his cold, leather trousers up his legs and hissed at the frigid temperature. Next, Tehl tossed on his shirt and clasped his cloak before jamming his feet into his boots.

He paused at the end of the bed and soaked in the sight of his wife one last time before he left. Stars, she was beautiful. He spun on his heel and moved into the war room area of the tent. Tehl spared a glance at the map but moved on.

Freezing air nipped at his ears, causing him to pull the hood of his cloak over his head. Two Elite silently followed him while two others took their place to guard the royal tent. They ghosted through the camp, the dark of the early morning only broken by a low fire here and there. Frost and icy snow crunched beneath their boots, as they made their way to the infirmary nestled in the trees.

He quietly entered the tent, followed closely by the Elite. The sight of the burned and injured men made him want to scream as they passed row after row. Upon reaching the back, he paused and took a fortifying breath before entering the room holding Gav. Sweltering heat slammed into him, and perspiration dampened the back of his neck immediately. He glanced around the room as his men took up silent posts on either side of the entrance.

Mira sat on the floor, her cheek leaned against the cot's edge, her fingers resting on the pulse at Gav's wrist.

"Mira?" he whispered. She didn't stir. Tehl approached her carefully and knelt beside the healer. "Mira?" he said a little louder.

She cracked an eye open and lifted her head. "He is all right, my lord. His pulse is steady for the time being."

Tehl's shoulders drooped in relief. "A fever?"

Mira straightened and placed the back of her hand on his cousin's brow. "Lower than it was. It spiked high a few hours ago. I brewed some special tea for him to reduce the fever."

"An infection?" Tehl asked, eyeing Gav's pallid complexion. Mira hesitated. "Be straight with me."

"Very well, my lord. Yes, likely."

He sighed. "We're long past you calling me by my title."

Mira grimaced. "It's hard to break a habit that was beaten into me." She brushed a sweaty strand from Gav's face. "It's normal for the body to run a fever when it's trying to repair itself. I did my best flushing out the wound, but there is a high chance there is infection. It's common with this sort of injury."

"Will he survive?" Tehl asked, the words bitter on his tongue.

"I can't say," Mira whispered. "I can promise you that I'll do my best to care for him."

"I know you will." He placed a hand on her slim shoulder. She'd lost weight. "Why don't you go get some food first and break your fast?"

"It's morning already?"

"More or less. Go."

"Is that a royal order?"

Tehl cracked a half smile. "If it needs to be. Get on with you."

Mira smiled in return and clambered to her feet. She stretched and groaned. "If you need me, I won't be far."

He watched her leave, passing the silent Elite, before he turned back to his friend. Gav was too still. Too pale. What he wouldn't do to have him healthy and whole.

"I wish you were well, my friend." Tehl settled himself on the faded rug, next to the cot. "Living in a world where you aren't alive and well is unthinkable. Plus, I could use your guidance." He stared down at his hands. "A decision was made last night to send Sage back to the warlord. It *feels* wrong, but I can see how it will benefit us. She'll give us a fair chance at destroying the ballistae. I wanted to talk her out of it, but her mind is set. I know she's putting on a brave face. I can see it in her eyes that she's scared." His fingers curled into fists. "What kind of man sends his wife into a den of monsters?"

Gav didn't reply.

"That's not even the worst of it." Tehl lifted his head and gazed at his cousin's profile. "I keep imagining what you went through after Emma died. You barely survived. You've never been the same. I don't know how I could bear it. What I feel for Sage…" He paused and tipped his head back. "It's too much, too big. She is my partner, but I don't want to treat her that way. I want to lock her away. Barbaric, isn't it?"

Still no answer.

He glanced at Gav, checking to make sure he was still breathing. "Part of me wishes I could go back to the time I considered Sage a traitor and spy. Shameful, I know. It was easier then. Things were black and white. If she dies," Tehl whispered, "I don't know if I can live with the knowledge that I let her go."

He felt sick even saying the words.

"When we were growing up, war was glamorized. It seemed like a heroic thing. Now, all I can see are the lives lost and the blood on my hands. Too many sacrifices have been made, and more will come. I will shoulder them to the best of my ability, as is my duty." A pale, sightless face entered his mind, the dead boy from the night prior.

He shook his head, trying to dispel the image. "I've spoken too much about myself. Sage tells me that I need to look on the positive side more often, and I realized that your attack, while horrible, has a silver lining. Last night, I experienced a soul-crushing blow from Scythia. I am thankful you were not there to witness the atrocity."

Tehl shifted around, so he could prop his back against the cot. "I'll stop speaking and let you rest. Heal quickly. You are missed."

Chapter Twenty-Six

Mira

Mira tossed her cloak over her shoulders and pulled her hood up over her blonde hair as she stepped outside the infirmary. Her breath fogged in the early morning air. Heavy, silvery clouds floated in the sky, only allowing shafts of moonlight to peek out here and there. The snow crunched beneath her boots as she moved around the side of the tent to her favorite spot to sit and gather her thoughts.

Just beneath the bow of frosted evergreens lay a fallen tree trunk. Mira pulled her cloak tighter around her body and sat. The snow and frost coated every leaf, branch, and tree as far as she could see. The clouds shifted, and a shaft of moonlight pierced the inky darkness, flooding the tiny glen with moonlight. It was so idyllic, like something from a fairy story. The world looked like it had been dripped in diamonds. An icy breeze bit at her cheeks, but she didn't care. Nothing could move her from that spot. Mira held her breath as if the smallest sound would shatter the magic around her.

Jacob had taught her to appreciate the little moments. Life as a healer wasn't an easy path. More often than not, you gave yourself to the job until you felt there was nothing left to give. Still, you pressed onward. From the moment Jacob had adopted her, Mira knew she wanted to be a healer like her papa. He'd readily taken her in, despite the reservations of others. A soft smile touched her chapped lips. Jacob never let anyone tell him what to do. A brilliant mind and willing spirit were enough for him. It never mattered that she was female.

Soft footsteps alerted her to the approach of another. She turned toward the sound. Raziel smiled at her, weaving his way through the trees, a steaming cup in each hand. He stepped over the fallen log and wordlessly handed her a mug. The heat warmed her cold fingers and seeped through the bandages of her wounded hand.

"Thank you," she murmured, lifting the earthen mug to her nose. Garlic, oregano, and pepper teased her senses. Mira glanced at the prince in surprise. "Soup?"

He shrugged his shoulders. "I figured you might be hungry."

"I am." She took a cautious sip, and the hot brew warmed her throat before heating her belly. Mira hummed in appreciation. "This is delicious."

"I'm glad you like it. It's one of my favorite recipes."

She lowered the cup and eyed him over the rim. "A family recipe?"

"One of my mother's. She made sure we all knew how to prepare it."

Mira's brows raised. "Did you cook this?"

"Surprised?" he asked with a smile, his golden eyes twinkling.

"Frankly, yes."

"Just because I am royalty?"

Mira snorted and took another sip of the delicious broth before answering. "More like because you are a man."

Raziel swiveled to face her, tossing a leg over the tree trunk. "Cooking is a skill every person should possess. I wouldn't want to get stuck in a snowstorm and not know how to prepare a meal to keep myself warm while it passes."

At the mention of snow, she shivered. While Mira loved the snow, she hadn't spent much time this far north before. Her only experience with snow was as a child, and it had melted in a day. It had seemed magical. She cast a glance around. She had a sneaking suspicion that the marvel of snow would wear off when it didn't melt away.

"What's it like, a snowstorm?"

"Cold. White. Dangerous. Beautiful."

Even talking about it made her colder. Mira took another long sip and watched the play of moonlight against the ice crystals. *Beautiful, indeed.*

Raziel shifted and his face creased in pain. He stretched his right shoulder.

Her brows furrowed. "Have you been injured?"

"Nothing that won't heal. I was on the coast and someone got the drop on me."

"Has someone looked at it?"

"Yes. My mother helped bandage me up, dearest. I'll be back to prime shape in no time."

Mira eyed him skeptically. Men were so damned prideful. She'd bet the wound was worse than he was letting on, but she let it go. Queen Osir was an incredible healer and she'd seen to her son. No need to worry.

They fell into a comfortable silence. A prickling feeling started on her left side, and she peeked at Raziel from the corner of her eye. His intense gaze was locked on her. She swallowed and tried to ignore him. It didn't work.

"You know it's rude to stare at a woman? Especially while she's eating?"

"I enjoy watching you eat."

Mira cut him an incredulous look. "Well, stop. It makes me uncomfortable."

"Why should I? Is it wrong for me to take pleasure in your enjoyment of the meal I prepared for you?"

He prepared the meal *for* her?

Mira twisted to face him fully. "You jest," she chided.

The Methian prince reached out and ran the tip of his finger along her cheekbone. "Why should I not cook for the woman I am courting? It is only right that I show her that I can provide for her as well as care for her well-being."

A damned blush began to heat her cheeks. The man was too smooth for his own good. "I can care for myself."

Raziel nodded, a deep wine-colored lock falling across his right eye. "You are more than capable. But just because you can accomplish a task, it doesn't mean you have to shoulder the burden all yourself. You deserve to be cared for."

Her jaw sagged. Who spoke like that? *A man raised right.* Those were few and far between. She'd seen the best the male population had to offer and also the worst. She'd given salve to women who sported too many bruises far too often and were worked to the bone.

Mira snapped her mouth shut. "Not many share your sentiment."

"Then they don't deserve to have a mate."

His vehement statement caused her to jerk, and she almost spilled her soup. She clutched the mug tighter. A sense of true camaraderie settled over Mira. She'd taken an instant liking to him when he'd begun to help the wounded. He always had a kind word or a way of drawing laughter from even the staunchest soldier. But to hear him speak about his own sex the way he did, it made her trust him. Trust wasn't something she gave often.

She finished her soup, relishing the herbs that had settled in the bottom—a final burst of flavor. "I like you," she admitted.

"It was the soup, wasn't it?"

Mira gave him a silly smile. "Most definitely." Her mirth waned, and she eyed him. "I think I trust you as well."

Raziel's smile faded. Intent and heat filled his expression, and his posture became languid, and yet predatory. She knew what that meant. Many a young girl had fallen for such a look and found themselves in a compromised position. While she trusted the prince not to take advantage of her, Mira didn't trust herself when he was looking at her like that.

She got to her feet slowly, so he wouldn't think she was running away. Mira stepped closer, her skirts and cloak brushing his left leg. He was so tall that sitting on the log they were eye to eye. She held out the mug.

"Thank you for breakfast and the wonderful company."

He pulled the cup from her fingers but held one of her hands. Her heart skipped a beat as he laid a kiss on the back of her fingers, his gaze never leaving hers.

"The pleasure is all mine, Mira."

She snatched her hand back. "You're not courting me," she blurted.

Raziel gave her a lazy smile. "Dearest, there's no deterring me."

Mira blinked at him. "It would never work. I'm a healer, and you're a prince."

"Blood is blood. You won't change my mind."

"And if I told you there was someone else?"

The Methian prince stilled, and his eyes narrowed. "Is there?" he asked softly.

"No," she admitted. Mira wouldn't lie to him. "But I'd like to know your answer all the same."

"If I knew you'd be well cared for, you were happy, and he was a good man, I would concede."

"Just like that?"

He smiled. "If you're looking for faults within me, I'm happy to share them. There are many. What you won't find is a jealous brute who will drag you off by your hair and ravish you."

Her pulse picked up. "I thought women enjoyed a good ravishing, every now and again."

Heat filled his gaze again. "Your wish is my command, my lady. Say the word."

"You're a rake," she accused, but with a smile. He was absolutely incorrigible. Sam would probably adore him. Mira waved a hand at him and strode toward the infirmary.

"Mira?" Raziel called softly.

She glanced over her shoulder. "Yeah?"

"The more you forget to eat, the more I'll arrive with food."

"Is that a promise?"

He stood from the log. "Care for yourself, or I will take it upon myself."

It kind of sounded like a threat, but she thought he meant it as a promise. Mira shook her head at his antics but couldn't keep the silly smile off of her face.

Princes. They were way too charming for their own good.

Chapter Twenty-Seven

Tehl

It was all set.

He wanted to break something.

Tehl paced outside their tent, his gaze darting toward the entrance every time he made another agitated pass. Night had fallen and, with it, a snowstorm. He scowled at the heavy snowfall. While it would make for the perfect cover, it also meant his time with his wife was up. She needed to make her move tonight.

He passed the entrance again. This shouldn't be the only way. No matter how many times he tried to come up with a better plan, there was nothing. Tehl trusted Sage. He didn't trust their enemy. The warlord corrupted everything he touched. The image of the warlord's hands on Sage's skin popped into his mind unbidden. His lip curled, and he kicked a stone that he'd uncovered with his pacing.

You're being a coward. Get inside and help her prepare.

Female voices murmured inside the tent, too faint for him to pick out.

Tehl paused and stared at the tent flap, ignoring the Methian warriors watching him. He rolled his neck and pushed through the entrance. The war room was empty. Most likely, all who were on the council were finishing up their last-minute tasks before they attacked tonight.

Stars help them be successful.

Pushing the flap back to his and Sage's quarters, he halted at the sight that greeted him. Sage stood with her back to him, wearing dyed cream leather and white fur, the Methian queen quietly speaking with her. She looked like an angelic warrior, sent to collect souls. He'd have given his soul to her in that moment if she'd asked for it.

Queen Osir glanced between them and pressed a kiss to his wife's cheek. "You're unbreakable. Good luck." She moved past Tehl and squeezed his arm once before leaving the room.

Sage slowly faced him, her green eyes dark in the low lamp light. Would this be the last time he ever saw her?

"Don't look at me like that," she whispered. "Or else I won't be able to do what I must."

"How am I looking at you?"

Her chin quivered. "Like you can't bear to part. Like you're as scared as I am."

In two steps, he had her in his arms. Sage melted against him, her cheek pressed to his chest. He licked his lips. "What if we were to run away?"

She chuckled. "What a wonderful fairy story. Where would we go?"

Tehl ran his hand down the thick plait of her braid, trying to memorize the feel of her. "To the desert, to explore for treasures and lost secrets. Then, we'd bathe in the sea and make love until the stars were envious of us."

"What pretty words, husband. Who knew you were such a poet?"

He smiled at her teasing. "I can become anything for my lady."

Sage pulled back slightly and tipped her head back. "You are and always will be my lodestone."

Cupping her cheeks, he slid his calloused fingers along her silky skin. "If you've changed your mind…"

"I haven't." Her smile was bittersweet. "It's the right decision."

It was the wrong decision, but the only chance they had. Waiting on Blair's troops wasn't a *real* option. "When this is over, we're taking a proper honeymoon."

The love of his life grinned. "Will it involve secrets, treasure, and naked, writhing bodies?"

Tehl hid his smile at her cheekiness. "If it pleases you."

"Rest would please me. I'm bloody tired. I would settle for a full night of sleep with you next to me."

Wasn't that the truth? "We'll not leave bed for a fortnight when this is through. Rest and play."

Her breath hitched, and he gave her a smile Sam would have been proud of. Anything to lighten the heaviness that threatened to drown them. He didn't want to say goodbye. Her cheeks flushed a pretty shade of pink when he pulled her tighter against him.

Tehl brushed an errant strand of her hair behind her ear. The lovely locks were always escaping their confinements. He pressed his nose into the crook of her neck and engulfed her in the tightest hug he could muster. She squeaked and threw her arms around his neck. Inhaling deeply, he drew her cinnamon scent into his senses. She smelled like home, like pure, unadulterated ambrosia.

Gritting his teeth, he fought the urge to tumble her back onto the bed one last time. To imprint her into his memory, to erase any fear she was hiding from him. She tipped her head to the side, baring her neck. Tehl surrendered to the urge to rub his cheek along her neck. Her fingers dug into the back of his scalp as he pressed a hot kiss to the skin, roughened by his whiskers.

Playing his lips over hers in the barest hint of a kiss, he pulled back just enough to whisper, "I love you."

Sage grabbed his head and laced her fingers in his waves. With a small cry, she crushed her mouth to his. He let out a muffled sound of surprise and slid his lips against her velvety ones, desperate to taste her. A whimper escaped her throat, and his brain ceased to care about anything around them. His only focus was the fiery woman in his arms. His tongue slid past her lips, delving into her mouth to dance over her teeth and duel with her tongue. Sage melted into him, letting him take want he wanted.

After too short a time, Tehl gentled the kiss and left butterfly-soft caresses over every bit of her face. His wife sighed and owlishly blinked up at him. A sense of smug masculine pride filled him at the well-loved expression on Sage's face.

"It's time, love."

Sage nodded, her happiness sloughing off, steel and determination replacing it. "Don't do anything foolish while I am gone."

"I'll do my best."

She slipped her hand into his and gazed around their small chamber. "I'll miss sleeping beside you."

He nodded. "Do you have everything you need?" Tehl frowned when he didn't spot the poison ring hanging from the chain at her neck. "Where is the ring?"

A devious look crossed her face. She turned her back to him and lifted the heavy fall of her hair. Plaited into the underside of her braid was the ring. Sage dropped her hair and faced him once again.

"I'll be stripped of all my weapons immediately. This is the safest place for it."

"He won't touch..." Tehl glanced away, his jaw working. He loved playing with her hair, and the image of the warlord doing the same made him sick.

Sage brushed her fingertips along his jawline. "He won't be laying hands on me, my love. Not unless he wants another wound to go with the one I gave him last week."

He shoved his anger and jealousy down deep. "If he touches you, cut off his hand."

She flashed him a bloodthirsty smile. "It is my deepest hope that he tries."

Voices neared their tent, and he knew their time for goodbyes was up. Tehl placed one last lingering kiss on her lips. "To the end, love?"

"To the end."

Chapter Twenty-Eight

Jasmine

"You can't go on like this!" Mekhl growled.

Jasmine didn't spare him a glance, just kept staring out the window at the sea. The waters churned, just like her mind. Out of the three Scythian warriors she'd been forced to live with, he was the hothead. It was best not to engage him when he was in one of his moods. A self-deprecating smile tugged at her lips. Time away from Scythia had not made her forget what they were like. Even if she wanted to.

"Phoenix, will you reason with her?" Mekhl demanded.

"Leave her alone," Phoenix rumbled.

Mekhl cursed, and a door slammed.

"Are you done torturing us?"

Jasmine snorted. "You're the ones holding me captive."

"We mean you no harm, as we've said over and over."

That got under her skin. She turned toward the largest of the Scythian warriors. His cinnamon gaze held her blue gaze.

"No harm?" Her words were a whispered accusation. He didn't flinch or look sorry in the least. "You know what you've done." Movement fluttered in her belly, and her hands dropped to her stomach. Phoenix's attention lowered to her abdomen, and his stern expression softened. "No," she hissed, stabbing a finger in his direction. "You do not get to look at me like that."

"You're a miracle."

It wasn't the first time Jas had heard the sentiment. It still changed nothing.

She turned away from him and stared out the window, her emotions on a thread. For the first few weeks, she'd screamed and fought against them. Once they'd gotten her on the ship, there was nowhere to go. While she prided herself on being a great swimmer, there was no way she could get past the leviathans that circled constantly. The sky was heavy with black, grey, and green clouds. A storm was brewing.

Her stomach lurched. Jasmine inhaled deeply through her nose. Her nausea was so much worse on the ship. The babe rolled again. She'd been doing that more often. Her fingers drifted over the big bump. At this point, Jasmine thought she would explode if the babe got any bigger. She'd been trying to put it from her mind, but her birthing time wasn't too far away. Would the babe be born here? Stars above, she hoped not.

"I don't wish to fight with you," Phoenix murmured.

"Then don't. Release me."

"I can't do that. Do you understand what that babe means to us?"

"Enough that you raped an unconscious woman," she snapped, facing Phoenix, her skirts swishing around her ankles. Phoenix's jaw clenched, but that was the only sign that she'd gotten to him.

"I don't think you understand how much danger you were in."

"Danger from you, you mean?" she retorted.

Phoenix stiffened and took one step toward her, pushing away from the bookcase. "I'm done tiptoeing around you. Orion is too soft, to tell you the truth, and you rile Mekhl up too much for him to think clearly, so I'll be the one to come out with it: you were given to us, as a war prize, as a gift for our service." His lip curled. "But that gift had strings."

"That's disgusting," Jasmine spat.

"You're not wrong."

She blinked. That was not what she expected him to say. "That does not excuse—"

"I'm not finished," he cut in. "You've screamed abuses at us for weeks, and, not once, have you thought to hear what we needed to say. You will now. The only reason the warlord kept you alive was because you were a means to an end."

Jasmine felt off-kilter. He wasn't telling her anything she didn't already know. She placed her right hand on the back of a wingback chair to steady herself.

"You were just another way to control his consort and to control us."

"Control you?"

He nodded. "On one of your ventures, Orion made a mistake. He trusted the wrong person, and I was summoned." His jaw flexed. "If we didn't follow the law, you would have been given to brutal, heinous warriors. He would have torn you away. You would have died in Scythia with no one the wiser. I couldn't allow that to happen."

"So you drugged me and stole my innocence?" God, she was going to be sick.

"We protected you when no one else would have."

"Protection?" Tears flooded her eyes. "You stole something that I can't ever get back!"

"I'm sorry."

"You're sorry?" Tears dripped down her cheeks. "That changes nothing."

"There wasn't any pleasure in it. I had to drink herbs just to accomplish the task."

"That's supposed to comfort me? That you didn't take pleasure in my unconscious body?" she scoffed. "Why didn't you just ask me?"

Phoenix held her gaze. "Would you have said yes?"

She wouldn't have.

He nodded. "That's what I thought. What we did was wrong, and we can't ever take it back. I wish things hadn't happened like they did. All I've ever wanted was a wife and children, but the warlord tainted that."

"I'm not your wife."

"No, but you are the mother of my child, and I intend to protect you until my dying breath. Keep on believing I am evil, I can bear that for my follies and sins. But I can't change the past, and I don't regret that you're safe and unhurt, out of that demon's grasp. We're all a product of his brutality and madness."

"Those are traitorous words, if I've ever heard them," she whispered. "Better be careful or you might be executed."

"I take the risk so you know my true feelings. Orion, Mekhl, and I were raised with women from the Pit who were taken as consorts. They suffered at the hands of our fathers. We never desired that for any woman. It's wrong. It needs to change."

"And yet you fight for him."

"For now."

Her eyes widened. What did that mean? "A few good acts don't negate the vile ones you've committed."

"True, but it doesn't mean nothing either." He blew out a breath and threw his shoulders back. "I'm getting off track. Your pain is ours. There are no words to express how sorry I am for the state of things. I wanted to let you know that Orion, Mekhl, and I have vowed to never touch you again. You need not fear us."

"How magnanimous of you." She rubbed at her temples, just moments from breaking down. "Get out."

"As you wish."

Jasmine turned toward the window, and the door closed with rough click. She bowed her head and began to cry. How could an act she couldn't remember hurt so much? Why did she understand his logic? What was wrong with her?

She sank to the floor and wrapped her arms around herself. She wanted Sam. Even if he was with another woman. Damn her.

She was broken.

***

Jasmine fell out of bed.

She yelped as the floor tilted, and she slid toward the bookcases. Her nails scrabbled at the ground as she fought to find a grip somewhere. She managed to grab the edges of the bookshelves, only to cause tomes to rain down around her. She curled into a ball, protecting her belly. The floor leveled out some, and she untangled the robe from her legs and squinted in the darkness, trying to get her bearings. What the bloody hell?

Lightning flashed outside, the wind howling. She forced herself to her feet and stumbled over to the window. Dread filled her as another streak of lightning lit up the night sky. The largest wave she'd ever seen raced toward them.

"Swamp apples." Jasmine dropped to her knees and crawled under the table that was bolted to the floor and wrapped herself around its legs. She grunted and clung to the table as the wave slammed into ship. The wood groaned and the floor buckled, causing her stomach to lurch. She puked. All over herself and the floor. Her gaze darted to the window, and all she could see was black water.

Full-on panic seized her. She would not drown in this room. She and her baby would get out of here. She couldn't leave Ethan and Jade without a mum again. Jasmine pushed through her panic and waited for the right moment. The bow of the ship dipped forward, tilting the cabin at an angle toward her bed. She forced herself to let go of the table and squeaked as she slid down the floor to the door. It was too damn heavy to open.

Jasmine glanced at window and steeled herself. She had to wait for the next wave to hit. It wasn't long. Her breath whooshed out of her as she released the latch, and the door barreled inward.

"Wicked hell." She gritted her teeth, using the arch of the doorway to pull herself into the hallway. The ship rolled again, and the swinging door switched directions. Jasmine let go of the doorframe right before the door would've slammed shut on her fingers. Her feet slipped against the wet floor. Her gaze locked on the stairway that led to the deck. Waves splashed down the stairs, spraying her with icy water.

Jasmine latched onto a nearby doorknob and planted her arse on the ground, shivering. How in the bloody hell was she supposed to get up the stairs? If she took a fall… She glanced at her belly. If she didn't get out, they'd both drown. She just knew it. Maybe if she slipped her robe tie around each of the planked stairs and crawled up on her hands and knees, she'd make it.

Releasing the doorknob would be one of the hardest things she'd ever done.

It's now or never.

She yanked the soggy tie from her waist and slid it around the fourth plank up, then wound each end around her hands. She only managed to get up five stairs when the next wave hit her. The breath was knocked from her as the icy water doused her. She gritted her teeth, quickly moved the tie up two more stairs and laboriously worked her way up. By the time she reached the deck, Jasmine was soaked all the way through and her knees were scraped and raw.

What she saw made her want to crawl back to her room.

Lightning cracked across the night sky, bathing the gruesome scene in stark light. Phantom-like fins sliced through the black water, as the creatures preyed on those unfortunate to be swept into the sea's dark embrace. Scythian warriors strained with ropes, shouting at each other.

Jasmine ducked her head and pressed as close as she could to the stairs, her fingers turning white against the red sash of her robe as the water rose over the edge and soaked her shivering form. She panted as water crashed over her head. Her skin was covered in goosebumps, and she gasped for breath as seawater dripped into her eyes, stinging.

She blinked as a dark figure strode her way, his steps sure despite the weather. Mekhl grunted when he spotted her, his expression grim.

"What *are* you doing?"

"I don't want to drown," she yelled.

He hauled her up and maneuvered her so they were behind another set of stairs on the deck. She watched through the gaps in the stairs, as the ship rolled to the side and bobbed back in the other direction. She vomited again. On Mekhl. He didn't say a word but tied a rope around his waist.

"Lift your arms," he commanded. She didn't hesitate. He secured the rope around her chest. "Listen to me. We're moving toward the coast. There's a lifeboat. We need to get to it."

She nodded, shaking from head to toe. Mekhl surprised her and brushed a wet, lank piece of hair from her cheek.

"Stop looking so grim. You're not dying today." A wry smile. "Although, you might get your wish. I might not make it." He paused, scanning the waves. "Move!"

Jasmine scrambled after him, her bare feet sliding all over the deck. It was absolute chaos.

"Damn it!" Mekhl changed direction and pressed her against the mast. He wrapped his arms in the rope and gritted his teeth. "Hold on!"

She managed to get a look at the oncoming wave and screamed. A wall of seawater crashed into them from above. She coughed and spewed. Mekhl groaned.

"Are you all right?" she yelled over the screeching wind.

"Fine."

Her eyes widened when he pulled his arms from the ropes. Blood leaked from cuts they'd made.

He caught her glance. "It's nothing."

Once again, they slipped and slid across the deck to where the lifeboat was secured. It looked tiny.

"Are you sure that will hold us?"

Mekhl spun, his wet braids slapping against his bare chest. "The beach is just right there. We can make it."

He tossed her into the boat, and her breathing grew shallow as the ship leaned to the side, the life raft almost touching the water. She'd sworn she'd seen a fin. "Please don't let me get eaten," she whispered.

"Please."

The warrior jumped into the raft and cut the ties. She shrieked when they were airborne for a moment, but then they hit the water.

"Lie in the bottom and scoot under the seat."

She did as she was told and gaped when the mast on the ship cracked and splintered as another wave struck. Their raft bobbed uncontrollably, but she couldn't take her eyes from the Scythian warship. It was as if a massive hand had punched a hole in the rear of the ship.

Where her quarters had been.

"Oh god," she cried out as another wave rushed toward them.

"We'll make it," Mekhl shouted.

They weren't going to make it.

The wave hit them and tumbled the boat over. The rope pulled taught around her upper body. She screamed, water filling her mouth. The salt water stung her eyes. She couldn't see anything until a shape moved beneath her. Mekhl's face entered her vision. With strength she didn't know anyone could possess, he maneuvered the little boat with frantic movements. Water sluiced from her as the boat was tipped back over.

Jasmine coughed and sobs wracked her chest. Was this her life? To escape one hell, only to journey into another one? She wiped at her eyes and reached for Mekhl's hand to help him into the boat. Her eyes widened when movement caught her attention.

Leviathans.

"Get in the boat," she shouted. He tried but his wounded arm failed. She pulled with all her might, her eyes not leaving the fin that streaked toward them. "Come on, come on, come on," she sobbed.

Mekhl gave her a tender look and cut the rope between them. "I'm sorry."

The monster struck, and Mekhl disappeared beneath the waves.

"No, no, no, no!" She couldn't believe her eyes. "Mekhl!"

The black water made it impossible to see anything. Another wave barreled toward her, and she ducked down into the bottom of the piddly boat, holding on for dear life.

Her screams were lost to the wind as the wild seas threw her about. The bottom of the boat hit something solid and cracked. She lifted her head. The small raft was lodged between two huge rocks.

Another wave hit. And another. And another.

The boat didn't move.

Jasmine found a rhythm. Breathe, breathe, wave.

At some point, she stopped feeling cold.

She stared at the roiling sky and screamed until she was hoarse.

She was Jasmine bloody Ramses.

Nothing and no one would be taking her from her babies.

Her stomach cramped, pain rendering her breathless. This could not be happening.

Labor was upon her.

CHAPTER TWENTY-NINE

Sage

Sage didn't know what disturbed her the most.

The empty maw of nothingness that numbed her, or the morose expressions on the soldiers' faces as she neared the edge of camp. Tehl's hand warmed her as he led her to their inner circle. Zachael, Rafe, Raziel, Hayjen, Blaise, and Domin stood or sat waiting, snow falling heavily around them.

Sage released Tehl's hand and strode to Blaise, who sat on a stump. She eyed her friend's splinted leg and dropped to her haunches. "How in the blazes did you get Mira to let you out of the infirmary?"

The Scythian woman cracked a smile. "I promised not to put any weight on it, and to use the burly one as a pack horse." She flicked a finger toward Rafe. "But, in all honesty, he's not a stallion, more like a jackass."

Sage sniggered. "How very accurate."

Blaise's smile melted, and her expression turned serious. "Are you prepared for what lies ahead?"

She wasn't. Who could possibly plan to face such a thing? "To the best of my ability."

Her friend seized her hands and pulled her closer. "Do you remember what I told you before we marched to meet the warlord?"

"How could I ever forget?" Sage sighed, her breath a puff of frosted air.

Blaise released Sage's hands and pulled a tiny jar from her cloak. She pulled the lid off and dipped her fingers into the onyx Tia warpaint. "Lean toward me and tell me who you are."

Sage closed her eyes. The paint was cold on her skin, but Blaise's movements were comforting as she swirled the paint across her cheeks and eyelids. "I am Sage Ramses. Warrior princess of Aermia. I am not the warlord's pawn. I am not his consort. I am his demise."

"Very good. Open your eyes."

Sage lifted her lashes and met Blaise's dark gaze. The Scythian woman drew a line over her lips, down her chin to her throat. "Who are you?"

"I am his judgement, his enemy, and his ultimate destruction."

Blaise smiled, but it wasn't nice. "You are his death." She kissed both of Sage's cheeks and then whispered, "You are not alone. Sisters in arms, yeah?"

Sage hugged her. "Always."

"I will see you soon."

She nodded and stood, her cloak disturbing the snow as she turned to face the rest of the group. Her hands opened and closed as she stared at some of her most cherished friends. What was she supposed to say?

Zachael approached first. He pulled her into a bear hug and dropped a kiss on the top of her hooded head. "Fight hard, Sage."

She nodded and gave him a squeeze before he moved on. Rafe stepped up next and clasped both of her cheeks. They stared at each other for a long time. She could almost read his mind, just from the look in his eyes.

"Don't make me hunt for you," he said gruffly.

"I won't."

He brushed his nose against hers before retreating so Hayjen could take his spot. Her uncle pulled her into a bone-crushing hug.

"Don't be stupid," he said. "Don't let your emotions get the best of you." He pulled back, his arctic eyes pinning her in place. "Find your nothing space and stay there. It will be your protection, *ma fille*."

Her heart twanged at the use of Lilja's pet name. "I promise."

She let out a sound of surprise when Raziel pulled her into a quick hug. "I have no words of advice for you." He flashed her a smile. "You're the strongest of us all. I'll see you soon, Sage."

Sage nodded at Domin, who was also wearing white, and turned to face her silent husband. His expression was completely blank, and, for once, she was so thankful she couldn't get a read on him. If she'd seen even the tiniest bit of fear, she didn't think she'd be able to go.

"To the end, my love?"

Tehl breached the space between them and pushed her hood from her head. "And back, my love." He kissed her softly in an uncharacteristic public show of affection and then brushed his nose against hers. "I'll be seeing you soon, wife."

Her smile trembled. This man. Tehl pulled her hood back up into place and stepped back, his arms crossed. She took one last glance at him and turned her back on him, facing the desolate stretch of battlefield ahead of them.

Lastly, she dropped to her knees and held her arms out. "Come here, Nali."

The leren slunk from the darkness and butted her in the chest with her head. Sage threw her arms around the feline and hugged Nali close. "I wish you could come with me," she whispered. Pulling back, she scratched the leren's ears affectionately. "You need to stay here and protect him." Nali's golden eyes blinked at her like she understood Sage's words. She gave the feline one last hug before standing.

"Domin?" she asked, turning to her Methian guard.

"Ready, my lady."

Sage inhaled deeply, and ignored the panic that was trying to creep up and freeze her in place. The time for fear was over.

She took her first step onto the battlefield and didn't look back.

Chapter Thirty

Tehl

Watching her walk away almost killed him. She never looked back.

Tehl stared until she blended in with the storm and disappeared from view. Even then, he didn't move.

Hayjen clasped his shoulder, and Tehl met the man's gaze.

"She will come back," Hayjen said.

An absurd statement. No one could promise that.

"He won't harm her," Blaise said, her smoky voice like black velvet.

Tehl looked to her. The Scythian woman pulled her cloak tighter around herself but met his gaze full on.

"My uncle won't kill her."

"And what makes you so sure?" he rumbled, hating that there was a little hope unfurling in his chest. He smashed it down, ruthlessly. To survive what was coming, he had to put her out of his mind.

"He's too obsessed with her to let her escape him, even in death. His demons wouldn't allow it."

"Blaise," Rafe chastised.

She glared at the former rebellion leader. "I am being honest." Her attention turned back to Tehl. "You can be thankful for that, at least."

A small favor—if he didn't think about what else the warlord would be doing with *his* wife. Tehl closed his eyes and sank into the quiet, calm place in his mind and counted to thirty. When he opened his eyes, everything was calm. He scanned the group.

"She's probably halfway there. We move now."

CHAPTER THIRTY-ONE

Sage

The storm swallowed Sage whole, and time ceased to exist. They could have been traveling for minutes or hours. She didn't know.

Her cloak whipped around her as she moved stealthily across the battlefield with Domin. Thank the stars he was with her or she would have gotten lost. She pinned her eyes to Domin's cloak and stumbled as she stepped on something too soft to be the ground. Her stomach rose, but she kept plowing on. The snow blanketed the earth in a white shroud, and, while that was a blessing, it was also a curse. One never knew if it was a natural mound or a forsaken body.

Shadows in the distance appeared.

Domin darted behind a boulder, and Sage followed him. They crouched and stared at each other.

"The camp is three hundred paces past this stone. We've managed to skirt by the patrol but..."

She understood. Sage laid a hand on his arm. "You need to go back. I'll go on from here by myself."

The Methian shook his head. "You're my lady. I go where you go."

"I will not be the cause of your death. You know the plan is for me to go in by myself."

His eyes narrowed. "Plans change when put into action."

"Not in this." She squeezed his arm. "You will long for death when he's finished with you. You will also be another way he will try to control me. We give him nothing," she said fiercely.

Domin slowly nodded. "May the wind be with you."

"And may the stars shine down on you," she whispered back in the Methian way.

Sage released his arm and peeked around the boulder. She didn't see any movement, but that meant nothing. The snow protected her, but it also obscured her enemy. She glanced over her shoulder at Domin. He was gone. What she wouldn't give for skills like that. He was almost as silent as Rafe.

She blew out a breath and crept around the boulder. Sage moved carefully across the open space. Her skin prickled at being so exposed. Her senses screamed at her to run, but she forced herself to maintain the slow pace. Her clothing aided in camouflaging her approach, but it didn't conceal her completely. A slow-moving object would attract much less attention.

The first tent appeared almost out of nowhere, and her heart thundered. Damn snow. What if it had been the enemy? She eyed the tent. Was there someone inside? If there was, would the snow dampen the sound of her approach? She didn't know.

Sage slowed down even further, making sure her steps were very careful. She slunk past tents at the south side of the Scythian camp without seeing even a hint of a Scythian. She chewed her lip. It didn't seem right. It was too easy. Every step she took, Sage waited for someone to shout the alarm.

She eyed one of the quiet tents and then her stark, white outfit. While it had helped her hide on the battlefield, she would stick out like a sore thumb among the warriors. She needed a cloak. Sage crept toward the nearest tent and listened. Not a sound.

Ever so carefully, she lifted the tent flap and peeked inside. Empty, as far as she could see. Sage slipped inside and hovered at the entrance. The tent held four pallets, a chamber pot in the corner, and a few articles of clothing. She grinned when she spotted a discarded cloak.

Quickly, she tossed the huge cloak over her outfit and pulled the hood over her head. It dragged on the ground and wouldn't stand up to close inspection, but it was better than what she had before. She blew out a breath and clenched her jaw, so her teeth didn't chatter, just as they were prone to do when adrenaline flooded her body. Sage took one last glance at the tent. It was funny how four walls brought a source of comfort. It was only canvas and wood. Easily burned or cut through, and yet she felt safer inside than she did wandering through the camp. Safe, at least, until the tent's inhabitants came back to rest in their beds. Staying in the tent wasn't an option, long-term.

Sage peeked through the slit of the entrance. The coast was clear. She crept from the tent, her filched cloak trailing behind her. Sage wove to the left of a tent when three Scythian warriors materialized ahead of her and blocked her path. Where the hell had they come from?

"What do we have here?" asked the Scythian to her left. He reminded her of a leren, all dark and feline-like. Contempt seemed to radiate from his person. "Did you think Scythians are so stupid they wouldn't notice a stranger prowling around in their camp?"

She kept silent. Let them have their words. They hadn't attacked yet.

"Do you know what we do to spies?" demanded the one in the middle, his sharp features making him appear hawkish.

Torture them.

"If you're looking to die, we're happy to oblige," the biggest warrior in the right crooned. "But we have a few questions we'd like to ask of you."

Sage crossed her arms slowly, so as not to spook the warriors into violence, the movement hiding how she was freeing the blades at her wrists. The Scythians all seemed to vibrate with anger, and she knew how easy it was to set them off. She needed to time it perfectly.

"Actually, I need to speak with your warlord. He and I have some business to discuss," she said cheerfully. "If you'd be so kind as to escort me to his tent."

The warriors frowned as her very female voice surprised them.

Gotcha.

Sage lunged left, clearing the far side of her attackers' line. She paused and waited on the balls of her feet. Sage jerked her head, and the hood slid to her shoulders. No reason to have it block her vision when the ruse was up. The soldiers moved in sync, hardly batting an eye at her prior burst of speed. They knew she was slower than they were. They were going to toy with her now. Sage held up one blade in front of her and one behind her, keeping her gaze on the trio that now circled her.

"What a pretty little thing," the big man taunted. He eyed her stolen cloak. "I'm sure my lord doesn't invite thieves to dine with him. I say we take care of this right here. What do you think, men?"

The others laughed, and the hair along her arms rose a moment, before the hawkish man came at her. He tossed a large knife from one hand to the other. A surge of relief rushed through her. Clearly, this one was still young. Any warrior worth his salt knew a soldier never let go of his blade.

Sage darted beneath his guard and knocked his knife from his hands. He swung at her, and she jammed one of her blades into his ribs. He bellowed and grabbed for her. She barely managed to duck in time and caught his eyes flicking right.

Damn it.

She cut the clasp at her throat and lunged forward, spinning to see the biggest man clutching the dark Scythian cloak she'd stolen. The feline man attacked from her right, and she snapped out a side kick, nailing him in the knee. A sickly snap sounded. He screamed and yet managed to grab her boot. He yanked, pulling her off her feet. Sage dropped to her back and twisted, dislodging her foot from his grasp.

A snick on metal caught her attention. She rolled, just as a blade plunged into the ground where she had been lying. Sage surged to her feet, knocked the biggest warrior's feet out from under him, and dumped him onto his back.

Her attention focused on the hawkish man who moved slowly, each step graceful and calculated. The biggest one was the loudest, but this man was the most dangerous.

Sage danced backward as he pursued her.

"Pretty little show," the man said simply.

She shrugged. "I do what I can. Take me to the warlord, and I will make sure he spares you." A lie.

He cocked his head but never stopped moving. "What makes you so special?"

"Nothing and everything."

"Playing with words." His lip curled. "Just like an Aermian."

Her muscles tensed, and he *blurred*. Sage didn't have time to prepare herself for the blow. The warrior hit her so hard, he slammed the breath from her own lungs. She sailed backward and remembered just in time to tuck and roll. Her left shoulder took the brunt of her weight. That would bruise. Sage popped to her feet and wheezed.

He hadn't used his blades. The warrior caught her glance and smiled. "Blades are too easy. It's more personal to kill someone with my bare hands."

Another psychopath. Delightful. "Your warlord won't be pleased if you don't take me to him."

The hawkish warrior studied her and held a hand up when the other two clambered to their feet and made like they were going to join in. "She's mine."

Sage sank further into a battle-ready stance. This wasn't going to be fun.

He took one gliding step toward her when a spear struck the ground between them, quivering, planted in the snow-covered earth. Another figure appeared from behind the hawkish warrior, his long braids just visible.

Blair. She wanted to sag in relief, but she didn't. She watched as the warrior looked back, to find the commander prowling toward them. The youngest warrior with the rib wound bowed his head and grimaced.

The hawkish man didn't bow but stood tall when Blair stepped into his space. "Do you know what you've done?"

"Protected our camp from an intruder, sir."

"You've attacked our liege's consort." Blair cracked a smile that was anything but friendly. All three warriors stiffened.

Sage kept her expression blank at her title, even though it made her skin crawl.

"We had no way of knowing," the youngest began to say.

"Enough," the hawkish warrior barked. "We will accept the punishment for our actions."

"Indeed, you will," the commander murmured. He moved around the warrior and took a couple of smooth steps in Sage's direction before halting. "Consort."

"Commander," she murmured. They gazed at each other, snow falling around them.

"I will escort you to our warlord."

She swallowed hard and tried to tamp down the fear growing in her belly. There was no turning back now. Sage rose from her fighting stance, her blades still in each hand. On wooden legs, she passed the biggest warrior and the youngest one, as they both stared at her in fascination. Sage paused next to Blair, eyeing the hawkish warrior. His eyes narrowed as he scanned her from foot to toe. She arched a brow.

"She's tiny," he muttered.

"True. Doesn't stop her from fighting a good fight, does it?" Blair pointed out.

The warrior nodded in agreement.

Blair looked down at her, his amusement draining away as fast as it had come. "Put those blades away, consort, unless you intend to challenge me."

Sage worked her jaw, but returned her blades to their places. She felt utterly naked without her weapons in her hands. At least he hadn't taken them from her. Yet.

"Very good. Now follow me. He's been eagerly awaiting your arrival."

Dread filled her.

There was no going back.

CHAPTER THIRTY-TWO

The Warlord

Three of his best warriors stood around his desk—Jacobi, Phenrir, and Demdai. He steepled his fingers and watched the three of them, his gaze blank even as he studied his commanders. Their army was making progress but... something about Demdai's posture was bothering him. His shoulders were just a little too stiff, his gaze a little too blank. Too much like his own.

What was his warrior hiding?

"Winter is setting in, my liege," Jacobi explained.

The warlord's lips twitched, and the overly tall warrior blanched. Satisfaction warmed him at the reaction. Jacobi wouldn't be rebelling against him any time soon. While the commander excelled at following commands, he was hardly a plotter.

"True," he murmured conversationally and waved a hand in

dismissal. Only a fool wouldn't have a plan. Zane's expression hardened a touch. He was not a fool. The years of bloodshed, rebellion, and death had trained him well.

Jacobi swallowed, his Adam's apple bobbing, but gathered his composure. "Of course, my lord."

Zane smiled at the man. He liked that about the towering warrior. A devious strategist the man was not, but he served in a more practical function of passing unbiased information among the warriors. A commander that followed his orders to the letter was difficult to come by.

His gaze slid over the other two warriors.

As for Demdai and Phenrir, both had their own agendas. Phenrir would never take the throne, but he had a son around Blaise's age. He wished for a union between them. That would never happen.

Traitor, the voices hissed in disdain.

His lips thinned. His niece had made a grave mistake in crossing him. She'd taken his consort from him. That wasn't forgivable.

Kill, kill, kill!

Her betrayal would not go unpunished, but not to the point of death. Zane steepled his fingers as he dropped his gaze back to the intricate map on his desk, his shuddered gaze hiding his glee from his men.

He had plans for the wayward girl. While he couldn't outright kill the only heir to his throne at the moment, the suffering and shame she'd experience when she was captured would be enough to have her fall in line. His lips twitched the tiniest bit at the remembrance of how his men hunted her down each time she set a foot on the battlefield.

Her woes were only beginning.

The warlord's eyes flicked to the haughty Phenrir. The warrior had too many ambitions—both he and his son—there would be no marriage between their families. He'd never let a sniveling wimp on his throne.

However, he did know of a warrior who might bring Blaise to heel…

"My lord?" Jacobi said.

"Continue," he said, waving his hand. Their reports to him each night were an exercise in humility. The warlord knew exactly what was happening on the battlefield and in his camp. Any good leader did. But it amused him to watch his commanders shift uneasily in his presence.

Jacobi opened his mouth to speak when Blair's deep voice sounded from outside his tent.

"Entrance, my lord?"

"Permitted," Zane answered.

His last commander pushed through the tent flap and hovered at the entrance, snow clinging to his dark braids.

"May I approach?" Blair asked respectfully.

The warlord's gaze sharpened. Here was a man who knew how to play the game properly. Blair *never* stepped out of line. That in and of itself was suspicious.

"You may," he drawled.

His commander approached the desk, not sparing a glance at the other three men staring at him with slightly veiled dislike. Another reason why he kept Blair around. His dutiful commander stirred the pot too much. They hated how many privileges Zane had given Blair. In all honesty, he hated Blair most days. The man was efficient, though, and the warlord couldn't find a reason to kill him. There were numerous fraudulent charges he could have heaped upon the good commander's head if he'd really wanted him dead. But Zane had learned not to be wasteful throughout his years.

He eyed the hostile glances being thrown from his other commanders. If his leading men hated each other, they would never unite against him.

Blair bowed deeply and straightened, locking eyes with him. "There has been a development. We have discovered a spy in our camp."

A spy? The hair at the back of his neck rose. There was only one so brazen to enter his camp. Slowly, he rose from his chair. "A spy?"

Blair nodded. "She's here."

The world slipped into silence; not even the voices whispered. His skin tingled. She was here. Sage. It was as if her name unlocked the chaos he kept tightly leashed inside himself.

Ours. Mine. Die. Possess. Pain. Ours, the voices roared.

Pain pulsed in his temples, and he glared at his men.

"Get out," he uttered softly. His warriors filed out, not one hesitating.

The warlord squeezed his eyes shut and grabbed the sides of his desk to ground himself. The wood groaned beneath his palms.

Ours. Ours. Punish. Ours.

"Mine," he growled out loud. *His.* She was his to possess and punish. His.

The warlord opened his eyes and inhaled deeply, barely holding on to the threads of his sanity.

Sage was here.

His vision dipped, and Zane bared his teeth through the howls echoing in his mind.

She was home.

The wood cracked and bit into his palms. The pain helped him focus. Slowly, he counted his breaths and released the edge of his desk, leaving smears of crimson behind.

The warlord rolled his neck and tipped his head back to stare at the ceiling of his tent.

She returned.

For once, he allowed himself a full smile.

He'd won.

She was his.

Chapter Thirty-Three

Sage

The night air seemed to thicken, as four hulking warriors exited the large canvas tent, Blair bringing up the rear. She kept her expression neutral, as one of the warriors approached from her right side. He halted an arms-breadth away and scanned her from head to toe. His lip curled. From his expression, he clearly didn't care for her.

"So, the consort returns," he sneered from his great height.

Consort. Sage hid her flinch at the title. *Get yourself under control. If you can't handle him, how do you expect to handle the warlord?*

He leaned into her space as if to intimidate her. Her initial wariness burned away while irritation and anger took its place. She'd danced with the devil and sat by his side in hell. He didn't know what *real* fear was. This man was just a giant bully. She could sense it.

The man gave her a terrifying smile and whispered, "I hope he rips your bloody throat out for what you've done."

She lazily arched a brow at him, goading him the tiniest bit. "Where would the fun be in that?" she murmured back softly, knowing that all the warriors were listening in despite her low tone. "Methinks you don't know your lord as well as you profess to." She scanned him from head to toe as he'd done to her. "If I was a betting woman, I'd say you're only a glorified bitch for the lord to kick around."

The warrior's face turned red at the insult. "You little whore!"

How unoriginal.

"If you don't watch yourself, you might be the one with his throat cut." Sage tsked. She slanted a glance to the tent and back to the warrior's expression, which had now drained of its fire but held bitterness. "I would watch what sort of labels you throw around in mixed company. I'm told all Scythians have an excellent sense of hearing. I'm sure the warlord more than most."

The warrior's jaw set, and he hissed into her face. Her heart pounded a little harder.

"Enough, Phenrir," Blair said, a clear command.

Sage didn't fail to notice the rage that ignited the warrior's eyes before he shuttered his expression and moved out of her space, his steps almost silent as he stormed away into the camp. So the haughty Phenrir didn't like Blair ordering him around. Good to know. Sage filed that information away for later.

Her shoulders slumped the smallest bit, and she felt like she could breathe again once he'd moved away from her, hovering to her far right. While Phenrir wasn't the warlord, he still wasn't someone she wanted to be close to. Sage dismissed him and focused back on the tent entrance.

He still hadn't arrived. Her stomach quivered. On one hand, it gave her time to think, but on the other hand, it ratcheted up her nerves.

Nervousness did not do her any good.

A fat snowflake dropped onto her nose, causing Sage to blink and to focus on the frigid feathers descending from the night sky. Snow fell around them, flurries dancing in a gentle breeze. She focused on one, and counted her heartbeats until the snowflake joined its brethren among the white shroud blanketing the ground.

The silence held a sinister edge to it. She studied the warriors stationed around her from beneath her lashes. They stood around her like stone sentinels, their dark gazes frozen to her. The only sign that they were alive were the warm puffs of breath that steamed into the chilly night air. How did they stand so still? Sage opened and closed her hands, keeping her fingers from stiffening up. Weren't they cold? Her toes had already begun to go numb in her boots as the snow piled up around her feet. How long did the warlord plan on leaving her out here?

Do you really want to see him so badly?

The temptation to fiddle with her shirt niggled at her, but she squashed the notion. She wouldn't give the men around her any indication that she was nervous. She readjusted her stance, and ignored the eyes that were watching her. The back of her neck prickled, but she didn't look behind her. Damn nerves.

You're more than nervous. She was on the brink of losing it.

Internally, she winced. Her mind had shut off during the journey across the battlefield. Her singular thought was to stay hidden. Now that the adrenaline was fading from her veins, her confidence seemed to wane as well. Sage surveyed her silent entourage. How was this the only option? What was she doing here? She'd asked herself that a million times already.

You're giving the people a chance.

At least, that was what she was telling herself. The pit of rage that rolled in her belly said something else.

She wanted revenge.

The hair along her arms rose at the sound of canvas flapping. The warrior to her left straightened just a touch—the first movement they'd made since arriving.

A shiver of awareness ran down her spine, and time seemed to slow, the snow halting midair. What sort of deviltry was this?

Her gaze sharpened, and the air in her lungs froze, as the tent flap lifted higher.

Out stepped her personal demon.

His dark eyes that she once believed were warm, met hers. His inky hair hung around his angular face, brushing his shoulders. He was beautiful. He was monstrous. He was pain and temptation.

"Consort."

His voice rolled over her, like thunder in a storm, all power.

She shuddered and released a slow breath. Everything about him called to her, from the straight, proud line of his nose to the stubborn chin and almond-shaped eyes. But it was more than his features; it was how he wore them. He was still the most stunning man she'd ever laid eyes upon.

And the vilest.

Time sped up, and Sage blinked once, the snow falling softly around them. Had she just imagined that? Surely, he didn't hold power over the elements?

Get yourself together.

Ice trickled through her veins, along with the blessed numbness that had been plaguing her for the last week. *Thank the stars.* Numbness would help her survive whatever he threw at her. Sage sank into it and tipped her chin up, still holding her monster's gaze. She wouldn't cower before him. Not here, not ever.

"My lord," she murmured through chapped lips.

He cocked his head and slowly perused her from head to toe. The temptation to tug her cloak tightly around her body to hide herself from his gaze almost overwhelmed her, but Sage held on. She wouldn't let him make her feel self-conscious.

"What a pleasant surprise. We've missed you while you've been visiting Aermia."

A smile lifted the left side of his mouth, making him appear boyish. Her spine stiffened and she forced herself not to look away. He was the furthest thing from a boy. Innocent, he was not. Her fingers twitched at the thought of slapping the smile off his face. She hadn't been visiting, and everyone in the silent circle knew it.

He lies. The warlord twists words. He killed Lilja, tortured you, and slaughtered wee ones. Don't let him manipulate you into giving anything away. Fight for those who have been lost.

The knot beneath her collarbone tightened at the reminder of his crimes. Sage tamped down her icy rage and sorrow and held her arms out, palms up as if she were surrendering. "I am here as you requested."

He studied her. "Has she been searched?" he asked without looking away from her.

"No," Blair answered. "Do you want me to strip her?"

Sage kept from blanching. She knew it was going to be brutal. There was no dignity in war.

The warlord teetered his head back and forth and then shook it. "No. Search her here. I'll strip her later."

Her pulse began to beat harder, and she wanted to shrink away from him as the unbidden memory of the warlord pressing her against the wall entered her mind. Her body screaming at the pain of being chained to the wall, his lips begging hers to play with his. The warlord's expression warmed, and something sensual flashed through his eyes like he was remembering it, too. It was enough to make her want to vomit.

Blair approached her and unclasped the white cloak from her neck. The wool fell to the ground, exposing her to the elements. The wind and cold cut through her linen shirt and leather pants, causing goosebumps to erupt on her skin. She'd never experienced the winter elements like this before.

"Hold your arms higher and spread your legs."

Sage did as he asked, her body heat slowly leaching from her clothing.

Blair impersonally ran his hands along her arms and down her sides. He relieved her of the daggers sheathed at her hips and one at her right thigh. It was the first time someone had touched her in that fashion, other than Tehl since her time in Scythia. While his hands never lingered, it brought back too many unwanted memories. Her mask never cracked, even as his hands traveled up the insides of her thighs and beneath her breasts.

"Boots."

Carefully, she pulled off each boot, her stocking feet immediately sinking into the snow. Sage staved off another shiver, and kept her head held high when Blair removed the last two daggers from her boots. She'd known that she'd be stripped of her weapons, but it was still unnerving. Sage hated to be without her blades.

The commander handed her back her boots, which she woodenly put on, her wet socks squelching as she adjusted her stance. Blair circled her and ran his hands along the back of her thighs, over her bum, and across her back. Sage forced herself to keep the bland, neutral expression on her face as he dug his fingers into her braid. The poison ring seemed to burn at the base of her skull. Regulating her breathing was a challenge as his fingers brushed over the cool metal. This was the true test of Blair's loyalty. Would he give her away? She hadn't doubted him, but in that moment, everything hung in the balance. One could really never tell who was the enemy these days.

"She's clean, my lord."

Relief washed over her, but she kept it tucked away.

Blair picked up her discarded cloak and examined the inside, including all the hems. He handed over her pale cloak, and she swung the material over her shoulders, clasping the garment at her throat, immediately thankful to have something to block the wind. A little fissure of delight wormed its way into her heart that Blair hadn't discovered the thin razor she'd stashed away in the lining.

Sage pulled her hood over her head, watching the commander when his gaze flickered. It was all the warning she received before a hand touched her chin. Sage startled and jerked back, but the warlord's calloused fingertips tightened and tipped her head back. He examined her face and leaned so close, his breath heated her own lips.

How she longed to spit in his face.

"This is just the beginning," he murmured.

The warlord's cool lips wandered across her right cheekbone. Sage's fingers clenched at her sides, desperate to be holding a weapon of any sort. It would be so satisfying to stab him in the chest.

"Consort, we have much to work through. I'm sure you'll soon earn my forgiveness." He gently pushed her hood back and pulled her thick braid over her shoulder, his fingers running along the silky plaited strands.

Bile burned the back of her throat. Him forgive *her*? After everything he'd done? He was clearly delusional.

"I am here," she said simply, praying that the three little words didn't give away how very much she wished she wasn't.

"An excellent first step, consort." His gaze sharpened, then he released her. "Sweep the camp. They wouldn't have sent her alone."

Terror filled her, but she kept her calm mask in place. The warlord wasn't stupid. Blair and three other warriors followed his command, silently prowling into the darkness.

Her monster turned his back on her, moved to the tent, and lifted the flap, warm light spilling onto the snow. "Come."

Everything inside her rebelled at the command, but she placed one foot ahead of the other, steeling herself for what the future held. Sage offered a final prayer as she crossed the threshold of the demon's lair.

Warmth immediately curled around her, and the tent flap closed. She stepped to the left to make room for the creature watching her like prey. Even though she'd moved, he still brushed against her.

The warlord moved farther into the room and paused at another tent flap. He slowly spun to face her. "Are you not coming in?"

What was she supposed to say to that? Best to go with honesty. "I don't know what to expect."

"Did you think I was going to throw you in a prison?"

"It wouldn't be the first time, my lord." Sage winced but didn't apologize for her comment. He needed her to be real. As much as she hated to admit it, he knew her. If she lied right now, he would know it.

"Things have not always been easy betw—"

An explosion rocked the earth and Sage stumbled a step. She gasped when hands curled around her biceps and yanked her from the door. Her teeth ground together as the warlord hauled her toward the second room faster than what should have been possible. Damn it. She forgot how fast he moved.

Her breath caught, as his midnight eyes caught hers and held fast.

Another series of explosions went off, followed by shouts and screaming. His fingers tightened— almost to the point of painful—around her arms and he pressed even closer.

"Was this your doing, wild one?" he whispered.

Sage prepared herself for what came next. She released the breath trapped in her lungs, and let loose the evil smile she had been hiding. Tehl and their men had succeeded.

"Just a little present like the ones you gave me," she murmured.

Any other demon would have punished her.

Her monster didn't rage. He didn't curse. He *smiled.*

"There she is," the warlord breathed. "I was wondering when my vicious Sage would come out to play. I was worried there for a moment that an ice queen had taken your place." He lifted his left hand and brushed her bottom lip.

She snapped her teeth at him. He was *not* allowed to touch her like that. *Ever*.

"So much fire," he whispered. "Welcome home, consort. Our war has only just begun."

Chapter Thirty-Four

Sage

The warlord could not be as calm as he was projecting. He dismissed her, turning to move farther into the room, his steps fluid and graceful. Sage gave the space a cursory glance, noting a large desk to the left of the room, only a map and lantern sitting on its worn surface. A wood stove sat in the rear left corner, and a massive low-sitting bed dominated the right rear corner.

Sage quickly glanced away from the bed and focused on the predator in the room. The warlord moved behind his desk and plucked a sword from behind the furniture. He ignored her as he belted it to his trim waist, and then pulled a black cloak from the back of the wooden chair that sat directly behind the desk.

"I hate to leave you so soon, but duty calls," he murmured, swinging the cloak over his broad shoulders and clasping it at the throat. The warlord glided around the desk, and her muscles tensed as he paused on her right side.

"Yes?" she asked.

His dark eyes narrowed. "Normally, it would go without saying, but our communication hasn't always been the best in the past—"

"That's because you're a liar." Sage snapped her mouth shut. She wouldn't win his trust by acting like a hostile shrew, but who knew? The monster liked confrontation and pain. It might just be what he wanted.

"Like calls to like," he responded, his expression softening a touch. "We have much to speak of. Now is not the time. Don't do anything we both might regret."

She swallowed. He had a way of making a warning sound like a threat. The warlord waited for her affirmation. Sage nodded slowly, her mind whirling.

"Be safe."

She eyed his lack of protection. "No armor?"

He smiled smugly. "I don't need any." With those parting words, he pushed through the tent flap and disappeared from view.

Her lips split into a grin as she stared blankly at the rear of the tent. His arrogance would get him killed. All the better.

A shiver wracked her body. Now that the immediate threat had disappeared, she became very aware that her feet were soaking wet. Stars, she hated the cold. Sage rubbed her arms, trying to create some warmth, and eyed the wooden stove. It would be nice to heat up.

She crept toward the tent flap and pushed it open. The war room was empty but for the giant table they'd passed. Her brows furrowed. No warriors. Odd. Unless he really didn't like anyone in his space. Sage dropped the flap, strode back to the fire, and held her hands out, the hearth warming her palms. Once her fingers had warmed enough, she stripped her boots and socks from her feet and set them near the brazier to dry. She turned her back to the heat and wiggled her frozen toes, all the while studying the space.

From first glance, there wasn't much in the room—a desk, chair, bed, and a chest sitting at the foot of the bed. Not much to make a weapon with. Sure, she could cut the bedding to create a rope to strangle him with, but that wouldn't do her much good. He was too strong. She eyed the chair. It would be easy enough to break it and create a shiv, but that was too noticeable. Sage craned her neck and examined the metal lanterns that hung high in the air. One of those could do nicely if she could reach them. Maybe if she stacked the chair on top of the desk, it would be possible to reach one of them. Then, there was always good old-fashioned burning. Scorching coals could do much damage.

Her heart slowed, and Sage sighed. She was never weaponless, nor powerless. If she kept calm and collected, her plan would work. Gain his trust, get close, and poison him. Plain and simple. Completely warmed, she quietly moved to the desk. Time to snoop.

Three drawers ran down each side and one sat in the middle. Gently, she tried all seven. It didn't surprise her that they were all locked. The monster was suspicious of everything.

Including you.

Sage crouched and ran her right hand along the bottom of the middle drawer, searching for any little catches or hidden spaces. Nothing. Sage raised her head and squinted at the edge of the desk. Two spots along the edges were cracked. She stood and inspected the damage. What caused those? They almost looked like... Holding her hands out, she placed a palm over each spot. A wicked smile curled her lips despite how chills ran up her arms at his strength.

He isn't as calm and unaffected as he pretends to be.

The drawers called to her, but it wasn't worth taking a chance. Even if she could, by some miracle, find something to pick the locks, there'd be evidence.

Sage sidestepped the bed, shying away from the memories it would surely provoke. She knelt beside the chest, her white cloak puddling around her, so she could keep an eye on the entrance, and tried the lock. Much to her surprise, the lock slid open. He obviously wanted her to find what was inside. Sage paused, her fingertips hovering over the lid of the trunk. Did she truly want to open it? Something truly horrendous could be inside. But on the other hand, she could not waste the opportunity to find something that could be used as a true weapon. A woman could never have too many tools in her arsenal.

Gathering her courage, she opened the trunk. Gorgeous fabrics were folded in neat stacks, every color of the imagination. It was as if the trunk held a rainbow. Sage ran her fingers over a luscious red silk. Was this his dressing trunk? She lifted the fabric and shook it out. A gasp exploded from her. It wasn't *his*; it was for *her*. The garment was more scandalous than anything she'd ever seen a woman of night wear. She tossed the garment back into the trunk and scrambled away, her heart pounding in her chest. Why in the wicked hell did he have those?

Don't be stupid.

Sage squeezed her eyes closed and inhaled a calming breath. Despite his beliefs, she was not his and if he tried to force her to wear one of those, she'd burn them all in the woodstove when he left her alone. In fact—her gaze darted to the fire—she could do it now, but that didn't strike her as wise. Clearly, it was a gift of some sort.

Sage approached the trunk of clothing like it held poisonous snakes and pulled each garment out, one by one, trying to discover if there was anything useful. Once it was empty, she ran her hands along the inside of the trunk. Her finger caught on a raised nail in the corner.

Perfect.

She wedged her thumb beneath the nail and tried to wiggle it. Not much movement. And while there wasn't any appearance of guards inside the tent, she wasn't a fool to believe the warlord was not having her watched. Sage began softly singing, praying that it covered up the sounds of her efforts. It took longer than she liked, and she was a sweaty mess, but the nail came free.

Quickly, she lifted the edge of the rug, still humming, and pressed the nail into the earth. With that finished, she put the garments back into the chest, changing the order of how they were folded. True, she could have put everything back in place like Rafe had taught her, but the warlord would already suspect her of searching the room. No need to pretend that he didn't know.

She carefully closed the box and turned, yelping as she came face to face with a leren. Her butt hit the ground as she scrambled back. The feline looked at her with golden eyes.

"Bloody hell," she breathed, placing her hand over her pounding heart. "Why did you sneak up on me, Nege?"

The leren just stared at her. She cocked her head and held out a hand. The beast released a low growl.

Sage snatched back her arm and slowly scooted to her right. "Understood," she whispered. "No touching. I can do that." Careful not to move too quickly, she rose from the ground, her bare toes sinking into the carpet. Nege eyed her but made no move to attack. "That's a good boy," she crooned, edging around him and putting the desk between them. Not that it would be much of a deterrent if he decided he wanted to eat her.

"I'll just stay here," she said conversationally as she skirted around the brazier. If there was anything that could keep the beast back, it would be the fire. He paced once and then lowered himself in front of the flap entrance. "You stay there."

He huffed and laid his head on his paws, as if to say he was laying down because he wanted to, not because she told him to.

Exhaustion seemed to slam into her from nowhere, and she scowled at Nege. She hadn't planned on sleeping in the first place, but with the prickly leren there, it was definitely not possible now. He closed both of his eyes. That was something.

She sighed and Nege cracked one eye. Sage scowled at him. "Excuse me if my sigh bothered you." A sharp longing rose in her chest for Nali. How similar the leren looked, but their temperaments were so different. Again, he huffed, and closed his eye, dismissing her. "You're just as bad as Nali," Sage muttered.

Nege's eyes sprung open, and he pushed to his feet, his tail flicking back and forth. She glanced around in confusion. Was someone coming? "What is it?"

The leren slunk closer, watching her. What had she done to catch his attention? *Nali.* "Do you remember Nali?"

Nege's ears pricked at that. Her breath seized when he halted no more than a handbreadth from her, his face level with her navel. She hissed when he butted his massive head into her stomach, causing her to stumble into the canvas wall. He released a deep purr and sniffed heavily.

Sage held up her hands. "Can you smell her on me? She's okay, Nege. I take care of her, I promise." To some it might seem odd to speak to an animal, but living with Nali had taught her that leren were far more intelligent than people gave them credit for. He arched his back and pressed harder against her, just begging for attention. Her heart squeezed when she noticed new scars marring his gorgeous coat. "Oh, handsome boy. I'm so sorry."

With care, she ran a hand along his spine and was rewarded with another rumbling purr. He twisted and bumped her so hard, Sage lost her balance and ended up kneeling, face to face with Nege.

"Don't eat me."

He blinked at her and then bashed his face into hers, purring loudly. Sage smiled and began to massage the feline, enjoying the experience, and yet... her gaze was glued to the entrance to the room, guilt tainting the moment.

It seemed her greatest weapon had fallen into her lap.

And possessed teeth longer than her palm.

***

Sage jerked upright, her eyes blurry and her heart in her throat. How in the blazes did she fall asleep, and what woke her?

Nege rumbled softly, his attention honed on the entrance. The warlord slipped inside silently and paused, pulling off his cloak. That was a nifty leren trick. She ran a hand over the feline's head that rested in her lap. Even if she couldn't detect when the warlord was lurking around, her furry companion could. Every muscle in the feline's body was tight, on edge.

So, we're of the same mind. She and Nege both knew who the predator in the room was.

Her focus moved back to the monster. The warlord was splashed with crimson, looking like a nightmarish creature that had crawled from the pits of hell. He tossed his cloak over his desk and placed his hands on his hips, his head hanging, raven hair hiding his features. Sage took the moment to study him. He looked *tired.*

"Judging me already, consort?" he asked, not looking in her direction.

She pursed her lips. "You can't judge something you care nothing about."

He chuckled. "So venomous with words. I'm surprised you weren't born from serpents."

Sage let the slight go and just shrugged. "I am who I am." Her gaze was once again drawn to the blood. Who had he slaughtered or wounded? Was it Tehl? Hayjen? Rafe? Her stomach clenched.

Don't think like that. You need to focus. If it were someone close to you, he would be gloating already.

The thought relieved and sickened her that she could know his mind so well.

"You've changed," he murmured, lifting his head and locking eyes with Sage.

"War does that to a person." She attempted to keep her tone even, but bitterness seeped through. There had been too many casualties.

"It also sharpens them and forges strength."

While he wasn't exactly wrong, there were other ways to go about it.

He moved to the desk and leaned his hip against the furniture, and crossed his arms. "It's not like you to hold back."

She blinked at him, his words filtering through. Her attention hadn't been on his words, but how he'd casually drawn closer. Sage shifted to get her legs beneath her. It was uncomfortable to have the warlord tower over her. It made her feel like a cornered animal. Nege growled softly at being disrupted.

Sighing, the warlord ran a bloody hand through his dark hair. "You're going to be difficult, aren't you?"

"I'm here as you asked, my lord." How was that for sidestepping the question? Sam would be proud.

"Zane."

Every fiber of her being rebelled at the name. Zane didn't exist. He was just a part the warlord played when he needed to. Her jaw clenched. In no way, shape, or form would she ever call him by his given name. Monster? Yes. Demon? Every inch of him. Bastard? Absolutely. But never, *never* Zane.

He must have read the mutiny on her face. He sighed again and then blurred toward her. She screamed and leapt to her feet as he lifted his hand and blew a purple powder into her face. Sage stumbled away from him and screeched as she landed on the bed, her eyes watering. Her fingers clawed at the silk bedspread as she scrambled across the mattress and over the trunk, cracking her knee against the wood.

Lethargy seeped into her muscles as she crawled over to the edge of the rug, desperate to get to the nail, but her body wasn't responding. Arms like steel wrapped around her waist and lifted her into the air. She weakly clawed at his arms and kicked his shin with her heels, wishing she had her boots on. Her head bobbed, seeming too heavy to hold up.

"What did you give me?"

"Something to help you sleep."

True terror filled her, and she released a wail of horror.

"Shhhh, wild one. I promise you'll feel better in the morning."

She wouldn't. "Why do you keep drugging me?" she slurred, her body slumping against his.

The warlord pressed his face into the crook of her neck and inhaled. Stars, it was disturbing. Her skin crawled, goosebumps rippling across her skin.

"It's better than chains, is it not?"

It wasn't. "Chains."

He released a huff of laughter against her shoulder. "You'd make too much noise. I need my sleep tonight. I can't worry about you trying to kill me in my sleep, and from the bags beneath your eyes, you need a decent night of sleep as well."

Sage rolled her eyes. As if he truly cared for her well-being. He was just playing another game. It was always a game. The world blurred a little more and darkness crouched at the edge of her vision.

"I hate you," she mumbled through lips she couldn't feel.

He nuzzled his face into the hair behind her ear. "As I hate you, consort. Yet, neither is whole without the other. Sleep well, my love. We can fight in the morning."

Her eyelids slid shut despite how hard she tried to keep them open. His haunting words echoing in her ears—words she knew not to be true. Then why were they ringing with truth?

Chapter Thirty-Five

Mira

All hell had broken loose tonight. The Scythians attacked without warning again. During a snowstorm. They were bloody insane—monsters whose only goal was to spill more blood.

Mira pulled the shard of metal out just before the wound began spurting blood.

"Wicked hell, no." She dropped the knife, pressed her hands against his stomach, into the blood, and threw her full weight onto the wound. Biting her lip, Mira pressed harder still, desperate to stop the bleeding as he began to thrash.

Damn it. "I need help," she hollered. Several soldiers rushed to her side. "Hold him still."

The men gathered around the cot and held down the wounded man's arms and legs, all of them wide-eyed and red-faced as they tried to keep him from rolling off the makeshift bed. The rickety cot beneath her wounded patient creaked and complained at the added weight, as the infirmary filled with the sound of their grunts and the man's groans of pain.

Mira lifted her head and scanned the room, searching for the queen. Nowhere in sight. Double damn. She was probably attending more soldiers as they arrived. She was stuck with untrained foot soldiers.

Blood bubbled up between her fingers, warm and thick. The metallic smell was strong and settled in her mouth. There was something wrong with the smell, but she was too busy to really focus on it. "Bandages," she commanded.

One of the men, a banged-up looking fellow, snatched a wad of fresh bandages from a nearby table and waved it in front of her eyes. Mira snatched it from his sausage fingers and crammed it into the wound, pressing down.

She had to get the bleeding to stop. The bandage turned crimson within a matter of seconds. Mira hissed out a distressed breath and refused to lift up when the wounded man screamed and thrashed hard, attempting to get away from the pain.

"I'm so sorry. Just a little while longer and the pain will go away. I promise," she soothed.

It didn't help.

The shortest soldier lost his hold on the patient's arms. Mira caught a glimpse of a flying arm before she saw stars. Her vision blurred for a few moments as her head rocked back with the blow. "Swamp apples," she choked out. "That one hurt." She'd have an ugly bruise across her cheek in the morning.

A blonde lock of hair slipped from her braid and fell into the blood that coated her hands. The soldier cursed, and wrestled the wounded man's arm back to the cot.

"Sorry, Mira," he gritted out.

"Hold him tighter," she bit out. Her voice was too sharp. Was she losing her touch? She'd never had a harsh word for anyone working with her. They weren't trained healers, and they were doing their best. Her gaze flicked to the burly soldier to her left whose face was pale and bloodless. He looked like he was one second away from vomiting. Bloody hell. Hopefully he would puke on the ground, not the wound.

Her shoulders and biceps tightened as she tried to increase the pressure. If she didn't staunch the blood, he'd bleed out. Where was the queen? She needed another experienced healer. Hell, she'd take some of the other inexperienced healers.

"I need help here," Mira yelled, not caring if she roused any of the other wounded.

"Mira? What's happened?" the queen's calm, strong voice asked from behind her.

Osir. Thank the stars.

The wounded soldier surged up again with a burst of strength he shouldn't have possessed, and the cot groaned in protest. If they weren't careful, the rickety thing would break.

"How is it possible that he's still fighting?" the burly soldier to her left gritted out.

"Battle rage." Something was triggered when men fought. It was as if they gained unearthly strength for a short period of time.

The soldier nodded, and leaned more weight onto the wounded man to keep him still. He yelled and then sagged back as the battle rage left him.

The queen muscled in and eyed the situation, her eagle-like eyes assessing. "What happened?"

"The shard came out clean, but he's bleeding," she answered breathlessly. Was there something still stuck inside? Mira hadn't seen anything else.

The queen grunted in a very unqueenly manner, and then leaned closer to the bloody mess. She pulled a deep breath in through her nose and pursed her lips. The man jerked again, and Mira gritted her teeth. While she loved the Methian woman, she also hated how she'd taken to giving Mira lessons during life and death situations.

"Do you know what's wrong?"

The queen made a noncommittal sound. "What will you do once the bleeding stops?"

Her voice was quiet. "Mira."

She didn't dare look at the queen.

"Mira, darling. You know what you must do."

The scent of waste in his blood was apparent. She closed her eyes for a moment and tried not to cry. Mira hadn't detected it at first, but she could now. It was a smell she'd become too familiar with. A strangled sob escaped her, and she released the pressure on the wound. The soldiers looked at her like she was crazy.

"What are you doing?" demanded the shorter soldier, his ginger hair sticking up in patches.

Mira gazed at him with sorrow. "I'm sorry."

He gaped at her, and then his lips thinned. "No."

The queen moved to his side and guided him away. The other soldiers released the wounded man's arms and legs and walked away. All but the burly soldier to her left. She ignored him as she moved to a washbasin. Meticulously, she washed the blood from her hands, the water in the bowl turning pink. Mira dried her hands and prepared herself for what came next.

She faced the cot and smiled gently at the last remaining soldier who'd procured a stool for each of them to sit on. Mira sat on the wounded man's left and the burly soldier on his right. Mira picked up the patient's hand and noted how his skin had cooled.

"Why did you stop?" the solider asked.

"Belly wounds that stink of waste mean a slow and horrid death. Sometimes, letting a person go is a kindness. Death isn't always the enemy." While her words were true, they still tasted bitter upon her tongue. There were so many limits to healing—to her abilities—she hated letting go. It felt as if she was failing. Giving up.

The soldier nodded.

"How do you know him?" Mira asked.

"I don't."

That surprised her. "And yet you're here by his side?"

The soldier shrugged. "War can be a cold and lonely thing. No one else is here for him. A man shouldn't die alone. The soldier needs someone to stand by his side when he leaves this world."

"Very noble," she murmured.

Her skin prickled as she stared down at the blood covering the front of her apron. Mira placed the wounded man's hand on the cot, and stood on trembling legs. She took a moment to yank off her soiled apron and rinse her dress of the worst of the blood, not that it would help things. The garment was stained to a point it should have been tossed in the fire. Since she'd arrived, she didn't possess a piece a clothing that wasn't covered in bloodstains.

Woodenly, she slipped a clean apron over her soiled garment and ran a cool, wet cloth over the heated skin of her neck. Stars, it felt good. Mira tossed the cloth in the basket of dirty clothes, and picked up a fresh bowl of water and a clean cloth before turning back to the dying man.

Carefully, she set the bowl on the ground and dipped the washcloth in the cool water before bathing the man's face. Her gaze darted to his belly wound. The bleeding had turned sluggish. Her heart squeezed. It wouldn't be long now.

The wounded soldier sighed, his muscles relaxing, and he pressed his cheek more firmly in her palm. This was always the hardest for her. When they gave up and accepted death, even before their mind fully comprehended what was happening.

Her father had taught her so many skills as she grew up to prepare her for this profession, but the one thing he couldn't train out of her was her soft heart. Each death pained her, and while she couldn't save him, she'd do everything in her power to offer him comfort in his last hour.

The soldier sighed again, and his breathing slowed. The water seemed to ease some of his suffering. Mira put down the cloth and steadied herself. Mechanically, she forced herself to rinse her bloody hands in the water, focusing on getting the blood from beneath her nails. The same pesky lock of hair fell from her shoulder, crimson tipped. Her lips tightened and she took a moment to scrub the blood from her blonde hair. With jerky movements, she pinned her hair back into place. While her papa loved her long locks, she longed to chop them off. They were always in the way, no matter what she did.

She was already considered a fool among those in the court, despite her training and family name. A woman doing a man's job. How scandalous. A hint of humor lightened her temporarily at the thought of chopping her hair off. They would positively lose their minds if she cut off her hair more in the fashion of a man's, like it somehow made her more male than female.

People were absurd.

Mira glanced around the quiet infirmary. Most of those healing had fallen back to sleep. Luscious rugs were strewn across the floor, decorative lamps hung from the ceiling, and every table was covered with jars and bowls of ointments and remedies. It was a blessing that the queen had given up her own tent to help care for the men. In truth, most of them probably hadn't ever stayed somewhere so opulent. Mira had fully expected the queen to take her trinkets and luxuries with her, but she hadn't. When she'd asked the queen why, the woman had patted her on the hand and told her it boosted morale. She eyed the bright colors. It certainly was a cheery house of death.

A small noise drew her attention back to her patient. His eyes fluttered open, his gaze glassy. Mira once again began to lave his face. As she worked, his gaze focused on her face, a question in his pained blue eyes.

She smiled, brushing the cloth along his dark red beard. "You are in the infirmary. You took a wound. Rest, please."

He licked his cracked lips, and his brows furrowed. "A spear to the gut. The tip broke off..."

She nodded, keeping all despair from her expression. She was here for his comfort. No need to speak. He knew.

He closed his eyes, then opened them again and for the first time, he seemed to really look at her. "Your father is a great healer. I am honored to have his daughter care for me," he wheezed as if the effort caused him pain.

She paused. There were very few who knew her father personally. The only way he would know her father is if he were one of the Elite. "How long have you been with the Elite?"

He didn't seem to hear her or notice the soldier to his left. "He was always a gentle sort of man, but tough as nails, your father. I've never seen one look so frail and yet act the part of a dragon."

Mira smiled at his description. Her papa did resemble a dragon when his patients didn't listen to him. "I assume you were a stubborn one?"

One corner of his mouth turned up. "What soldier isn't?"

"So true."

His arm trembled as he tried to lift his hand. Mira caught it and held it between hers. "Tell him goodbye for me, and that I won't miss him sewing me up anymore."

"I will make sure to pass that along," she said softly. "Is there anyone else you want me to speak to?"

The soldier slowly shook his head. "Family is all gone."

Mira swallowed, and her smile felt like it was frozen on her face. "What is your name?"

"Micah."

"I promise I won't forget your message, Micah." Mira squeezed his hand for emphasis. A hand that was much too cold.

A wave of pain crossed his face. "Thank you, fair lady." He seemed to gather strength somehow, and he squeezed her hand and gave a slight tug. Mira lowered her hand to his mouth. The soldier pressed a kiss to the back of her hand, a roguish smile touching his mouth. "No better way to go than with the taste of a woman upon the lips."

The soldier sitting to his left chuckled. "Amen to that, brother."

Her patient winked at her and sighed. "I think I'll take a little nap."

Mira held back her tears and smoothed the hair from his face. "I think that's wise. Rest for a while."

He smiled and embraced death, even as his hand slipped from hers.

She blinked down at him, her body flashing cold and then hot. "He's gone," she heard herself mumble. "Please retrieve some men to help move him."

Her legs quivered as she stood and walked away, her steps jerky. Heat filled her eyes, and Mira held tears back, quickening her pace. She burst from the infirmary and rushed into the nearby darkened wood. Moonlight briefly peeked from between the dark clouds and spilled over her favorite spot, but she hardly noticed its usual beauty as the torrent of tears broke free. Salty droplets rolled down her cheeks, and she tipped her head back, trying to keep the sobs at bay.

Her papa loved her, but he always said she was too soft at heart. Sure, she could cut open a man and not blink an eye, but not being able to save a human being? It tore her apart. Her chest shook with silent sobs, and Mira wrapped her arms around her waist. The past few weeks had been brutal. So much death. It was despicable. What was it all for? Logically, she knew they needed to protect their land from the warlord, but he'd only played games with them. Had Tehl been able to destroy the war machines? Was Sage safe?

Mira halted in that line of thought. She could not go down that road. Her friend could take care of herself and if Mira thought too much about what Sage was going through... well, it would be easy to become distracted with worry and make a mistake while she was healing a patient. She needed to focus on her job and trust her friend to do the same.

You know what the warlord did to her. In what state will you find her this time? If you ever see her again?

Mira shoved that thought deep down, locked it in a box, and then tossed it into a bottomless pit in her mind. Her heart stalled for a second when the moonlight disappeared, a creature soaring above. A fiilee. Mira wiped at her wet cheeks as the flying feline circled closer and landed in her little glen. The feline stretched his wings, and his rider slipped from his back.

Raziel and Skye.

Frozen to the spot, she watched as Raziel murmured softly to Skye, who stared straight at her, his white whiskers twitching. Mira admired the way the Methian prince cared for his beast. He didn't look upset. If anything, he looked invigorated and proud with a smile on his face. That meant they succeeded.

She swallowed the lump in her throat, pushed her own problems aside, and stood. Raziel twisted, and their eyes clashed. His smile slipped from his face, and he darted underneath Skye's midnight wing. Mira held a hand up. If he asked her any questions, she might break down again.

He paused and cocked his head, his brows furrowed. "What's wrong?"

Giving him a wobbly smile, all she could do was shrug.

His frown deepened. "Was it bad tonight?"

Her bottom lip quivered, and she bit the betraying flesh.

Sorrow crossed his face. "Oh, Mira. I'm so sorry, sweetness. What happened?"

"I can't," she croaked, shaking her head.

"Can I hug you?" he asked.

No. That would just make it worse. If he wrapped his arms around her, she'd break.

Mira shook her head. "Sorry."

"Don't be sorry," he murmured, concern lacing his tone. "I understand that some things are just too raw to speak about." The prince shifted and glanced back at Skye. "You know, Skye has been working hard tonight. I'm sure he would love some attention, or a hug or two."

Her gaze moved to the winged feline. Skye crouched and released a loud rumble, as if he knew what was being discussed. Before she made a conscious decision, her feet were already moving through the crisp snow, her steps crunching as she flew toward Skye. The fiilee crouched and tucked his wings back, ruffling her hair. Mira threw her arms around his thick neck and sank her fingers into his luscious, silky fur. Skye released a loud purr and leaned into her, as if hugging her back.

That was the last straw.

Tears pricked her eyes. She pressed her face into the feline's fur and cried, her shoulders shaking. What was wrong with her? Why couldn't she be more like her papa? Why did she have to feel *everything*?

Skye tilted his head and rubbed his cheek against her arm as heat suffused her back and strong arms wrapped around her waist. Raziel rested his chin on top of her head and just held her. He didn't say anything, for which she was grateful. He let her have her cry until there were no more tears.

Exhaustion washed over her, and Mira turned her head to the side. She watched as more snow drifted from the clouds that had covered the moon. It was there one moment and gone the next. Fleeting, just like life. Combing her fingers through Skye's fur, she soaked in the comfort.

"Better?" the Methian prince asked.

"Better," she whispered. Sometimes, a woman needed a good cry to be able to move on, and it was only appropriate for her to mourn the soldier. He had no other family. "I won't forget you." Her words were only a shadowy whisper in the night.

Raziel shifted, making her very aware of the man holding her. Mira scowled when a little blush heated her cheeks. She tamped down the urge to twist out of his grasp and focused on petting Skye's black and white spotted fur.

"How did it go tonight?"

"Well."

It was almost as if she could hear the smile in his voice. He lifted his head when she glanced over her shoulder. "How well?"

He smiled, his white teeth a flash of brightness against his swarthy skin. "The war machines have been destroyed."

Mira sagged in relief. With the infernal death contraptions gone, hopefully the war would end sooner. "That's the best news I've had all day. Did everyone make it out safely?"

The Methian prince released her, so she could fully face him. His expression said everything.

"Tehl?" she rasped. *Please let it not be him.*

"He's okay. We lost a few, including William."

She placed a hand over her mouth and shook her head, a sense of numbness creeping through her veins. William was one of her father's oldest friends. It didn't make sense that he was gone. "He can't be."

Once again, Raziel said nothing, but pulled her trembling form into his arms and held her close.

"How will I tell my father?" Her tremors grew worse, and she finally began to feel the cold. "I'm so cold."

Raz cursed and yanked off his cloak before tossing it over her shoulders and sweeping her into his arms. "When is the last time you slept? Or ate?"

Mira didn't know. All she could do was blink up at him.

"Damn, woman. You're going to get yourself killed. How will you help others if that happens?"

She didn't answer, her teeth were clacking together too hard.

Chapter Thirty-Six

The Warlord

Her body lost all tension and Sage sagged against him, her head lolling forward. He adjusted his grip on her and swung her fully into his arms. Her head was cradled against his chest, her braid dangling over his arm. In sleep, she was beautiful, but she was absolutely breathtaking in the heat of battle.

Fierce. Lovely. Ours.

He hitched her closer to his body and slowly moved toward the bed, the one she'd darted across like it was hot coals. The wrinkles on the bed bothered him. Chaos wasn't solely bad, but he didn't like it in his space. His attention moved back to his consort. She was proof that he liked a little chaos.

Nege hissed as he drew closer, and he slanted a glare at the feline. The leren lowered its head repentantly and backed away. Zane watched the feline slink toward his desk before using the toe of his boot to push the blankets back. What was it with this woman that inspired such devotion? Nege hadn't acted out like that in a very long time. It seemed the feline forgot who was dominant in the relationship. He must need some punishment.

The warlord lowered Sage into the bed and unclasped the cloak still secured around her neck. He scanned her head to toe. Despite the gifts he'd given her, she hadn't changed. His jaw twitched at the slight. It would be so easy to redress her while she was sleeping.

Touch. Kiss. Taste, the voices crooned.

He ran a finger along her delicate collarbone and stopped at the laces of her shirt, her breasts rising with each breath she took. Saliva flooded his mouth at the thought of tasting her skin once again. It had been too long since the last time.

His fingers tangled with her laces, and he began to pull one loose, his blood heating with excitement.

Claim, the voices urged.

The warlord froze, his body stiffening. What was he doing? How long had he waited for this woman? Was he really going to ruin everything by being weak and giving in to the voices?

His hand shook as he pulled away, breathing hard. Zane stared at his hand like it had betrayed him. Something wasn't right. He needed to take his draught and check his levels. Leaving her side was harder than it should have been. Rage at his lack of control triggered his berserker rage.

He stormed from his chambers and through the war room. The frigid night air did nothing to cool his skin. He glanced at Jacobi who stood to the left of the tent entrance. "The prisoner?"

His commander didn't bat a lash at the warlord's snarl. "The forest."

He smiled and, this time, Jacobi did flinch the tiniest bit. "Let no one inside, or everyone you hold dear will suffer in ways you've never experienced before." His tone was light, but his commander understood the gravity of the situation.

Nodding, the warlord set off for the forest.

Spilling a little bit more blood might just take the edge off.

Chapter Thirty-Seven

Sage

Sage slowly woke up and blurrily stared at the canvas wall of the tent. The air was cool. Not frigid, but cold enough that her nose was frozen. She snuggled deeper into the covers and pushed herself against Tehl to soak up his heat, her mind in a morning fog. When was the last time they'd stayed in bed? It was utterly glorious. She yawned, her jaw cracking in the process.

"Good morning, consort," the warlord whispered.

Her body stiffened, and all grogginess fled as reality set in. She was not in her bed. It was not her husband pressed against her with his arm around her waist, his hand resting dangerously close to her left breast. Sage tossed the covers back and tried to spring from the bed, but her body didn't comply. The room spun, and she found herself on her back with the warlord hovering over her, looking rumpled, his dark eyes staring at her with concern.

"Take it easy," he crooned. His thumb ran along her ribs, and she shuddered at the sensation. It was just a little thing, but it disturbed her immensely. "It will take time for the powder to wear off."

"What did you give me?" she demanded, her mind flipping through the memories of the prior night. The nail. Nege. The blood. The drugs. Her mind returned to the nail. She needed it. Her hands brushed her body, and relief filled her. She was still in her same clothes as the night before. Nothing had happened. Unless he redressed her, which was always in the realm of possibilities when dealing with the deceitful demon.

"Just a little something to make our first night back together easier." He touched the skin just beneath her right eye, causing Sage to flinch back. "You needed rest."

Rage flared in her gut. How. Dare. He. "Don't *ever* do that again," she hissed. If only she could get to the damn nail.

The warlord smiled."It was for your own good, wild one."

Sage wriggled away from him and put as much space between their bodies as possible. She attempted to control her breathing and school her reaction, but she failed utterly. "You have no idea what is best for me. How could you take my freedom like that?" It was a dumb question to ask, but fear and anger caused the words to pop out anyway.

He sighed. "Freedom is overrated. Sometimes freedom must be taken away, because it can cause so much harm."

"So says the man with all the power," she retorted, fingers clenching and unclenching. "How would you feel if someone rendered *you* completely helpless?"

"I know the feeling well," he replied calmly. Leaning closer, he forced her to meet his gaze squarely. A powerful emotion that she refused to acknowledge passed across the warlord's expression. "You have completely undone me."

Her skin crawled, and all she could think of was getting away, if only her body would cooperate. Part of her wondered why she wasn't losing her damned mind. He was the monster that plagued her nightmares. Unconsciously, her weak hand lifted to her throat, and the warlord's gaze followed the movement. His lip curled, and fear flashed through her. This was the terror she'd been looking for. She shied away as he brushed a gentle finger along the twisted scars around the base of her neck.

"I can fix this," he murmured.

What an odd thing to say. Unbidden heat filled her eyes, but Sage blinked it back. This demon did not deserve her tears. She'd made peace with the scar, and she now wore it as a badge of survival.

"I have a balm that will—"

"No!" The vehemence in her voice surprised her.

"No?"

"No. I want no more of your potions. I want *nothing* from you."

But his death. The ring dug into the back of her head as she tried to relax. Could she possibly retrieve it and stab him now? No. Too risky.

His expression shifted. "You presume to dictate to me?"

Sage lifted her chin proudly, refusing to be cowed by the darkness shadowing his expression. He may have drugged her, but he was not in control of her. She'd never give him that power again. "It's my body." That was supposed to be the end of her argument, but more stupid words flooded from her mouth. "And you deserve to look at these scars. You can't erase your crimes and pretend they didn't happen. I will wear your cruelty and depravity around my neck for all my days, to serve as a reminder that not all things can be fixed. You're not all-powerful." His eyes flashed, and his hand tightened around her neck, a snarl twisting his lips. He pressed his weight along her side and leaned so close that all she could see was the pain he promised in his expression, and the madness glinting in his eyes. Her heart galloped, and her lungs screamed for air. Sage clumsily lifted her arms and yanked at his fingers. Her left hand moved to the back of her neck where his fingers overlapped. This was not how it ended. He was the one who would die. If only she could get to the ring.

Her fingers brushed the silver ring as the warlord cursed and rolled from the bed. He stormed to the desk, and pulled a key from a pocket inside his shirt. The warlord yanked open the bottom drawer from his desk and pulled a bottle from it. He turned his back to her. Sage gasped for air, her throat already aching.

What in the bloody hell was that? She was not sticking around to find out. Sage forced her muscles to work and clawed her way out of the bed. Her hands and knees crashed onto the cold floor, but she barely felt it. With her gaze on her predator, she pulled the nail from the dirt and stood on wobbly legs, determined to get out.

He slowly faced her and cocked his head. "Where do you think you're going, consort? Come back to bed."

No way in hell. "I will never be biddable."

"I never wanted you to be."

Sage snorted and edged toward the entrance to the room. "You and I both know that's not true. You can't help yourself. You want everyone to bow to you, to obey you. I will not."

He took one gliding step toward her and sighed, his bare chest rising. "I'd hoped we would have enjoyed a nice lunch together before we arrived at this part of our journey."

Her palms began to sweat. There wasn't a chance she could outrun him, but when he pursued her—and he would—it would give her the perfect opportunity to stab him and escape.

"Things will get better. You just need to let go of the past. It's not healthy."

"The past?" she whispered. "Which part am I supposed to let go? The torture? The pain? The loss of my friend and family?" She swallowed and stared him down. "I know what you did in the northern village of Aermia."

He blinked slowly, not giving anything away.

"You slaughtered them." Her throat constricted at the memory of little toes. "They were children. Children, Zane!" Her voice rose, and she stumbled back a step when his name flew from her lips, a name she swore she would never use again. "How could you?"

"I was not there."

Lies. She shook her head. "And the children outside my camp?"

He arched a brow. "They were soldiers."

"They were *children*, and you know it. What happened to your lofty principles of protecting women and children?" she yelled. "Is every word you utter a lie, a twist of truth?"

"Do you remember what I told you when we were at the Nagali palace?" he rumbled.

"You said many things."

"I gave you my word that I would not hurt you and yours as long as they did not hurt me." His jaw clenched. "You *left*. You betrayed *us*. You struck first."

Us? Unease slithered through her belly. "Do you hear yourself? Look at my neck. You chained me like an animal. From the moment I was kidnapped and taken into your kingdom, I was mistreated and manipulated. Don't you dare lay your crimes at my feet. There's only one monster in this room." Her back touched the tent flap. So close.

The warlord nodded, his expression thoughtful. "So, you hate me?"

"Hate is too weak of a word to describe what I feel for you. I am disgusted and destroyed by what you've done. You can't come back from that."

"True. But why would I when it's led me to everything I've ever desired?" He gave her a small, soft smile that confused her. It was the only warning she got before the warlord moved.

Sage spun and sprinted forward into the outer room. She made it only four steps when he caught her. Terror exploded in her chest, but she fought it back. This was part of the plan. She screamed and fought, thrashing in his arms as he lifted her from the ground.

"We love a good fight," he murmured in her left ear. "Please keep struggling, we'd love to punish you. It's what you deserve, after all."

Chills ran down her arms at the use of *we.* Sage swung her right arm across her chest, her sweat-slicked fingers holding tighter to the nail and slammed it into his neck once, twice, three times. The warlord grunted, and his arms loosened. Sage darted from his grasp and spun to face him. He blinked at her and growled while pulling the nail free. He held it in the air and squinted at the weapon.

"You're always a surprise," he rasped, smiling like a maniac. Dropping to his knees, he clutched at his neck, crimson liquid spurting from between his fingers.

Sage blinked at the liquid. It was red. It disturbed her. In her mind, she imagined him to have black blood running through his veins. Blood bubbled on his lips, and she stood there numbly watching.

Everything faded. There wasn't anger, triumph, relief, or joy. Just numbness.

He gurgled, and the haunting sound pulled her back to reality. She needed to get out of there now. Sage ran around the table and darted back into the bedroom area of the tent and tugged on her boots and then her cloak. Where was Nege? There wasn't time to find him. Hopefully, with the warlord gone, he'd find a better way to live.

She eyed the entrance to the rest of the tent, terrified she'd find the warlord standing on the other side of it. It was too risky to take any chances. Sage yanked at her braid and pulled the ring out. She pushed it onto her finger and steeled her nerves as she lifted the tent flap. He was now lying on the floor, eyes closed. Her escape was so close, but she couldn't leave without accomplishing her task. With strength she didn't know she possessed, she approached her fallen monster and slapped him on the side of the neck, her ring pricking him. How long should she wait? Her gaze darted to the exit of the tent. Every moment that passed was another she could be caught.

A whisper of sound pulled her attention back to the warlord. His pitch-black eyes stared up at her, that insane smile still on his face. Sage blanched and scrambled back, her boots slipping in the blood and her fingers tightening against the ring. She fell against the wall as he tracked her movements. How was he still alive? He'd lost so much blood. Wicked hell, she needed to get out of there.

Just as he began to rise to his knees, she backed up to the exit and another pair of hands encircled her biceps. Sage growled and kicked at the hateful commander who'd snuck up on her.

"Going somewhere?" the warlord whispered through blood covered lips. His grin grew, baring scarlet-stained teeth. "Remember, you attacked first, consort. I promise you that I won't enjoy this next part, and it will hurt me more than you. Just pray you can take the pain your people will suffer. Retribution will rain from the sky."

Chapter Thirty-Eight

Mira

Mira pulled the bandage from Gav's leg. It wasn't looking good. The wound had festered, and pus oozed out . Angry red lines fanned out from the wound across the skin like an insidious spiderweb. Poisoning of the blood. It was starting.

"You need to take it," a masculine voice said from behind her.

She glanced over her shoulder at the newcomer. Virdan, the Methian healer. He was only a handful of years older than her, but he acted like she was just a child. "Keep your voice down," Mira commanded softly. Gav hadn't been sleeping well, and she'd be damned if she let that haughty healer wake him.

Turning back to her friend, she plucked the rag from the bowl of water sitting next to her left foot. Gently, she dabbed the wet cloth across his forehead. Immediately, Gav's brow smoothed. At least there was something she could do to soothe his discomfort. She focused back on the airing wound.

"It needs to be done," Virdan said, rounding Gavriel's bed. The Methian healer brushed his dark hair out of his eyes that were more silver than grey.

She ignored him. His leg didn't need to be amputated.

"Don't ignore me. It has to be done, and you know it."

Mira glared up at him, hating that he was towering over her. She stood and rounded the cot, her skirts swishing with her jerky movements. "I won't do it."

He crossed his arms. "It's your job to do it."

"We're not to that point yet," she reasoned, trying to keep her temper in check. Virdan was already getting on her nerves, and he'd only been working with her for three days.

"Look at the lines, Mira. He's worsened."

"You've been here for only a short while. Don't presume to tell me what to do with my patient."

His silver eyes pinned her to the spot, his lips thinning. "If we don't amputate, he'll die."

"You don't know that," she argued. "And do you know how many survive such a surgery? Not even a fifth of the wounded survive. *A fifth*. I cannot take that risk."

Virdan's eyes narrowed, and he studied her in a way that made her feel naked. "Is he your mate?"

She blinked slowly. "No." Why in the blazes would he ask something so preposterous?

"You're emotionally attached to him."

"He's a friend."

"So, let me do this."

"No."

He shook his head. "You're going to kill him."

Mira's spine snapped straight. She'd never felt like slapping a man more than in this moment. "How dare you," she hissed. "Get out!"

"When you get yourself under control, let me know." Virdan stalked out of the small room.

What a pompous, arrogant, self-righteous bastard. What he was suggesting was dangerous for a healthy man, let alone Gavriel, who was full of infection. What was that brute thinking? Amputation rarely worked. Most times, the patient died, or—she swallowed hard—they just gave up. Life was not kind to someone who was viewed by some as broken. They were shunned, made fun of, or accused of the worst crimes just because of the way they looked. Mira would spare him that sort of prejudice and pain by keeping the leg as long as possible. People could be so small minded. A disability didn't make one incomplete.

A hand seized her skirt, startling her. Her gaze flew to Gav. His lavender, bloodshot eyes held wildness. "Don't let them take my leg."

Mira dropped to her knees and pressed his heated hand between her two palms. "I won't."

"Promise me!" he demanded, sweat dripping down his neck.

She swallowed hard and lied. "I promise." While now was not the time to take the limb, if there came a point where it was either his life or the leg, she knew what she'd have to do. Stars help her if it came to that.

Gav closed his eyes and sank back into a restless sleep. Mira pulled away, collected her cleansed scalpel, and called for help. Two burly soldiers entered.

"Wash up and then hold him down. We need to cut out the infected flesh."

They did as she bid, and Mira gently placed a piece of leather between Gavriel's teeth before picking up a wickedly sharp blade. She ran it through the fire in the corner and then approached the bed.

"Don't let him move." She knelt by his ear and whispered, "Don't fight us. If you want to keep your leg, you need to let me cut out the dead flesh." Mira moved to his thigh and placed the tip of the dagger on the edge of his jagged wound. "Ready? One, two, three!"

***

"Damn it, Gav. It's been a day. You have to fight!" Mira said harshly, her head in her hands. "I'm not taking your leg. I'm not doing it!"

She pushed dirty hair from her face and lifted her head. Gavriel thrashed on his bed, murmuring something incoherent. She leaned her cheek on the mattress, making sure not to put pressure on her black eye, and stared at the brazier burning in the corner. When she'd lanced his wound the day prior, he'd come out swinging. He was lucky she'd pulled the blade away swiftly enough when he'd backhanded her across the face, or she could have caused more damage to his leg. Mira wiggled her jaw. It hurt. Even her gums and teeth seemed to ache. The man knew how to throw a punch.

She frowned and wrapped her fingers around his wrist, his hot skin heating hers as she checked his pulse. His fever had skyrocketed in the last day. None of her efforts had done anything. The fever had just climbed and climbed. Today, the wound didn't seem worse, but his fever worried her. Had the infection spread? Was Virdan right? What use did she have if she couldn't heal him? How many had she lost already?

Mira squeezed her eyes shut and inhaled a shallow breath. *You can't allow yourself to think that way.*

Logically, she understood that no one could save everyone, but of late, it seemed like everyone she laid her hands upon died. A lone tear dripped down her cheek. Gav couldn't die. Although they hadn't been best friends growing up, he was still her friend. They'd practically been raised together, running around the palace and stables as young children. His wife Emma had been one of her few close friends before she died. It still killed Mira that Gav had sent Isa back to his estate when Emma died. Mira hadn't even recognized Isa when she'd come to her for healing a few months back. If Gav died, who did that little girl have?

"Mmmm..." Gav mumbled.

Quickly, she sat up and scanned his pallid face. "Gavriel?" His eyes moved beneath his lids, but he didn't wake. She pulled a waterskin from the small table sitting to her left and dripped a little liquid between his parched lips. He gurgled but then swallowed the water. As she pulled her right hand away, his hand snapped up, his fingers curling around her wrist.

She froze, staring down at him. "Gav?"

He mumbled, and his calloused thumb stroked the delicate skin of the underside of her wrist. Mira jolted at the soft touch.

"Need more," he murmured.

"More water? I can do that." She stood and lifted the waterskin back to his lips, but he didn't drink. "What do you need—"

He jerked on her arm, causing her to tumble onto him. Mira cursed and tried to backpedal, her knee bumping his leg.

"No," he moaned, sinking his other hand into her hair.

She gasped and tried to pull back, but she was effectively trapped. "Wake up!" Sweat broke out across her skin as she struggled to get up without hurting him.

"Don't leave me," he whispered.

Her gaze flew to his face at the quiet plea, just as he leaned in. Mira shook her head, but Gav's hand buried in her hair kept her immobile. Hard lips captured hers, brutal and ravenous. A kiss of possession.

What in the bloody hell was happening?

She opened her mouth to protest, but he took the opening she'd unintentionally given him. His silky tongue slipped into her mouth, all heat. A tremble worked through her at the sensation, his taste of mint and lemon on her tongue. Mira struggled against him, managing to turn her head to the side to suck in a breath. Gavriel's roughened cheek rasped against her throat.

"You need to let me go," she commanded, panting. Her heart pounded like a drum when he released her wrist but slid his arm around her, bringing her into a powerful embrace.

"I'll never let you go, Emma," he murmured.

Mira's heart shattered for him. She clasped his cheeks between her palms. "It's a dream, Gav. It's Mira, not Emma. Open your eyes. You need to let me go so I don't hurt your leg further."

He didn't open his eyes. Instead, his hand slid up her back, locking her into place as he hauled her closer and ran his tongue down her neck toward her cleavage and nipped her tender skin.

That was not happening.

She grabbed fistfuls of his hair and yanked his head back. "That is enough of that! Wake up!"

Gav groaned and blinked his eyes slowly. He stared at her face, his pupils blown wide. Mira looked down at him, her breath rushing in and out of her lungs. For a moment, time was suspended as they both watched each other. Slowly, reality started to creep in, and with it, his awareness filtered in. His brows slashed together in a confused frown.

"What are you doing on top of me?" he asked, his tone holding suspicion.

Mira flushed and gritted her teeth. As if she'd assault a sick, unsuspecting man. "You asked for water, and I was helping when you tugged me onto your bed."

His scowl deepened, and it felt like he was accusing her of something.

She glared down at him. "You were dreaming."

"Dreaming?"

"Yes," she said sharply. "Now release me."

He still did not. "I don't understand."

Mira blew out a breath and winced when she realized she'd have to give him more. "You were mumbling Emma's name. Now, please remove your hands from my person. I need to check your wound."

His expression flattened at the mention of Emma's name, and his fingers flexed. She squeaked when she realized the hand that used to be on her back was cupping her bum. "Kindly take your hand from my arse, Gav."

He jerked and tore his hands away from her. Mira hissed and scrambled off him, conscious of his wound. The blanket covering his nude body had shifted, and she pointedly looked away while he recovered himself, panting with the effort.

"How's the pain?" she forced out, a little breathless. *Get yourself together.*

He didn't answer, only stared at the ceiling of the tent. Mira shook out her dress and moved around the bed, back to her stool. "I need to check the wound again," she said as she sat.

Gavriel's jaw clenched, but he didn't answer.

She forced her mind away from what had happened and checked his leg. It didn't look worse. Lowering the blanket, she wiped her hands on her apron and stood. "I'm going to brew some tea to help with the fever. I'll be right back."

He still didn't look at her, his gaze shuttered.

She bustled toward the exit, her skin feeling tight and itchy.

"Mira."

She paused and stared at the tent flap.

"I would never have done that if I was in my right mind."

Mira flinched but nodded. "Understood. No offense is taken." Her first kiss, and he admitted that, in his right mind, he would never have looked in her direction. That hurt. She didn't even care for him that way, but it still hurt.

She bustled from the room, catching the queen's eyes as she moved through the infirmary. "He's awake and needs some willow bark tea. I need to take a break." Mira lengthened her stride and exited the infirmary, the winter air biting her flushed skin. Tipping her head back, she counted to one hundred and focused on slowing her galloping heart.

Her first kiss.

And he'd ruined it.

Bastard.

CHAPTER THIRTY-NINE

The Warlord

Sage had stabbed him.

The iron taste of his blood still lingered in his mouth.

While he'd known that she'd make her move, he hadn't believed it would have been in the fashion it was. Liquid dripped down his throat, and he spat blood and saliva onto the pristine snow, ignoring the fearful looks being tossed his way.

They were not worried for him, but for the punishment that would come.

Punishment, the voices crooned softly.

For once, he agreed with them. Sage had shown that his expectations of forging her into a proper consort were futile until she learned her place. She had to know her actions would have consequences.

He glanced at her from the corner of his eye. She begrudgingly padded next to him, her movements stiff as she took in his camp—or what he was allowing her to see. Cuffs circled her wrists, and the chains clinked together in the silence. While she portrayed a calm demeanor, he knew better. Power and rage boiled just beneath the surface. A satisfied smile crossed his face.

From the first moment he'd laid eyes on her, Zane had seen her potential. He'd molded her slowly over time—now all that was left was to put her into the flames of the forge to truly transform her into something remarkable. As they moved to the back of the camp, his warriors stopped what they were doing and joined the entourage.

His consort ignored them all and held her head high. Pride swelled in his chest. She was a work of art. She ignited something inside him. Jacobi pressed closer from the right, and Sage jerked away from his commander almost stumbling into Zane.

Mine, the voices snarled.

As if he too heard the voices, Zane's commander glanced in his direction. Horror flashed across Jacobi's face, and he put space between himself and Sage.

That was better.

No one touched what was his.

As if drawn by a loadstone, Zane glanced at his consort's stony expression.

She wouldn't enjoy what was coming, but *he* would.

His enemies always got what they deserved.

CHAPTER FORTY

Dor

Three days had passed since Dor visit Illya.

Seventy-two hours since Maeve had exposed the truth of who Dorcus really was.

It felt like a lifetime had come and gone.

Tomorrow, the Scythian rebellion marched on the warlord. Maeve wanted Dor to speak to the people of the Pit, to convince them to join them. She didn't know how to do that. In the three days that had passed, not once had she been able to speak to her mother about what she had learned.

Her foot scuffed against the smooth marble floor. She wiggled her toes, her feet a stark contrast against the pale stone. After spending years not wearing footwear, she couldn't bear to wear shoes above the surface. It made her unbalanced.

Dorcus brushed off the thought and nodded to the two guards stationed outside her family's room. She pushed the heavy wooden door inward. Another bizarre detail that made her feel even more off kilter. Her entire life consisted of open spaces, damp stone, and curtain entrance coverings. No one was truly shut away from each other. It led to a certain sense of community. Here, everyone shut themselves off from each other. Just another divide between people and other cultures.

Her mum sat in the corner of the room, rocking in the rocking chair. Her softly sung lullaby loosened the fist that squeezed around Dor's lungs. At least this was familiar. She gazed at the precious bundle in her mum's arms, and then to the wealth of shocking red hair that her mum boasted. How different she and her mum were, and yet the same.

Dor leaned against the wall. "You didn't tell me."

Her mum pulled her attention from the babe in her arms, her fingers running around his black downy hair. Her green eyes met Dor's, very solemn. She said nothing.

Her mum had always been an honest woman. Hell, she had raised Dor to be honest, and yet she'd kept one of the biggest secrets one could keep from her daughter. Even now, it was hard for Dorcus to even fathom what Maeve had revealed to her in the dragon's lair.

Dragons spoke.

Dragon Songs could understand them.

The heir to the Nagali throne still lived.

And she was both the heir and a Dragon Song.

"You raised me. My whole life you kept my heritage from me. Why didn't you tell me?" she asked quietly so as not to wake the babe. Dor already had her suspicions of why, but she needed to hear it from her mum.

Her mother sighed and shifted in the rocking chair. Dorcus's little brother murmured softly in his sleep before snuggling back against his mother's chest.

"Love, it was better if you didn't know. The secrecy was to protect you."

She nodded slowly. Her mum was right, of course. A rueful smile touched Dor's mouth. She'd always been a hellion growing up. The knowledge of her bloodline would have made her more reckless. Recklessness in the Pit meant death. While she could understand why her parents had kept the secret, it still hurt. It was as if they'd robbed a part of her. She didn't know who she was any more.

"I don't know what to do," she whispered and held her hands out. It was too much. Maeve wanted her to help with the remaining dragons and to unite the people of the Pit. Her people demanded freedom, but where would they go? Nagali was just ruins and fables. Then there was the war. Aermia was weakening according to Maeve. If a stand wasn't made soon, the warlord would sweep through the remaining kingdoms like a plague of locusts, devouring everything in its path. Where would that leave the people of the Pit?

Still enslaved.

There was truly only one option.

To fight.

"Take it one day at a time, precious," her mum murmured. "I know you will do well."

Dor snorted and ran a hand down her face. "I'm so lost. I don't have a place. I'm neither Scythian nor Nagali, slave nor master, commoner nor royal. I'm lost somewhere in between." Her breath stuttered out and she shook her head. "I don't know who I am."

"That is part of life. No person is ever only one thing, love. We're transient beings. Hold on to your morals and conscience. Let them guide you. You've been trained well. Trust in that." Her mum smiled. "You've grown into a strong woman. You have more skills to accomplish on the hard road ahead of you than you know, but you're not alone."

It felt like she was. The room took on a more stifling air, and she turned to pull open the door. "I need to think." And she wasn't ready to have the royal conversation with her mum yet. What did it even mean for her?

Her mum nodded and gave her an encouraging smile. "It is a lot to take in, love. When you're ready, I'll be waiting to answer all of your questions. This conversation is well overdue."

Dorcus nodded and slipped from the room. Two Scythian guards materialized on either side of her, their steps quiet as the group moved down the silent hallway. The back of her shoulders prickled, and she glanced over her shoulders. It felt like someone was watching her, but it was only the two guards. Spending time with Maeve was clearly getting to her. That woman was suspicious of everyone.

She focused on the high, arching ceilings and the clean, white, smooth lines. At first, the Scythian palace had inspired awe. Now, it made her uneasy. It was the opposite of everything she'd been raised with. The Pit was dark, wet, porous. Here, it was too bright. Dor felt exposed. Then there was the lack of sound. One would think with all the soaring hallways that echoes would be common, and, yet, there was nothing.

It was as if everyone was skulking around, and with the way Maeve had been executing dissenters, skulking was a high possibility.

Dor's paced picked up, and she arrived at the immense circular entrance that led to the pit. Six warriors—three on each side—guarded it. All formidable. Her lip curled as she caught sight of Darius on the end. The meddlesome warrior. He grated on her nerves more than she could express.

"I need to pass," she said sternly.

"Do you think that's wise?" Darius asked.

She glared at him and pointed at the entrance. "Behind this wood is my home. I've lived there my whole life and never feared the people. The only thing we had to fear was *you*."

Darius scowled, his lips curling slightly. Even angry, the warrior was attractive. She scowled at the thought.

"If you wish, but you won't go in alone."

"These men will die if you send them in with me. They stay here."

His jaw clenched. "Then I will go in with you."

Dor barely kept from rolling her eyes and nodded once. It would be easy to lose him along the interwoven hallways, and Darius knew how to take care of himself. If he got into mischief, she wouldn't feel the least bit guilty.

He removed a key from his throat and unlocked the door, the metal groaning as he pulled it open just enough so he could slip through.

"It's safe," his deep voice murmured. He popped his head back in and handed the key to the next warrior before beckoning her forward. She slipped quietly through and crept down the wet tunnel, ignoring the Scythian at her side. The tension in her shoulders loosened as she inhaled the familiar scent of wet stone, crushed plants, and mold. She was home.

Dorcus ghosted through the maze of hallways by memory, with one destination in mind. Jadim's home. Her heart squeezed at what he must think of her. She'd gone missing weeks prior and never sent him a word of what she was doing. In honesty, she'd been so wrapped up in the insanity around her, and just trying to survive, that she hadn't had time to think of her best friend and almost bond-mate. Her steps slowed. What would he say when he saw her? Their circumstances had changed. She wasn't required to produce a child so there wasn't any reason for them to marry. Their lives were going in opposite directions now. Her heart squeezed. The thought hurt.

"Something wrong?" Darius asked softly.

She jerked at the gently asked question, realizing she'd stopped in the hallway. "I need some privacy."

The Scythian warrior was already shaking his head. "I cannot allow it."

Her temper boiled over. Dor stalked up to him and planted a finger against his chest. "Until three weeks ago, my future consisted of being given to a warrior to be bred and then abandoned. The man who was supposed to be my bond-mate has been trapped in the Pit without any news from me or what our future holds. We need to speak about our changing circumstances." Her voice cracked. Damn it. "I need to do this *alone*. I owe it to him, to our friendship."

Darius scanned her face, and, to Dor's surprised, he pulled her hand from his chest and squeezed it once. "I understand. I will make sure you're safe and then disappear."

She snatched back her hand and nodded. It wasn't exactly what she wanted, but the compromise wasn't horrible. "His home is just around the corner."

Her mind spun as she led him to Jadim's home. She hesitated at the curtain that covered the entrance to his cave. Darius laid a hand on her shoulder in another surprising display of apparent understanding and entered before her. She followed. The home was similar to her own. A medium-sized room with a table and two chairs to the right and a bed in the far left corner. An arched entryway led to a small section that held another bed.

Dor stood in the middle of the room as her Scythian protector searched the room before nodding.

"It's safe. I will leave you in peace. Just scream if you need me."

He moved to leave.

"Thank you," she murmured.

"You're welcome," he rumbled and then disappeared outside.

Idly, she moved around the room, running her fingertips over the trinkets Jadim had collected. Her hand hovered over the cover of a faded book she'd given him when they were children. They'd been friends for as long as she could remember.

Voices interrupted her revelry and drew closer. Dor darted to the small bedroom and hovered in the dark. The voices grew louder, and the rustle of fabric alerted her to the fact that they'd entered Jadim's home.

"The people have spoken," a gruff male voice said.

"Our people are divided. They don't know what they need or want," a sharp female voice retorted. "They don't understand the cost of what will happen."

Dor's brows furrowed as she listened.

"We need to fight," the male voice growled.

"We would only die," the woman cut in. "Do you think we could really win against the Scythian army? Our population consists of weaker people."

Something crashed, causing Dor to flinch.

"We are not weaker or inferior!"

"That is not the way I meant it, and you know it, you old coot. They have taken everything from us. Do you want to put the women and children in danger?"

"We are not speaking of war," Jadim's calm voice interrupted. Dor flinched at his familiar chastising tone. "We're speaking of peace and freedom. The princess has guaranteed that—"

"You think we can trust that monster? She's worse than the

warlord," boomed a new, deeper male voice. "She's playing all sides."

"There can be no peace with those who use us as slaves. They need to be eradicated from this planet," the first man rumbled.

Chills ran up and down Dor's arms at that sentiment. She hadn't been invited to be part of the conversation, but she wouldn't sit by and listen to such ridiculous talk.

She stepped into the doorway, arms loose at her side. "And that hate is what will ruin us."

Five people stood in the room. Two men, two women, and Jadim. She spared him a glace. He watched her with a serious expression, his eyes shuttered. He was angry. He only ever hid how he felt when he was about to lose his temper.

And rightfully so. You deserve it.

Dor fully entered the common room when no one interrupted her. "What you speak of is exactly what the Scythians did to the Nagali people all those years ago. Do you truly want to walk in their footsteps? If we choose that path, we will become what we're seeking freedom from. How would that make us better than them?" Silence followed her question. "Not all Scythians are bad."

The shorter woman with dark curly hair snorted and crossed her caramel-colored arms. "The scars on my body prove otherwise and so do the children that they took from me." The woman's sharp tone broke. She coughed and quickly wiped the tear that escaped her right eye.

Compassion filled Dorcus. "I cannot comprehend the pain and suffering you've gone through. I'm so sorry." She remembered well how much her mother agonized over what would happen to each of her children. "I'm not saying as a whole they're good or without blame, but I will not condemn them all. My father is a good man."

"Agreed," the gruff, older man said. "He's fighting for us. We need to fight."

"He is fighting for us, but he is also working with the warlord's handmaiden."

"We can't trust her," the other woman interjected, shaking her head, her thin ginger hair floating around her pixie face. "She's like a serpent. When you think you've got ahold of her, she wiggles from your grasp."

"True, but I've spent time in her presence since the first revolt. She hates the warlord as much as we do. She is on our side."

"For the time-being," muttered the short, skinny man whose deep voice was almost shocking. He could almost pass for a small boy.

"Change is upon us." Dor took in a deep breath and eyed the group.

The curly-haired woman dipped her chin and cocked her head. "Did they tell you who you are?"

Her words seemed to hang in the air.

Dorcus swallowed hard but kept her head held high. "They did, and I'm prepared to do what I must. I've been gone long enough. I need to know what is happening. Time is short, and we must decide which path we choose."

The woman dipped her chin, her dark, springy curls bouncing with the movement. "Our people have been waiting for this moment for a long time. My family has helped protect your bloodline for over five hundred years."

"Thank you," Dorcus said. The words felt insignificant. She glanced around the group. None of them seemed to be confused. They all knew she was the Nagali heir. Her attention snagged on Jadim. Hips lips turned downward, but he didn't avoid eye contact.

"How long have you known?" she asked.

"Since the beginning."

Dor stiffened. For their entire friendship, he'd know what she was and he'd never said a bloody word. Was he really her friend or had he been planted to keep an eye on her, to guard her? Her jaw clenched as another thought slammed into her.

The bonding.

"Did you *want* to bond with me?" It was an absurd question to ask at the moment, but she needed to know the answer. Had he been another line of protection or had he cared for her?

"You have always been, and will always be, my best friend," he said softly.

It was only half an answer.

It was as if someone had kicked her in the ribs. Her parents had always been a suspicious and protective pair. Had they orchestrated this? Her stomach clenched. Jadim never had a choice to bond. He was just doing his duty.

Dor swallowed down the bitter truth and turned her attention back to the rest of the group. Personal feelings would have to be dealt with later. "I need to speak with our people. They deserve a right to voice their opinions on their future."

"*Our* future," the woman with ginger hair whispered. "It's surreal to say that."

"Maeve's men are going to move against the warlord tomorrow." Dor scanned the group. "Before I speak with the people of the Pit, you need to know that I've made up my mind and I will be fighting with them. The warlord must be stopped for the good of all."

"The good of all," Jadim repeated. "Will you ask if our people will fight with you?"

Dorcus nodded.

"They won't. There's too much bad blood." Jadim crossed his arms.

"Maybe," Dor said. "I know prejudice and hurt won't fade in the blink of an eye, but I won't stand by and perpetuate it. It's time we started fighting our wars together."

"As the monarch commands," the curly-haired woman said, standing tall.

"Your name?"

"Terra."

Dorcus smiled. "Well, Terra. Are you ready to change the world?"

Terra smiled, flashing crooked, white teeth. "I was born ready."

Chapter Forty-One

Sage

It was done.

She had stabbed him.

Yet, he still lived.

It should have been impossible. A normal man would have died from the nail alone, let alone the poison ring—yet the warlord now strode next to her side, impossibly tall, his expression hard. If it wasn't for the dried blood staining his clothing, one would never have known he'd been drowning in a pool of scarlet ten minutes prior. The skin on her arms prickled at the reminder.

What sort of creature was he? Had he truly come from the pits of hell?

The snow lessened as they worked their way into the forest where the towering trees acted as a tent above them. Her breathing sounded harsh to her own ears, her steps overly loud. For one second, she thought about taking off into the forest. She'd accomplished her task. The war machines had been destroyed and her monster poisoned. But even as she formulated a plan, reality stared her in the face. The forest crawled with the warlord's warriors. She'd have to wait to escape.

Which meant facing her punishment.

As much as she tried to hide it, fear swirled in her belly. What horror awaited her?

A familiar lanky, black feline crept through the forest to her left.

Nege.

Even though he wasn't quite her friend, the leren made her feel less alone.

The trees stopped abruptly, which was anything but natural. The manmade meadow was covered in snow and opposite her, the ground rose up to form the mouth of a cave, a gaping maw of darkness. Her pulse leapt as a memory slammed into her.

"Where does that lead?" she asked. No one answered. Wherever it was, it was not somewhere she wanted to be.

One by one, they entered the black hole and disappeared. A calloused hand wrapped around her bicep. She winced at the tight hold and leaned away from its owner.

"Don't cause trouble or you'll regret it," Rhys threatened.

Her skin prickled at his proximity, and her heart galloped. He was unhinged; it was boiling right under the surface. Sage dipped her head in what she hoped was a respectful way, and wished he would release her throbbing arm.

"Good."

Sage blinked back into the present. Was it an entrance to another city? Surely, there couldn't be one so close to the Aermian border?

One thing was for sure, she wasn't going inside. Her gut told her that if she entered that cave, she'd never leave it.

The warlord cut her off and moved toward a platform she hadn't noticed. Obediently, she followed him, searching the area for any clues as to what was going on. Her lips thinned as she spotted a pole standing in the ring with chains. Did they plan to beat her in sight of all the men? She squared her shoulders. What were a few more scars to replace the ones that had already disappeared?

Her boots thumped up three slick, wooden stairs onto the dais, ice crunching beneath her feet. The warlord moved to a black, stone throne with a dragon carved at the top. He attached her chains to the bottom of the throne and wordlessly faced her.

Sage froze and stared back at him. This was where their battle truly began.

He wanted to break her. Sage refused to be broken. She would bend, but she wouldn't break. Not for him. Not for anyone.

The warlord sat in his throne, his dark gaze pinned to her. He pointed to his lap "Sit.".

Her jaw tightened. Sage took slow steps in his direction and halted next to the stone monstrosity, then sank to her knees, head bowed. The chill from the snow seeped through her pants. From the outside, it looked like she was humbly serving the sovereign. In truth, it was a battle of wills. He was a proud demon. It was only smart to push him so far, especially with his men looking on.

Sage flinched when his hand touched the top of her head. His fingers caressed her ear, then ran along the edge of her jaw. He put gentle pressure on her chin, and she tipped her head back. The warlord leaned closer, his hair falling around his face, creating a curtain of sorts, so all she could see was his proud, ethereal face.

"Do you know why we are here?"

"Because I attacked you."

"No."

"No?" she echoed, surprised.

"It's been some time since we spent time with each other. I need you to understand the gravity of your actions. I want to protect you from mistakes that will make our lives difficult."

She slowly blinked at the use of the word *our*. There was no *our,* but she kept that thought to herself.

He released her chin and nodded at someone over her head.

"Get your filthy hands off me!" growled a familiar male voice.

No.

She glanced over her shoulder and bit back her denial. William. The old general looked like hell. The Scythians dragged him through the circle and chained him to the post. He cursed at the warriors and leaned heavily on his right leg. Every inch of his exposed skin was covered in cuts and bruises, both his eyes were black, and his lip had been split.

"William will suffer for your actions," the warlord murmured.

Sage briefly closed her eyes and sucked in a sharp breath. Why did it have to be her friends? She faced the warlord and lifted her hands to his knee. "Please," she begged. "Take me instead."

He caressed her cheek, looking at her tenderly. "This pains me as much as it pains you. I'm sorry, but I must do what is best for you. You must learn your place." He straightened and stared over her head. "Watch, or I will be forced to drag it out."

Bile burned the back of her throat, and she almost puked right there. With strength she didn't know she possessed, she pivoted on her knees and faced her friend. William shouted slurs and insults until he caught sight of her.

Aermia's commander lost some of his color. "No."

Tears blurred her eyes. "I'm sorry."

William shook his head, his eyes sad. "Nothing for it." He gave her a small smile. "Don't stop fighting."

Sage swallowed down her tears.

"Enough," the warlord said, his hand landing on her left shoulder.

William's gaze narrowed. "In my country, touching another man's wife can be a death penalty."

"You know nothing," the warlord said simply. "Call it."

It?

A warrior pulled a horn from his belt and blew. A haunting sound echoed around them. Nothing happened for several moments until two warriors on each side of the clearing pressed heavy levers. The snow began to move, and two enormous chains emerged from the earth. Sage's pulse ratcheted up a notch as a groan came from the ground and the chains began to be pulled in their direction, disappearing into the ground. A coiling mechanism? All thought fled when a hiss came from the cave. The hair at the nape of her neck rose.

Green reflective eyes appeared in the darkness of the cave right before an emerald, scaled beast moved into the light.

A dragon.

It looked nothing like the one she'd come across when fleeing Scythia. This poor beast was covered in scars so deep that his scales looked like they'd cracked. Her heart squeezed when the base of his wings flared slightly. His wings had been completely hacked off, just leaving bony stumps at the base of the beast's sinuous neck. An immense collar circled his neck as he crept from his cage, his hostile gaze darting around the meadow. Warriors edged the clearing with crossbows and wicked-looking spears.

Sage looked over her shoulder. The warlord stood from his throne, his thigh brushing her shoulder. "William of Aermia, you have been accused of murder, espionage, and are deemed a traitor to the Scythian throne."

William didn't blink but instead laughed, pulling the dragon's attention to his chained body. The older man shook his head, then glared defiantly at the warlord. "*You're* the traitor. You'll never rule the kingdoms. There will always be those who fight against your tyranny." He dismissed the warlord and met Sage's stare. "Be strong, love. Don't look."

It was like his words released a dam inside her. Sage lurched to her feet and jerked forward, the cuffs biting into her skin. An inhuman scream came from her throat when William turned to face the dragon that was now right behind him.

"No," she wailed, fighting to get loose. Her friend couldn't die. She couldn't sit here and do nothing. The dragon and man studied each other for several seconds before the obviously starving beast lunged. The rushing of waves filled her ears, and her skin flashed hot then cold.

"No," she whispered. "No."

Sage dropped to her knees, tears falling down her cheeks.

Just like that, William was gone forever.

She bowed her head, her body shaking with silent sobs. He'd been one of the first to accept her into the council when Tehl had proposed she join them. William had always supported her. He was her friend.

The dragon hissed.

Lifting her head, Sage watched as the Scythian warriors corralled the starving, scarred dragon back into the cave. For once, she let every ounce of hatred show in her expression, not for the beast, but for the men. They were the reason the animal had been reduced to these dire circumstances. The dragon hadn't killed her friend. The warlord had.

The dragon roared when a spear struck its underbelly.

Nausea swamped over her. Sage bent forward and placed a hand on the icy dais to catch her breath as saliva flooded her mouth. The cruelty was disgusting.

The beast released another pained, mournful cry that tugged on her soul.

Without meaning to, Sage began to hum her mother's lullaby softly while she got herself under control. When she lifted her head, the dragon had stopped struggling and was focused on her.

His emerald eyes clashed and held her own. She felt a kindred spirit with the dragon. *We are both scarred but not broken. He will never break us. I will free you.*

Sage pulled herself to her feet and turned away from the dragon, refusing to look at the warlord as he unclasped her chains from the throne. She moved to the edge of the platform without a word. Sage paused at the top, the chains tightening between them.

The warlord peered up at her, a brow lifted. "Something on your mind?"

She smiled at him. "I was thinking you look good dressed in blood."

He returned her smile. "I forgot how amusing you are."

She wouldn't be so amusing when she danced on his grave.

Chapter Forty-Two

Sage

Sage's moment of rage had passed and grief had replaced it.

Silent tears had turned to full-on sobs as the warlord led her through the forest, back toward the camp. The warriors kept casting glances in her direction, but she didn't care. Shame had no place here. William deserved to be mourned. Another ugly sob wracked her body, and she halted, not able to move another step. She turned in the direction of the meadow.

I'm sorry.

How she wished she could have done something more.

"Leave us," the warlord commanded softly.

She was acutely aware of how the men melted into the forest, not one sound betraying their movements. Strong arms wrapped around Sage from behind and gently pulled her against a wide chest. Sage trembled with banked rage but didn't attack. She had to choose her moment.

"He's gone, and there's nothing to be done about it," the warlord whispered. "It will be okay." His words did nothing to soothe her, and her stomach rolled when he ran his hand along her tangled mass of hair. "I'm so sorry."

That was the final straw. He didn't get to hold her and pretend he cared. He was the murderer, the monster. She lifted her hands and raked her nails down his forearms.

The warlord hissed and released her. Sage scrambled forward, determined to put space between their bodies. The monster jerked her chains, sending her sprawling to the ground. Sage squeaked as she landed on her belly.

Bastard.

Her fingers dusted the ground and curled around a rock just as he bridged the gap between them. Sage rose to her knees and swung, but he caught her manacled wrist easily, his thumb digging into the tender underside of her wrist.

"Let the stone go."

Sage gritted her teeth, refusing to release the stone. She'd never willingly give him anything he wanted ever again.

The warlord sighed and brutally squeezed her wrist.

Pain ricocheted through her fingers, and she dropped the rock. He hauled her from the ground and looped the excess chain around her arms. Sage cursed and struggled to get away as he pulled her close.

"He's gone, wild one."

"Because of you," she spat, leaning so far back that her spine cracked.

"He was an old man. It was only a matter of time before he departed this earth," he reasoned, like death by a starved animal was a natural course of life. "He died a warrior's death. There's honor in that. I wanted to give you that much."

Her jaw sagged, and she shook her head, hardly believing what she was hearing. The warlord looked at her with sympathy that she wanted to destroy. The sudden silence became stifling, so much so that she felt as if she were going to drown in it.

"You need to let me go," she murmured, bile flooding her mouth. His calloused hands on her skin made her nauseated. He released her just as she pitched forward and vomited onto spiny plants to her right. Tears rushed down her cheeks and dropped onto the dirt as she heaved.

How many more would die by his hand? How could someone survive the wounds she'd given him? Why hadn't the poison worked? Would she be stuck here forever? Sage heaved again at the thought.

The warlord's hand touched her shoulder, but she shrugged it away with a whimper. William told her to fight. She was trying her best, but every time she stood up to him, the monster knocked her down again. Her stomach lurched again, and she emptied the last of its contents onto the forest floor. Tears and snot ran down her face.

The warlord squatted beside her and brushed her hair out of her face. Sage refused to look at him.

"If only you had listened to me," he lamented, his voice filled with sadness and regret. "I hate that you're in so much pain, but you left me no choice. This hurts me as much as it hurts you. Do you think I wanted things to go this way? You brought this on us, on that man. If only you had been obedient, you could have spared him."

His words sucked the air from her lungs, and all the guilt she'd buried, from everyone she'd lost, rose to the surface with acute anguish. She slapped him as hard as she could, her chains rattling.

The warlord hissed and slowly lifted a hand to his cheek. "You're in pain, so I'll forgive you for that today. Don't ever strike me again, or you won't like what happens next."

His softly whispered words caused chills to run up and down her spine. Sage's chest heaved in and out when he removed his hand and she got a good look at the nail marks on his right cheek. She'd marked him just as he'd done to her. The scars around her neck pulsed in memory of the pain he had bestowed upon her.

"You deserved it," she said. He cocked his head, but she ignored him, wiping her mouth. She leaned onto her heels. "There's nothing in you that is good, is there?"

His dark eyes leveled on hers. "Disobedience cannot be tolerated." A pause. "No matter how much I love you, I can't let this go. His life is the price you paid for your rebellion."

Love?

Tears squeezed from the corners of her eyes. "Love? This is how you treat the ones you love?" Even *speaking* about love with this *creature* made her nausea return tenfold. "You know nothing of love!" She forced her legs to stand.

The warlord stood, towering over her. He tipped his head and leaned closer. "I've been through this before. You will work through it. You made a mistake, but I forgive you. We will right all the wrongs in the world. Together."

He was utterly delusional. "Do you really believe all wrongs can be reversed?" she asked. "How can you say such a thing? There's so much blood on your hands that you leave rivers of poison in your wake. You speak of love, and, yet, death trails you. I will never forgive you. *Never.*"

Her monster walked closer and touched her chin. Sage jerked her face away and took two hasty steps backward.

"I forget how young you are." He shook his head and sighed. "It is you who knows nothing of love. Love has a price, and it requires sacrifice. It's not easy. Love is *pain*."

Rage flashed through Sage, and her arms began to tremble. Losing any lingering fear, she stepped closer to him and tipped her head back so she could stare defiantly into his eyes. "I would never intentionally hurt those I love."

"That's the funny thing about intentions. They change over time."

"Is that how it started with you?"

"You know nothing." His expression hardened a touch. "Time changes one's perspective."

She refused to be cowed. "I know enough to promise that I will always fight for my friends and family. I will protect them and my people until my dying breath."

"On that we can agree, consort." He studied her face. "You're angry now, but it will abate. It will slowly fade into a distant memory. I promise you."

Sage held his gaze, sickened. "I can promise you it won't and that I *will* kill you." Her words seemed to hang in the air.

The warlord smiled, and she shrank back at the tender, knowing gleam in his gaze.

"Hate is a strong word, full of passion. You care for me, even if you won't let yourself admit it." He pushed past her, the chains slithering on the ground. "It will be as easy as breathing to slip into our future. We are on the right path, wild one."

There was only one path: the path of destruction.

CHAPTER FORTY-THREE

Sage

Sage pulled her cloak closer around her body and numbly walked into the warlord's tent. The sun had set, but the war drums kept on going. Her heart gave a pathetic thump. Were her people okay? Tehl? She shut down that line of thought. She couldn't think about him. If she did, she'd break.

The room was just as she'd left it in her mad dash to get away. The chest lay open, emerald green silk draping over the edge. The dragon's tortured green gaze flashed through her mind, along with William's final smile. Her stomach cramped, and she bent over, dry-heaving. Everything was such a mess.

Sage straightened and glanced at the entrance. The monster had disappeared once a healer had seen to the lacerations around her wrists from the cuffs. Without his shrewd gaze on her, it was easier to study the camp around her. The rear of the camp that butted up against the forest wasn't well protected. Her lips turned down. The warlord's tent was a different matter. Every two paces a Scythian warrior stood guard. At least she gained some useful information as to the layout of the camp.

Feeling cold, she drifted toward the woodstove. She lifted the bottom of her cloak and fingered the wide hem. Her rusty nail was gone, but at least she still had her hidden blade.

Not that it will do you much good.

Prickles of uneasiness ran across her skin at the thought. If she stabbed him in the heart, would he die? The nail and poison had only slowed him down. She frowned. In fact, the wound to his thigh that she had given him only days earlier wasn't affecting him. Any normal man would be limping.

He's not normal.

As if her thoughts would conjure him, she glanced back at the entrance. Whatever type of monster he was, he shouldn't be walking among them. The bloodstain in the other room was proof of that.

Unnatural. A demon.

Chills plagued Sage, and she moved closer to the heat. Exhaustion crashed down on her as the fire warmed her. She needed to figure out how to get out, but her mind was muddled. The bed hovered on the edge of her vision, like a siren call, but she ignored it. There was nothing that would entice her to sleep on the mattress. While she believed the warlord wouldn't outright violate her, a lot had changed since she'd been in Scythia. It wasn't worth the risk.

With a curse, she yanked a pillow and blanket from the perfectly made bed and curled up between the woodstove and battered wooden desk on the floor. Plopping the pillow over her lap, she leaned her head against the tent post and closed her eyes.

Just a little sleep.

Her eyes sprang open at the sound of movement. Her tension drained away when Nege peeked his head around the desk and crept toward her.. He bumped her left shoulder with his nose and released a chest-rattling purr.

"Hello," she whispered, running her fingers between his ears.

The feline maneuvered himself and plopped down, curling around her like a half moon, becoming a wall of man-eater between herself and the warlord whenever he decided to sneak up on her.

Sage stroked Nege's silky coat and spine. Her heart clenched at the scars her fingers passed over. Even with the abuse he'd suffered, Nege still offered her protection and comfort. Gratitude flooded her.

"Thank you."

He rumbled softly and laid his head on his paw, his golden eyes closing. She may not be able to hear the warlord coming, but Nege would warn her of the demon's arrival.

Sage closed her eyes. Just a little sleep, and then she would figure out where to go from there.

***

The rattling of glass yanked her out of her deep sleep. Sage's eyes flew open, and she peered through the fringe of hair that had fallen into her face. The warlord muttered something unintelligible. His hair was in disarray, like he'd been running his fingers through it. The bloody shirt had been replaced with a black one that was open at the throat, revealing burnished skin and a leather necklace that disappeared under his clothing. Sage focused on the little crease between his brows. Was something wrong?

Again, he mumbled something to himself, and then pulled a small leather book from inside his shirt. He sat heavily in his chair and leaned over his desk, scratching something into it with a feathered pen. Her curiosity deepened when he removed the necklace from his neck, and she saw a key attached to its end. The warlord opened the bottom desk drawer.

Interesting. He kept the key on his body. What was so special he kept locked away?

The warlord drew out a golden tincture and tossed its contents back, his profile only visible. His face slackened and his eyes closed. Sage shifted uncomfortably with the debauched image he portrayed. He seemed too comfortable.

"Spying on me is never a good idea," he mumbled, licking his lips as he opened his eyes. He shot a glance over his shoulder at her.

Sage abandoned her pretense of sleeping, and watched him as he put the empty glass back into the drawer. Carefully, he shut it, locked it, and put the necklace over his head, once again hiding the key.

"What was that?" she asked softly.

Silence met her question.

The fire crackled in the brazier, and he scratched something down in his little book before closing it and tucking it inside his shirt.

The warlord swiveled to face her and braced his elbows on his knees. He set his chin on his left palm and watched her, rubbing his fingers across his mouth as if deep in thought. "Something for healing."

Her brows rose in surprise. She hadn't expected him to answer her question. His gaze roved to the bed and back to her.

"You know that the bed is for you? I had it made for you."

She shook her head, uncomfortable. There was no way she was getting in that bed.

He nodded absentmindedly and then stood. Her whole body went on alert. Would he force her? Before she could do anything, he plopped down on the other side of the tent support, Nege's bottom separating them. The warlord propped his left foot against the floor and sighed. Her tongue stuck to the roof of her mouth. In that moment, he looked like a lounging dark god.

Sage twitched and hated that she allowed herself to think such a thing. He rolled his head to the side and looked at her with a tired gaze. It hadn't been noticeable before, but dark smudges shadowed the skin beneath his eyes and faint lines bracketed his mouth. He'd lost weight. He looked sick.

A fissure of hope burst in her chest. Was the poison working?

He huffed and then tipped his head back once again to stare at the low burning lanterns above. "You understand that hurts me, too, when I have to punish you?" His voice was soft and almost apologetic.

"How?" she asked.

"I don't like seeing you pain."

She swallowed hard and had to look away. It was bloody unfair that he looked boyish, sad, and vulnerable. The warlord was none of those things. He was a killer. He'd hurt her in more ways than she could count. She needed to keep that in mind. The pretty shell wasn't distracting enough to make her forget about the ugliness it concealed.

Sage settled with, "I don't know what you want me to say. Is it forgiveness you seek?"

"I don't want your forgiveness. I want your acceptance."

She jerked. "My acceptance? How can I accept a monster?"

"A beauty and a monster. Poetic, wouldn't you say?"

A moment of silence lapsed between them before he turned to fully face her. Sage still avoided his gaze and stared at the desk, her hand absentmindedly running across Nege's back.

"I want peace," he said finally.

"Peace?" she questioned. "How could there ever be peace between us?"

"I could give you anything and everything. The world would be yours."

"Mine," she mumbled. "Do you really believe that?"

"Scythia has many gifts to give. We can change the world for the better."

"If you truly believed that, you would've already helped make positive changes. Yet, all you have done is cause misery and pain. You have hurt people. You have hurt *me*." The words tasted like ash on her tongue, but she said them anyway.

"Pain is a part of life." He sighed. "But I am sorry for the pain you've suffered."

Everything in his tone suggested he was sincere, but Sage didn't believe him for one second. Intrigued with the line of conversation, she carried on. "How can you do it?"

He examined his hands, uncharacteristically quiet. "Because I must."

"That's not an answer."

"You're young, wild one. You were blessed with a good family. I was raised by monsters. You call me a monster? It is an apt description since that's who created me. *I* have the power to eradicate people like that from the start. Could you imagine a world with perfect families? Children who never suffered abuse?"

Sage swallowed, feeling sick to her stomach. "And the children of the northern Aermian village?" The horrors of that place would haunt her until her last day.

"Those women and children would've died a long, painful death. I gave them a clean death. I gave them peace."

Not able to hear another word of his lies, Sage shot to her feet, startling Nege. She stepped over the disgruntled feline and spun to face the master manipulator.

"A clean death?" she hissed. "They suffocated."

The warlord slowly rose from his position on the floor, his boyish impression sloughing off as the predator took its place. This was the monster she knew. She could fight him.

"The village was deep into poverty. They were all starving to death. The children were undersized and the men weak. Even if I had given them any of my tinctures, it was too late for them. What was *your* king doing for them? His people are dying. How could I leave that village, those babes, to perish in such a barbaric way? I may be a monster, but I don't lie about what I am. I spared them pain."

Like a child, Sage wanted to put her hands over her ears to block out his web of lies. It was just deranged enough that he could delude her into believing his muddled logic.

"Do you even hear yourself, Zane?" The use of his real name startled her so much that she stumbled back a step.

Don't you dare go there, Sage. Don't let him reel you in.

The warlord moved around the leren and ran his finger along the corner of his desk, before leaning a hip against the old piece of furniture. "You know, I never wanted someone like you."

"Then why do you keep coming after me?" she cried desperately. "Just let me go!"

"I cannot." He shrugged a shoulder and gave her a wry smile. "They demand we keep you, and I have become attached to you."

"They?" Who was he speaking about?

"Things will get better," he said, ignoring her question.

"They will." *When he is dead.*

"Why do I get the feeling there was more to that thought?" She didn't answer. The warlord smiled and shook his head. "The pain of the past will fade."

"I don't think it'll be so easy," she retorted.

"You will be surprised how time passes. It'll be easier than you think to accept your fate. Our future is bright, consort, which is why I am going to share a secret with you. Today was not easy on either of us. I'm not completely cold, and I know how important family is, which is why I have a gift for you." He straightened and held his hand out. "Come with me."

Inside, she'd frozen over. *Family?* "What have you done?"

"It's what I *haven't* done. Take my hand, consort."

Sage didn't believe she had a choice, so she placed her fingers in his and let him lead her away.

Chapter Forty-Four

Sage

Trepidation filled her as they trekked farther from their tent. Sage's lip curled. From *the* tent. The horrors of the day and using his given name had thrown her for a loop. Snow crunched under her boots, and the bitter chill of winter bit at her cheeks. She glanced around the moonlit darkness, trying to take in as much of the camp as she could.

The warlord squeezed her fingers and tugged gently on her arm. Disgust wormed its way into her belly as she stared at their clasped hands. Why was she doing this? Every time she gave in, things became more muddled. His rough callouses rubbed against her own. She couldn't stand it anymore. Sage tugged her hand from his, avoiding his gaze as he scrutinized her despite the darkness cloaking them.

Her teeth ground together as his attention lingered on her face, his black gaze seeming to note every micro expression that she tried to hide. They continued their quiet trek, Sage following the warlord. Some might have mistaken her for being meek as she held her head down and stayed close to his side, but really, she was cataloguing information. Escape was imminent, and, when she left, she'd take a wealth of information back to her people.

Disquiet settled over her when they moved into the forest. Her skin crawled, and the back of her neck prickled. She was being watched. Her anxiety went up a notch when they rounded a thick tree trunk and a lone tent came into view. What was it doing out here?

The warlord didn't acknowledge the two warriors stationed outside the tent they approached. He paused and pushed back the first tent flap for her. Sage squared her shoulders and didn't hesitate as she strode inside, not knowing what to expect.

The room was similar to the warlord's. There were a few chairs scattered around, a thick rug across the floor, and two lanterns hanging from the ceiling. Nothing special. Her attention zeroed in on the additional warriors hovering near the next flap.

Her stomach dropped. Why was there another set of warriors when there was a pair stationed outside?

The warriors straightened and bowed. The one to the right lifted the second tent flap at their approach, revealing only part of the inner room. Her pulse began to hammer in her neck. What was he hiding?

The warlord leaned close. "You first, wild one."

Sage forced her legs forward and she ducked into the next room of the tent. Her breath caught. To the right, two tables held an assortment of sharp, deadly-looking tools and weapons, but that didn't shock her the most. She blinked several times, not believing her eyes. "I'm dreaming."

"You're not," the warlord murmured.

In the far left corner were two huge stakes buried in the ground.

Chains hung from the tops of them and attached to the wrists of a crumpled figure on the ground.

Lilja.

Sage rushed forward and crashed to her knees beside her aunt. She fluttered her hands over Lilja's bruised body. "Lilja?" she whispered hoarsely.

Her aunt didn't open her eyes.

She placed her fingers on Lilja's neck and leaned closer, listening for breaths as she tried to detect a pulse. Her aunt wheezed softly.

Lilja was alive.

Tears blurred Sage's eyes, and she shuddered with soft sobs. "How is this possible?"

The fall of his boots alerted her to his approach. The warlord stood by her side, placing a hand on her shoulder. "I know how important family is to you. I didn't want you to lose her, so I kept your aunt safe for you."

"Safe?" Emotion clogged in Sage's throat. Lilja was a bloody mess, but she was alive. Sage didn't know how to work through her thoughts and emotions. Part of her was so thankful that her aunt lived, but the other part was horrified. The bruises and cuts across her aunt's body couldn't have been from when Sage saw her last. They were fresh. She'd been beaten and tortured.

Sage brushed a limp lock of silver hair from Lilja's bruised cheek, her fingers ghosting over the damaged skin. What sort of horrors had her aunt suffered?

Losing Lilja had broken Sage's heart, but there was peace in death. She could make peace with it, because she knew her aunt wasn't suffering, but the idea that she'd been at the mercy of the warlord and his men for over a month was too much.

Sage put a hand over her mouth, feeling like she'd throw up. This was worse than death. How was she supposed to get them both out? Especially with the condition her aunt was in?

"She needs medicine," Sage croaked.

"The Sirenidae will get what she needs now that you are here. You will be her savior. Her life rests in your hands."

To someone else, his words might have sounded reassuring and pretty.

All she could hear was the threat: if she learned her place, Lilja would be safe. If Sage acted out, her aunt would be harmed.

"She's been a thorn in my side. Sedating her has been the only option several times. I'm sure since you're here, she'll be better behaved as well."

Sage closed her eyes. Lilja wouldn't want Sage hurt, and Sage didn't want her aunt assaulted. The warlord had played them both.

Sage chuckled, the sound rusty and dark. When would his depravity and cunning manner cease to amaze her? He would go to any lengths to control and manipulate those around him. How was he always one step ahead?

"I have to give it to you. You surprised me." Her words were hollow.

Her monster reached for her hand and pulled her to her feet. "It's late. Time to go."

Sage shook her head. "I don't want to leave her."

"I can understand your reluctance, but today has been trying for both of us. There are things we need to discuss." He reached out and traced her cheekbone, liquid heat filling his gaze. "Come along, wild one."

She froze. She knew what that look spelled.

Her head spun as she tried to see a way out of the situation. It wouldn't do anyone any good if she fought right now. It was about picking her battles.

Sage nodded, kissed her aunt on the cheek, stood, and strode out of the tent.

I'll be back. I promise.

Angrily, she wiped the remaining tears from her cheeks. The warlord's hand curled around her bicep, stopping her.

He stepped close. "Consort," he crooned. "It's time. We've patiently waited long enough."

We?

Sage's jaw set, and she glanced away, staring at the darkened forest, her breath frosting the air. "You wish to speak of sex after I lost my friend today and you exposed me to my abused aunt? I will not give you one more thing."

His finger crept under her chin and forced her to look up at him. "Not sex, but love." He smiled, his expression soft like a lover's. "It's been a long time coming, and we shouldn't wait any longer. Time is so short."

"Short for what?" she asked. "I thought you said we had all the time in the world?"

His smile turned smug. "I wish to go into battle tomorrow with the taste of you on my tongue. It will make Scythia's victory all the sweeter."

Victory? Her body flashed hot and cold. "What are you planning?"

"It matters not." He pressed into her space, his breath heating her lips. "I don't wish to be apart from you any longer."

An eternity seemed to pass as she stared up at her monster. He truly believed that she would give herself to him. Tehl's face flashed through her mind. There was only one person who got to see that side of her, and it wasn't the demon before her.

Deep satisfaction rolled through her, and a smile lifted her lips as vile, ugly words rose to her tongue. Sage released the full force of her utter disgust, loathing, and hatred. "You will *never* have that part of me," she said resolutely.

He cocked his head, a small indulgent smile on his face like he was amused by her outburst.

"You kissed me in Scythia and in the Nagali palace," he murmured, his voice dripping sin. "I didn't imagine the affection you held for me, nor the way your body curved against mine any time we were in bed. Let go of what holds you back. Your body already belongs to me. Give me your heart, too."

Sage laughed without humor. "You think you can take everything around you? You presume that you are the lord of all, but you are not."

Some of his smugness leached away. His fingers tightened on her chin. "I can take whatever I want, and I know you'll give in. You're young, and I've practiced seduction for longer than you can imagine. Admit it. You're *mine*."

She stepped closer to him, her head tipped back so she could meet his dark gaze. "It brings me pleasure to say this to you, but you will never have that part of me. I am not yours. I gave myself away freely," she paused, "*eagerly*, a long time ago to someone who is capable of love." Her chest lifted and fell with her heavy breaths.

The warlord stilled at her declaration. It was if his body was made of stone. The fingers around her chin dropped away and wrapped around her throat. Terror flooded her, but it didn't take away the satisfaction of watching the warlord start to unravel.

His grip tightened, and he leaned into her face. "You would not do such a thing."

Sage's smile widened. "I was never yours. I belong to myself, but I gave my husband a part of me that you will never claim."

The warlord's gaze snapped shut. "You didn't," he whispered, pained.

His hand spasmed, and she wheezed for a breath.

"I know," he snarled, talking to someone Sage couldn't see. His eyes closed. "She's ours."

She grabbed his wrist when the pressure increased and his eyes opened, insanity shining through.

"You gave it to that mutt," he said harshly. He bared his teeth. "If you're so free with your body, you shouldn't have any problem sharing it with me." The warlord slammed her against the tree trunk, pressing his body against hers as she scrambled against his hold. "I'll remove his stain from your body, from your soul, if I have to. You're *mine*! You're ours!"

The back of her head cracked against the tree, and she lifted her blurry gaze to the edge of the forest. Escape was so close. The war drums marched with the beat of her heart as the demon tore at her cape and shirt. Buttons popped and scattered across the forest floor.

Sage turned her gaze to the sky and blinked slowly. The moonlight cut out, and a flying figure formed. Her brows furrowed even as her monster pressed his cold hands against the warm skin of her bare back. The shadow was too large to be a fiilee. Her breath caught.

A dragon. A *free* dragon.

Its wings flared, and Sage smiled.

If the dragon had escaped the warlord, so could she.

She cocked her head to the side and latched onto his ear, biting as hard as she could while simultaneously slamming her knee into his crotch. The warlord gasped, and his grip on her faltered. Sage wiggled away as the warlord grunted. Dots crossed her vision. She fell to her knees and grabbed her cloak and a rock.

Get off the ground. You're too vulnerable.

She stood and staggered as the warlord reached for her. Sage swung the rock with all her might against his skull, and he stumbled as she reached for the hem of her cloak. He grabbed her by the braid.

Sage screamed as he wrenched her body against him, her back against his front.

"Don't worry, consort. We consider bloodshed part of foreplay."

She didn't think, just reached back and grabbed his crotch and squeezed. He yelled and flung her forward. She crashed to the ground, striking her head on something hard. The world tilted, and she curled into herself, her shaking fingers groping for the hidden blade in the hem of her cloak.

The breeze kicked up, blowing snow into her face. Sage squinted as the dragon landed, wings outspread before the opening of the forest.

A feminine figure slid off its back and down its wing, landing in a crouching pose. The woman lifted her head and smiled.

"Hello, brother."

Maeve.

CHAPTER FORTY-FIVE

Tehl

"I refuse to leave her for one more moment!" Tehl growled. He glanced at the men and women surrounding the war table. "It's been long enough. The war machines are no longer a threat." A pause. "Raziel."

The Methian prince pulled his attention from the map on the table. "Yes?"

"Have all your fiilee been pulled from the coast and are ready to be deployed?"

"They are," Raziel murmured.

"Good."

"Do you think it's wise to push forward without a signal from Sage or Blair?" Queen Osir asked.

"We can't wait any longer. It's been three days." Tehl hadn't slept since his wife disappeared into the storm. He stared stonily at the table. Something had gone wrong. He could feel it in his bones.

Hayjen pushed in through the tent flap, his icy blue eyes bright. "I have news. Blair's warriors have arrived and are in position." He rubbed his hands together. "It's time."

Tehl sagged in relief. A turn of luck. Finally. He glanced around the table, his heart heavy. It was too empty. Sage, Gav, Lilja, William, Blaise, and Garreth were all missing. This could be the last time he stood with what currently remained of the war council.

He smiled at them all. "Thank you," Tehl said softly. "Your dedication, sacrifice, and hard work will not be forgotten."

"It's no more than you have done," Rafe said gruffly.

"This is our last stand. Be safe and give them hell. I'll see you on the battlefield." Tehl locked eyes with each person before they filed out of the tent.

All except Hayjen.

Sage's uncle moved closer to the crown prince's right side.

"Are you ready to go get our girl?" Hayjen rumbled.

Tehl lifted his head and wiped a hand over his mouth. "I am."

"But?"

"I'm not ready for this next leg of bloodshed."

"Lilja and I have been fighting for a long time." Hayjen paused, his face creasing in pain. "We *fought* for a long time. Many lives had already been lost before you or I were even born. This fight isn't just about our people now, but for the ones who didn't get justice in their time. Today, we serve that justice."

Tehl nodded. "May vengeance be served."

"May the warlord die a horrid death," Hayjen snarled.

The men shared a smile.

The end was upon them.

Chapter Forty-Six

Mira

Mira sat wearily beside Gav's cot. His fever had spiked once again, but it wasn't as terrible as it had been a few days prior. She pulled back his bandage and hummed. It didn't look better, but it looked no worse.

"Gav, I think we're through the worst of it," she mumbled. Her friend didn't answer her, likely too lost to his fever dreams. Her mind flashed back to the kiss. Mira blushed and then scowled. "Leave it to you to steal my very first kiss and think I'm someone else."

She rewrapped his wound and pulled the blanket back over his bare leg. While Mira had managed to keep his leg, Gav would never walk normally. He would walk, but with a limp.

Laying her arms on the cot, Mira pillowed her cheeks against her hands. Stars, she hoped he didn't blame her. At least he was alive. The war had already claimed so many lives. War was a brutal, ugly thing.

Her eyelids began to droop, but then a hand settled on her left shoulder, startling her. She glanced up, meeting Raziel's eyes, concern plain on his face.

Mira smiled at him and patted his hand. "I'm all right," she whispered.

He nodded and absentmindedly ran a hand over his face, uncharacteristically serious.

"What's wrong?" she asked. Had something happened to one of his family members? One of his friends? Mira gasped. "Is it Sage?"

Raziel shook his head. "Nothing like that, love." He held his hand out. Mira took his hand and stood, her body complaining. She groaned and stretched. No good deed went unpunished.

"Tonight, we attack," he said softly, pulling her toward the piping-hot woodstove at the rear of the tent.

Mira shivered, despite the heat. More men would be entering the infirmary. Raziel brushed a damp curl from her cheek, his fingertips lingering on her jawline. He scanned her face.

"I may not come back," he said bluntly.

She blinked slowly, and a fist seemed to tighten around her lungs, making it difficult for her to breathe. Mira shook her head. "Don't talk like that. You've made it so far, and there's no one stronger than you are."

A half smile curved his mouth. "What an extraordinary creature you are."

Mira slipped her hands into his. "The feeling is mutual. Be safe tonight."

The Methian prince nodded, his smile fading away too quickly. "Do you remember what I said?"

She gave him a silly smile. "That you'll force feed me if I forget to eat?" It didn't lighten the mood. He moved in closer.

"I already spoke of my intentions before. They have not changed. Goodness and kindness radiate from your soul and touch the lives of those around you. I admire and respect you."

Mira swallowed at his sentiment and tipped her head back to stare into his eyes. "I care for you, too."

He paused, tenderness playing across his expression. "I *like* you, and it will be easy to love you." Raziel released her fingers and slid his hand behind her neck, cupping the back of her head. His fingers tangled in the soft, tiny hairs at the nape of her neck. He leaned closer. "If you'll let me."

Her heart thundered as he breached the tiny gap between them. Warm lips brushed her own. Her breath shuddered, and the world stilled as Raz kissed her. It was so light, a ghost of a touch, the whisper of silk against her skin. Mira's lips parted on a gasp, and, as if that was all the permission he needed, his hands cupped her face and mouth covered hers.

The prince kissed her slowly, as if they had all the time in the world, like she was everything he needed and wanted. The first brush of his tongue caused Mira to shiver. Her hands rose to his chest, hesitating. What sort of madness was this? She never felt like this—all hot, shivery, and weak.

"Please kiss me," he whispered against her lips.

His plea destroyed any hesitation inside her. Mira seized the front of his shirt and kissed him back, brushing her own tongue with his, tempting him to play. She jerked when he groaned, her eyes flying open.

"Did I hurt you?" she squeaked. He was the first man she'd ever kissed, other than Gav, and that didn't count, because she hadn't kissed him back. Had she done it wrong?

Raziel smiled lazily and brushed his nose across hers, then pressed a kiss to her temple. "No, love. It was perfect."

Her embarrassment disappeared at his praise, and she sank into his embrace, enjoying the wonderful hug. He felt... safe.

"I need to go," he said.

She squeezed him tightly once more. "Please be careful." Mira pulled back reluctantly.

Raz touched her cheek and gave her a charming smile. "I'll be back to annoy you before you know it, Mira. I'll see you soon. We can talk then."

It was more difficult than it should have been to watch him walk away. She lifted her hand over her mouth, her lips tingling from his kisses. He'd become her unlikely friend and suitor. And while she did like him, there was no future for them; he was a prince, and she was a healer.

Tears misted her eyes. She should have told him the truth. Babies weren't in the cards for her. A crown prince required an heir, and Mira couldn't give him one.

She'd tell him when he returned.

If he returned.

A lone tear ran down her cheek, and she closed her eyes.

Please, please stay safe.

Chapter Forty-Seven

Sage

The world tilted and spun.

Maeve strode forward, her expression as serious as ever. The warlord's boots entered Sage's vision, and she shied away. Who knew what he'd do to her in this state? She angled her head to get a better view.

He straightened his rumpled clothes and brushed his black hair away from his angular face. He cast a glance down to her, his gaze calculating. "Don't move."

She shivered as he moved away and held his arms out, moving to meet his sister.

"You finally arrive at last. Do you have what I asked for?"

"I oversaw the fermenting myself." Maeve smiled and pulled a small glass bottle from her pocket. "I came as soon as I could." She approached him, all lethal grace and power. Sage blinked. Their features weren't too similar, but their mannerisms were, so much so, it was eerie.

Sage lay on the ground, trying to make the earth stop moving. She pulled her cloak closer to her body and tried to crawl to the nearest tree. The warlord embraced his sister, and Maeve looked over his shoulder, locking eyes with Sage. An eternity seemed to pass between them. Sage owed the woman so much for getting her out of Scythia.

Maeve nodded subtly and, in the space of a second, she released a hidden blade from her sleeve and stabbed her brother in the neck. The warlord bellowed. Sage's jaw dropped as the warlord's sister jerked the blade forward. His shout turned to a gurgle. He yanked his own weapon from his thigh, and stabbed Maeve between the ribs. Maeve jerked but never lost eye contact with Sage.

"Run," she mouthed.

Sage stumbled to her feet. The world rolled and lurched. She touched the lump on the back of her head and used the tree to catch her balance. She glanced toward the dragon—toward her best chance of freedom—then back to the tent in the distance. Leaving Lilja wasn't an option.

She crashed toward the tent, well aware that there were four Scythian guards. Time to come up with a plan quickly. Surely, they'd heard his scream? Sage exaggerated her limp and let her sobs break free when she rounded the last tree.

"They attacked," she sobbed, and purposefully tripped over her own feet. "Please help him."

Warriors emerged from the tent, and all four entered the forest silently.

I'm sorry, Maeve. Please be safe.

Sage waited until she heard shouts from Maeve's direction and rushed into the tent. She panted as she pocketed as many sharp tools and weapons as possible, shoving them into every available opening.

A small blade made its way into her hands, and she set to work on unlocking the cuffs encircling her aunt's wrists. It was tedious, and every sound Sage made ratcheted up her nerves. Sweat dripped between her breasts when the first cuff released. She moved to the second one. It was stubborn.

Each second felt like a year. "Please work," she whispered. The final lock clicked, releasing the cuff around Lilja's right wrist.

A hand seized her by the hair and yanked her back. Sage screamed and dropped her blade, clutching at the hand.

"Did you think you could run off that easily?" the warlord spat. "We will always be able to find you. You belong to us. There's no escape."

Sage released his arm and pulled a dagger from her pocket. Twisting, she slammed it into the inside of this thigh. He grunted and tossed her to the ground. Her head collided with the floor, and her vision danced. The air in her lungs fled as he threw himself on top of her, pinning her to the floor.

Revulsion struck her, as blood dripped onto her from the ghastly wound at his throat.

"Look at me," he roared, his spittle and blood spraying her face.

Her gaze snapped to his face, and Sage swore she was looking into the pits of hell itself. This was it. The end. Her monster bared his teeth. "I will not let you ruin everything. Why can't you accept me?" he demanded, his tone changing. Something vulnerable fluttered across his face. "Does no one care for me?"

She flinched as if struck. All she could see was him telling her about his past. About the monsters his parents were.

Don't let him fool you.

"You've brought this on yourself," she whispered. "You have had many chances to love, but you've chosen power, hate, and violence over and over. How can anyone love a monster?" she spat.

He leaned closer and ran his lips along her cheekbone. "'Til the bitter end, you defy me. Why do I still want you?"

"Because you're sick."

The warlord lifted his head as Maeve burst through the door. He sprung up just as his sister slammed a rock over the back of his head. He dropped to the ground, moaning. Sage scrambled back on her hands and knees as his arms clawed at the dirt. How was he still moving?

Maeve let the rock fall to the ground, and tugged another bottle from her trousers. She jogged to Lilja's side and pinched her cheeks, forcing her mouth open. Quickly, Maeve uncorked the bottle and poured the liquid into Lilja's mouth.

"You need to get her out."

Sage shook from head to toe and nodded. Her eyes widened when Lilja's lashes fluttered and her gorgeous eyes opened up. The warlord's sister cupped Lilja's cheeks as her eyes opened and locked on Maeve's.

"Old friend, it is time that you go," Maeve said. "I know you're hurting, but you need to gather your strength. I've given you something. Leave with your niece."

Lilja nodded, her pupils blown wide. "Ruuuunn," she slurred.

Sage forced herself to her feet, her gaze darting to the warlord who was trying to stand. Sage and Maeve each took one of Lilja's arms and stumbled to the first tent flap.

Maeve released Lilja and met Sage's gaze. "Go. I will stay."

Sage swallowed. Determination was clear on Maeve's face. She didn't plan on surviving the encounter. "Thank you," she choked out, knowing it wasn't good enough to express how thankful she was.

"Traitor," the warlord hissed.

That was her cue.

It took everything she had to leave Maeve in the tent, but the slither of the warlord's voice made her flee. Sage and Lilja stumbled down the path, her aunt dragging at her side. Sage gritted her teeth as she tried to balance both of them. She didn't examine the carnage of the dead warriors they passed. Silently, they moved toward the immense dragon twenty paces away.

Sage hesitated and eyed the surrounding forest. It was thick. There was no way she'd get Lilja through that to get around the winged beast.

"It's just a dragon," Sage mumbled. He was Maeve's friend. He wouldn't hurt them. Hopefully.

Lilja rolled her neck and crooned softly, a series of clicks and hums. The dragon clicked back, lowering his head so his silvery eyes were level with them. His hot breath washed over them. Sage had only experienced something like this once, with the leviathan.

"He cannot leave this place yet, but he can give us shelter under his wing."

"You speak to dragons?"

Lilja smiled sloppily. "Pirates can do anything."

The dragon lifted his leathery wing. Sage glanced around, sure that the warlord would appear behind them. There was no one.

They stumbled toward the dragon and lurched beneath his wing. He lowered his wing, cocooning them against his side. Sage paused, her eyes widening as she caught sight of another refugee barely visible. Another girl leaned against the dragon, her raven eyes watching them. She lurched away from her spot and grabbed Lilja's other arm.

"Thanks," Sage wheezed, her ribs and head pulsing with pain.

Together, they gingerly lowered her aunt to the ground. Lilja slumped against the dragon, his breathing moving her body.

"So warm," Lilja murmured. She stroked a hand down his side. "Thank you."

The girl glanced from the dragon to Lilja and then to Sage. "She speaks to dragons?"

Sage shrugged. "She does a lot of things I can't explain."

"What happened to her?" the girl asked, pushing a braid over her gorgeous midnight skin.

"The warlord," Sage whispered. She still hadn't had time to process that Lilja was alive. It still seemed unreal, like a dream. "Thank you for your help," she murmured, turning back to the girl. "Who are you?"

The girl smiled, her white teeth bright in the darkness. "Dor."

"Dor," Sage repeated and then held her hand out. "I'm Sage."

The girl's expression melted into one of recognition. "I've heard of you. The consort."

Sage flinched and then gave the girl a hard stare. "I am *nothing* to the warlord. Nothing."

Dor nodded. "My mistake. I apologize."

Remorse flooded Sage. "I'm sorry, my—"

The sounds around them changed. The forest quieted. Sage's brows furrowed. Something wasn't right. She held her finger to her lips and then pointed to her ear. Hopefully, Dor understood to be quiet. The Scythians had uncanny hearing. One word could destroy them.

The dragon clicked.

Lilja's eyes fluttered open, and a true smile flashed across her face. "They fly," she whispered.

Sage stiffened. "Who?"

"The fiilee and the Dragon Songs. The tide changes tonight."

Chapter Forty-Eight

Mer

The ship with the black leren was nowhere to be found.

Until Mer dove to the bottom of the sea.

She swallowed hard and darted toward the submerged ship. She prayed that she wouldn't find Jasmine in the wreckage.

Mer squeezed through the jagged, broken window at the rear of the ship. Bed linens floated in the water like specters, but no bodies. A rattle hovered above the floor, and her heart seized. Had there been children aboard? She steeled her nerves as she approached the door and yanked.

No bodies, just a hallway that was lined with doors and led to a set of stairs. Laboriously, she checked every room. Nothing but abandoned belongings and weapons.

She made quick work of the rest of the ship, thankfully empty.

While she was relieved she hadn't found Sam's wife in the ship, she couldn't shake the sense of urgency that plagued her. Her gaze flew up to the tempestuous surface, dotted with bobbing debris and bodies. Dark shapes glided above silently.

More leviathans. Damn.

Stars, she hoped Jasmine wasn't in the water or bleeding.

Cautiously, she drifted toward the surface, humming a tune so that the leviathans wouldn't mistake her for the enemy, but recognize her as an ally. She broke the waves, careful to keep her gills in the seawater. Her stomach clenched when the fingers of a corpse touched her arm. Mer shied away, her senses screaming at her to leave the watery graveyard. She soldiered on.

Time slipped by as she meticulously searched through the debris. A Scythian moaned, and clung tighter to a piece of driftwood as a wave crashed into him.

Mer caught his eye. "The Aermian vessel will be here to collect any survivors within the hour."

His lip curled. "They won't find me."

She nodded to one of the dorsal fins that disappeared beneath the water not twenty paces from them. "You're right. If you keep kicking like that, they won't find you." The warrior paled and froze. "Movement draws them. Keep still, and you might survive." Then, Mer moved on. She passed three more warriors in similar situations—all of whom were not happy to see her.

The wind howled, and the waves turned rougher. Mer dove into the water, still searching. Her heart stopped when gauzy fabric caught her eye. She kicked harder and brushed the fabric away from the body it concealed.

It was a girl, but it was not Jasmine.

Mer gazed at the unseeing eyes of the young woman who couldn't be older than herself. What a waste of life. How did she end up here? Had the Scythians captured her while raiding Sanee? Or was she a slave? She touched the girl's cheek, then guiltily continued on. The young woman didn't deserve to be lost at sea.

Mer swam to the surface again and eyed the floating fragments of the ship. No Jasmine.

"Help," a hoarse voice called.

Mer twisted in the water, her hair floating around her. She locked eyes with a huge Scythian warrior who clung to a barrel. His entire face was one big bruise. A gash over his left eye bled profusely. Other than that, he looked fine. She made sure to keep a bit of distance between them. No sense in courting danger, and this warrior screamed danger.

"The Aermian vessel will be here soon to collect any of the survivors."

"Not for myself," he whispered. "There's a woman. She's pregnant."

Mer's anger ignited, and she darted forward with a snarl, grabbing the warrior's face and digging her nails into his cheeks. "Where is she?"

He didn't fight back or pull away, just held her gaze, sorrow lurking in his dark eyes. "They managed to escape into a life raft. Their destination was the cove. I don't think they made it."

She released him, her attention moving to the far-off lagoon. The weather only hours ago would have made it nearly impossible to reach the bay. Mer kicked forward, already dismissing the warrior.

"Please find her," the warrior pleaded.

The desperation in his tone had her glancing over her shoulder at the man once more. There was something in his eyes. He didn't harbor a hatred for her, nor was there any malevolence in his gaze.

She nodded once and dove.

Chapter Forty-Nine

The Warlord

Sage had attacked him. Twice.

He rose from the floor and stared at his sister, his chest aching. Maeve held her hand to her side where he'd stabbed her, blood seeping between her fingers.

"Why?" he demanded.

She met his gaze, no remorse. "You know why."

"Because I killed your dragon?" His lip curled. "He was turning you against me. You know he had to go."

His sister shook her head. "You committed genocide."

"I was protecting the world," he spat, blood running down his neck. Why wasn't he healing faster? The serum wasn't working as well as it should have been. Suspicion pricked him.

We've been betrayed, the voices hissed.

He pulled a sword from the table and examined it. "It's been you this entire time." Maeve didn't deny it. "You would betray me, your brother, your one true protector, over a handful of imperfect slaves?"

"My brother died the moment he slaughtered innocent people. *Children*." Her voice hardened. "You know what our childhood was like, and yet you committed the most heinous crime. All children deserve to be protected, you told me that."

"They were tainted by association. Do you truly believe we could have taken them in? The children would have grown into adults who revolted." He ran his finger along the edge of the cutlass. "I trusted you."

"You shouldn't have."

He faced her. "It was you and I against the world."

"No, Zane," she whispered. "It was you trying to *destroy* the world. It stops here. I won't let you hurt anyone else."

"So, this is the end?"

End her, the voices howled.

Maeve pulled a short sword from the sheath crossing her back. "For you, it is."

Then, she attacked.

***

He walked slowly from the tent, his sister's body swaying in his arms. Her blood seeped through his shirt and ran down his body. A lone tear dripped down his cheek. It had been years since he'd cried.

Zane glanced down at her pale face, her eyes closed in death. They'd spent close to a millennium together. It was unreal to think he'd never see her glare at him or utter something sarcastic. Even in her last gasping moments, she'd spared no affection for him.

"It is only a matter of time before you join me," she'd said. "There isn't enough suffering for you to endure to make up for what you've done." Maeve had smiled. "I was the one who let Sage go." With that final statement, the life had faded from her eyes.

He lifted his head and dropped to his knees in the forest. The betrayal cut too deep. The warlord placed his traitorous sister on the ground, threw his head back, and screamed. It didn't release his anguish or rage.

His hands shook when he tightened the bandage around his neck. The war drums beat an incessant march, and the sounds of battle filtered to his ears. Aermia had made its move.

He caressed his sister's face once, then stood. He strode toward the dragon and smiled.

Pain, death, triumph.

"Indeed." He tossed his head back and laughed before shouting, "I will find you, consort!"

She couldn't be far away.

Neither could Scythia's victory.

Chapter Fifty

Sage

"I will find you, consort!"

The warlord's voice cut right through, and, without realizing it, Sage seized Dor's hand. Sage widened her eyes and shook her head. They barely breathed as the warlord strode past the dragon, sputtering madness and curses. The hairs prickled along her arms, and her pulse thundered in her ears.

Sage turned her neck and stared at the dragon's wing. Was the warlord waiting just on the other side? A shiver ran down her spine.

Enough of this.

With difficulty, she battled back the fear. If her monster was lurking outside, he would have already been taunting her.

"We need to get out of here," she whispered. "It's not safe."

Dor nodded. "How do you plan on getting her out?" She pointed to

Lilja.

Sage eyed her aunt who had passed out again. She grimaced. Getting them both through the camp would be nearly impossible with the warlord hunting them. Although the chaos in the camp might be enough to conceal their escape, it wasn't going to be easy.

"Unless you plan on coming with us?" Sage asked.

The young woman shifted her dark eyes back to Lilja. "I cannot go with you. I must get Illya into the skies. Someone is bound to come back to harness him. I can take your kin with me." Dor turned back her. "You can come as well. Illya can take us all away from this place."

Freedom.

It was so temtping, but she had to see this through. The warlord could not be allowed to continue his tyranny. While it would be so easy to fly away on the dragon, it would be cowardly. She couldn't run away.

"I can't," she said with regret. "I must fight with my people."

Dor squeezed her fingers and released her hand. "That, I understand. I will take the Sirenidae somewhere safe and return. I will be watching over you from the skies." She clicked softly, and the dragon clicked back. "It's clear. I'll get your kin onto Illya, and you get as far from this place as possible."

"I can do that."

The women crawled to each side of Lilja and threw her arms over their shoulders. Sage gritted her teeth, as pain ricocheted through her ribs when they lifted her aunt. It was uncoordinated, and Sage kept looking over her shoulder when they crept from beneath the dragon's wing. They managed to get Lilja settled behind Illya's haunches, with Dor right behind her.

Sage tried to climb down from the dragon gently, but ended up sliding down his leathery wing. She landed in a crouch and smiled at

Illya. "Thank you."

The beast blinked its silvery eye once, and she took that as an acknowledgment. "Be safe," she whispered and stepped back. The child in her wanted to stay and watch the dragon take flight, but she knew that would be a mistake.

Sage jogged to the nearest tent and peeked inside. No one. She slipped inside and scanned the room. It was a disaster: weapons, armor, and clothing lay everywhere. Once again, she stole one of the cloaks and tossed it over her own soiled ensemble, the filched weapons clinking in her pockets.

Shouts ruptured the air, and she froze. With silent steps, she lifted the tent flap slightly. The dragon had opened his wings and sprung from the ground. A grin curled her lips. Lilja and Illya were out of the warlord's grasp. That felt *good*.

She let the canvas flap close and tiptoed to the rear of the tent. Carefully slipping her blade into the canvas, she cut a slit and peeked out. Sounds came from every direction, but it didn't seem like danger was heading specifically for her. Sage crept away and slunk through the sea of Scythian tents.

More snow began to fall, and she shivered, pausing when warriors jogged toward her from the right. Sage pressed herself against the nearest tent, and prayed it was enough to conceal her. Her enemies bypassed her without so much as looking toward her shadowed spot.

Releasing her breath, she tipped her head back. Her eyes rounded, and her mouth gaped. Fire lit up the *sky*. It seemed like liquid flames poured from the belly of a dragon. What the bloody hell? None of the dragons she'd read about as a child could accomplish something of that magnitude. Fire and ice battled with each other, along with the shrieks of man and beast.

The sounds of pain, death, victory.

Sage caught her breath, keeping a steady eye on her surroundings as she slipped from her hiding place. She stealthily wove through the camp, observing the Aermian force pushing the Scythians deeper into their camp. Smoke filled the air, and her eyes began to water. Her people were right there. She could join them.

You can't let the monster escape.

She panted. Even though he was evil, she still didn't want his death on her hands. It would be just one more nightmare to haunt her for the rest of her days. It was a selfish thought.

Finish this.

"Consort!" the warlord's voice roared.

Sage shuddered and stiffened. It was as if he could sense that she was thinking of him. He couldn't know where she was. Her feet were rooted to the ground, as if his voice held complete power over her.

"You cannot run from your destiny. This is our legacy. You cannot run from me! I will always find you!"

That was her worst fear. No matter what she did, he always seemed to come back.

Don't let fear cripple you. He is just a man.

Her hands trembled as an idea formed in her mind. He needed to be drawn out, and she was the key to that. The Aermian line wasn't far, and the warlord was weakened and unstable. A well-placed swing could end his life.

"I'm crazy," she muttered.

Sage eyed the area around her, trying to muster up the courage to reveal her position. Once she did, he'd be onto her. She'd only have moments to get to where she needed to be.

The war drumbeat synchronized with her heart, and she barely paid any mind to the Scythian soldiers that ran past as orange flames danced along the tops of tents in the distance. The time for stealth was over. It was time to fight.

"I've never been yours!" she shouted, her legs already in motion as she sprinted through the tents toward the battlefront. Even with the noise, she knew he'd hear her.

One heartbeat.

Two.

Three.

Sage put on a burst of speed and bolted toward the thickest fighting. She almost stumbled when she ran past the last line of tents. The earth and sky were teeming with motion—not only that, but the Scythian resistance had arrived.

"That is enough," a deep voice rumbled.

Sage skidded to a stop, and yanked two daggers from her pockets as she spun and faced the monster. The battle seemed to freeze in a watercolor painting as she faced her most bitter enemy.

Ten paces separated them.

It wasn't enough.

The warlord panted hard, his body almost swollen, like he was too big for his own skin. His obsidian eyes had now lost any pretense of civility, holding only rage and hunger.

"What are you?" she murmured.

He smiled. "Everything and nothing."

He held his hand out. She noticed how it trembled. Was he on the edge of losing himself to the berserker rage? The scars at her throat throbbed in phantom pain. Time to tread carefully.

"You cannot leave. You know your place is here." He tipped his chin toward the battle. "We can stop this bloodshed once and for all. This is our future." He held his hand out farther, bidding her to come closer and join him. "Come."

Once again, Sage was at a crossroads. The last time he'd offered his hand, she'd almost taken it, nearly believing his lies. The only thing she felt this time was disgust.

Sage squared off and shifted into a defensive position. She couldn't allow him to get to her. He was too far gone. If the warlord got his hands on her, he'd kill her.

"Fighting me until the bitter end." He chuckled. "How like you, wild one. I will enjoy breaking you more than I should. Just know you brought the pain upon yourself and those around you."

She snorted. He was the only demon here.

"I only wanted what was best for you," he whispered. For a moment, he looked like a lost little boy. It threw her off-kilter.

Then, he *blurred.*

She threw both her blades at his heart and yanked two more from her pockets when he halted two steps from her. Her mouth bobbed as she stared at one of her daggers buried in his chest, along with five arrows. He took another step toward her, and more arrows hit him.

Sage ducked, and bile burned her throat as his pained gaze met hers.

"From the moment I saw you, I knew you'd be my downfall," he wheezed.

Rooted to the spot, she flinched as he brushed his bloody fingers along her left cheek. This couldn't be real.

He stumbled forward and dropped to his knees before her. The warlord reached for her, and it broke her from the mental ice that had kept her captive. Sage skittered back several steps, and stared as blood leaked from the corner of his mouth.

What the bloody hell had happened? Where had those arrows come from? Her hands shook, and she dropped the daggers. Was this really how his reign of terror ended?

"Please," he gurgled. "Don't leave me."

A last plea.

A final time, he held his hand out, looking completely vulnerable. Heat pressed at the back of her eyes and tears spilled down her cheeks. All she could see was the abused little boy that he used to be.

Sage dashed away the tears and hardened her resolve. He didn't deserve anything from her. Abuse did not excuse the vile choices he'd made. If any other criminal had made the same last request, she would have granted it, but not him.

"You deserve to die alone," she whispered harshly.

Sage backed away, making sure he couldn't come after her. He toppled onto his side, his mouth forming words she didn't want to see. She turned her back on him and walked into battle. Blair and Hayjen stalked toward her, both wielding bows. She touched her uncle's side as he passed her, but she kept moving toward battle.

The warlord would never take anything from anyone again. He would never hurt her again. Her conscience nagged at her to look over her shoulder, but Sage didn't. She kept her attention straight ahead.

He's gone.

Even in death, she wouldn't give him one more second of her time.

Scanning the battlefield, she numbly watched as the war raged on, all the warlord's soldiers completely ignorant to the death of their leader.

It was fitting that the monster who had terrorized the world for so long had disappeared from the earth without a sound.

She pulled two more wicked-looking daggers with serrated edges from her pockets. A warrior caught her eye and charged.

Sage smiled—more of a dark slash of her lips, baring teeth—before diving into the fray.

No rest for the wicked.

CHAPTER FIFTY-ONE

Tehl

Tehl shouldn't find death so beautiful.

He stumbled to a stop as he caught sight of the most stunning thing he'd ever laid his eyes upon. His wife fought two warriors, her complete focus on the enemy. Each moment was almost too fluid and fast for him to track.

Hell's handmaiden.

Rafe appeared to his left, panting. He took one look at Tehl's expression and followed his gaze. "Finally."

"So, what's the plan?" a deep female voice asked.

Tehl glared at Blaise. "What the blazes are you doing on the battlefield?"

The Scythian woman gave him a gleeful smile. "Fighting."

"And your leg?" Rafe eyed said leg, which was weeping blood. His lips thinned.

"Nothing some herbs and rest can't heal. Both of which I can get when this is over."

Tehl pressed his lips together so as not to smile. Blaise was one of the fiercest people he'd ever met. "We'll come around back. We can't afford to distract her."

Blaise scanned the fray. "Where is he?"

"That was my question," Rafe muttered. "I can't see the warlord."

"Where Sage is, he's not far behind," Tehl murmured. "Keep an eye out. Let's move."

In tandem, they began working their way toward Sage. But with every enemy they felled, another took his place. He spun, thrusting his sword backward into a warrior as Sage caught Tehl's eye. His heart stopped, and everything went silent around him. She didn't smile. There was no expression on her face.

What happened to you?

Years seemed to pass as they watched each other. Like the sun thawing ice, her expression melted into a gorgeous smile. Covered in mud, snow, and blood, she was his picture of perfection.

They crashed together, and he couldn't help himself. Tehl captured her lips in a quick, rough kiss. "Are you okay?"

"He's gone," she whispered.

He couldn't have heard that right. Before he had a chance to ask her more, they were swept into battle once again.

A battle cry tore through the air. Tehl frowned. Where the devil had that come from? Almost as soon as the thought went through his head, soldiers burst from the Scythian camp and *attacked* their own warriors.

Blair's rebels.

He smiled.

It was a beautiful conglomerate of mankind fighting against evil.

And they were going to win.

Chapter Fifty-Two

Mira

Gav's fever broke.

And she wept. Like a baby.

Once again, she placed the back of her hand over his brow, just to check. It was a normal temperature. She sighed and pulled her hand back. The morning light warmed the east side of the tent, and she stretched.

Her brows furrowed when Gav's breathing became louder. Her attention snapped to his chest. He wasn't breathing any differently. What the hell?

Then it dawned on her.

He wasn't breathing louder. It was *silent* outside. The war drums were silent.

She'd become so accustomed to the incessant beat of the Scythian war drums that she couldn't remember a time without them. Her hands shook, and she took one of Gav's hands in her own as hope unfurled in her chest.

"They've done it, Gav. They've done it," she whispered.

"Done what?" his deep, rusty voice rumbled.

Mira's lips parted in surprise as his eyes opened, his purple gems locked on hers.

"They've defeated Scythia," she murmured, beyond happy to see him awake. Her breath caught as he gave her a huge smile and squeezed her hand.

Today, miracles did happen.

CHAPTER FIFTY-THREE

Jasmine

Jasmine pulled her arms close to her torso, her whole body shivering. She tipped her head back and wheezed out a breath, staring at the dark skies that were beginning to lighten. The worst of the storm had passed, but the sea was still angry.

Another wave crashed over Jasmine, dousing her with icy water. The little boat groaned, but held. How much longer, she didn't know. She eyed the two rocks that pinned the boat in place. Thank the stars for the rocks. If it hadn't been for them, she was sure she'd have died hours prior.

It was still a possibility.

There was still so much distance between herself and the shore, not to mention it was littered with sharp rocks and coral. One wrong wave, and she'd be dashed to pieces against the stones. She had to do something. The labor pains were coming faster now, and she was already so exhausted.

Jasmine ran a shaking hand over the swell of her belly. "It's okay, little one," she said, her teeth chattering. "I will make sure you're all right."

The sea swelled and pulled back toward the open ocean. *That wasn't good.*

Jasmine glanced over her shoulder, her eyes widening as another huge wave rushed toward her.

Bloody hell.

She managed to curl in on herself as the wave crashed into her. The little boat cracked and splintered apart. Jasmine tumbled forward, her side scraping against the rock. Water rushed into her ears, and her hair caught on some coral and was torn from her scalp. She clawed at the water, and her head broke the surface. She sputtered and managed two breaths before another wave hit, once again shoving her beneath the water.

Something sharp sliced into her leg, and she cried out, water flooding her mouth. Jasmine kicked as hard as she could, her lungs desperate for air, and she managed to make it to the surface again. She gasped and tried to tread water. She didn't have much of a choice now. It was sink or swim.

Despite the fatigue saturating her limbs, she managed four strokes before her belly contracted again. She glanced to the left, just catching a fin as it sank beneath the waves, and she turned in that direction, while trying to breathe through the pain. Jasmine gritted her teeth and fought to stay as still as possible. The pain passed after a minute, but she didn't actively move from her spot. She just treaded water. Panic and fear held her in place. She didn't want to do anything to attract the leviathan's attention.

He already knows you're here. Just move slowly. You can't stay here.

She released a small whimper and kicked her legs. Exhaustion pressed down on her, and her limbs faltered. She made it only a few paces when the next contraction slammed into her. She grunted at the immense pain and crossed her legs. She lost all coordination and wrapped her arms around her belly, sinking beneath the surface. The agony seemed to go on forever.

Tiredly, she fought her way back to the fresh air, and she cried softly. The shore was too far away, and the closest rock looked impossible to climb.

She hissed when she felt the contractions coming again. A short scream flew from her parted lips as she tried to stay afloat, but she just didn't have the energy.

Jasmine began to sink again. She tipped her head back, trying to get as much air as possible, just as hands wrapped beneath her armpits. She let out a loud sob when the person maneuvered her so her back was against their chest, keeping her afloat. She moaned through the rest of the pain, hands fisting in her torn robe and nightgown. Her body sagged when it was over.

"That's it," crooned a deep, sensual female voice. There was only one group of people Jasmine knew with a voice like that. A Sirenidae. "You're doing amazing."

She leaned her cheek against the Sirenidae's chest and breathed in her amazing scent. "God, you smell good."

The woman chuckled. "I've been told that before."

Jasmine wheezed a laugh that turned into more sobs. "I can't do this."

"Yes, you can. You're so strong."

She didn't feel strong. Her eyelids lowered. "I'm so tired."

"I know, *ma fille*. Just take a little rest. I'll keep you and the babe safe."

Tears of gratitude rushed down Jasmine's cheeks. "I can't. The pains are too close."

"Just focus on your breathing," the Sirenidae crooned.

Jasmine nodded and tried to regulate her breathing. Her belly contracted again, and she squeezed her eyes shut. Her breath was completely robbed from her when the pain became so acute she thought she'd surely pass out. She opened her eyes and screamed when she caught sight of two dorsal fins that were too close.

"Peace," the Sirenidae said. "They are welcoming the child you bring into the world. The beasts are sensitive to such things and usually observe our births beneath the seas. It's an honor." She began to hum a soft melody that vibrated through Jasmine's shoulders.

It didn't feel very honoring, more like terrifying. But the agony was too intense for her to focus on the leviathans.

"That's it," the woman crooned. "You're so brave. Just breathe."

The pain receded but still crouched low in her abdomen. That could only mean one thing. Her eyes widened. "How close are we to the shore?"

"We've just entered the cove."

Jasmine gazed around, just realizing the waves had gentled to a soft lap against her wet skin. "The babe is going to drown," she cried.

"No. I've seen such things in the past. Giving birth is natural. The babe won't even realize she's parted from your womb."

"Except for the frigid water."

"Don't worry. There's a place just ahead."

Another pain hit Jasmine.

Then another.

And another.

She hardly noticed as the cove narrowed, and the water warmed significantly.

Jasmine shook, and she blinked dazedly around when her feet touched the sand beneath the water. She sighed, enjoying the brief moment of reprieve. "Thank you," she whispered as heat began to enter her limbs again. "The water is warm."

"A natural spring," the Sirenidae explained. She rotated Jasmine until she carried her like a bride. Jas blinked at the woman. She looked like the woman Sam had been kissing. She shook her head. Her luck couldn't be that bad.

She doubled over when the next wave of pain hit her. "I think it's time, and I don't know what I'm doing."

"You're doing great. Birth is natural. Your body knows what it's doing."

"But it's too soon," Jasmine cried, clinging to the woman.

"Everything will be okay." She settled Jasmine with her back against a log that had fallen at the edge of the water, then moved to kneel between Jasmine's floating legs. "When the next one comes, you push."

Jas nodded and bore down with a grunt.

"Wonderful," the Sirenidae crooned. "A few more like that and your babe will be here."

Another contraction and more pain, burning. Jasmine grabbed the log and squeezed it, her teeth gritted.

"The head is crowning. You're doing amazing, Jasmine. Just a little more."

Jasmine pushed and yelled, her voice echoing around them.

"The head is out. Just the shoulders."

The pain retreated and Jasmine sucked in ragged breaths. "I'm so tired."

"I know, *ma fille*. Your babe is almost here. Now push!"

Jas tipped her chin down and pushed with everything she had. One moment, she was in agony, and the next, there was relief. Her jaw dropped as the Sirenidae caught her babe.

"It's a girl!"

The woman lifted the infant from the water, rolled her onto her belly and thumped her on the back. The infant coughed up liquid and then released a piercing cry. Jasmine smiled, tears running down her cheeks as the Sirenidae handed the babe to her.

A daughter.

The infant nuzzled into her chest, and Jasmine pulled the cloth away so they were skin to skin. Her daughter was so tiny, petite rosebud lips puckered. All she could feel was love.

"You did it."

Jasmine tore her gaze from her daughter and held her other arm out to the Sirenidae. "Thank you so much."

The woman wiped tears from her own cheeks and then held her hand, moving closer. "She's beautiful."

Beautiful was too pale of a word.

"What will you name her?"

Jasmine stared at her daughter's closed eyes. "I don't know." Her brows furrowed. "What's your name?"

"Mer."

"Mer," Jas murmured. "That's pretty—a sea name. I think she needs a sea name, don't you?"

"I think a sea name would be fitting for your little warrior."

She smiled, brushing a finger across the infant's black hair. "I don't know any."

"What about Lana? It means calm as still waters," Mer whispered.

"Lana." She tested the word on her tongue. She liked it. "Is Lana your name?" she crooned to the baby. Her daughter sighed and cuddled closer. "I think she likes it."

Jasmine's own eyelids began to lower, and her body sagged. She was so tired. Mer wrapped an arm around her back and wedged herself between the log and Jasmine, so her long legs bracketed Jasmine's. Mer enfolded her arms around Jasmine and Lana.

"Rest for a little while. I'll watch over you."

That was the last thing Jasmine heard before her body gave out.

Chapter Fifty-Four

Mer

"Mer."

She opened her eyes and turned toward the familiar voice.

Her grandfather stood waist-deep in the spring, his long silver hair hanging in wet ropes. She eyed him, trying to get a read on his mood. His magenta eyes so similar to her own, gave nothing away.

"My lord," she replied, overly respectful. It never hurt to be respectful, especially when one had committed treason.

"You went against my wishes," he said softly.

She swallowed around the lump in her throat. Even though his words were softly spoken, it felt like a slap. Growing up, he'd never raised his voice, but the disappointed tone he used seemed worse than physical punishment. She'd let him down. But even knowing that, Mer wouldn't go back. Going behind his back had been wrong, but so had his choice to leave the kingdoms at a disadvantage to the Scythians. Mer lifted her chin the smallest bit and refused to cower. Whatever punishment she received, she'd take it with her head held high.

Jasmine moaned and stirred in her arms but didn't wake. The poor thing was exhausted. Mer's heart beat a little faster when she thought about what could have happened to Sam's wife if she hadn't discovered Jasmine in time. The babe sighed and snuggled closer to Jasmine's chest, pulling her grandfather's attention. His expression softened, and he drew closer, water rippling around them.

"How was it?" he asked.

Mer smiled. "While the babe was a hard time coming, Jasmine fought. They both are worn out but healthy. Aren't they beautiful?"

Her grandfather gently drew a large, damp finger across the infant's downy little head of dark hair. "Children are a blessing."

She couldn't agree more. Mer gazed down at the pair with wonder. A new life was an absolute miracle. What Jasmine had accomplished was nothing short of extraordinary.

"Her name?"

"Lana," Mer whispered, resituating both babe and mother more comfortably in her arms.

"That's a good name," her grandfather murmured, his musical voice sweet in her ears. He pulled away and both fell into silence as the morning sun broke the patchy clouds. "You know I cannot let this go without punishment."

Mer's lips thinned, and she nodded.

"Many Sirenidae lost their lives. There must be justice for those souls." His heavy hand landed on her shoulder and squeezed. "I love you, but tough decisions will be made in the future. Ones that will hurt me as much as they will hurt you."

Had that statement come from anyone else, she wouldn't have

believed them, but her grandfather loved her, and he meant what he said. Going against her grandfather's wishes would ultimately lead to her banishment from the sea—from her parents—from her people. Her heart squeezed painfully, but she knew she'd done the right thing.

"I'm sorry I hurt you." That much, she was very sorry for.

"I know, *ma fille*. As am I, as am I."

The resignation in his tone caused her eyes to burn. He was telling her goodbye. The next time they met, he'd be exiling her.

"This is the Spymaster's wife," she said softly, changing the subject. "I cannot leave her alone. Would you please let him know where we are? He's aboard the *Dauntless*."

"It will be done."

He leaned close and kissed her forehead. Mer closed her eyes, her tears trying to break free. This was their final moment before everything changed.

"I love you," she croaked.

He pulled away and smiled tenderly at her. "I love you far more than you could ever know." Then, he turned his back and disappeared silently into the water—ripples the only proof he'd ever been there.

Mer tipped her head back and peered up at the sky, just as soft morning light began to peek over the trees and cascade over the spring. Her heart hurt, but at least she knew she wouldn't be alone. While Lilja was gone, she still had her uncle, Sam, and... her gaze dropped down to Jasmine and Lana.

A family. Even if part of hers was gone.

Ream had died and Lana was here.

One life extinguished, one lit.

In that moment, she let herself cry for everything lost, and for everything gained. A wobbly smile touched her lips as tears coursed down her cheeks, mouth, and chin. No matter where she was, she'd find family.

CHAPTER FIFTY-FIVE

Sam

Sam pulled on the reins. His horse slowed to a stop and he swung his leg over his mount and landed on the ground with knees bent. He briskly strode through the foliage, not taking his normal care to silence his steps. All he cared about was getting to his wife.

His heart raced in his chest, and the air seemed to be thinner. After the hellish night before, he'd only expected more bad news when the Sirenidae king had appeared on his ship, morose and wet. When the king revealed the news about Jasmine, it was almost impossible to believe. Sam hadn't given up looking for her; he just hadn't expected the information of her whereabouts to drop into his lap.

It had taken him ten seconds to board a rowboat and head toward shore. As soon as his feet touched sand, he'd hit the ground running, grabbing the first mount he came across. Technically, he was a thief, but he'd pay the family handsomely and return the horse once he retrieved his wife.

And child.

Sam swallowed hard. The king hadn't revealed much other than Jasmine had borne a child, and Mer was protecting her in the cove with the warm spring.

The babe had arrived early.

His anxiety ratcheted up and his strides lengthened. Was Jasmine all right? Was the babe healthy? He'd seen when infants were born before their time. They weren't always whole. His lips thinned. Even if the child wasn't what his world considered normal, he'd love the babe all the same.

The sound of water lapping at the shore reached his ears, as he pushed through the last vestiges of thick shrubbery and trees. Sunlight danced over the gently rippling water that kissed the white sandy edges. It was utter paradise. But that was not what stole his breath.

Mer sat waist-deep in the water, leaning against a log with her arms wrapped around Jasmine and the small bundle in her arms. Sam was rooted to the spot as he soaked in the sight of his sleeping wife. Her dark lashes rested against her cheeks, paler than normal. She was covered in bruises and scratches, but nothing serious-looking. His attention dropped to the infant nestled in her arms, cuddled against her bare chest, wrapped in Mer's sealskin.

"You can come closer," Mer's melodious voice whispered.

Sam jerked out of his stupor and yanked his boots and socks off before wading into the warm water. He was careful to move slowly so as not to create more ripples in the spring. Heat pressed at the back of his eyes when he caught sight of the tiny babe sleeping in his wife's arms. He'd never forget this moment. Ever.

"Come meet your daughter, Sam."

A daughter.

He sank to his knees, white sand mixing with the water around them. Sam reached out and hesitated only a moment before running one fingertip across the dark fuzzy hair that covered the infant's head. So soft.

A tantalizing scent caught his attention, but he ignored it the best he could. Just the Lure. "How did you find them?" Mer didn't answer. He pulled his attention from his family and studied Mer's profile. She gazed blankly ahead. "Mer?"

"I found her floundering in the waves with the Leviathan circling her." Although the words were softly spoken, they struck fear into his heart. "It was a lucky thing that I came upon her when I did."

His gaze dropped back to his daughter and wife. He had been so close to losing them, and he hadn't even known. "How did you know where to look?" he rasped. "Or did you come upon them in your patrol?"

"A Scythian survivor pleaded with me to find her. I knew it was Jasmine as soon as he spoke about her pregnancy."

While her words rang true, Sam couldn't help but feel like there was something she left out. "The warrior?"

"Probably being picked up by one of the patrols now."

His lip curled. Probably one of her abductors. "They will regret—" His growled words disturbed his daughter. The babe squirmed and released a small squall.

Jasmine roused and cuddled the infant closer, crooning softly, "It's okay, precious." Her stormy gaze wandered to his, and his heart began to race once again. Stars, she was stunning. "Are you really here?" Her voice was scratchy, like she'd screamed herself hoarse.

Sam's lips trembled as he smiled at her. "I am, Jas."

One tear coursed down her cheek as she stared at him with huge, tired eyes. Sam leaned forward and cupped her wet cheek. She sighed and pressed her face into his palm.

"I can't believe you're here," she cried, bottom lip wobbling. "You found me. You finally found me."

Sam swallowed the lump in his throat. "We made a deal, remember? We stick together."

"The twins?" she asked.

"Missing you, but healthy and safe."

More tears coursed down his wife's face faster than he could wipe them away. Jasmine adjusted his daughter in her arms, water rippling around them. The babe blinked her tiny eyes, revealing blue orbs just like her mum.

"She's stunning, love," Sam whispered in awe, and a lone tear escaped the corner of his eye as the babe's gaze latched onto his own. It was as if she knew who he was. Extraordinary. He gently ran his thumb over his daughter's tiny ear. She was so small and perfect.

"I know we hadn't settled on a name," Jasmine said softly. She glanced over her shoulder at Mer and then back to Sam. "But it seems fitting to give her a sea name because of how she was born. What do you think of Lana?"

"Lana," Sam whispered. "What does it mean?"

"Calm as still waters."

His daughter still hadn't looked away from him, placid as a lake. "I think it suits her." He touched her little fingers. "Hello, Lana. I'm your papa. I'm sorry I wasn't here to welcome you into the world, but I promise to be here every moment from now on."

"Sam," Mer said.

He forced himself to break his stare off with his daughter, and for the first time noticed how haggard and broken his friend looked.

"What's wrong?"

"Nothing." Mer tried to smile, but it didn't fool him. "We need to get Jasmine and Lana back to the castle. She needs to see a proper healer. If you take Lana, I can carry Jas."

Jasmine held out the bundle, and he gingerly took Lana from her arms. She was even littler in his arms. Mer stood and helped Jasmine to her feet, water dripping down their bodies. His friend swept Jas into her arms, and Sam shook his head. He always forgot how strong the Sirenidae were.

"You have a cloak?" Mer asked, flowing toward the opposite shore.

"I do," he mumbled, preoccupied with taking slow, cautious steps so as not to jostle his daughter.

They moved back to the stolen horse, and Mer sat Jasmine gently on the ground before wrapping his cloak around his shivering wife. Jas looked one second from passing out. Mer held her hands out, and he reluctantly released his daughter into her care. He bent down and smiled at Jasmine, quickly stealing a kiss.

"You're amazing," he breathed as he lifted her onto the horse. She groaned. "Are you okay?"

Jasmine winced. "I have to be."

He frowned and wished he had a coach or something. Sam mounted behind her and gazed down at Mer, who was singing softly to Lana.

"Be good for your mum, *ma fille*. I'll see you soon." The Sirenidae carefully handed Lana up to Jasmine. His wife tucked Lana inside of the cloak, crooning softly at the fussing infant.

"Thank you," Sam murmured. The words were too plain for what he felt. If Mer hadn't found his wife, Jasmine and Lana wouldn't be here. "I owe you more than I can express. Whatever you need, if it is within my power, I will give it."

Mer nodded, her expression grave. "I may need a place to sleep in the future."

"Done," he said. "You will always have a place with us."

She smiled. "Goodbye."

Sam guided the horse around and set a gentle pace toward Sanee.

"Are we going home?" Jas rasped.

"Yes, we're going home."

Where they belonged. Together.

Chapter Fifty-Six

Sage

Blair stood to Sage's left, and Tehl to her right.

It had taken only two days to secure the rest of the Scythian army.

Now, Blair's men brought three chained Scythian commanders before them and forced the warriors to their knees. She stared at their handsome faces, unaffected. Beauty often hid the ugliest qualities of a person.

From the corner of her eye, she caught sight of mud-caked boots. Sage forced herself not to look in his direction. The warlord's body was a garish sight after the rebels had gotten ahold of him.

Blair stepped forward. "Jacobi, Demdai, and Phenrir. Your warlord has fallen, and Scythia is now under the command of Aermia."

"You traitor," Phenrir spat. "I always said the way you treated your *gift* was unnatural. You would sacrifice your kingdom for a half-blood wife and her spawn?"

The commander didn't react to the taunt, even though Sage wanted to slap him across the face for such a remark. She glanced down the line to where Dor stood, her dragon a hulking, silent threat. Sage wouldn't be insulting a woman with a dragon if she was him. Illya was looking at Phenrir like he'd be a great snack.

She focused back on the Scythian commanders kneeling in the dark slush.

"Are we to be executed?" Jacobi asked mildly.

His tone surprised Sage. Almost every Scythian she'd met, who supported the warlord, wore an air of superiority. This man, however, did not. Interesting.

"This is not an execution," Blair said sternly. "We are not without mercy. Living under the warlord and his laws was not an easy life. That being said, you can fall into line or go to prison for the crimes you've committed against your people as well as the kingdoms of Aermia, Methia, Sirenidae, and Nagali."

It was still bizarre to hear the name Nagali. It boggled her mind that the warlord had been able to keep a remnant of the Nagali people hidden for hundreds of years. While she was thankful, it also broke her heart for what they must have suffered.

"While I appreciate your words, it's not you I would like to hear them from." Jacobi turned his coffee-colored gaze on Sage. "With the warlord dead, you are now our ruler. What are your orders?"

Sage blinked slowly. "I am married to the crown prince of Aermia."

Jacobi nodded. "That being said, the warlord declared you his consort, and in the event of his death or his inability to rule, leadership of our kingdom shifts to you."

That couldn't be true. She looked to Blair, who winced. Sage smoothed her expression as her mind scrambled.

"You expect me to bow down to the warlord's Aermian consort?" Demdai finally spoke up. "She's a foreigner. I could tolerate him tumbling her, but ruling our kingdom? She'll be killed before the week is over."

"Is that a threat?" Tehl murmured.

Demdai glared at Tehl. "Not a threat but a fact."

"Enough," Blair said softly. He held his hand out to Sage, his gaze steady, seemingly asking her to trust him. "Consort."

She prided herself on the fact that her expression didn't change and that her fingers didn't tremble when she took his hand. "Commander."

"Today, you are charged with the care of the Scythian people."

"Mark my words, the people will rebel. *I'll* rebel," Phenrir snarled.

Sage glared at the insolent warrior, putting on her best scary face. These men had only ever known fear and manipulation. Maybe it was the only thing they understood.

"You don't have much of a choice," she hissed. Sage pointed a finger at the warlord's body. "I'm sure death doesn't scare a big warrior like you." She smiled. "But what if your family lost all its wealth, and your sons were taken into Aermian captivity indefinitely?"

The man paled slightly even as he glared daggers at her. Not her best negotiation, but it got him in line.

"Your camp will be disbanded, and anyone hostile will be taken prisoner or killed." She straightened and stared at them. "This week, a treaty will be drafted, which I will sign, and then I will appoint a capable regent." Sage paused, making sure she had the attention of all three warriors. "If you think to take advantage of my generosity by not executing you on the spot, or you get it into your head to rebel or break the treaty, the power of the united kingdoms will invade Scythia, and you'll never recover. Do you understand me?"

"Yes, my lady," the men muttered.

She nodded and turned her back on them, barely able to stand. What had just happened?

"Long live the lady warlord!" shouted Jacobi.

Sage snarled. By the time she was done, there would be no warlords left.

Chapter Fifty-Seven

Hayjen

He couldn't take his eyes off her for one moment.

Hayjen held her warm hand between his own, and tried to imprint every detail of her face into his mind. In the time since he believed her dead, his memory had distorted her face slightly. Nothing too serious, but enough to surprise him for such a short time.

Lilja sighed and opened her eyes, revealing the magenta orbs that had struck him speechless the first time he'd seen her. She smiled at him, her whole expression lighting up, robbing him of his breath. Tears gathered in the corners of his eyes, and her expression softened.

"Hey, handsome," she crooned. Lilja cupped his left cheek with her other hand, her own eyes filling with tears. "I missed you."

He slid from his stool, landing on his knees, and scooped her body against his, burying his face in her silver hair. "I thought you were gone," he choked out. His shoulders began to shake with silent sobs, his tears wetting her hair. Lilja stroked a hand through his hair, murmuring lyrical nonsense.

What had he done to get so lucky? They'd received a second chance. "Don't ever leave me again. I can't bear it."

"Never," she whispered. "Never again."

"Where you go, I go." He lifted his head, wiped his face with the back of his arm, and stared down into her beautiful face. "Promise me."

She studied him, her own face damp. "Where you go, I go. That's the way it's always been, yeah?"

"Always."

"Is it really over? Is he gone?" Lilja asked.

"He's gone," Hayjen said gruffly, not wanting to spare a moment of thought for the demon that had taken his wife from him.

She closed her eyes. "He can't hurt anyone else."

"That's right, love."

"We've been fighting so long to rid him from the world, it's almost surreal." Lilja sucked in a deep breath. "You're sure he's gone?"

A dark emotion that he didn't want to acknowledge slid through his chest at the remembrance of putting three arrows into the warlord's back. "He's gone. We left his body to rot on the battlefield. Soldiers have been guarding the corpse to make sure no one tries to give him a proper burial, that the monster doesn't deserve."

"May I enter?" a deep voice called from outside.

Hayjen turned toward the entrance as Blair pushed into the tent. His attention zeroed in on Lilja, and he grinned, love clear on his face. At one time, Hayjen had been jealous of Blair and Lilja's relationship. It took several years for him to understand the depth of their connection. While they loved each other deeply, they were never *in* love with each other. Their experiences had bonded them.

Blair moved deeper into the room, knelt by Hayjen's side, and pulled him into a brief hug before caressing Lilja's cheek. "How are you feeling, Lil?"

She grimaced. "Better and worse. I need to get to the sea."

Blair nodded and pulled his hand away. "I figured as much. Are you—"

"I'll survive." Lilja smiled at her oldest friend and then turned her attention back to Hayjen. "He'll take good care of me." She flicked a glance toward the entrance. "I met your daughter."

"So she told me," Blair said.

"A Dragon Song," Hayjen whispered. He couldn't believe it. Lil had spoken of such things as being real, but hearing about it and seeing it in person was another thing. "We owe her much."

"It is nothing among family," Blair murmured.

"What are you going to do?" Hayjen asked.

"Do?"

"She's the heir to the Nagali throne, is she not?"

Their oldest friend sighed, looking years older. He hung his head and rubbed his forehead. "She has her own path to forge. I have done my best to train and raise her, but I worry for her. Restoring Nagali will not happen in a day."

"Will you not go with her?" Lilja asked.

"Not immediately. Scythia still needs me, but the Nagali people need her."

Hayjen mulled that over. Dorcus would need guidance and protection. He slowly focused on Lilja, who was already staring at him. Words didn't need to be said. He could almost read her mind. She wanted to go with Dor—to protect Blair's daughter. She was ready for a new adventure, and... his gaze wandered to the entrance again. Sage was settled, more or less. His niece had come into her own and didn't *need* them anymore.

"We will accompany Dor to Nagali," he said.

Blair blinked slowly, relief coloring his expression. "It would put my mind at ease to know both of you were looking out for Dorcus and counseling her."

"We will care for her as if she were our own," Lilja rasped. "It would give me nothing but pleasure to get to know your daughter."

Their oldest friend nodded, his gaze suspiciously shiny, and pressed a quick kiss onto her forehead. "You were always a blessing."

"I love you," Lilja uttered.

"And I you."

The two friends shared a look of understanding before Blair clasped Hayjen on the shoulder one last time and stood. "There's to be a meeting of the kingdom rulers. I will pass this information on to them. Is there anything you wish for them to know?"

"Just that she's awake," Hayjen said. Sage would want to know.

"It will be done."

He hardly noticed as Blair disappeared, his whole focus on his wife. "Are you really ready to throw yourself into another scheme? Don't you need time to heal and relax?"

"Resting is for the old and decrepit. I'm not quite there yet. There's exploring to do."

"A wanderer's heart," Hayjen teased.

A glimmer of mischief entered her eyes. "A pirate's heart."

His smile grew. "Well, you did steal my heart..."

Lilja released a throaty chuckle. "Nineteen years of marriage and you're still a charmer."

"I aim to please," Hayjen whispered before brushing his lips against hers.

Life had never been so sweet.

CHAPTER FIFTY-EIGHT

Tehl

"What the bloody hell?" Tehl growled, glaring at Blair. "A little notice would've been nice."

He flicked a glance toward his wife. Sage stood near the round war table, scowling at the map at the figurines that represent the armies and their leaders. She snatched up the leather bag from the surface, and one by one put the pieces away until all that was left was the warlord's leren piece. She stared at the feline figurine as the rest of their council filed in. Her jaw clenched, and she snatched the warlord's piece off the surface, then tossed all of them into the woodstove.

So, she wasn't as composed as she was pretending.

Sage moved back to his side, her expression placid. Other than their initial reunion, they hadn't spoken much in the last two days. He still had no clue what she'd experienced, or what went on in the Scythian camp. But she was too quiet. It was unlike her, and it bothered him. A lot.

"There wasn't much time to give you any warning," Blair responded. He ran a dirty hand over his haggard face. "In all honesty, it slipped my mind until Jacobi mentioned it. I'm sorry for not giving any warning."

The girl with onyx skin moved closer to Blair's side. Tehl scrutinized Dorcus. She looked nothing like her father Blair, except for the high cheekbones and the slope of her nose. He kept reminding himself not to stare. It was like he was in a fairy story. A Nagalian princess was standing in his tent—her dragon just outside. He glanced at the tent flap at the thought. He was still a little uneasy having the beast so close. It wasn't because Tehl was afraid, necessarily, but the way Illya had looked at him... it held true intelligence and understanding.

"She cannot rule in Scythia," Queen Osir said softly, both her sons flanking her. Zachael stood just to her right, nodding.

"I agree," Tehl said, glancing once more in his wife's direction.

"They would not accept me even if I was keen on ruling Scythia. I would be assassinated by the end of the week." Sage flashed as sharp smile, a bitter twist of her lips. "The Scythian commanders weren't wrong." She scanned the group of leaders in the tent, her gaze resting on Rafe and then finally focusing on Tehl. He jolted at the weary look in her emerald eyes. She was barely holding on by a thread. "The only choice we have is to appoint a regent in my stead," Sage continued. "Aermia still needs to have a presence in Scythia, but we cannot rule the kingdom."

"You're right," Tehl acknowledged. "If we tried such a thing, there would be rebellion and more bloodshed. That's the last thing we need." Too many lives had been lost already on both sides. Healing of their kingdoms needed to begin. As far as a regent...

Tehl examined the people in the room. Most of the occupants were monarchs of their own kingdoms or heirs. His mind turned to Gav. If his cousin was healthy, he would have suggested him, but Scythia was too dangerous for a wounded foreign man and his small daughter. There was only one true choice. He paused on the figure sitting in the corner.

Blaise.

She stared at the floor, idly picking at one of her nails, not meeting anyone's gaze.

"Blaise," he rumbled softly.

She lifted her head, her dark eyes meeting his. Blaise grimaced, shaking her head. "It won't work."

"You are the solution," he murmured.

Sage nodded and eyed the Scythian woman. "You know he's right."

Blaise shook her head. "I've not been trained to rule, and I have no *desire* to rule over Scythia." She rose to her feet and glanced around the room, holding her hands up. "This is a bad idea. What makes you think they will accept me? I've been working with their enemies. I'm a traitor."

"That's exactly why you should be ruling," Queen Osir cut in. "You fought for the rebels. You fought for the freedom of *all*. Those who supported the rebellion will welcome you with open arms."

"And those who supported the warlord?" Blaise asked.

"They will begrudgingly accept you because of the blood flowing through your veins," Rafe answered. "Scythia is in disarray. Even the staunch supporters of your uncle will not want civil war. You are the medium."

"Blair has more experience than I do," Blaise pointed out, crossing her arms. "He should be the one to rule."

The man in question shook his head. "I am the real traitor. They wouldn't tolerate me on the throne, any more than they would accept one of the warlord's former commanders. Then there is the matter of bloodline. I'm not royal. It has to be you." He dipped his chin. "But I will stand at your side and protect you with my life. You will not be alone."

Blaise ran a shaking hand through her hair, tears glossing her eyes. She blinked them away. "This would be so much easier if my mother was still here," she rasped.

Tehl's heart squeezed. He knew what it was like to lose a mother. "We will all support you in this. You're family."

The Scythian woman swallowed hard.

"You'll not go in alone," Sage murmured softly. "Not only will you have Blair, but we'll also send in someone to counsel you and keep an eye on your back."

Tehl hid his amusement as Rafe stilled, his attention completely focused on Sage. The Methian prince was a little too focused on the conversation—on Blaise. Intriguing.

His wife nodded to the group. "Aermia isn't the only one to have a stake in what happens in Scythia. I think it wise to have someone who isn't Aermian to stand by her side." Sage arched a brow as she held Rafe's gaze. The two seemed to share a private conversation. Her lip curled slightly. "I nominate Rafe."

He stood a little taller and turned to Blaise. Her face blanched but she quickly schooled her expression, not quickly enough that Rafe didn't catch her reaction. Poor bastard.

His expression didn't reveal anything as he respectfully dipped his chin in deference. "If that is what everyone wishes. I will happily go to Scythia."

Queen Osir smiled. "Go with my blessing."

"If no one opposes the appointment, let's move on," Tehl said. He stared at Blaise, giving her the option to request someone else. She didn't. "So, it's settled. Blaise will rule Scythia as regent, with Rafe as a mediator and counselor until a time when Scythia is stabilized." He turned toward the silent Dorcus. "You have many decisions ahead of you. Do you have a plan?"

The Nagali princess looked at her father and then focused on Tehl. "We refuse to go back to the way things were before."

Blaise limped from her corner and bowed deeply to Dor. "I know it will never be enough, but you have my most heartfelt apologies for the atrocities committed by the Scythian people." She straightened, holding her chin high. "I promise things will be different, and that you are no longer beholden to Scythia. You never should have been in the first place. Every culture should be treated with equality and respect."

"Something we agree upon," Dor said softly.

"Know Methi will support you in your ventures. Do you plan to stay in Scythia?" Queen Osir added.

"I'm not sure," Dorcus answered. "Many just desire their freedom. Scythia, however, is the only home they've ever known. While there will be many who will want to return to Nagali and begin restoring our homeland, I know there will be some who wish to stay behind as citizens."

"Consider it done," Blaise cut in. "Any who choose to stay in Scythia will be granted full citizenship."

"I don't want to be the bearer of bad will, but many of the warlord's supporters will not like this." Raziel held his hands up. "Slavery is a vile, evil practice that should never have been instituted. What I am saying is that there will be those who accuse you of crippling your kingdom. It is something you'll need to address."

"We will figure it out," Rafe cut in, side-eyeing his brother. "They may not like it, but it's the way it's going to be."

Blaise chuckled darkly and pushed the loose braids from her cheek. "For once, the high court will have to do their own work like the rest of the world has been doing for generations."

Rafe shared a shark-like smile with Blaise, and Tehl hid his satisfaction. While the two might irritate each other, they would be a force to be reckoned with when they united against a common enemy.

Tehl turned his attention back to Blair and Dorcus. "If you do not wish to stay in Scythia until your people are ready to make the expedition back into the Nagali homelands, you may find refuge in Aermia."

"Thank you," Dor said, her cocoa-colored eyes warm.

He glanced at her father, brows furrowing. Blair had said he would stay with Blaise in Scythia. If that was the case, who would go with his daughter to Nagali? "You would leave Dorcus without your guidance?"

"Tehl," Sage admonished.

He shrugged a shoulder. Better to be blunt than to have miscommunications.

"I appreciate your concern for my daughter. She will not be going on this journey alone. I've spoken with Hayjen and Lilja. They have agreed to accompany Dorcus and those who wish to go with her to Nagali." Blair smiled. "There's no one I trust more than those two with what is precious to me."

"She's awake?" Sage breathed.

Blair's smile widened. "Yes."

"Thank the stars," Sage whispered.

Tehl brushed his fingers against the back of her hand, and she flashed him a relieved smile.

"If that is all," Queen Osir said, "then I will fetch a scribe and have him draft a treaty to include all that was agreed upon today. You will be able to proof it tomorrow morning. For the time being, rest and enjoy your respite before the real work begins tomorrow—the cleanup."

Chapter Fifty-Nine

Sage

Sage couldn't stay in bed another moment. Too much restlessness ran through her blood. She pressed a kiss to Tehl's cheek and quietly crept from bed, wearing her clothing from the prior day. The night before she'd been so tired that she'd just crawled onto the mattress and passed out.

She grabbed her cloak and daggers from the chair, and slipped her boots on before sneaking from the tent. Snow crunched beneath her boots and the cold air stung her lungs, but it felt good. For the first time in months, it was as if she could pull in a full breath. Domin sat in a chair to the left of the entrance. He arched a brow in silent question.

"I'm fine," she mumbled as she belted the daggers around her waist. "I couldn't sleep any longer. Did you get any rest?"

"I did. Thank you, my lady. My shift just began."

Her nerves settled some once her weapons were in place. Sage swept the cloak closer to her body to ward off the chill of the early morning. She peered toward the east, the sky just starting to lighten. A new day.

The tent flap whispered, and Sage turned her head toward the sound. Tehl silently stepped out, his inky hair mussed in a way that caused her heart to flutter. He pressed against her back and wrapped his cloak about the both of them, his chin resting on the top of her head. Her husband curled one arm around her waist, securing her against his body, and laced his fingers with hers, his callouses catching against her own. Sage sighed and settled into his warmth. He wasn't the kind of man she ever expected to marry. Blunt. Quiet. Awkward. But he also offered comfort and love in a gentle way she'd never experienced before. He made her feel cherished. Whole.

"You've been quiet," he rumbled, his voice deeper than normal.

She shrugged. "I'm tired."

He huffed a silent laugh against her hair. "Understatement of the year." A pause. "Are you almost ready for that break we spoke about?"

"Almost," she murmured, playing with his fingers. "There are a few more things I need to tie up."

"Oh?"

"I need to go back to the forest today." She turned in his arms and gazed up at him. "Would you come with me?"

He scanned her face, his deep-blue gaze fathomless. "Are you ready now?"

She'd been ready during the middle of the night, but that hadn't seemed prudent. Sage nodded.

Tehl gently tugged on her hand and began leading her through the quiet camp, Domin and three Elite quietly following behind them.

They arrived at the corral, and she whistled softly. Peg parted from the herd and trotted to the fence, immediately pressing her nose to Sage's pocket.

"Hello, sweet girl," she crooned, running her hand down the mare's silky nose. "I don't have any apples." Peg nickered as Sage climbed over the fence. "I promise a bucketful of oats when we return."

She used the fence to mount the mare just as Tehl cantered to their side atop Wraith, his black warhorse. Their men circled them, and their group exited the corral and wound their way through the sleepy camp. A fiilee on the edge of camp stretched, flexing its wings. Skye—Raziel's flying feline.

"Raziel?" she called softly.

The Methian prince in question stood from the ground and approached, carrying a mug of steaming liquid that smelled nutty. "Going somewhere, Sage?"

"I need to return to the forest."

He scanned their entourage. "Expecting issues?"

"No, we just need some muscle. Would you be willing to come and possibly bring Rafe if you can find him?"

Raz chuckled. "My brother is always lurking about somewhere. I'm sure if you spin around three times and call his name, he'll appear."

Her lips twitched. Brothers. Stars, she missed hers. "We're heading out. I'm sure you'll catch up."

He downed the rest of his brew and nodded. "We'll be right behind you."

Sage urged Peg forward and directed her toward the huge dark lump that rested near the evergreen trees at the edge of camp. Her mare tossed her head and sidestepped as they approached Illya.

"It's okay," Sage soothed, not moving any closer. The dragon opened one silver eye that reflected the fire burning in the small camp set up near his side. Blair rose from the log he was sitting on and Dorcus followed. Apparently, no one was sleeping when they should have been.

Sage smiled. "If you're willing, we have a rescue mission this morning. Would you be willing to lend us your translation skills, Dorcus?"

Dor's brown eyes grew round. "You have knowledge of another dragon?"

Sage winced. "I do, but he's in bad shape. I promised him I would release him, but I want to make sure there are no casualties when I do so."

The Nagali heir turned to Illya, who clicked softly. "We'll do it," she said, turning back to them. "I'm new to this Dragon Song thing, so I'm not sure if I'll be able to understand him."

Her humility and humor caused Sage's smile to widen. She liked Dor. "We're meeting on the outskirts of the forest."

Tehl wheeled his mount toward the battlefield and they pressed on. Passing over the battlefield was a quiet affair. The ground seemed to be stained red. She had no doubt that the earth would be painted with blood—both ally and foe—for quite some time.

The sky lightened, and she smiled as she caught sight of Raziel and Skye soaring above, Illya following behind. Dragons and flying felines.

"It's seems unreal, doesn't it?" Tehl asked.

"I can hardly believe it."

"So, a dragon?

Sage glanced at him as they skirted the former Scythian camp and moved into the forest, forming a single line. It still was so bizarre to see snow meet forest.

Minutes passed before Peg grew frisky and tossed her head. They were close. "We leave the horses here," Sage commanded.

All dismounted, and Sage felt unsteady on her feet. Being surrounded by trees caused goosebumps to break out across her skin. The last time she had been here, she'd been running for her life. She placed a hand on the nearest tree and steadied herself.

Tehl's hand ran down her braid. "Do you need a moment?"

"I'm okay," she huffed. Sage shook off the memories and pointed in the direction they were going. "Straight ahead, gentlemen. Don't enter the ring," she warned as Raziel and Rafe caught up, leaving Skye in a small meadow. Three Elite took up the front while Rafe, Raz, and Domin brought up the rear.

"Blasted ferns," Raz grumbled. "Always in the way."

His blasé comment loosened some of the tightness in her chest. What they were doing was something good; happy, even. "Dorcus?" she asked.

"She's soaring through the sky with her dragon. Her father instructed her on where to meet us," Rafe supplied.

The trees thinned, the meadow just visible.

"What the bloody hell is this?" Raziel asked when they'd exited the tree line.

"Looks like an execution ring," Rafe growled.

Sage didn't look at either brother as she stared up at the dais and stone throne. She seethed inside. It needed to be torn down. *One thing at a time.* From the corner of her eye, she caught Tehl studying her. She could almost see the questions running through his mind, but he uttered none of them. And she was thankful for it.

Her stomach dropped as her gaze skittered over the post where William had been murdered. The pulse at her neck began hammering, and sweat beaded at the back of her neck. Sage pointed to the levers on the north and south sides with a shaking finger. "Three men on each side. Pull the lever toward the west and stay out of the ring."

Silently, the men followed her command and Tehl stepped closer to her right side when Dor and Illya soared above them before landing on the south side of the dais. The Nagali princess slid from her dragon's back and moved to flank Sage's left side.

"Pull the levers," Sage said.

The ground groaned before the taut chains began moving toward them and disappearing into the ground on either side of the circle. An emerald scaled snout was the first thing to exit the cave on the east side of the meadow. The dragon hissed, its hostile green eyes darting around the circle.

Dor sucked in a sharp breath when he was fully emerged. "His wings," she choked out. "So many scars."

Sage watched as the dragon homed in on Illya and seemed to swell in size. She took three steps forward, pulling the hostile dragon's attention. Gasps erupted around her, but she didn't pay them any mind as she locked eyes with the beast.

"That's far enough," Tehl murmured softly.

She paused and slowly unbuckled the daggers at her waist before tossing them behind her. The dragon was angry, but she could see his intelligence. Sage held her hands out and knelt, making herself as nonthreatening as possible.

"I made you a promise the last time I was here." She paused and then touched the scars at her throat. "He is gone. He can't hurt you any longer." The dragon's gem-like eyes glittered. "I plan to release you. Please don't eat anyone here. We're friends, not enemies."

Dorcus clicked, and the dragon hissed, his gaze focused on the girl. The dragon released a series of terrifying growls, hums, and clicks.

"What does he say?" Sage asked.

"She hates eating humans, so she won't bother with your men unless they attack her."

A female dragon. It would explain the size difference between the emerald dragon and the massive Illya.

Sage smiled. "It's a pleasure to meet such a fierce dragoness. I'm sure you wish to be gone from this place. Nagali is uninhabited; if you wish to be undisturbed, you should settle there. Although, you will be welcomed in any of the kingdoms."

The dragon clicked again, seeming more agitated.

"She won't leave this meadow. It's her territory," Dor translated. "Also, Illya says her wings are too damaged for travel."

Sympathy swamped Sage. It was a cruel thing to mutilate such a stunning creature. "If you'll allow it, we'll relieve you of the chains. We don't have the equipment to rid you of the collar today."

Dorcus, Illya, and the new dragon spoke in a way that reminded Sage of rough song. She eyed the chains. "Can Illya rip the chains from the ground?"

"I think so. He's much larger than the female."

The dragoness hissed.

"No disrespect intended," Dor murmured. "Give Illya room!"

Sage retreated to the edge of the forest, along with the men, when Illya scooped the chain into his mouth and crunched down. Her eyes widened as metal squealed and snapped like a child breaking a small stick.

"Wicked hell," Tehl breathed.

Illya lumbered to the other side of the meadow and repeated the action. The female dragon held her head high and reluctantly tipped her chin upward so that Illya could repeat the process on either side of the collar. As soon as the deed was done, she scuttled backward, and spines along the ridge of her back flared.

That wasn't good.

"It's okay," Dor whispered. "She's just defending her territory."

Illya held his ground but retreated eventually.

The emerald dragon scanned the tree line, and her eyes seemed to pin Sage in place. She clicked and then waited. Sage glanced at Dor, who blinked slowly.

"She says you're foolish and should leave."

For some reason, that made Sage chuckle. Staring down a dragon was on the tame end of foolish things she'd done in her lifetime.

"As you wish," she called and turned to leave.

The dragon clicked.

Dor quirked a smile, her brown eyes glittering. "Her name is Dia, and she says the little fool can visit sometime."

Sage smiled over her shoulder. A fool she was, because she'd be back.

"I'll see you soon, Dia."

Chapter Sixty

Mira

"I need to be there," Gav bit out.

Mira shook her head, dipping into her well of patience that she reserved for especially troublesome soldiers. "And I said no. You need to be on bedrest for weeks to come."

His purple eyes flashed in anger. "I cannot miss it."

"And you can't afford to lose your leg," she retorted. Mira inhaled sharply. What happened to biting her tongue and controlling her anger? In the three days since the fever had broken, Gavriel had been an utter nuisance. The charming prince was nowhere to be found, and in his place was an absolute troll. She placed her hands on her hips and met his glare. "If you attempt to leave this cot one more time, I'll tie you to it myself."

His lip curled. "Do you really want to threaten a prince?"

That got to her. Mira leaned down into his space, her loose hair pooling on his chest. "I don't see any princes in this room. Only a grouchy, defiant patient who is making my work harder." She straightened and calmly walked toward the exit. She'd already wasted fifteen minutes arguing with him, and she'd be damned if she humored him any longer.

"Don't let him get up," she mumbled to one of the soldiers standing by the tent flap. The soldier nodded once and glanced quickly over her shoulder. Mira scowled. "Don't you be looking at him. He's not in charge in this room. My credentials trump his in this situation."

Mira tossed her head and sent Gav one last glare over her shoulder. "Don't cause any more issues or I'll sic Osir on you. She's not nearly as nice as me."

"Anyone would be better than you," he mumbled.

She gritted her teeth and kept her stride, even as she moved through the infirmary, grabbed her cloak, and exited. Her breath came a little easier as she inhaled the crisp, clean air. The midmorning sun cascaded light across the ground, the ice sparkling like a thousand diamonds. Beautiful.

Tucking her cloak closer around her body, she turned, lifted her eyes, and locked gazes with Raziel as he rounded a tent. His stride lengthened at the sight of her. Mira's heart fell. She did not want to have this conversation now.

She turned on her heel, and fled toward the glen she frequented for quiet time. Part of her hoped he wouldn't follow, but the practical part knew he would. At least no one else would learn of her shame.

"Why do I have the feeling that you're running from me, dearest?"

Mira gathered her misplaced anger and spun to face him, her plain cloak flaring around her boots. She flung her hands out and pointed a finger at him. "I am *not* your dearest." Her soul withered from the hateful words spilling from her lips.

Raz slowed to a stop and an awkward silence began to stretch between them. He scanned her face, his expression revealing nothing of his feelings. His brows furrowed, and then determination filled his face like he'd come to a decision. He stormed toward her, and Mira braced for what he would say. A squeak escaped her when he pulled her into a bear hug, her body held tightly against his.

"What is going on?" he asked softly.

Mira held herself stiffly. She began counting, and only made it to thirty before she gave in and sagged against him. After being berated by the creature that had inhabited Gav's body for the last three days, it was nice to be held. Her face pressed against his cloak, and she soaked in the comfort he was offering, even though she shouldn't be. It wasn't right for him to be holding her. They couldn't be anything to each other but friends.

Raz petted her wild hair, his fingers sinking into her tangled locks, pulling a few baby hairs at her nape. The pain helped her clarify a few things.

"I can't do this," she mumbled into his chest.

He tipped her head back and stared down at her face. "Can't do what?"

Heat filled her eyes, but she battled the tears back. "This." A rueful smile touched his mouth as she waved her hand between their chests. "It won't work."

"Give me one good reason."

"I'll give you five." She held up her first finger. "For one, I'm not royalty."

He shook his head, looking slightly amused. "I know you aren't, but it doesn't matter. We've already spoken about this. Who sired you doesn't matter in my culture, and—" another handsome smile "—I've asked around and discovered the laws in Aermia require someone who is of royal blood to marry someone of common blood. So, by your own laws and mine, we're just fine."

"You're not taking this seriously," she accused. That wiped the smile from his face.

"You're wrong. I take everything seriously when it comes to you." He gazed down at her soberly. "Tell me what is really wrong. You're skirting around the issue."

Mira pushed out of his arms and walked two steps away to gather her thoughts. Once again, she faced him, and her stomach rolled. Why couldn't he just let it go?

"I can't marry you," she whispered.

"You know what I think?" Raziel murmured. "I think you're looking for excuses not to be happy. You keep saying you *can't*, but I say that you *won't*." His lips pursed. "Did I read the signs wrong? Do you not like me?"

"Of course, I like you. You're funny, and you care for those around you with such compassion and love. You're an amazing friend."

"More than just a friend, surely?"

"More than a friend," she admitted, a sneaky tear leaking from her left eye. There was no way around it. She needed to lay it all out there for him. "I can't give you children," she said bluntly.

Raz stiffened and blinked once, slowly. "What do you mean?"

She huffed out a breath. "Exactly what I said. I cannot have children," she choked out. "So, no heirs for Methi if you were to take up with me. Your wife needs to be able to give you children, and I can't—" Her voice broke.

The Methian prince rushed forward and once again pulled her into his arms. His kindness unleashed the torrent of tears lurking just beneath the surface. Mira clung to him and cried, releasing all her pain and anguish. It had been some years since her father had told her the brutal truth, but it was only just now hitting her hard.

"I'm so sorry, dearest," he crooned, rocking her back and forth.

"An accident right when I was on the bloom of womanhood stole my future." She hiccupped. "Papa said I would never have children." Mira's chin trembled as she tipped her head back and forced herself to meet Raziel's gaze. "You understand why it's impossible for us to marry."

He dropped a small kiss onto the tip of her nose. "I don't need to have children of my own."

Her eyes flew wide, and she tried to pull away, but he didn't let her. "You don't know what you are saying."

"This war has robbed many children of mothers and fathers. Regardless of if I sire my own children, I plan to adopt those that I can care for. You needn't bear me children."

Mira was so shocked her mouth dropped open. She didn't know what to say. Having an heir was important to secure the throne. "Does your family have the same values?" she rasped.

"We will make our own family." He didn't answer her question, so a resounding *no*.

"I can't let you do that," she said finally.

"Will you rob me of my own choice?"

Mira, although saddened, smiled at the prince. He really was the best. "You don't know what you're saying. Right now, it may be easy to say you don't want your own children, but what about down the road? We've known each other a short period of time. I don't want you to regret having chosen me, and more importantly, I don't want you to lose out on having your own child. It's a miracle. I would not have you suffer loss." Mira cupped his whiskered cheek. "I care for you, and you've become one of my closest friends."

"More than that," he interrupted.

"You're right, and it's because I care for you that I'm saying no. Also, the selfish part of me couldn't handle it if you eventually looked upon me with disappointment. I want you to have every happiness in the world, Raz."

"This was not how I imagined today going." He huffed. "I had hoped to formally announce our engagement. You really won't consent to marry me?"

Stars, this is hard. "I won't." She pulled her hand away from his cheek and hugged him. "Aermia needs me. I've been trained my whole life to become the next Royal Healer." Her thoughts turned to her papa. "And I cannot leave my father."

Raziel pulled her closer and they stood quietly in the glen. "I feel like this is goodbye," he muttered. "I don't want it to be goodbye."

"We've been good friends this entire time," Mira said. "Do you think we could carry on as we did before?"

"Maybe not immediately, but I think we can be friends. The best of friends."

She smiled and squeezed him. "The best."

Things didn't always go according to plan, but sometimes even when they were bitter, they were sweet.

Chapter Sixty-One

Sage

It was done.

She stared at the signed document once again.

"We did it," Tehl murmured.

They did. It was surreal. The warlord was gone, the Scythian army subdued, and a real peace treaty signed between all the kingdoms.

She traced her finger over the Nagali princess's signature. A culture they all had thought lost was reborn like a phoenix. It was hardly believable.

"I have some other good news," her husband said, moving around the table to face her.

Sage smiled at him. "I don't know if I can bear anything else. I might just implode."

Tehl gave her a devastating smile. "You'll welcome this. Sam sent news. Jasmine has been found."

She stilled. *Finally*. "Is she okay? Where was she found? And the babe?"

He held up a hand. "She's in good health, and so is their daughter!"

"Daughter?" she whispered, her eyes growing damp. *A daughter*.

"You're an aunt, my love. Little Lana was born four days ago."

"Lana," Sage murmured before promptly bursting into noisy tears. Jasmine had been on her mind for days. She'd feared the worst. It killed her not to be able to search for her friend. Tehl pulled Sage from the chair and hugged her.

"I wasn't expecting this reaction."

She wiped at her face. "Women cry for all sorts of reasons."

"This is a happy cry?"

"Yeah," she croaked.

"That doesn't make any sense," Tehl mused. "The body is a bizarre machine."

Sage laughed. He wasn't wrong. She pulled away and wiped at her face. "I'm okay. Go get into the bath."

His eyes heated. "Get in with me?"

"Perhaps." She nodded toward their room of the tent. "I'll give you a few minutes."

Tehl dropped a kiss on her temple and moved through the tent flap to their room. She turned back to the bare table, holding a copy of the treaty. Once again, she gently ran her fingers over the document. In the beginning, she'd set out only to make a difference in Aermia. She'd never anticipated the far-reaching effects of her actions. While change had been brought about... a fist squeezed her lungs, making it harder to breathe... It had come with the cost of so much blood.

Never again would she see William smile or experience his gruff hugs.

Nor would Maeve's eyes twinkle with a well-thought-out plan, or train with her daughter.

Nor anyone hear one of Garreth's raunchy jokes that always inspired laughter.

No one had been left untouched by the war. Everyone was scarred in some way. Her fingers brushed the scars along her throat. Hers were more visible than others, but no person was alone in their pain and loss. *Stop being ashamed. Wear them like a badge of honor.*

She'd survived and come out stronger. They all had.

"Bloody hell!" Tehl yelled.

Sage sprang from her chair and launched into their room, daggers in hand, her reflexes taking over. She skidded to a stop at the foot of the bed and blinked, then shook her head to make sure she was seeing things clearly.

Tehl stood naked in the tub—a blade in one hand—his attention locked on the leren on the bed. A feline that *wasn't* Nali. *Damn cat.*

She slipped her weapons back into their sheaths and placed her hands on her hips in exasperation. "What are you doing, Nege?"

The feline in question growled and plopped his butt on their bed like he owned it.

"When did you acquire a new leren, love?" Tehl said through gritted teeth.

"I didn't, but I was wondering when he'd show up." Sage scowled at Nege and pointed to the rug. "Get off the bed."

He eyed her and then stretched out, gazing at her with challenge in his golden eyes. She narrowed her eyes at the beast. "Now you've done it. You are marking Nali's territory. Don't come to me whimpering when she boxes your ears."

Sage shot a glance at Tehl, and heat filled her cheeks. Bloody hell, he was a handsome man. Sage hid her smile when he didn't immediately sit back in the bath, his attention locked on the maneater. The man sure didn't like surprises. "You can sit down now."

He curled his lip and slowly sank into the water, covering all his glorious muscles. "Could have told me there was another one."

She hid her smile. "He's just a big ol' kitty cat," Sage said. "He won't hurt you, will ya, Nege?"

The feline huffed and turned his back on them, kneading the bedding with his front paws, the fibers catching on his claws. *Rotten bastard.*

"Some kitty cat," Tehl growled. "One that could eat me."

Sage moved around the end of the bed and stood beside the tub, smiling at Tehl, who still hadn't taken his gaze off the leren. "You just going to stare at him all day?"

"Don't trust him," her husband muttered.

Gently, she pulled his dagger from his wet hand and tossed it onto the chair before kicking off her boots. Tehl's attention focused on her, and she preened when his gaze sharpened as she untucked her shirt. Carefully, she leaned over the edge of the tub and kissed him gently. "Make room for me?"

"Always."

Sage grinned against his lips. "You love me?"

"Always."

She pulled back. "Is that the only word you know?"

Tehl's dark-blue eyes creased at the corners as he full-out smiled, leaving her breathless, her heart racing. "No."

"No?" she asked, wiggling out of her leather pants.

"I know two more. Come here."

"Your wish is my command, my lord."

"If only," he muttered.

Sage tossed her head back and laughed. Despite her heavy heart and the weight of loss, there was good in life. She planned on seizing it with both hands.

EPILOGUE

Mer

Mer kept her head high. This was it. They had kept her under confinement for the last month while the council deliberated on her punishment. She'd been informed that this was just a preliminary hearing.

"You're exiled for a duration of thirty days until the council comes to a unanimous agreement," the Sirenidae king announced. Gone was her loving grandfather, in his place the powerful sea monarch.

They hadn't outright banished her. Her brows rose in surprise. She hadn't expected that, or the emotion that came with the judgement. Since Ream's death and her imprisonment, Mer hadn't felt much of anything.

"You will leave our territory immediately. If you are caught in our kingdom, you will be put to death. Do you understand?"

"I do." Mer bowed low. It was done. For now.

Her gaze flicked to her parents once before she swam from the throne room, the judging gazes of the court scouring her skin. Guilt pricked her, but the ever-present numbness swallowed it up as she departed the city and swam toward Aermia.

Her mind wandered while she made the lonely trek from the deep sea. Mer blinked slowly when the sandy ground began to angle toward the surface. She glanced over her shoulder in the direction of her former home.

There was no going back.

Everything had changed.

Sage

Sage soaked in the warmth; the winter day uncommonly warm. A light breeze stirred her cloak as she walked along the beach with Jas, Mira, Isa, and the twins.

"That's far enough, Ethan!" Jasmine shouted.

"You too, Isa," Mira called from Sage's right.

Sage hid her smile when Ethan halted and then took one more step, the two other children looking from him to Jas. He'd been testing her boundaries since Lana's arrival.

Jasmine growled and shot Sage a glare. "Don't think that I can't see you smiling. Just wait until it's your turn."

"It will be a while before that happens."

Mira snorted. "If you say so. I'm not even married, and I have the responsibility of a parent." She paused, looking thoughtful. "Not that I don't enjoy spending time with Isa. I didn't mean it that way."

Sage placed a hand on her friend's arm. "No one could ever doubt how much you love that little girl."

"I do." Her lips pursed. "Even when she's pushing me... like now." Isa edged closer to the surf, her red curls waving in the wind. "I just can't keep her out of the water," Mira grumbled. She sped up, leaving Jas and Sage behind. "That is close enough, Isa Ramses! How many times have I told you that it is too cold to be in the water? You'll catch your death!"

Jasmine sniggered as Mira attempted to round up all the children but ended up following them to a tide pool. "Glad I'm not the only with disobedient children."

"They're all good kids." Sage scrutinized the black bags beneath Jasmine's eyes. "How are you doing? Getting enough sleep?"

"Sleep?" Jas chuckled. "I don't know what sleep is anymore."

"You know I'd take the children whenever you need a break," Sage offered. She loved the wee beasties. Being an aunt was the best.

"I know. Sam keeps telling me to pick a governess, but I don't like the idea of someone else raising my children."

Sage nodded. "I can understand that. Does Sam have Lana right now?"

"Yeah." A goofy smile touched Jasmine's mouth. "He passed out with Lana sleeping on his chest. They didn't even move when we left."

"He loves that baby," Sage remarked, scanning the sand for any shells to add to her collection. She'd never seen a man dote on his children as much as Sam did. Gone was the rake and seducer. Well... she wouldn't go that far. Sam would always be Sam; mischief maker, lover of women, Spymaster. Speaking of which, Sage needed to talk to him about their partnership. Now that she'd returned to the castle and war was no longer on the horizon, it was time she stepped up her involvement with his spies. She'd never wanted to be a soldier. Spymistress suited her much better.

"Mer!" Jade screeched. The little girl raced to meet the Sirenidae. Mer rushed from the waves and dropped to her knees in the wet sand, catching Jade in a hug.

"She's beautiful," Jas murmured.

Something in her friend's tone pulled Sage's attention back to Jasmine. She looked defeated. "What's going on?"

Jas shrugged and pasted on a fake smile. "Nothing. Let's go say hello."

What the bloody hell?

JASMINE

She plowed through the sand toward the Sirenidae, determined to be civil, despite her heart feeling like it was going to break into a million pieces at the sight of her. Over the past month, Sam had been so attentive and loving, but that didn't mean he was in love with her. Her husband loved all women, and she couldn't get the image of him and Mer wrapped up in each other from her mind. Every time he disappeared, Jas wondered if he was with her.

The hardest part was that Jas couldn't find it in herself to hate the woman. She was stunning, kind, and funny, and Jasmine owed Mer her life as well as Lana's. It was time to say thank you. She hadn't seen Mer since Lana's birth.

Jasmine steeled herself and strode right up to Mer as she put Jade down. Jas threw her arms around the Sirenidae and hugged her tight. "Thank you so much for what you've done. There aren't words sufficient enough to express how thankful I am." She pulled in a deep breath to continue and frowned when the most delicious scent she'd ever smelled washed over her. "What *is* that?" Jas pressed her nose against Mer's shoulder and inhaled, heat blistering her cheeks. What in the bloody hell was she doing? "I'm so sorry," she muttered, but she sniffed the Sirenidae again. She couldn't help it.

Mer chuckled and gently pulled back, holding Jasmine at arm's length. Her magenta eyes twinkled. "It's just the Lure."

Jasmine's brows furrowed. "The Lure?" Stars above, her mouth was watering. It was like chocolate, pears, and something exotic that she couldn't put her finger on. "I could just lick you," she blurted. Mortification slammed into her as Sage sniggered behind her.

Mer smiled. "The Lure. When our skin is in contact with seawater, we release a pheromone of sorts. It's something all Sirenidae have; a protection, if you will."

"Pheromones?" Her jaw dropped.

"Don't feel bad. You're not the first or the last to invade my personal space. In fact, Sam has accosted me a few times, though he's stronger than most to resist the Lure." Mer's smile widened. "Although, I'd welcome a hug from you anytime."

Jasmine stilled, and she bit her bottom lip to keep it from trembling. Her eyes grew glassy. "You… and Sam… you're not?"

Sage's laughter cut off abruptly.

"No!" Mer said fervently.

Tears spilled from Jasmine's eyes. All this time, she'd thought he'd been…

"I would never, *never* do that! I love Sam but he's like my brother, and you, family by extension." Mer yanked her into a hug, her lovely scent curling around Jas once more. "He loves you, only you."

"I'm such an idiot," Jasmine moaned.

"Maybe you should go take a nap, too…" Sage murmured. Jas pulled away and glanced at her friend. Sage arched a brow and jerked her head toward the castle. "I'll keep the wee ones. Their uncle wanted time with them anyway."

"You're a lifesaver." Jas jogged to Ethan and Jade, kissing them both on the top of their heads. "Be good for your auntie. I'll see you a little later."

"Speaking of time," Mira said softly, "I need to get back to the infirmary." She held Isa's hand. "You ready to go, little lady?"

"I wanna stay with Jade," Isa whined.

"I can take her, too," Sage offered.

Jas didn't hear anything else as she practically sprinted for the palace. All she could think of was getting to Sam.

***

They were still in the same position as she'd left them.

Jasmine closed the door softly and padded across the luxurious rug, then skirted around the massive bed. She unclasped her cloak, tossing it on the striped chair in the corner before kicking off her boots. Carefully, she climbed onto the bed and lay beside Sam, her cheek pillowed on her hands as she stared at his profile.

"Are you really going to stare at me?" he whispered, not opening his eyes.

Jas rolled her eyes. The man was impossible to sneak up on. "Did you get some sleep?"

"A bit." He turned his head and opened his gorgeous blue eyes, a sleepy smile on his face. "Did you have a nice time?"

"The best," she murmured, and her eyes dropped to his lips, then shifted back to his eyes.

The sleepy look in his gaze disappeared and something hot filled them, causing her to shiver. Her knees weakened, and Jas was thankful she wasn't standing. He was too attractive for his own good.

She licked her lips, and he followed the movement. A thrill ran through her and she shifted closer, so they were practically sharing the same breath.

"I discovered something," she mumbled.

"Oh, yeah?" he asked, brushing his nose against hers.

"I love you, and I have for quite some time."

Sam blinked, and a blinding smile lit up his face. "Finally."

"Excuse me?" That was not the reaction she was expecting.

"Just been waiting on you, sweetheart." Sam adjusted Lana on his chest, making sure the blanket covered the sleeping infant before focusing back on Jasmine. "Didn't want to push."

"What are you saying?" Her heart pounded in her chest.

"That I've loved you for a while. I was just waiting for you to catch up."

This man. Jasmine closed the distance, her lips crashing against his. Sam's right hand wrapped around the back of her neck and adjusted the angle of her head. He kissed her with gentle bites and nips, as if he wanted to savor her mouth. Jas pressed herself against his side as he devoured her.

Lana mewled, and they both froze.

Jasmine opened her eyes slowly, her breath as ragged as Sam's. He smiled and released her neck, rubbing a gentle hand down their daughter's back. "Duty calls. I'll have to ravish you later."

She grinned. "Maybe *I'll* ravish *you*."

Sam smirked. "Promise?"

SAGE

"Help me!" Tehl called. "I'm being attacked!"

Sage grinned as Ethan, Jade, and Isa climbed all over Tehl.

"One more time!" Ethan cried.

Tehl groaned but smiled and hauled himself to his hands and knees again. "Once more, and then this horsey is going to the stable."

The three children crawled onto his back as he did his best impression of a wild horse. Mira leaned over and bumped her shoulder against Sage's, smiling at the silliness. "Thanks for keeping Isa. I didn't want her to have to spend another afternoon in the infirmary."

"How is he doing?" Sage asked.

Mira's nose wrinkled. "Still being a stubborn ass."

"Still giving you grief, huh?"

"Some days, I swear he hates me." Mira's jaw clenched and she looked away. "I know it's part of the process. The pain and loss he is dealing with is extreme. It's just… difficult when it's someone you know."

Sage pulled her friend into a side hug as Tehl bucked the children off his back and tickled them. "I'm so sorry. Even if he's not appreciative now, he will be. You saved his life and his leg."

"For now he just thinks I'm the witch hellbent on making him suffer." Mira squeezed Sage's back. "But if it means him walking and riding again with his daughter, I'll play that role." She pulled away and clapped her hands, moving for the entrance. "Okay, beasties. It is time for dinner. You hungry?" Mira opened the door. "Mer is here."

"Yay!" they chorused.

Ethan popped to his feet first, followed by Isa, and then Jade. All three children ran for the exit of the study. Jade switched directions last minute. She quickly hugged Tehl and then Sage.

"I'll see you tomorrow." Sage ruffled her niece's hair and then gestured to the books lining the walls. "We'll read one of your favorite stories."

"'Kay!"

Jade disappeared out the door, the children's happy chirps fading as they moved away.

Tehl groaned as he stood, rubbing his knees. "I'm getting too old for that."

Sage rolled her eyes. "If your father can do it, you can do it too."

"I heard from Raziel," he said conversationally as he began to stalk her. Sage quickly maneuvered herself, so the desk was between them.

"Oh?"

"Methi has been in contact with the Sirenidae."

"Interesting." She moved around the desk as he slowly took another prowling pace. "Blaise wrote to me. She wants Rafe gone already."

"Knew that was going to happen. They'll work it out."

"How do you know?" she asked, watching her husband like a hawk. It was the quiet ones you had to look out for.

"We did." Two little words that meant everything. "If we could work it out and be incredibly happy, then they can too."

Warmth unfurled in her chest. "Such sweet words. I still won't go easy on you."

"Do you really think you can escape me?" he asked, a challenging glint in his gaze.

She smirked. "Catch me if you can!"

She feinted to her left, then darted to the right and was out the door. Tehl cursed, and she released a peal of laughter, putting on a burst of speed, rounding a corner to her left. That was where their strengths lay. He could catch her on a straight path, but she was nimbler when it came to obstacles. Sage took the servants' stairs and arrived at their room. No sign of Tehl.

Sage slipped into their chambers and scanned the room. There weren't many places to hide. She heard running footsteps, then ran around the bed and dove underneath it. Her heart raced, and she covered her mouth with her hand to hide her breathing. The door slammed open, and Tehl strode inside. Her heart skipped a beat when he closed the door and locked it.

No escape now. Not that she wanted to.

She shivered and watched as he checked the bathing room and then the closet. His booted feet paused at the end of the bed. She held completely still. A smile played about her mouth when he moved onto the balcony. He hadn't found her yet.

Suddenly, his hands closed around her ankles and yanked her from beneath the bed. Sage stared up at him with shock. She didn't even hear him move.

"Found you," he murmured, sapphire gaze glimmering.

She grinned. She loved Tehl's playful side. Not many got to see it. "What do you claim as your prize?" she asked breathlessly.

He hauled her into his arms and stood, as she wrapped her legs around his waist. "Don't need anything," he said simply. "I have everything I need in my arms."

Sweet man. Sage playfully narrowed her eyes at him. "You, good sir, are a liar. You said you weren't good with words."

Tehl tugged the collar of her shirt aside so he could kiss the curve of her shoulder. "Telling the truth is easy," he murmured against her skin. "What isn't is getting these leathers off you."

She tossed her head back and laughed. Life wasn't easy. It was gritty, dark, and sometimes painful. But sometimes, it offered priceless gems; like a partner who woke you from nightmares and soothed you back to sleep, a friend who sacrificed herself to keep you safe, or a future you weren't sure you deserved.

Sage kissed both of Tehl's cheeks. Despite everything, she counted herself lucky.

"You love me?" he asked, sitting her on their bed.

"Always."

The End

Coming 2021

The Aermian Feuds: Banished Queen

Also by Frost Kay

THE AERMIAN FEUDS

Rebel's Blade

Crown's Shield

Siren's Lure

Enemy's Queen

King's Warrior

Warlord's Shadow

Spy's Mask

DOMINION OF ASH

The Stain

The Tainted

The Exiled

The Fallout

TWISTED KINGDOMS

The Hunt

The Rook

ALIENS AND ALCHEMISTS

Pirates, Princes, and Payback

Alphas, Airships, and Assassins

MIXOLOGISTS & PIRATES

Amber Vial

Emerald Bane

Scarlet Venom

Cyan Toxin

Onyx Elixir

Indigo Alloy

Thank you for reading COURT'S FOOL. I hope you enjoyed it! If you liked this book, please review it BECAUSE the review rating determines which series I prioritize. If you want the next book in this series soon, review this book♥ Thank you!

If you'd like to know more about me, my books, or to connect with me online, you can visit my webpage https://www.frostkay.net/, check out my Facebook group Frost Fiends, or follow me on Bookbub to receive news about my new releases.

You've just read a book in my AERMIAN FEUDS series. Other books in this series include REBEL'S BLADE and SIREN'S LURE.

If you love SCI-FI, TWILIGHT ZONE, and ALIENS, check out my MIXOLOGISTS & PIRATES series! (More info on the next page!)

www.ingramcontent.com/pod-product-compliance
Lightning Source LLC
Chambersburg PA
CBHW020304030826
48979CB00027B/2091/J

* 9 7 8 1 6 4 9 7 0 3 6 5 1 *